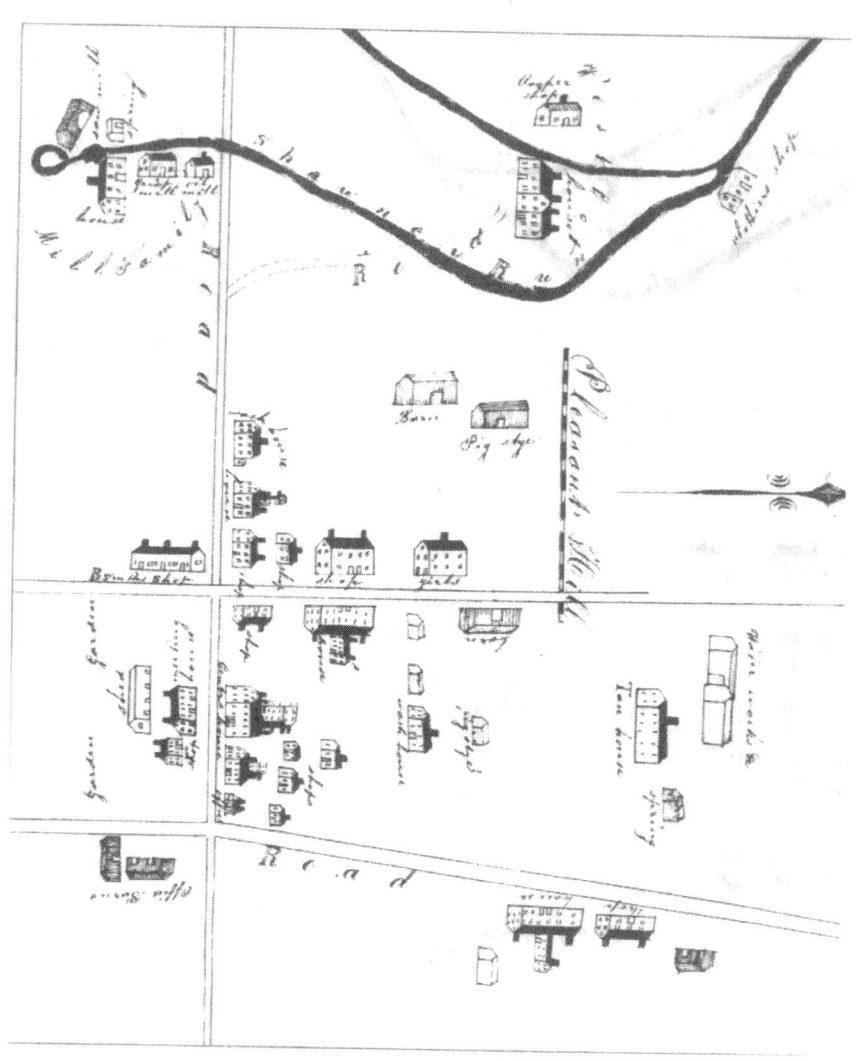

Copyright © 2015 by Thomas Rain Crowe

All Rights Reserved

FIRST PRINTING

Sections of this novel has been previously published in:

Cover photo collage by Thomas Crowe—taken from photos by Thomas Croweand Shaker archival history.

Designed by CreateSpace and published for amazon.com and Kindle Books.

ISBN: 978-1511466455

LOC Card Cataloging Number:

Contacts for book orders and for New Native Press are at newnativepress@hotmail.com and www.newnativepress.org or at 828-293-9237. NNP/PO Box 2554/Cullowhee, NC 28723.

The Watcher

Like Sweet Bells Jangled

to all those who have loved,
and lost,
and loved again -

"And I…

Now see that noble and most sovereign reason,
Like sweet bells jangled, out of tune and harsh;
That unmatch'd form and feature of youth
Blasted with ecstasy…"

--Ophelia

William Shakespeare
from *Hamlet: Prince of Denmark*
Act III, Scene 1

ACT I

Scene I.

From his vantage point of a narrow stairway hidden inside the wall and through a small window that looks out over the large, impeccably unfurnished hall, The Watcher can see everything. The uncontrolled choreography of feet. The way bodies move and awkwardly fall in contortions of anti-flight. The illicit glances. Returned glances withheld. Eyes upturned revealing only white orbs of trance-like reverie. Lips that utter languages unknown even to the skilled and lip-reading. As his eyes move over the room, they settle on a young man with tousled blonde hair who sits on the *fastener* bench near the door. The young man has been to Shakertown many times before and is familiar to the elder man watching from his window in the wall. From behind the waves in the pane of blown glass, he strains to focus on the young man's eyes. He tries to read the expressions in his face and the body language of his limbs. He watches the boy who, in turn, watches the plain-clothed men and the women in their lace caps moving askew in discombobulated lines in a kind of bewitched choreography that resembles very little what is still referred to as The Shaker Dance.

As a member of the elite Ministry, and positioned in the stairwell on the incarcerated side of the glass, The Watcher has been given the time-honored task of keeping an eye out for any indiscretions, over-earnest transcendentalism, or when a potential convert is swept-with-spirit and ready to be plucked. The position of being an elder in The Ministry was not one for the impatient nor those of restless spirit--cloistered, often, there in the claustrophobic stairwell, watching... while the other members of his community dance and sing in various states of jubilant dis-grace.

Wilford Ranks had come into the larger American Shaker community soon after his twentieth birthday--from a small rural town in Bucks County, Pennsylvania, having heard a strange-clothed man singing Shaker hymns on a street corner in Philadelphia. He had immediately returned home only to leave the next day headed for the Mother village of Shaker communities in New Lebanon, New York. Here, he became indoctrinated into the Shaker ways and beliefs, making a devout life for himself in the tradition of disciplined devotion and strict celibacy. Now, almost forty years later, he finds himself in the bluegrass hills of eastern Kentucky at Pleasant Grove, a newly-appointed member of The Ministry.

As one of the elite group-of-four, Wilford Ranks watches from his window the mayhem down on the Meeting Hall floor. His years in New Lebanon and now more recently at Pleasant Grove have been good years, he thinks to himself, as he watches the young blonde-haired boy sitting there with his comrades from town on the *fastener* bench. He sees the boy's eyes begin to disappear behind the eyelids, as if he is in an awakened state of sleep. He watches the boy rise from the bench, join the men's line and begin to dance. To dance and then to whirl. Arms uplifted and stretched out as if to caress an imagined bodily form. From where The Watcher sits, looking down like a curious raptor from his window, it seems to him that the blonde-haired young man is "with spirit" and, therefore, vulnerable and possibly ready to be plucked.

With a single wave of The Watcher's hand, a short, balding man seated in the back of the room below rises to his feet and moves quickly toward the blonde-haired boy. The solitary dance of the young man is now a tango of two, as the older man keeps time and perfect step with the boy's every move. This unlikely *pas de deux* of old man and beautiful blonde-haired boy moves round and round the men's half of the room until The Watcher notices that the boy's eyes have disappeared behind his open eyelids and into the top of his head, as his lips part and strange sounds and words begin emanating from his mouth as inspired speech.

"Oh have you seen beyond the veil, young man, to the other side?" the older man asks in his inquisitive yet catechismic tone. "Are you filled with spirit, boy? Are you ready to be called? Are you being called? Can you hear the voices, boy? Can you hear them?"

The boy is whirling like a dervish and babbling like a newborn hungry for his mother's milk. Struggling to keep pace, the old man places his palm in the middle of the boy's back--keeping him upright and balanced in a room inebriated with 100-proof dance and indecipherable speech. But amidst this pagan-like pageantry, and in a split second of unexpected lucidity, the blonde-haired boy raises an elegant hand and waves the old man away. Dismisses him. Moves forward in the Shaker line. And with a smile on his face, continues to dance.

1842 had arrived in Pleasant Grove (or "Shakertown" as it was casually known to the locals) amidst a new, livelier spiritual renaissance in the American landscape and among the Shaker faithful in particular. Since 1837, the "spirit" in spirituality had come alive and the "Era of Manifestation," as it was being referred to from New Lebanon, New York, to South Union, Kentucky, saw the ritual of Sunday Meeting change from a controlled transcendentalism to a "Carney" sideshow, as seen from the perspective of people living nearby the expanding Shaker communities. A "sideshow" that included, simultaneously, spontaneous visions, speaking in tongues, exorcisms and ecstatic dance. It was no wonder that on Sundays along the large dirt highway that bisected the Kentucky Shakertown community, there was a long line of wagons sitting idle, having deposited their passengers at the Pleasant Grove Meeting House. And with guests to the Sunday Shaker services being welcomed--even encouraged--the people of Herodsville and other adjacent towns thronged to Shaker Meeting in increasingly greater numbers with each passing week of warm weather as winter began its annual transfiguration into spring.

Sitting on the *fasteners* which were built into the peripheral walls of the large meeting room, the townsfolk watched, transfixed, as the men, women and children of Shakertown twisted, bowed, and sang in spiritual ecstasy and angst. And all the while from his secluded window-seat on the stairs, the Watcher watched--like a beneficent alien from another dimension. Like a Greek god. Taking curious pleasure in the proceedings from his self-imposed prison in the wall.

Asher Pope, whose name in Hebrew meant "fortunate, blessed and happy," had been born the son of Matthew Pope, a Baptist minister named after the patron saint of tax collectors, and had spent his whole youthful life in the town of Herodsville, only eight miles from the Shakertown commune. Unlike the other members of his family, he was a different sort. A young man, now, who still lived with his parents and his two younger sisters, he very much looked forward to the day when he could, in good conscience and the security of some kind of permanent work, leave his Baptist nest. While in the presence of his family, in truth he lived mostly in books and spent almost all of his free time in the out-of-doors. In his imagination. In waking dreams. Dreams not unlike his trips to Shakertown on Meeting Day--to be witness to and participant in the spiritual orgy of the Shaker dances which reminded him of places and cultures he had discovered in books. Places far away and in the past--to which he was curiously and irrevocably drawn.

There on the large-planked wooden floor of the Shaker Meeting Hall on this particular Sunday, as he spins around the room like a flesh-covered top, Asher is having a revelation. The revelation of wonder. Of possibility. Of freedom from constraint.

For weeks he has watched a dark-haired girl and her effortless whirling during the Sunday dances. Hears her speak in a strange language by barely even moving her lips. Sees the light that surrounds her body as she moves about the room in ecstasy, with graceful ease. He is attracted to this. He watches her, week after week. He watches her move. He listens to her voice, which seems amplified and separate from all the other voices and sounds in the large hall. He likes the sound of her voice. He likes what she says even when he can't understand an inkling or a word. He comes each Sunday to watch her. To listen to the sound of her voice. And, now, he, too, is dancing. Is whirling. Is mimicking her language. He likes this language. He likes the feeling of being "taken" by something outside of himself. And for the first time he feels free. He feels like he is where he belongs. With the people with whom he belongs. And as he feels these feelings and as he thinks these thoughts, he gently, but confidently, pushes the elder Shaker man away.

Gliding across the leather-worn floorboards of the Meeting House, Asher has been cut-loose. Cut loose from his past. Cut loose from the enforced conformity of his upbringing. Cut loose from anything he has known. He is in unknown territory. It is a strange place. A place only of windows. Windows looking in. Windows looking out--into light. "Is it sunlight?" he is asking himself. Or is it something else. Whatever it is, it feels good. The whirling dance seems to go on for hours. But Asher feels no fatigue. And when the singing and the dancing stop, he is standing in the center of the great wooden hall. When he opens his eyes, what he sees is a face. The face of a girl staring back at him like an image in a mirror created by the flood of light pouring in through the windows on the far wall of the room. Locked into her eyes. Or are they his? In that mirror-of-the-moment he is facing, he sees hair. Hair that has fallen from the veil of her bonnet and is illuminated by the sunlight coming from the windows. Hair that is long, thick and golden brown. A mane. A Rapunzel-like rope he feels the urge to climb.

Spirits talked through Kitt Leigh. Many spirits. During the preceding year she had seen lights and un-bodied spirits and heard the sounds and seen the forms of angels flying, but none more important than that of Mother Ann Lee. Of similar name, Kitt had become Mother Ann's voice that spoke to the other Believers in the Shakertown society. Because of the reverence in which Mother Ann was held by all Shakers as the cornerstone and founder of the Shaker movement in America, these transmissions were taken most seriously, and Kitt's position in the Pleasant Grove community was quickly elevated from that of being a "younger sister" to that of a chosen instrument at the center and at the head of the Society. So celebrated had she become and so integral to the Era of Manifestation practices that the members of the Ministry would wash her feet to purify her and prepare her for the occasion of her "visits" with Mother Ann.

In these "spirit talks" Kitt listened and then recited the words of Mother Ann warning the Believers of "a great day of impending judgment" when the unbelievers would invade the ranks of the Shaker societies creating dissension and anarchy. Mother Ann's message urged the Pleasant Grove members to focus on God and to meditate upon his name, and to pray for protection. In Kitt's trances, she would even name names of those who might be acting out of line or were in danger of falling from grace. The members of the Shakertown Society had never heard such uplifting and inspired speech. There was much weeping and crying accompanying Kitt Leigh's recitations, which would sometimes last for hours--the energy of such occasions moving like an electric current through the assembly, accompanied by what some present described as "heavenly sounds."

For a number of years, now, the spirit manifestations had been on the rise with the young women experiencing their fair share of visitations. But it wasn't until Kitt began "visiting" Mother Ann Lee dressed in white robes and with a crown upon her head in her "big square building" with the thirty odd-shaped chairs and the book "as large as a twelve light window," that the Pleasant Grove renaissance and Kitt's prominence in that spiritual renaissance took its full grip upon the community.

"Keep order, be neat, don't think too much of yourselves, be solemn, and labor with thoughts of God in mind. Repent and be humble, stop quarreling and telling lies. Don't waste anything. Keep order and be neat," Kitt pronounced to gatherings large and small during that year. And the members of the Pleasant Grove society listened raptly while taking her words to heart.

Treated as something of a local saint, Kitt was really only a girl of eighteen. A girl born in the Blue Ridge mountains of Virginia, whose parents had died when she was young. She had been taken to Pleasant Grove by an aunt and uncle in the Shenandoah Valley who were too destitute to look after her. At the age of eighteen, she was still a virgin, just like most of the other young women of her age in the Shaker camps. When she had started bleeding, several years before, she began feeling certain attractions for the older boys. As the years went by, she had learned how to deal with her yearnings. How to suppress them. How to fill her mind with thoughts of God and with beams of purifying light. Despite her self-imposed discipline, the thoughts and the yearnings remained, and she wondered why, after all the ritual and the recitations and the denial, these feelings had not gone away.

Standing there, oddly motionless, in the center of the Meeting House floor and looking into this strange boy's eyes, Kitt realizes that in her uncontrolled whirling and singing, her hair has been shaken loose from her net-like woman's bonnet and now hangs fully and voluptuously past her shoulders covering her breasts and back. In this moment of realization, her eyes meet his and she is instantly distracted from doing anything about her hair. Instead, she just stands there lost in the reverie of magnetic blue eyes slightly covered in a tangle of golden-white hair. He reminds her of the angel she has seen in one of her early visions. "A creature with the head and face of a man, a long neck and feet and legs like a man--very beautiful, but difficult to describe--covered by white feathers and with a ring of golden feathers about its neck. The angel both walked and flew." She has described the other-worldly being to a gaggle of her girlfriends by moonlight, long after the time when all candles were to have been extinguished and all conversation and activity were to have ceased throughout the community.

Who is he, she wonders to herself, in that long moment--when time has seemed to stop and everyone in the room has ceased to exist except the two of them, both standing there lost deep in the endless eternity of the other's eyes. Clearly not the angel of her vision, he does, however, seem so familiar, like family. She thinks that she has seen him before. But with her mind still swirling with indescribable emotions and celestial sounds from the afternoon's Meeting and the Shaker Dance, she can't make the connection. Her knees begin to buckle and she feels the heat of a light rouge color begin to fill her face. She is snapped back into the world of man-made time and consciousness, and in that moment she becomes aware of the folly of her hair.

Hurriedly, she pushes her flowing reddish-brown mane of hair to the top of her head, covering it all the best she can with the Shaker bonnet that clutches to the mane with a single hair hitch--so that only a few long tell-tale strands hang loose and free from the prison of the cap. As she pushes the only other hitch she can find into place, securing her hair underneath the respectable cap, she notices that he is still watching her. Staring at her hair. Staring at her face, and then looking downward at her body--looking at her breasts, her waist, her hips, her legs and feet. Then back up the same route until finally looking, again, and locked, into her eyes. And just as her image of him becomes something she feels might be real, and as a strange unfelt-before lump begins to swell up in her throat, she sees the older, balding man move up to the boy, say something in his ear, and he quietly, yet forcefully, leads him away.

Brother Wilford Ranks saw all of this transpire from his vantage point behind the stairway window and was quick to signal the elder man again to intervene. While he saw the potential for a possible indiscretion between the boy and Kitt, and had, he thought, nipped it in the bud, what he hadn't seen was the invisible thread of recognition, of connection, that passed between the two young people. The slow sensual dance that begins with only a glance and the well-timed unveiling of a shock of hair.

For the most part Shakertown had a good relationship with the nearby town of Herodsville. Although there were minor disagreements and technical and philosophical skirmishes over boundary lines and matters of theological debate, the general mood of the large river valley where both of these communities existed was accepting and sober. Just the same, there were very clear lines drawn in the sand between the two communities and any untoward social interaction between the two meant a clear crossing of that line. This thought flew through Brother Wilford's mind as he watched the short Shaker man lead Asher away from the Meeting Hall floor and deposit him back on the *fastener* bench with his fellow townsfolk. One of Brother Wilford's principal charges was to maintain the peace between the townsfolk and the members of the Pleasant Grove society. At the same time, he was sworn to due diligence concerning the primary principles and ethics of his own people. Herein lay a delicate balance, and it took a special kind of person to hold the line.

In all of his years of being watched and then becoming the one who was doing the watching, Brother Wilford had developed a keen eye. While his vision was physically failing due to the nuisance of middle-age, his insight had only sharpened over the years. It was the subtle things that stood out to him, now. It was because of this honed ability to see deeply that he had noticed what could have been an awkward, even dangerous moment there on the floor that afternoon between Kitt Leigh and the blonde-haired boy. He had acted swiftly and decisively in alerting his man on the floor and avoiding any impropriety.

Wilford Ranks was nothing if he wasn't a team player. Loyal to church and family in every way, he was also human. A man. With manly desires. He had, more than once in his life, had to suppress his feelings for various women. During his years at New Lebanon, he had been tested sorely, by the lure of one Anne Marie Goff, whom he likened to the young Kitt Leigh. Both had the ability to talk with spirits, both had innate charisma and good looks. When Kitt's hair had fallen from her cap at the end of the dance, Ranks was taken aback by that sudden flash of beauty. It was that explosion of beauty embodied in Kitt's long auburn hair that had sent him back in time to his days at New Lebanon and his feelings for Anne Marie Goff. He was not only frightened by how much Kitt resembled Anne Marie in that moment, but somewhat stunned by the familiar feelings it brought up in him. Feelings that he thought had been buried years before.

With the situation on the floor defused, Watcher Ranks had his eyes on Asher Pope, watching him like a hawk observing its potential prey. Watching for anything that might give him useful or telling information. He watched the blonde-haired boy as he sat soberly there on the *fastener* bench talking from the side of his mouth to a boy of similar age who was also from the nearby town. Ranks wondered what kind of soliloquy the blonde-haired boy was offering to his comrade. Driven by his curiosity and haste, Ranks reached over and took hold of the brass handle on the side of the window and unlatched it, opened the glass into the humid human air of the room. This gesture did not go unnoticed, especially by those on the far side of the room on the *fasteners* facing The Watcher's wall. While the members of the Shaker community were used to a sudden opening of the window in the wall and paid it little mind, the townsfolk, being more like young rabbits in the brush, were instantly alerted to the strange movement from above, and quickly dozens of heads turned upward in The Watcher's direction, and were all eyes.

As much as he strained to hear, strained to read the lips of Asher Pope who carried on his monologue with his young friend there on the bench by the door, the-one-who-watched was unable to decipher what Asher said, so loud was the general chatter in the room. In earlier days, there would have been very little and probably even no talking at the end of the Shaker Dance when the parishioners were filing out to make the silent walk across the dirt road to the Centre Family Dwelling and the dining hall. There they would, still in silence and with all the other members of the community, partake of their Sunday meal. Now, however, with the advent of the Era of Manifestation in 1837 and its subsequent impact on Shaker communities, things were quite different. This particular Sunday, Wilford Ranks found that he was feeling a bit nostalgic for those simpler days and their relative peacefulness, and above all the prevalent silence. In such times as those he might have been able to hear at least some of Asher's soliloquy. Even a few tell-tale words heard coming from his lips might have been translated by Ranks as something useful. Something to justify the scores of hours he was obligated to spend crouched uncomfortably on a wooden stair-step as the Society's omniscient eye.

Scene II.

While in Herodsville the Baptist congregation of Reverend Matthew Pope abhorred the practice of dancing as a general rule, dancing on the Sabbath was considered nothing less than heresy. So, when the word got out that there was dancing and all manner of irregularities going on at the Shakertown Meeting Hall on Sunday afternoons, Herodsvillians began coming in droves to witness for themselves the "shaking Quakers."

The Shakertown Society members tolerated outsiders because it provided them with an opportunity to attract converts and to dispel inflated rumors that the Sunday services included naked dancing and the sacrificing of children. In an attempt to keep peace in the valley, after the bretheren and sisters had filed into the Meeting Hall through their separate entrances and had taken their seats on opposite sides of the room, some sort of welcome was delivered to the spectators from the surrounding community. This welcome was often followed by a lesson on the importance of the separation of the sexes, after which the dance would begin. "The forsaking of carnal pleasures, liquidating lust, and the crucifixion of the flesh" were often phrases that passed from the lips of whoever was leading the Sunday service. While Rev. Pope's flock of Protestant puritans might have agreed with such notions in principle, the idea of anyone actually carrying out these eremitic credos of monasticism was unthinkable. And so the townsfolk came in ever-increasing numbers to watch and be watched by The Watcher.

If the sexual innuendoes attributed to the brethren and sisters of Shakertown weren't enough to bring townsfolk out on Sundays, then the whole business of the divinely inspired visionists and spiritism was more than enough to make up the difference. Wilford Ranks, at a previous Shaker service, had loosely counted more than six hundred people in a group where the spectators outnumbered the Believers to such an extent that some of the townsfolk were forced to sit in the Shaker seats. And he had seen dozens more peering in the windows from the out-of-doors. To the locals, this was exciting theatre. And Sunday afternoon was the high point of their week, there amidst the Shaker Believers and their "strange sexual ideas and bizarre religious practices," as Rev. Pope was wont to say earlier in the day from the puritan pulpit of his church just down the road.

Despite the ironies of the local Baptists gathering on Sunday afternoons in great numbers at the Shakertown Meeting Hall, the fact remained that the Era of Manifestation and all that went with it was the best ticket in town. And since the price was right, the escalating numbers of people coming out to the Shakertown services was serving as a kind of incentive for recurring, if not expanding occurrences of visions, visitations and messages from the unseen world.

As the whole Meeting House scene escalated week after week, month after month, the nature of the spirit manifestations became more and more elaborate, more and more outrageous. In recent weeks Wilford Ranks had observed girls talking with departed friends, Believers visiting with the damned in hell, all manner of bowing and shaking, writhing in agony and groaning in heartache. In all cases those receiving the visions swore to experiencing "living intelligent beings invisible but in a state of conscious existence."

But while most members of all the Shaker societies were enthralled and enraptured in the aura of manifestations occurring almost daily, such behavior was not without it detractors. One visitor in the spring of that year had written a letter-to-the-editor in the local newspaper in indignation: "The visionists were clearly beyond self-discipline. Several women appeared to be thrown into violent hysterics, and in particular, one girl of seventeen threw up her handkerchief into the air, tore off her cap, and required the care of two or three of the older women to hold her down. In another case, one of the Shaker sisters wrenched her head nearly over her shoulder on one side and the other, and then jerked it nearly to her knee. She stopped at the end and varied it by spinning like a dervish, twisting her arms round her head like snakes.

Doubtless they regard her as a saint, for I saw a faint imitation of it in others."

During this same period in Herodsville, Rev. Matthew Pope was pontificating to his congregation against the blasphemy and evil practices occurring at Shakertown, using the words, "Why, these aberrations are nothing more than the contagious frenzy characteristic of camp meetings, a triumph of enthusiasm over reason and order. Why these people are nothing more than a handful of miserable fools and bedlamites making themselves ridiculous."

While testimonials like these were often seen and heard outside of the Shaker communities themselves, within the societies this sort of behavior was not only becoming commonplace, but was encouraged. The Ministries of the various Shaker societies from New Hampshire to Kentucky saw this new Era as something of a necessity and a needed injection into the family of Believers--something to heighten their enthusiasm during a time when a kind of lethargy was increasingly becoming prevalent.

The fact was that by 1842 in Shakertown and many of the other Shaker communities, the key "instruments of manifestations" frequently delivered messages to the entire society, and often directly to the Ministry or village leaders. These transmissions were often specific injunctions and were to be incorporated into the strict rules of the society. In this kind of environment and under these kinds of circumstances, instruments such as Kitt Leigh rose to a kind of prominence never before seen in the heretofore egalitarian confines of any Shaker community. And it was because of this "rise to prominence" that The Watcher and the other members of the Shakertown Ministry were so attentive to her and protective of her every move.

Riding on the passenger's side of the driver's bench in the buckboard wagon as they made their way home from the Shaker meeting that evening around dusk, Asher engaged his friend Caden in conversation.

"Forget it. You don't have a prayer--no pun intended. She's so well protected with her society's chastity belt that any love-bullet you were to shoot at her would bounce off like rain from a duck's back. And besides, she's way too pretty. Pretty girls only marry money, and all you've got of that sits in your pocket, jangling, as we speak," Caden warned.

"But did you see the way that she looked at me? I'm telling you, she was talking with her eyes. And though mostly hidden behind her great hair, her eyes were inviting me in. Begging me, in fact. I'm telling you, disguised in all that beauty, there is a simple Shaker girl whose body is crying out to be touched. Whose heart and soul are crying out to be loved. Love of the flesh. Not all this mad religious stuff. I'm telling you that look was like a kiss."

"Show me the imprint of her lips, friend. Where it was her lips touched your skin. You're dreaming. This girl is famously guarded by her clan. You'll never get that close to her again. Did you see how fast that old man got to you and dragged you off the floor? It's kind of spooky--that old guy sitting up in the window. You best forget her. They've got their eye on you, already."

"How am I supposed to forget her? How can I forget that hair? How can I forget those eyes?"

"She's a Shaker girl. You think you're just going to show up in your wagon and they're going to let you take her to the square-dance on Friday night in Herodsville? These people are all about celibacy. In case you don't know what that word means, it means 'no sex'!"

"I'm not even thinking about sex. I just want to be close to her. Bathe in her shadow. Feel the wisdom of her breath blowing in my hair. Hear the sound of my name as it bursts from her lips."

"Sure you do. Try and tell me you aren't thinking of what she looks like underneath that long dress of hers. The size of her breasts. The soft muscles in her calves. I'm telling' you, you need to look somewhere else, closer to home, if you're going to get some. What about Darci? What's she gonna say when she finds out you've got eyes for this Shaker girl?"

"To call her body beautiful is an understatement. Her Shaker clothes are but a mask that the eyes of her breasts long to look through. I have looked into her eyes and I have come away blind. All I see is her face. It stays with me. Now a blind-man, how will I ever see the faces of other girls? And in memory, none until now even closely compares. Blindmen have great memories. I cannot forget her face."

"As you wish, my friend. I don't know how to teach you to forget. I'm not one of those saints your father preaches about every Sunday. All I know is that you're headed for trouble if you keep up your obsession about this girl. Ah, here we are. Home again. Some food and a good night's sleep is all the cure you need. Trust me. By tomorrow morning this whole day will seem like a forgotten dream. Now get your backside down from this wagon. I don't want to hear any more of this silliness."

At the same moment that Caden's wagon was pulling up to Asher's parents' house, Kitt and her girlfriend Eden were talking as they walked down the main road in the village to the Centre Family Dwelling to partake of the Sabbath meal.

"I was worried about you, tonight," says Eden. "All that head-shaking and contorting. And then at the end when your cap fell off...."

"Did you see him, Eden? Who was that boy? Like a blonde god standing there afore me. I felt like a statue, so focused was his gaze. Do you know who I mean? The tall blonde boy at the end, there in the middle of the room."

"How could I have missed him? So quickly did old Mr. Spires escort him off the floor and back to the *fasteners*. I don't think you'd even gotten your hair back into your cap before the old man was there between you--shot like a gun from his seat on the other side of the room. I don't think I've ever seen the old man move that fast! I thought your blonde-haired boy was going to cry as old Mr. Spires took him away. What was it you said to him to bring those invisible tears to his eyes?"

"I said nothing. Yet in my eyes there must have been a kind of language leaking out and which he was translating back to me as we stood there for that momentary eternity--until Brother Spires got in the way. His eyes--I swear they were singing some sweet song. A thrush's song, perhaps. Or a kind of sparrow. But the look of his eyes was more like that of an eagle. For a moment, I thought that he would pounce on me. Like a raptor would sight and seduce a small rabbit into some frozen motion, making it an easy prey. Who was he? Do you know his name?"

"What does it matter? He is a townie. He comes from Herodsville. I saw him leave with another boy his own age. The both of them have been here before. In fact, many times according to my count."

"How do you know such things? And if you know them, why do I not?"

"My eyes and mind are more on simple things--unlike yours, that are so attuned to the realm of spirits and the voice of Mother Ann."

"Am I so out of touch? So out of tune? What else have I been missing all these weeks and months?"

"I don't know, Kitt, but I will ask Sister Wicks at supper tonight, as she seems to know everything that goes on in Herodsville and who comes from town to our meetings. I'm sure she will know who this blonde-haired god of yours is. For now, enough of this inquisition, and this trivial talk that can only lead us astray."

Later, Asher and Caden sit on the front steps of Rev. Pope's house. They had been served one of Mrs. Pope's legendary Sunday suppers and were attempting to talk and eat at the same time.

"Well, has your mother's good meal satiated that hunger which, earlier, was stuck up in your eyes?"

"No, Caden, the one hunger satisfied, has only made the other worse. The second makes my mom's cobbler seem almost bitter by comparison."

"Your comments border on heresy," says Caden, with the taste of Mrs. Pope's cobbler still fresh on his lips. "Can you hear what you're saying?"

"Even out here in this spring night's air, with my stomach full of supper, I feel like I've been wasting away in prison for weeks without food. I can't get her out of my head. I guess my own good fortune has become my misery. What would be her name, Caden? If only I knew the letters of that name and could speak that language."

"I can read. And the book of this girl's religion is a murder mystery. And I can see no happy ending for you, there."

"Then I shall turn this afternoon's tears into fire, becoming a kind of sun that will shine back on myself, so she be blinded and can not turn away."

"Where is all this poetry coming from? I've never heard you talk this way."

"I doubt there has ever been a woman this beautiful. God must have been having a good day when he created her!"

"Really, Asher, let me fix you up with one of Mandy's friends. And then you can compare. I think the cobbler has gone to your head. There are other beautiful fish in the Kentucky River. You'll see."

"Ok, sure. Go ahead. But you're gonna lose this bet. My money is on this Shaker girl who has no name."

Kitt and Eden had eaten their Sabbath supper with the rest of the Shakertown community, and having finished their dishwashing chores for the evening, they are now sitting out on the steps of the Centre Family Dwelling.

"I think I would swear, Eden, if swearing were allowed. I swear I cannot get his image out of my mind. I see him standing there and all I want to do is to ask him if he'd like to dance. You know, a "slow dance" I think the people from town call them--when a boy and a girl dance together."

"Be careful, Kitt, you're treading on thin ice with this kind of talk. You wouldn't want anyone to hear you saying such things. You never know when one of the older sisters might be upstairs in the hallway with the window open on a warm night like this, and might hear your words."

"I don't think that if I were to live for a thousand years I'd ever forget the look on his face."

"But, Kitt, he is from Herodsville. What good to think even another thought of this boy? And even if you were to come face to face with him again, what then? And if you were to be found out? What would Brother Wilford and Sister Daniella do? You know this kind of thing is not allowed."

"I want you to do me a favor. I want you to find out his name. Where he lives. Who his parents are. And anything else you can find out about him. Will you do this for me? I just want to know. Maybe if I know these things, that will be enough and I shall never think of it again. If that's the case, you will be doing me a great service. Will you do it?"

"It is against my better judgment. But if it will get your thoughts off of this subject and get this boy out of your mind, it's probably worth the risk. For I must be careful, too, you know. I've already told Sister Mary that I wanted to speak with her about her shopping trips into Herodsville. And we have planned to meet tomorrow upstairs at the Sister's Shop. She told me that she will be there alone tomorrow and that we can talk in privacy. There will only be two other women working the looms, downstairs, tomorrow, and the noise of the shuttles banging will drown out our voices upstairs. And, you know how Sister Eleanor and Sister Karen love to talk!"

"I will see you tomorrow night after dinner and we can talk about your meeting with Sister Mary while we are washing dishes. No one will be able to overhear our conversation. Then, I will hear his name in harmony with the musical sound of the rattle of plates. I only hope that his name is not known to me too late."

*A*s Wilford Ranks ate his meal that evening in the Centre Family Dwelling, he was watching. From where he was sitting in the Ministry alcove of the basement dining area at a four-board birch trestle table, he could see the whole room. There was typically no conversation during mealtime and little movement about the room. The servers and cooks were all moving about and taking care of things while the rest of the community quietly ate. Silence being the virtue that it was in Shaker doctrine, many of the important and essential acts done by Shakertown members were done in silence.

Silence: noiselessness, quiescence, taciturnity, extinguish, overcome, suppress, refute, hush--all synonyms for this non-act which is at the center of all Shaker doctrine and practice. Also, "quiet, still, peace and whisht"--as the Irish and the Scots referred to this kind of self-imposed muteness. In Pleasant Grove society there were many of Scots-Irish descent and one could hear the brogue and occasional Gaelic words from the Old Country slip from the lips of these members of the community--when they weren't holding their tongues.

In his state of inaudi there at the Ministry table, Brother Wilford watched his three compatriots as they eat. Observing how they went about eating their food. Watches Sister Daniella Darrow sitting across from him at the trestle table as she took long sips of fresh cow's milk that had been brought in from the milking barn that day. How the milk, after each sip, covered and enlarged her lips in a white lipstick before she licked it off with her tongue. Catching himself in this bit of erotic visual eavesdropping, he felt a little ashamed. But only a little, as he noticed there was, now, a rise in his pants--behind the buttons of his fly where his loins were emitting pleasurable heat.

The Watcher quickly forced his gaze away from Sister Daniella and the thoughts that were becoming jangled in his mind, and looked around the adjacent room until he found Kitt Leigh at one of the women's tables near the far wall. His thoughts went immediately back to the afternoon's meeting and dance and the sight of the sister's shock of auburn hair.

Scene III.

It was true that there was beginning to be some concern in the ranks of Shakertown society about the excesses that were going on involving not only community members, but the visitors from the nearby town of Herodsville, as well. The number of visitors to the weekly Meetings was continually growing and the attendance at Meeting had gotten so large that it was becoming a hinderance to the carrying out of the actual religious practices of the Shaker society. And, recently, visitors from town sitting in the *fastener* benches had been getting up from their seats and taking part in the more active parts of the service. Since this had started, the floor of the meeting hall during the Shaker dances had become so crowded with enthusiastic and exuberant townsfolk and their rappings that physical accidents were no longer occasional, but becoming ordinary. At one of the meetings there occurred a massive wreck in the men's line, and from up in his window-seat Brother Wilford, again The Watcher, had counted no less than eighteen bodies lying on the floor at one time--some of them still speaking in unknown tongues.

It was during these months of the year 1842 that an apparent split began to occur in the theretofore good relations between the townsfolk of Herodsville and the society members of Shakertown. As the worship services grew more ardent, outsiders became less respectful, as evidenced by the recent "train-wreck" incident. The rationalization by the townsfolk was that the hullaballoo of the Shaker services and dances was, in fact, a kind of built-in therapy to assuage their eccentric beliefs and to extinguish the burning fires of sexual desire.

But the growing divide only grew wider when one of the Shakertown faithful, Brother Jerah, had received special revelations which had then been transferred and engraved onto a special stone that stood in a fenced-off area beside the Meeting House. It acted as a kind of "Ten Commandments" stone for the Pleasant Grove community and was touted to be the direct words of God. Called "The Groveland Stone," it was the site of both personal and group gatherings, often attracting Society members before and after Sunday Meeting service. A kind of Old Testament liturgy, the message inscribed upon The Groveland Stone used the words "Let the stranger from afar, and the traveler, behold this work with sacred reverence and pass by in solemn fear of his God."

Both the fact of and the message upon the stone flew in the face of many of the pious
townsfolk, who saw in the stone little more than a form of heresy, or worse, an attempt to usurp the importance in biblical scripture and historical fact of Moses' visit to Mount Sinai and the resulting tablets bearing the Ten Commandments. This stone and its implications were not lost on Rev. Pope. At Herodsville First Baptist Church on Sunday mornings, he railed away against the very existence of the stone, so close by. He termed it a blatant defamation of God's character, if not "a kind of blasphemy created by nothing less than heathens worshipping false idols."

Since that fateful day when Asher had had the encounter with Kitt on the Meeting House floor, he had been back to the Shakertown Meeting Hall several times, and weeks had gone by. In each case he had gotten up during the Shaker Dance and participated, dancing in the long line of men and amidst all manner of shaking and quaking. In more than one occasion he had gone 'round in the line and ended up close to the women's group and had passed Kitt at close range. In each case their eyes had met, like stars passing in orbit in the night sky. Each time this happened, it seemed to Asher that the glance, the gaze, was increasingly more intense coming from Kitt, as it was certainly more intense coming from him. As he would see her coming up in the women's line from the other direction, he would channel all his energy into his eyes and project pure emotion towards her as she glided by.

While they had still not had a chance to meet or speak formally, the glances they threw at one another during the Shaker Dance were preludes to what would come. At each of these events Asher noticed how the short balding Shaker man stood always nearby, watching him. He noticed The Watcher up in his window, eyes locked on him in a kind of omniscient exchange as he sat on the fastener bench. Always watched.

During that spring, Asher's conversations with Caden focused almost exclusively on his longing for the girl. Caden still thought Asher was barking up a fruitless tree. But as the weeks passed and as Asher's resolve increased, Caden had finally come to accept the fact that Asher wasn't going to let go of this lusty bone he was chewing on. And with this newly-formed, if half-hearted, alliance, the marrow of a secret plot were planted between the two.

Caden's father owned and ran the Herodsville General Store. Caden had been working there since boyhood and was working there full-time since his graduation from school. The Herodsville Store was the center of community interaction and gossip, so Caden knew more than he wanted to know about almost everyone in town. And in his capacity as "assistant grocer" he had, on more than one occasion, waited on members of the Shakertown society who occasionally would come to town to shop for the few necessities that they didn't produce for themselves. It was during one such encounter that he had met and talked for a short time with Sister Mary Wicks on one of her errand-runs into Herodsville to get some out-of-season asparagus, as the Shakertown garden asparagus beds had run their course a couple weeks prior. She had also come into town to pick up some screws and bolts for the racks in the Dry House--in anticipation of the upcoming growing season and the heavy load of fruit and vegetables that would be processed there. From across the counter, Caden and Sister Mary exchanged pleasantries, did their business, and then a strange thing occurred. Sister Mary, out of the clear blue, asked Caden if he knew of a young man with blonde hair who had been regularly attending the Shaker meetings.

So unexpected was Sister Mary's question that Caden dropped the wrapped package of asparagus that he was handing her onto the wooden countertop next to the cash drawer. Off guard, but making a quick recovery, Caden made a survey of the store to see if his father or mother, who occasionally helped out in the millinery section, was anywhere in sight. Seeing that he was alone in the store for the moment, he awkwardly responded to Sister Mary's question.

"Blonde hair? Do I know anyone with blonde hair? And what name would there be to go with this blonde hair, ma'am?"

"No name, sir, only the color of his hair and that he is seen every Sunday afternoon at Shaker Meeting--oftimes partaking in the dance. For fact, I have seen you there, too, at his side on the fastener bench."

"Yes, ma'am, I do have a friend of that description whom I do sometimes accompany to Shakertown on Sundays."

"Well, sir, does this friend not have a name?"

"Name? Oh, ah...yes, ma'am. He has a name."

"Would you give it to me, sir? There are those I know who have inquired and have asked me to do their bidding, today, as I make my rounds in town."

"Is he in any trouble, ma'am? Is he in disfavor amongst your kindred in Shakertown? I know of no thing that he has done that may have brought him discredit there."

"No, lad, your friend has done no harm in Pleasant Grove that I know of. My question comes not from The Ministry or from "The Watchers" as I understand you call them here in Herodsville. My questions come from one of the members of the women's group, who has noticed him during the dances. She has asked me to find out his name and what he might be about. I have told her I would, but only because she is held in such high esteem in our community and to deny her this small favor would be unlikely and unkind."

"Ma'am, my friend's name is Asher. Asher Pope. The last being a kind of irony and joke amongst some inasmuch as his father is the preacher of the Baptist church here in town. There, now, in saying only this I have told you much already."

"I thank you, sir, and is there any more information on your generous tongue? This young woman would love to know more."

"Love, ma'am? Did you say 'love'?"

"Love meaning like, sir. She would *like* to know more."

"And what would this young woman you represent *like* to know? It seems strange that a young woman of your society would be asking about a young man from Herodsville. Given.... Well, you understand my meaning, ma'am."

"She would like to know his name, sir, and his status in your society. Nothing more, really. She has noticed him at the Sunday dances and says that he seems to have noticed her, and her curiosity seems to have prevailed. Hence my mission for today and this conversation that we share."

"And does your 'young lady' have a name, ma'am? For Asher will surely want to know, as I am duty-bound as his friend to share with him this conversation that we are having. He has, in fact, mentioned to me on more than one occasion of his own curious interest in a certain young woman whom he sees at the Meeting Hall on Sundays. Might this girl who has caught Asher's eye be one and the same as your 'young lady' ? He talks often of her auburn hair."

"That would be my lady, sir. She is known in the women's quarters for the quality of her long brown hair. But how would your Asher know this? Her hair, like mine, is always hidden by this cloth cap."

"He talks all the time--and there is seemingly no end to his telling--about an incident during one of the dances some weeks ago, now, where a young lady's cap came off and her full head of hair was revealed. 'A glowing mane' he is wont to refer to it."

"Oh, yes, I seem to remember this incident. It was the subject of some talk for a few days thereafter. But only in jest and in a teasing kind of way when brought up to Sister Kitt."

"Her name is Kitt, then? And would she have a surname? "

"I'm afraid I've already spoken too much. But, in fairness, you should know the name of the one who asks for your friend's name. Her surname is Leigh. Her full name is Kitt Leigh. She is held in high regard by everyone in Pleasant Grove, due largely to her ability to communicate directly with our beloved founder Mother Ann, who is no longer with us. I tell you all this in the strictest of confidence, sir, as nothing untoward should ever come of this conversation--either in your society, or mine."

"You can count on me, ma'am. Asher's ears, alone, will hear these words. And he will be very pleased to hear them, ma'am, and to know her name. He is a gentle soul, ma'am, and wouldn't hurt a flea. So, you can sleep peacefully tonight and therefore not worry. And here is your asparagus, ma'am. In your hands, rightly, this time."

"Thank you sir, and for your confidence. It will help Sister Kitt to rest, too, I can assure you. Til we meet again, then, my good boy."

"Goodbye, ma'am. Nice to have talked to you."

That evening Caden and Asher are sitting in the hayloft of Caden's father's barn smoking an illicit cigarette that they were passing back and forth between them.

"Well, Asher, my boy, your wishes have been answered."

"What do you mean? Speak plainly."

"Today at the store, I had a very interesting little chat with one of the women from Shakertown. The one who comes in once in a while and does all the shopping for the folks up there. We've talked about her, before."

"Yes, I remember. Well, come on, tell me, what did you talk about?"

"About your "Shaker girl." What else?"

"About THE Shaker girl?"

"None other."

"Well, come on, tell me what she said. Did she tell you her name?"

"Yes, but first things first. The Sister started the conversation while she was buying some asparagus and just kinda matter-of-factly asked me about YOU! Said she was asking for a 'young woman' whom she knew. I was so taken aback by this question that I dropped the package of asparagus I was in the process of giving her."

"She was asking about ME?"

"You got it. Said her 'young woman friend' wanted to know your name. 'Course I told her. And then she leaked the name of the girl. I don't think she meant to, but out it came."

"Well, then, what is her name?"

"Let's see if I can remember it."

"Don't play with me, out with it!"

"Britt.....no....Whit....no....."

"Come on. Come on. Stop with your hedging. I'm gonna bust that lip of yours if you don't quit this and tell me her name."

"Oh, yeah, I think she said it was Kitt—with two Ts."

"Kitt?"

"Yeah, that was it. Kitt. Kitt Lee--or something that sounded like that Army man over in Virginia we've been hearing about lately. You know, Robert E. Lee everyone calls him. She must be kin to him somehow."

"Kitt. That's got a nice ring to it. You know it brings to mind young foxes and wild cats. 'Kits' my granpa calls them. Kitt Lee. So, she's got a name after all. Was beginning to wonder. Those folks up at Shakertown are so strange anyway, and I was wondering if they even had normal names and such. Guess so."

"And I told the Sister your name, too. I'd never have gotten her name if I hadn't. So, when she asked, I told her. But she wanted to know more. Said this Kitt girl had sent her on a special errand and wanted to know. I told her about your dad being a preacher and all. And that you were a good person—'cause she seemed concerned about that, her bein' all secretive and all. But in the end I got the feeling that she was satisfied and pleased that she'd found out what the Kitt girl had sent her to find out."

"What else did she say about the girl? Anything else?"

"Somethin' about her being real important and highly respected up there in Shakertown amongst folks. And somethin' about her talking to ghosts or somethin'. I think she said that she could talk to some old dead woman named Mother Annie, or somethin' like that. And that she was kinda famous up there for being able to do that. I don't know, sounds kinda strange to me. But I didn't ask any questions, as I didn't want to cause her to stop what she was saying, since she seemed kinda shy about talkin' in the first place."

"I've heard about this kind of thing that goes on up there. They call it "manifesting" or some such term. The people there that talk to spirits are called "instruments." My dad talks about all this at dinner sometimes. Says it's the work of Satan. And it's all part of all the stuff that goes on at the Shaker dances--with all the janglings and the rappings, the hollering and whirling about. So, this girl does that? I could see she was special. Could see it in her eyes. A kind of faraway light shinin' through them. Like it was comin' from somewhere else. So, what else did the Sister say?"

"That's it. Nothing else. Just wanted to know your name and who your people were. And she didn't offer nothing else about Britt.....I mean, Kitt."

"Did she say anything about talkin' to you again, or talkin' to me or anything?"

"Nope, just only what I've told you."

"Does she come into the store often? Like on a regular day or anything?"

"I haven't been taking notes, but seems like she comes in about every two weeks or so and buys only a few things from the grocery, but almost always gets something from the other side of the store. You know, hardware and stuff. And it seems like it's fairly regular, like today, on a Tuesday."

"Your dad gonna need any help at the store Tuesday after next? I can work it so I can get off from my janitor job over at the church and help out some on odd Tuesdays for a while. What do you think?"

"I'll say something to dad and let you know. Like I said before, you best not be gettin' in over your head with those Shaker folks. Your dad's already aggravated about your goin' up there every Sunday with me to 'watch them heathens dance,' as he says. Best to forget about this girl, man. Becky was in the store the other day and she came right out and told me that she'd be willing to go out with you. Now, how can you turn down an offer like that?"

"Talk to your dad, and see if he needs any help on Tuesdays. And I'll see what I can do about getting off at the church. We best get down from this loft and get home. I'll talk to you tomorrow."

The room in the old East Family Dwelling is packed, and Kitt, stands at the front of the room, has not moved in several minutes. In preparation for the meeting, Kitt has not eaten that day and her feet have been washed by two of the elder Sisters just prior to the evening's events. There is no talking and no rustling about and the energy in the room is of anticipation. Slowly, Kitt opens her eyes, which have been closed all this time, and begins to speak:

"Oh my sisters and brothers   Ye are not called to become defiled and polluted and to wallow in fleshly gratifications as a sow walloweth in the mire   There is a better way to act the part of a mother and a bosom friend to your companion   That superior way involves care and cheerfulness in household duties   Lay your hand to the distaff and know that it is the diligent hand that maketh rich and idleness is the sure threshold to destruction   Avoid a clamorous tongue and do not seek amusement abroad and keep a clean habitation   Hands to work and hearts to God   These are thy cleansing gifts   Everyone should work diligently with their hands according to their strength for the public good of the society--to build community identity and equality   Your work is the root of your achievement   So eat not the bread of idleness   Let no idle hands be seen   This is your Mother's wisdom   Through the hand of a medium I will send you an image: of a tree bearing fruit   This shall be your reminder   This tree rustles with a living spirit   In it you will get your daily strength   Like your houses it will show a peaceful mansion at rest   And so you shall be also   At peace in your work   At rest in your work   Let thee not be idle   For in work is our connection to the Divine

Hands to work and hearts to God   This be your credo   Hands to work and hearts to God   Sing this to yourselves as you work and in your songs   These words I leave with you as they have been certified by ancient prophets holy angels and all of the divine presences above   If you could only hear the angels sing!   They sing for you   I and the angels are one   So be not separated   Be as one and think of God and your Mother Ann and pray to them for protection   Do these things and fear not the fear of famine or of terrible winds   In the future I shall send you sacred and divine edicts   These will come through a spiritual witness in the form of a spiritual mother who is in your midst   A female witness   When the scriptural passages come--listen and take heed   Those who obtain this gospel shall inherit the earth and are assured a peaceful mansion of rest when they are done with the things of time   Hands to work   Hearts to God   May the fruit be bountiful on the Tree of Life   Hands to work   Hearts to God......"

As all those who had heard Sister Kitt's transmission from Mother Ann made their way back to the Centre Family Dwelling or to their rooms there in the East Dwelling to their "peaceful mansions of rest." Kitt sat on the back steps of the East Family Dwelling eating a large piece of rhubarb cake made from some spring shoots of the tart plant and talked with Sister Mary.

"I swear Sister, your words from Mother Ann tonight did take my breath away, and then I have had to run to the Centre House to check on the young girls and get them into bed and then run back here to catch you lest we might never be together and alone again on this night."

"Sister, I am sorry for your trouble. I did not mean to steal your breath or your energy tonight, but I saw a small opportunity for us to talk of matters of interest--at least of interest to me. Sister Eden has told me that you have recently been to town and have some news for me as a result of your visit."

"Yes, Sister Kitt, and I will tell you only in strictest confidence, as you know how some of the sisters love to wag their tongues. Should they know of this meeting or of what we will soon talk, gossip would fly around this village like leaves in a storm of wind in fall."

"Pray, sister, do tell me what you know."

"I would do no such favor for any other, dear sister, 'cept you. But for you, our voice of Mother Ann. Pray that this bridge I've walked is a sturdy one. For neither one of us would likely survive such a fall."

" 'Fall', sister? What sort of fall do you mean? A fall from grace? A time of year? You speak strangely and answer my simple question in an odd way. Do tell me what is on your mind, dear sister."

"I have been to Herodsville and to the grocery there. The young man who waited on me there is the son of the man who owns the store. We found ourselves alone in the store and so while I was buying some asparagus and hardware for the Dry House I asked him if he perchance knew of a blonde-haired boy who comes regularly to the Meeting House on Sundays. He swore he did, as he is, in fact, a close friend to such a young man. When I asked the blonde boy's name and his station, I revealed too much and told your name in the same breath. Seeing that I had confided in him your name, he was gentle and offered his friend's name, too."

"Go on, go on, sister. Let's not make a novel of this tale. Where is thy ending?"

"A happy ending, dear sister, as the young man in the shop has given me his name--to be given, in turn, to you. He mentioned his friend would be delighted to know that you had been inquiring about him, just as he, apparently, has been inquiring about you. You see, my girl, what a happy ending our story has?"

"Sister.... Is there a character with a proper name in this long fiction!?"

"Nay, not a fiction, dear, but more of a history have I brought for you this evening. A drama backed by a history as recent as only this week. An oral tale much akin to the early pages of one of your favorite plays, I do believe. Sister Eden tells me you read often from the works of Brother Shakespeare."

"Sister Eden has told you much. Too much, I fear. But, the name Sister Mary, the name!..."

"The blonde-haired boy's name is Asher Pope. He resides in Herodsville. He has noticed you, according to his good friend who works at the grocery, and has spoken about you on many occasions to his friend. So far our story is on a steady foot. Ah, but here's the rub.... His father is none other than the minister of the Herodsville Baptist Church. And it is known to us that he preaches against our ways, and especially against the manifestations and those who are instruments of voices from beyond. I fear your blonde-haired young man is from the enemy's camp, my dear, and not among those who would be friends of The Society."

"Asher. It has a kind feel to it. Like snow falling through a clear sky. Don't you think so, sister? And Pope, that, too, would indicate a kind of religious heritage. While not our particular path, here at Pleasant Grove and in our sister societies, it has promise, does it not? Asher Pope. Asher Pope. I hear this name as if it were lifted in voice by large cheering crowds. Ash-er Pope. Ash-er Pope. Ash-er Pope.... Can you hear the lyric quality I do, sister? And what else? Did the grocery boy say more?"

"Only that asparagus was high last week, as it would soon be past its season. And that he was sorry for having dropped my package when I spoke your name."

"This is all? Are your sure?"

"He did say he would be talking to your Asher that very evening and would pass along the fact of your inquiries and your name."

"Sister Mary, you have made a good day even better with this news--this tale of yours and its Shakespearian telling. And I thank thee for thy troubles and any tribulations it may have caused."

"It's ok, girl. I actually enjoyed myself and the errand of espionage. It added a little flavor to an otherwise tasteless trip. So, for that, I should be thanking thee.

"But I fear the innocence of this play's first scene belies portent of not-so-pleasant scenes to come. I worry that much as in your *Romeo & Juliet*, there is no happy end. I hope you have learned well from your many readings of this tale."

"I know it well, sister. But my heart is way ahead of my head, I'm afraid. And there is reason, I intuit, in this madness, which will reveal itself soon enough. For now, it's getting late and there is much to do tomorrow in the Dry House to get ready for the coming garden season which will be upon us before we know it."

"Yes, I expect we are at the end of our winter's reprieve. But I'm worried where all this sleuthing leads. From Shakers and Baptists, a happy ending we'll not get. It gives me mind of Montague and Capulet."

Scene IV.

A warm spring afternoon. Another Sunday. Another Shaker service. Wilford Ranks crouched on the stairway in the wall of the Meeting House. It had been a long day of exhausting correspondence with members of the Ministries in the other Societies up north. Not the usual fare for "the Lord's Day," but brought on by certain urgencies and concerns being voiced and debated at arm's length and over considerable distances amongst the supposed Shaker elite. In his state of fatigue and hunger (Sunday supper was yet a few hours away), Ranks was experiencing a kind of unpleasant euphoria and at the same time feeling a little dizzy. The dizziness took on hallucinogenic qualities as he looked down through the waves and ripples in the small window onto the large room filled to capacity with townsfolk and society members. It was as if he were looking through a window into another realm. Another world. A fantasy. A dream.

Later that evening, feeling satiated but hardly what he would call clear-headed, Wilford Ranks wriote his mixed impressions of what he had seen that day into his Ministry Journal.

Worship growing wilder. Outsiders taking part. Less respectful. Gifts being displayed openly. Pleasing. Disorder. Dancing going on outside. Sister Gates shaking wonderfully. Sister Matilda very powerful as she went round Sister Miranda at a surprising rate. Sister Abigail jerking around. Sister Elizabeth beating on everything in sight. Sister Sidle much wrought upon. Sister Sarah bowing and singing at the same time. Sister Miranda spinning the whole time without stopping--jerking and motioning with hands and arms in inhuman poses. Hasn't eaten (says Sister Darrow) since the 25th. Sister Sally flying about under operations. Sister Samantha, Brother Dean and many others in much distress, and I don't know how many more. Counted at least fourteen brethren and sisters and every boy but one under operations. Spirits seem to be everywhere. Angels? Many wailing and in tears. Women laying prostrate. Strange roaring sound in my ears. Songs of Indians. Whole assembly drunk on spiritual wine. Bordering on the bizarre. Sister Sarah being used like a mop being scrubbed across a dirty floor. Brother Prentis shakes mightily while stooping down and eats simplicity off the floor. Public showing of affections amongst the women. Kissing. Ghosts rising up from graves. Strange lights. Building moving. Shaking. Building is alive? Small earthquakes. Wind. Fire. Unknown tongues. Six young boys in trance. One urinating. Another spitting. Indiscretions everywhere in front of the world's people. The world's people interacting with people of the Society--jerking, bowing, shaking, arms flying in all directions. A Carnival. A Mardi Gras of souls. Amazing grace. Uplifting. No! Want to stop service. Can't. Time stopped. No Time. Everything in motion. Nothing in motion. Open window. Deafening roar. Too loud. Close window. Blonde-haired boy nowhere to be seen. Sit on steps for a while. Stairway shaking. Light-headed. Go to door to get air. World's people dancing in the grass. Laughter. Children looking in windows. Big eyes. Rain coming. No one leaves. Outside dancing in the rain. Carriages all along the road--all the way to river. Circle dance around Groveland Stone. Sacred stone used as Maypole. Bacchanal. Tribal. Uplifting! Natural. NO! Back inside at window. Motion to Brother Spires, Sister Beth, others to stop the service. Takes thirty minutes to calm room and get everyone to stop. Few still jangling. Several lying on the floor after others have left building. Take some to Centre Dwelling talking in tongues. Eat supper late. Couldn't sleep.

Sitting on one of the highest promontories in Mercer County along the Kentucky River, Shakertown was fairly typical as a mirror image of most other Shaker settlements. Stone, board and brick buildings of hefty size and structure arranged aesthetically and with geometric good taste were positioned comfortably in amongst the lovely rolling Kentucky River landscape. In Shakertown, every member of the village society had a job to do that was determined by a rotating work schedule which changed with the seasons and provided new experience, the learning of new trades, as well as being an antidote to tedium or boredom. The doctrinal ethic of work and overwork as an antidote to overcoming "the sins of the flesh." Shakertown society was not only a model of semi-self-sufficiency, but was fertile ground for architectural and industrial creativity.

Some society members were especially adept at certain scientific and technological trades and had brought current trends into the community from outside or had kept abreast of the latest advances in those fields through their reading. In the end, everyone, in a highly organized, but not oppressive fashion, shared in the idea of the daily business of self-reliance, which was something of an obsession within the society as it was their open door to living outside of and slightly separate from mainstream America and "the world's people."

Nowhere was their entrepreneurial savvy more evident at Shakertown than in their herb and seed industry. Cottage industries were a major economic staple for many of the Shaker communities and the members of the Shakertown community excelled in the selling of seeds to farmers and gardeners. Seeds were sold in bulk and in small packets by Shakertown peddlers who traveled established routes in the fall and winter months with their two-horse wagons filled with seeds. In 1842, Shakertown's logs for the seed business showed that about one-tenth of the village's total income came from the sale of seeds.

Using the apprenticeship system for teaching the trade, young men, and even a few women in Shakertown learned the skills of carpentry and Shaker design. Using techniques that emphasized harmony and proportion, the Shakers produced furniture that gained nation-wide recognition. It was prized by urban as well as rural households and by members of the American landed gentry as well as early collectors. Shaker chairs, trestle tables and candle stands could be found in 1842 throughout the United States and in every dwelling in Shakertown.

While the occupants of Shakertown believed in and aspired to a strict separation from the rest of the world with regard to temporal matters, in reality, their drive for self-sufficiency ended up being somewhat dependent upon the market system of the dominant culture. In the process of producing, selling and bartering for certain products, they also bought or bartered for goods from the outside. As time had gone on, this kind of economic co-dependency had become more prevalent, despite the doctrines of separation and well-meant sectarian strategies of economics. So by 1842, the Society of Pleasant Grove found itself in a situation of increasing interaction with surrounding towns and peoples who were not believers. Weekly trips to Herodsville by members of the Pleasant Grove society were not uncommon. Nor, as was evident by the large local attendances at Shaker worship services and dances, was it uncommon for local folk to be seen up in Shakertown on Sundays, or on other occasions. While this sort of interaction bothered some, such as the Rev. Matthew Pope, it was a boon for the local farmers and merchants like Caden's father who owned and operated the Herodsville General Store.

On Monday morning following Sunday's "bacchanal," and as Wilford Ranks entered the word "missing" into his journal, Asher was at home in his upstairs attic room writing a letter. A letter that would, two days hence, be delivered by Sister Mary Wicks to Kitt Leigh.

Asher had always believed in the organic, yet metaphysical, power of words. He sat there at the small table composing words in his mind that would become the potion that would become the spell that would turn the head of Kitt Leigh. As he sat there facing the blank piece of paper, he could see her face, like the gesture of her hands reaching up into the stream of light coming into the Meeting Hall from the large windows nearby. He could almost feel the memory of the caress of those hands, those long womanly fingers that seemed to curl around the beam of light. With these thoughts and visions rushing through his mind, he began to write. Began writing the letter. The alchemy of the words he had been rehearsing became fluid, and he rolled around in the waves of that liquid language like a playful seal. Before he had begun to write, he had reached into the drawer of his small desk and from the very back part of the drawer he had taken out a few pieces of almost transparent onion-skin paper his father sometimes used to write his Sunday sermons. He had also taken from the drawer his rarely-used fountain pen which had been his present upon graduation from school, and which to his good fortune and delight is still full of an indigo ink. The correspondence of ink, paper and words was the perfect alchemy he imagined would make the magic, creating the desired effect.

While his words went down upon the sensuous paper, he knew immediately that nothing he had ever written contained this much power. He had always believed that the art of letter-writing was the purest and most profound form of literature. And the way he had leapt onto those pages of onion-skin, the way the indigo was running out from that pen like a river, the way the words fell into place like a dance, he knew he was writing his best work.

In the end there were four pages of perfection. As much a visual piece of art as it was pregnant with profound language. He had written this letter to work!

Dear Kitt,

This letter which you hold in your hands, I have been writing in my head all this time-since our first encounter at the Shaker dance, and after. All those sidelong looks and gestures.... They all had meaning for me. I wonder if you meant them this way. In any case, all this has endeared you to me. I only hope that this letter has a similar effect, but upon you.

I love the co-incidences that seem to occur so effortlessly between us. They are like valentines. I wonder, do the people of Shakertown send each other valentines? Is this allowed? We hear such odd things about your lives, but always from unreliable sources. Maybe, if you will write to me, I will learn the truth about these things. And more!

My friend Caden says that the Sister who shops sometimes at his father's store told him that you can see and hear spirits. I've never known anyone who has had this kind of experience. I would like to know more about this if you would tell me. Do you actually talk to these spirits? Can you ask them questions that they will answer? Since they are dead and not living in our kind of reality, is their existence timeless? And if it is, can they see into the future? Maybe you could ask them (is it "them" or only one?) what the future holds for us. I would want to know. On the other hand, I'd be afraid to know if the answer was not positive. So maybe we should just keep our conversations between the two of us and not bring in any third parties. Keeping things simple is usually better, anyway.

In case you want to know about me–my family, on my mother's side, all came from Scotland–from up in the Highlands of northern Scotland. They are from Clan McDhai, which is sometimes, now, called Clan Davidson, and from a "wee place" (as the Scots often refere to it) called Dingwall, which is about an hour or so northwest of Inverness. Dingwall is the seat of Clan Davidson–which are my people. My mom says that our ancestors are notorious poets and direct descendants of King David in the Bible. Where are your people from? It wouldn't surprise me a bit if your people also came from Scotland and that we were related–in a very distant way, of course.

It is starting to rain, so I guess I won't get outdoors to do the work I intended to today. While I enjoy sitting here and writing this letter to you, it goes against my nature not to be moving and doing something physical–which is why my dad gave me the job of working as the janitor at the church. I guess he knows that it's hard for me to sit still. But I can sit still when I'm writing, or reading. I like to read and write poetry. Do you read? What do you like to read? Do they let you read what you want there in Shakertown? I've been reading the poetry of the Scots poet Robert Burns. (In Scotland they call him "Rabbie" Burns.) My mother has a book of his poems. She used to sing me some of his songs when I was younger. Maybe your mother did the same. After reading his poem "The Lass That Made the Bed to Me", I wrote my own poem. When I was writing it, I was thinking of you. I guess in a way it's a kind of valentine.

The Lass With The Bright Brown Hair

One eve amidst a crowd I was
Inside a Shaker's lair,
And when my eyes they glanced eon up
I saw a lass so fair.

Her hair aglistened in the light,
Her lips apart did lure.
And when her eye it did catch mine
My heart did beat most pure.

We talked and danced all through the night
Until 'twas time to part.
And on our parting I did sigh
And left her with my heart.
Now, time has gone awandering
Since then we've been apart.
But ne're a day it has gone by
I've not thought of her and start
To dream of days and worlds where we
Will together be entwined.
And I will court her, flawlessly,
O'er haggis wined and dined.

O where art thou, my mountain maid
Who has run off with my heart.
I think ye are in forest glade
Where first we made our start.
And one day I will pledge ye troth
And take you by the hand.
And we will go, together,
And in Scotland make our stand.
Where cattle graze and heather blows
About in misty wind.
And I will show thee Whence I came,
My land of kith and kin.

For thee I make this little rhyme
For on this special day. When Rabbie Burns did walk among
The Scots in Highlands play.
His favorite pipe and best-laid song,
For every ear to dream.
Of all the years and all the things
That each we did not glean.
But I will glean ye, yes I will.
My promise you do have.
For on my horse I'll come the road
That leads up to your door.
And then, my lass, we will depart
For Scotland, O so fair.
Where I can run my yearning fingers
Through your silk brown hair. And
I will run my fingers through your silk brown hair.
Your silk brown hair my fingers run
Like rivers from my soul.
To rest in tidal pools, Your lips,
Those luscious little bowls.
That speak the words of poesie
Our hearts and ears do know.
That speak the words of poesie
Upon which this love does grow.
That speak the words of poesie
Upon which my love for thee doest grow.

  As you can see, this pen is giving me a fit. So I'll cease to persist with my rhyming nonsense and all my questions. I hope you will write to me. I will if you will. There is still so much I want to know about you. Meanwhile, stay warm on these cold spring days and nights and I'll look forward to seeing you, as ever, on Sunday.

your Asher

Dear Asher,

As I would much prefer to speak with you directly, I will write you, instead, this letter, which I will send through Sister Mary Wicks. Your friend Caden must be having some fun being the go-between in all of this. What a story he will have to write some day. Is he a writer like yourself?

I have to say, that your "Rabbie" Burns poem made me blush. No one has ever sent me anything like this before, much less written it themselves. It made me want to run to the library and try and find some of Robert Burns's poetry--which I did and which I found. I am sending you one of his poems at the end of this letter which I think may just be the poem you had been reading before your wrote you poem to "The Brown-Haired Girl". If so, it will be another "coincidence" as you call it--that I should find that very poem.

How strangely the world does work! The day I got your letter, I had had a dream that we had actually met. I won't tell you the details, here, of this meeting, as I don't want to jinx it or ruin it for the day that we finally do meet. Does that make sense?

I missed you at the services on Sunday. At the service

on two Sundays ago, you seemed shy. You didn't look at me as much as you have done before. It seemed to me that you were holding back a lot. I certainly was nervous, but I tried to look at you as we passed in line and even searched for you about the room when we weren't near one another. I saw you with your friend (or should I say "our" friend Caden?) on the fasteners before the dancing started. It's good to know what he looks like. He looks like a nice person and I'm glad to know, now, who he is. I wonder if all three of us will ever be able to get together and just enjoy each other's company? All this sneaking about, while I must say it is exciting for me, is not normally something I would do. I've never done anything like this before, so am probably not very good at it.

    Yes, I too feel we may have a lot in common. It almost feels like we have known each other before. Maybe in another lifetime, or in the world of spirits. But, Asher, I have no illusions about what the nature of our relationship will be in this world. While I do feel we have a definite attraction for each other and have much to share with each other, I doubt that we can ever be together in any normal sort of way. The Society does not allow such things, and especially, for me, with men outside of the community. You can come and go as you please, but I am duty-bound to stay sequestered, here, and to live a life which is regulated by the doctrines of The Society as set out by our Mother Ann. While you can visit our "Pleasant Grove" on Sundays, I would never be allowed to come to town on a casual visit or even to services on Sunday at your father's church--as much as I'd like to. Either of these things might be construed as grounds for expulsion from The Society. The Society has been my family for most of my life. While I was not born in Shakertown and my parents are no longer living, I am, in a sense, married to this place and these good people. It's a good life, if not perfect. And the brethren and sisters of Shakertown count on me to be diligent in my devotion and chaste in my behavior. So, it would seem that in this lifetime we will have to be satisfied with passing by one another in line during the Shaker Dance and these letters. Anything else would cause great suspicion and great problems for both of us, I fear. Perhaps if we pass through this phase of curiosity and attraction, we can get to know each other as good friends. Even though there are all these restrictions I'm deeply happy that we are connected.

    I'm not sure what you meant by not being used to things happening so fast between you and me. Were you comparing me to your experiences with other girls? As for how quickly things have developed during these last few weeks that have led to my writing you this letter, it may be because I am now secure in my relationship with the Shakertown community. Because of my connection with Mother Ann, I have been shown a lot of respect from almost everyone in the community. This has helped me to become stronger and it is only now that I could have even dared to have done anything so risky as what you and I are now doing--even if it is only through letters. In the past, I would have been too concerned about creating problems for others in the community by communicating with you. But, for some reason, now, I feel secure enough in my situation and my role in The Society to have taken this leap. I feel very privileged to be able to hear intimate stories and thoughts of people who have passed on. And also to serve the people in the community who are the salt of the earth. Good-hearted farmers and workers, who take pride and great joy in what they do and what they create. While there is a great deal of satisfaction and joy in what I do, here, in Shakertown, there is also a great deal of responsibility. And I must not lose sight of this. I hope you can understand.

Now, here's the Burns poem I found. I will print it so you can read it more easily. I wonder if it's the one you were referring to? I am blushing as I write these words.

The Lass That Made the Bed to Me

When January wind was blowing cold,
As to the North I took my way.
The darkening night did me enfold,
I knew not where to lodge till day.
By my good luck a maid I met
Just in the middle of my care,
And kindly she did me invite
To walk into a chamber fair.

I bowed full low unto this maid,
And thanked her for her courtesy;
I bowed full low unto this maid,
And made her make a bed for me.
She made the bed both large and wide,

With two white hands she spread it down.
She put the cup to her rosy lips,
And drank: "Young man, now sleep you sound."

She snatched the candle in her hand,
And from my chamber went with speed.
But I called her quickly back again
To lay some more below my head:
A pillow she laid below my head.
And served me with due respect
And, to salute her with a kiss,
I put my arms about her neck.

'Hold off your hands, young man,' she said.
'And do not so uncivil be;
If you have any love for me.
O, wrong not my virginity!'
Her hair was like the links of gold,
Her teeth were like the ivory,
Her cheeks like lilies dipped in wine,
The girl that made the bed for me.

Upon the morning, when we rose,
I thanked her for her courtesy.
But always she blushed, and always she sighed,
And said: 'Alas, you have ruined me!'
I clasped her waist, and kissed her then.
While the tear stood twinkling in her eye.
I said: 'My girl, do not cry,
For you always shall make the bed for me.

She took her mother's fine Holland linen sheets,
And made them all in shirts to me.
Blythe and merry may she be,
The girl that made the bed for me!
The lovely girl made the bed for me.

The lovely girl made the bed for me!
I will never forget till the day I die,
The girl that made the bed for me.

yours in Scotland,

Kitt

P.S. Have you always had blonde hair?

Scene V.

Wilford Ranks' movements were uneasy as he made his way from the Ministry's workshop to the doorway that would take him into the east side of the Meeting House and up the stairs to the residencies on the second floor where he and the three other members of the Ministry lived apart from the rest of the community. The others resided either in the Centre Family Dwelling or the East Family Dwelling in spartan, yet pristine dormitory environments. The work and the worry of the past few weeks had begun to take its toll on him as he was much too fast approaching his sixtieth birthday. The seemingly constant correspondence, and more recently, visits from members of the Ministry at New Lebanon, had placed an added burden on him. A weight he had never felt before in his capacity as an elder at Pleasant Grove.

With the Era of Manifestation burning like a wildfire through the Shaker communities, the comments from one of the elders from New Lebanon had particularly taken him off guard. The Brother's comments deriding excessive spiritism and advocating a return to the original Shaker doctrines and practices were antithetical to the direction the Society had chosen to take in recent years, and if instituted at this juncture would create problems unforeseen before in the ranks of the Believers. But it was something else the member of the Ministry from New Lebanon had said that caught his attention even more. The Brother from New Lebanon had said something to the effect that he thought the Society doctrines relating to celibacy needed to be re-evaluated and probably altered due to changing mores and sexual attitudes in the American society and what this would mean for recruiting new members. On the one hand, the member of the New Lebanon Ministry was advocating a return to a more conservative doctrine, yet on the other he was asking for a more liberal and permissive doctrine where sexual matters were concerned.

The more he tried to wrap his mind around this seeming

contradiction, this kind of "chop logic," the more he found his own personal beliefs wavering in terms of where he stood regarding both of these issues. On the one hand, he found himself in agreement with the New Lebanon brother that Shaker services and dances were getting out of hand, especially the Sunday services. But he had firmly embraced the idea of spiritism and the visitation of spirits and the messages and teachings that resulted from such contact. He had watched these past few years as vehicles such as Sister Leigh had been able to contact Mother Ann, and he valued the messages that had transpired as a result of Sister Leigh's remarkable telepathic gifts. He, personally, felt he could adjust by going back to "the old ways" and a simpler, more reserved and formal form of worship, even if it would make his job as community elder a more difficult one. But it was the issue of the loosening of sexual mores and practices that had really thrown him off. Not that he was such a puritan in his thinking about the issue, but because of moments of heightened sensual attraction he had experienced in recent weeks and the increasing difficulty he was having in overcoming those uncomfortable, yet exhilarating feelings of passion.

In recent face-to-face conversations with Sister Daniella, he had found, unexpectedly, that he was physically attracted to his fellow Ministry member. He caught himself, on several occasions, looking at her physical body. The quality of her skin. The glint in her eyes. He imagined the size of her breasts beneath her clothes. He noticed her slender figure and imagined the shape and musculature of her legs. He even, on one occasion, caught himself lusting over her lips. Even the sound of Sister Daniella's voice had taken on a siren-like quality that he found appealing. Nothing like the ringing bell-like quality of Sister Kitt's, for instance, but attractive just the same. All these thoughts, these feelings, these impulses worried him. He felt, in some ways, that he was slipping from grace. Back-sliding. Losing his faith.

He tried to fight his sexual feelings. He increased his time spent doing spiritual practices. He did more manual labor and heavy work in the Workshop, hoping his over-working would exhaust his desires. He even spent more time in prayer. With all of this attention being paid to getting rid of his newly discovered sex-drive, it seemed to only increase the amount and degree of attention he ended up spending on the subject and to heighten the kinds of passions he was trying, so desperately, to quell. He had even caught himself during one of the Sunday services lately, watching one of the local women on the fasteners in an untoward manner. Having "thoughts" about her. Admiring the slight amount of skin that was revealed when she had shed her coat midway into the service when the room had gotten warmer from the massive amount of body heat generated from the Shaker Dance.

On top of his lustful longing, Brother Wilford was finding his job as arbitrator and liaison with the local community of Herodsville increasingly difficult, as the lines between Shaker doctrine and the secular beliefs and practices of the local community began to blur. How, in good conscience, could he speak for the residents of Shakertown as a voice for strict Shaker doctrines if he, himself, was in such a reckless state?

As the days and weeks passed, there were more letters from New Lebanon. Questions about the spiritual direction of the Society. Hints toward a need for change. These correspondences only heightened Ranks' increasing ambivalence and uncertainties. His sensual thoughts continued. The sexual feelings did not go away.

In the year 1842 and the Era of Manifestation with all its eccentricities and, some would say, excesses, there were remarkable goings-on all throughout the Shakertown community. Much like the news that was coming from the New Lebanon community, manifestations were also disrupting daily life in Shakertown. Wilford Ranks' Ministry Journal was filled, almost daily, with longer and longer entries chronicling unusual and increasingly odd events.

A counting was made in the large Centre Family Dwelling, where there are fifty adults living and only a little less than half are experiencing spirit manifestations. Sometimes almost this many will be overcome by spirits at the same time. With this sort of thing going on and with these numbers, I don't know how they (and other Family Dwellings in the community) manage to keep up with their daily work and meal routines. But they do.

For some days now, at least a dozen members of the East Dwelling have been carrying on what is being called "The Midnight Cry." They march, at midnight, through every room in every building, gathering up everyone for active worship that goes on sometimes until as late as four o'clock in the morning. On one morning, recently, all the male members of the community were woken in the middle of the night and made to walk the boundaries of the property lines. And all this in frigid temperatures.

I heard from Brother Joseph that some of the instruments are doing nothing but receiving visions. He says "they shake wherever they go; whether at work or at table, and sometimes their shaking is so violent that it is nearly impossible to get any food into their mouths and they have to leave the table without eating." Brother Joseph is worried that some of the bretheren are receiving so many spirit messages that they have almost no time left for their usual duties.

Sister Darrow has reported to me that on this past Wednesday night "one of the women rose in the middle of the night receiving a spirit message and the whole wing of the house got up to hear the inspired words. There was much wailing and tears. Our quiet quarters became bedlam. Many were so overcome with their weeping and wailing that they cried out aloud as a little child might after being spanked. A great part of the second-story floor of the building was eventually covered by those who lay prostrate and the house resounded with a heavy roar."

I list here other aspects of various manifestations that have occurred of late. Brethern drunk on spiritual wine. Visitations by ghostly menageries. Visitations of howling Indians. Evil spirits were, on one occasion, driven off with 'hot warfare.' Evil and suggestive dancing and operations. Stinginess and the hoarding of food. Forgeries. People sleeping outside of their sleeping rooms...

In some cases we have had to put monitors in rooms where there has been much disruption, and in some cases change sleeping arrangements to other rooms. This has not been popular amongst some, as they have become accustomed to being in one room or one building or another for a long time. We have had to do this to keep proper surveillance on things.

Spiritual drawings are ever increasing, illustrating spiritual gifts. Flowers, vines, doves, "streams of love," trees of life, grape arbors, fountains, golden chains, harps and other images have been the result of much time and energy amongst believers of late. Last week a 'spiritual valentine' was made up and given to every member of the Pleasant Grove Society. On each was a saying or an image. It must have taken the instrument of this offering many hours, if not days, to create so many of these 'valentines.' In one case, of this past week, I was told of one sister who became an instrument and spent a whole week writing inspired material. I have seen these writings and it is hard to tell how much of this writing is divinely inspired and how much is not. My concern is that all this sort of thing is taking up an inordinate amount of time. And with more and more brethern and sisters participating in spirit manifestations and as instruments, I fear that the balance in our society is being compromised and that much necessary work is being left undone. I will have to look into this in more detail.

In addition to excessive actions there was also the issue of the actual messages that were being given to members of the community by the instruments. As time had gone on, more and more power had been given to those who were transmitting profound messages and doing so with flair and theatrical abilities. These messages were often taken as gospel and incorporated into the written or unwritten community by-laws and doctrines. With some of these messages being extreme, it was, by the spring of 1842, causing not only concern amongst the Elders, but confusion and dissension amongst the ranks.

In addition to the messages, which were followed to the letter by the community, were a set of instructions and regimens which included early rising, eating bread and water, total fasting on given days, kneeling in prayer facedown, walking in a solemn march from place to place, abstaining from all labor, mandatory repentance.

With all of these spiritual "innovations and inventions" the Watcher's job as Elder and overseer of the Pleasant Grove community was getting more and more complicated, if not difficult, and adding to his growing vexation and concern.

Meanwhile, the train of letters between Herodsville and Pleasant Grove continued, being perpetuated primarily through Asher's zealous pen.

Dearest Kitt,

Since I received your last letter I have been able to think of little else. I only wish I had received it before the Shaker service last Sunday, as I would have made more of an effort to get your attention (if that had been possible) during the dance and lesson. I did notice that you were able to steal a glance over my way during the lesson. I hope you saw my smile. I don't think The Watcher saw us, as I looked up right afterwards and he was looking toward the speaker's corner and seemed to be trying to hear what was being said, as he had his little window opened out into the room.

You are really something. Such patience and understanding. Is this really true, or are you, underneath the words, reeling and rocking at my attempts to equal your lucid prose. (I got the word lucid from my father's thesaurus. It means "translucent," "clear," "elegant." Are you impressed?) Most girls would have already written me off as a result of my romantic insinuations. But you seem to have gotten past all that and have come to terms with your feelings and your situation in Shakertown. I consider myself lucky to have connected with you at this time in your life. You are who you have become. And I like the "you" who you are. And this includes how you look. You don't need to apologize at all for that!

Yes! You got the Burns poem right. The one you sent was the one I found in the book, which inspired me to write my own "Burns" poem. I'm very happy that you liked my poem and weren't too taken aback by its forwardness. I re-read my poem after I had given my letter to Caden to give to Sister Wicks and worried that it might not have been good enough to send.. But on further reading, it still seemed to hold up alright. Glad I was right about that, as you would be the ultimate judge of its success or failure since it was written to you. There's more where this came from, if you will only write to me once in a while. Your letters are an inspiration to me. As is your presence at the Sunday service.

Please know that I respect you and would do nothing to compromise your position in the community. This is why I have not urged you to try to come into town, where we might meet. Caden has told me that he would be our watchdog if we wanted to try and meet at his father's store during the week sometime. But I've refused his offer more than once, as I don't want you to get in any trouble. As much as I wish to see you, to talk with you, to look unselfconsciously into your eyes, I won't try and lure you into town. At the same time, if you should come up with an idea as to how we might meet, I would very much like to hear it. I would move heaven and earth to get to you if it were possible.

Tell me more about your Mother Ann. I have been paying attention to the sermons at the Sunday meetings these many months and am becoming more familiar with your beliefs and practices. While there is much reference to Mother Ann in the lessons, I still don't know very much about her. She seems to be so revered by everyone. You seem to know her best. Maybe you could say a few things to me about her in your next letter. Do you actually see her? Or simply hear her voice? I'm not sure I understand how this all happens, since I've not been able to attend one of your "manifestations." Although, I have seen how some people during the dances seem to start speaking strange words and languages and appear to be in a kind of trance. Somehow, though, I don't see you as going through all these gyrations in your sessions. Anyway, tell me more. Curious is my middle name.

My father talks more often about the goings on up at Shakertown. He seems to have become obsessed with all this. I think he thinks it's becoming a bad influence on the people of Herodsville. I don't see that as being true, but he has something about "the evil practices" at the Sunday services in almost every sermon he gives. I have tried to talk to him about this and to speak respectfully about your beliefs and all, but I guess I don't know enough about religion—either orthodox-Christian or Shaker-Christian—to be able to hold my ground in this kind of debate. I wish I could be more convincing in my arguments and when speaking about my own experiences and feelings on the subject, but speaking out (or any kind of speaking, for that matter) is not my strength. My intellectual and vocal skills come through my pen and not through my mouth. I feel competent in what I write. I'm not a good debater or public speaker like my friend Caden. Ole Caden can sell anybody just about anything. He could talk the eyeballs right out of a man who can't see.

Well, guess I've gone on long enough, here. I need to stop, anyway, as I've got to go over to pay my respects to one of our neighbors who has just turned ninety-four-years-old. She's one of the Hoopers who live here in our valley. She has a huge flock of guinea hens and chickens, and she usually can use some help around her place, and since the sun is shining I best be on my way.

Hope to hear, again, from you soon—and better still : to see you!

always, Asher

PS Yes, I have always had blonde hair.

Dear Asher,

I hope you will forgive me, but this letter won't be long.

We're overwhelmed at the moment with work preparing for this year's gardens. And Sister Ella is laid up sick and I'm having to do her chores in the milk-barn in the mornings, which puts me behind in my other duties, then, for the rest of the day. I've found a little time, alone, today in the Dry House, which is where I'm spending about every Wednesday, it seems, fixing the place up and repairing the drying racks, as soon we will be drying some early crops. If anyone ever wanted to find me on a Wednesday, that's where I'd be. I can't write from the Family Dwelling, as there are too many people around all the time, and at night we have a strict policy of blowing out all the candles at bedtime. And since I can't write very well in the dark....

You needn't worry about your "Burns" poem and all the images and associations with the flesh. As you saw in my letter, I wasn't shy about writing all those descriptive lines in the real Burns poem. While "sins of the flesh" is a constant topic of conversation, here, I'm not nearly as pious and fixated on that subject as some are--especially the elder women. And I think they feel so superior in that regard to the younger women because they don't feel, any more, the same desires as the girls. Most of the older women won't even joke about the subject of sex, while the girls my age talk and laugh about it all the time.

I'm glad you liked what I said about my being deeply happy that we are connected. I meant what I said. And I am always thinking about the next time I will see you--even if all we ever get to do is to steal a glance at one another. Meanwhile, there are the letters. And you don't have to feel that you must answer all my letters, as I don't expect you to. I'm kind of old-fashioned about correspondence. This probably comes from my Shaker up-bringing. So you don't have to write a reply unless there is something you would like to say, or know. Since we have never had an opportunity to really talk to each other, there always seems to be at least something I want to say to you. I wish they would change the rules so we could talk to outsiders at Sunday service. It seems only logical, with so many of the World's People coming and participating in the meeting these days. But....I have to admit that I would be disappointed if Sister Mary should return from town on Tuesday without one of your letters in her pocket. I notice that you are not using the lovely onion-skin paper you used to use when we first started writing. I guess you have run out, or maybe you were borrowing it from your father's desk (?) To keep writing as often as we do and using that kind of paper would be expensive for you. I don't want you to go broke on my account, or feel you need to spend that kind of money on me. I'm not interested in your money, Asher, since there would be no point in it. I'd settle for just once being able to run my fingers through your blonde locks.

 Send me another poem!

  Yours in spirit,

   Kitt

Scene VI.

Due to all the excesses of behavior as a result of the plethora of manifestations and "spirit business" going on at Shakertown and the Ministry's perceived necessity of policing certain living quarters, events, and persons, a tension began to grow between visionists and those who were wanting to control them. In a few cases there were even incidents of hostile behavior where an actual "we" and "they" attitude was developing amongst the members of the community. Ringleaders emerged on the visionist side, who spoke openly about fighting against the "old establishment" authorities, accusing them of standing in the way of the spiritual progress of The Society. From the perspective of the Ministry and many concerned elders in the community, things had gone too far with all this "visioning." A certain amount of policing seemed necessary to discourage pretenders-- those who feigned visions and transmissions for their own personal purposes.

These were matters that were not only relevant to the Shakertown Shaker community, but were fairly universal throughout Shakerdom in the year 1842. In a letter written to The Watcher that spring, Isaac Newton Youngs, in the New Lebanon Shaker community, wrote, "I have watched these gifts and operations closely to see if any pretense went undetected. There have been some cases of overstepping of the real gift. It is my concern that a gift found to be fraudulent would prompt many Believers to question the validity of all manifestations. And this is my confidence in the present manifestations, that no imposition or forgery will be suffered to pass." In response to Brother Youngs's letter, The Watcher had responded: "We, too, continue to watch for forgery. There are those among us, here at Pleasant Grove who are also concerned about these matters. While I have been reluctant to actually challenge those with 'gifts' who are having visions, others like myself who have doubts seem to want to go along with the visionists so as not to upset the sense of union in the community.

"There is a growing consensus amongst the elder members of our society, here, that gifts and inspirations should be restricted to formal worship services or specially-designated times. We worry about the timing of indiscretions and that manifestations often occur in common view in front of the world's people--in sight of Believers and unbelievers, alike. There is even talk of closing the Sunday worship services and dances to the public."

This growing schism between the visionist camp and the elders was precipitating a perceptible division, with the younger members of the settlement by-and-large siding with the unregulated visionist beliefs and practices, while the older society members leaned heavily on the side of restrictions, monitoring and the more conservative doctrines and regulations of the past.

There were calls for more Roundtable meetings among members of the Ministries from the various bishoprics, as well as General Meetings for all Shaker societies in order to address and to deal with the growing problems of manifestation in all its forms. Clouds had appeared in the skies over the Shaker world. Storms were predicted.

It was Tuesday and Asher's friend Caden had gotten him a part-time, one-afternoon-a-week job there in the Herodsville General Store. It had been a slow day and Asher and Caden had been busy cleaning and stacking shelves in the grocery. While they worked, they talked.

"Asher, you finished yet?"

"I don't care if I never see another shelf ever again. Yeah, I'm about finished over here. What you need me to do next?"

"It'll be closing time soon, and since it's not been too busy today, we can start cleaning up. Go get that mop and bucket in the back and you can start-in mopping the floor. Meanwhile, I'll finish up with all this shelving. You having any fun, yet?"

"About as much fun as a man could have! You don't think I took this job for fun and games, do you? Work's not supposed to be fun, you know. Least that's what my dad says. 'Work is serious business, son. It's the Lord's chores we're doing down here,' It's fine enough, and I thank you for getting me the Tuesday afternoon job. I can use the cash and I'm hoping it will pay even greater, non-monetary dividends in the end, if you know what I mean."

"I still think you're dreamin'--about that 'foxy-named' Shaker girl. And I haven't seen the old Shaker lady in here for a couple weeks. She may never come back again, and then you'll be out of luck. Or maybe they've decided to start sending some younger woman to do the town shopping. No matter how you cut it, it's a dead-end street for you, my friend. Like mixing apples and oranges. You ever hear of anyone ever eating an 'orange pie'?"

Asher pretends not to hear and disappears into the back of the store to fetch the mop and bucket, leaving Caden over in the grocery up on a ladder with a large duster, cleaning the top shelves. About this time, a small bell hanging on the inside of the door frame sounds its singular alarm and the front door to the store opens. Sister Mary enters with a couple of net bags and a cloth tote-bag hanging from one hand. Not able to turn to look and see who it is that has entered the store, Caden is still up on the ladder dusting shelves when Sister Mary makes her way across the store and over to the counter. Sister Mary addresses Caden, who is so startled that he almost falls off the ladder.

"How are you today, Brother Caden?"

Caden tries to respond as he steadies himself on the wooden ladder. "Ummm, I, I'm doin', doin' okkk, Sister Mary. And you?"

"Faring pretty well today, young man, since I got shed of that ole croup I've had for the last week or two. Thought I'd die, I felt so poor last week. Guess maybe you thought I had, since I've not been in the store lately."

"Yes, ma'am. I mean, no ma'am. I mean--I really haven't given it much thought, ma'am. But now that you mention it, guess it has been a while. What can I do for you today?"

"As Kitchen Deaconess for the Center Family, I'll be needing some more of that fresh asparagus if you've still got it--after you get down from that ladder. We've got a big celebration coming up and the kitchen crew put in a special order for this week's list. Oh, and some of those dried beef strips you had about a month ago. Brother Wilford liked those so much he asked me to get him some more."

"I've got the beef jerky, ma'am, but I'm afraid we're out of the fresh asparagus. Ol' Will Shelton was in on Saturday with an armload of asparagus, but said that this load would be his last--for this year, at least. I'm sorry, ma'am."

"That's ok, young man. If you would wrap the dried beef strips up in that special paper you have back there for me. And you can just set it in this cloth bag--while I go over to the other side of the store and look for some needles and thread. I'll be right back."

"Yes, mam. Help yourself, ma'am."

About this time Asher emerges from the back of the store with a mop in one hand and a bucket of hot water in the other as Caden is wrapping the strips of beef jerky at the counter.

"Caden, did I hear you talking out here with someone?"

Caden rapidly raises the index finger on his right hand up to his lips, silently telling Asher to say no more, then points in the direction of Sister Mary on the other side of the store. "Shhhh....the Sister is here, over there. Quick, go back in the back before she sees you."

"Sister? What sister?" Asher replies, also speaking in infectiously hushed tones.

"Sister Mary--from up in Shakertown. The one who does their town-shopping and who has been bringing me those letters from that Shaker fox of yours. Quick, get back in there before she comes over here to pick up her groceries."

"Brother Caden, did you say something to me?" Sister Mary asks from across the room. From a distance, Sister Mary spies Asher and sees that Caden is not alone. "Oh, Brother Caden, I see you are not alone. I guess you were talking to your friend. Excuse me for interrupting."

"No, ma'am. It's ok. I was just telling Asher where he needed to begin mopping the floor. He's been working here on Tuesdays since the last time you were in, and is learning his way around the store."

Carrying, carefully, a handful of small merchandise, Sister Mary makes her way across the store toward the grocery counter where Caden and Asher are standing. Caden is looking at Asher, wide-eyed, telling him with his eyes to disappear. Asher is looking, shyly, at Sister Mary as she makes her way across the room and approaches the grocery counter.

"Young man, you look as if you've seen a ghost," says Sister Mary to Caden in a concerned voice.

"Uh, er, no ma'am. I was just trying to remember what the total was on your groceries, as I got distracted."

"What did you say your friend's name was?"

"Uh, um, it's, it's Asher, ma'am. Ma'am, this is Asher Pope. His dad's the minister over at the Baptist Church. You know. This is THE Asher Pope, ma'am. In the flesh."

"Oh, my goodness. So....we have finally met THE Asher Pope. He actually DOES exist, after all! A pleasure to meet you, sir. Seems I've known you for some time, but it's a pleasure to finally meet you face-to-face."

"Yes, ma'am. The pleasure's all mine, ma'am. I mean, pleased to meet you, ma'am."

"Well, let me look at you, then. You do seem fit enough. Cleanly. Blonde hair, most definitely. Everything Sister Leigh has said. You pass the physical inspection, young man, but are you well-spoken? Our Sister Kitt says that you write a nice hand. For, I, of course, have not read your letters for myself, but this is what she tells me. So, what do you have to say for yourself, young man?"

"What would you like to know?"

"Are you an honest man, sir?"

"I think so, ma'am. Yes, ma'am. Most of the time."

"Most of the time?!"

"I mean all of the time, ma'am."

"And are you a noble man, sir?"

"I am not from nobility, if that is what you are asking, ma'am. I come from fairly humble origins. My father is a Baptist minister. My mother takes in some sewing at home and does charity work."

"And do you make a living for yourself? You certainly look too old to still be in school."

"I work as a janitor at my father's church and here in Caden's father's store on Tuesdays, and I live at home--for the time being—ma'am."

"Thank you, young man. I will quiz you no more. I know this must be uncomfortable for you, and I won't prolong your discomfort with more probing questions--for which I already know most of the answers. You have passed this little test, and, besides, we must get to the matter at hand: the business of the letters."

She reaches into a pocket which is skillfully sewn into her long grey dress and pulls out a small sealed envelope.

"This should look familiar to you, Brother Asher, as I have delivered several of these, by now, to Brother Caden, who says that he has been passing them on to you. We both know who this letter is from. And this one, like the others, is also for you. As you can see from the envelope, it is in Sister Kitt's hand."

"Yes, ma'am. And I thank you for all the letters you have delivered. You have been a true friend to both Miz Kitt and myself. How can I repay you?"

"Payment would only tarnish further what already lingers in a very grey area of acceptability. I would do us both a disservice by accepting any recompense from you. Please accept this letter, and all the others, as a gift."

Asher sets his bucket down on the floor. Sister Mary hands the small brown sealed envelope across the counter and places it in Asher's outstretched hand.

"Thank you, ma'am. I am forever in your debt."

"Not mine, my boy, but one greater. By the grace of God these letters come to thee. I am only a messenger in His work. If I did not believe this, I would be riddled with guilt. For these kind of *hidlings* are most uncommon amongst our society and would be looked upon with much disfavor by many. So, please be discreet, Asher, to whom you speak about these meetings and to whom you show the words of Sister Leigh."

"Oh, yes, ma'am. Sister Mary, ma'am. I will be discreet."

"You best be, my boy, lest we all be in a heap of trouble. And above all we don't want to soil Sister Leigh's good name. Can I trust you in this? Will you give me your word--that none of this will go beyond the four walls of this safe house? Will you, too, Brother Caden, join in this sacred bond of secrecy?"

"Yes, ma'am."

"Then, all join hands and let's end our heavy working for today. Then be set free to recast working into play."

Sister Mary clasps the outstretched hands of the two young men. Pays for the things she has purchased and puts them in her cloth sack and exits the shop. Without saying a word, Asher picks up the bucket from the floor and, with the mop still in the other hand, disappears through the doorway into the back room of the store. Caden is still standing behind the counter with Sister Mary's money in his palm and has not spoken--looking somewhat puzzled. He collects himself and goes about putting the money in the register drawer and returning the ladder to the corner of the room. A few minutes later, Asher appears from the back room. Looking radiant, he addresses Caden with uncharacteristic enthusiasm.

"I know Sister Mary has warned me about being discreet in terms of who knows the content of these letters, but you gotta hear this. It will shed some light on this subterfuge."

"Sub-what? Where are you getting all these fifty-cent words you're using lately?"

"Sorry, but I've been using the Dictionary to write my letters to Kitt, and when I come across interesting words, I read what they mean and try to learn them. But this is off the subject. Where was I? Yes. So...What I show you will be only between me, you, and the floor that I've not yet mopped. Agreed?"

"Do I have a choice? I think that you are going to tell me no matter what I say."

"Agreed, then, my friend. Here's what she reveals and what I have to say.

"Here, in her letter, she has confided her feelings for me. I feel that a door has been opened. And I, for one, intend to walk through that door. She also says--in a very suggestive way--that she works on Wednesdays at a place there in the Shaker village called "The Dry House." Here, right here in her letter she says, 'If anyone ever wanted to find me on Wednesdays, that's where I'd be.' What do you think? Does this sound like an invitation to you, or what? Am I reading more into her words, here, than are actually there, and is this just wishful thinking on my part? In any case, I've got an idea and I want to run it by you.

"What do you think if I were to go up to Shakertown disguised in Shaker clothes and go to this Dry House to find Kitt? You know, and surprise her. Wouldn't that be some fun? I mean, she said right here in her letter that if anyone wanted to find her--meaning me, of course--that she'd be there. So, I'm thinking maybe you and me, we could put together some sort of costume from the clothes for sale here in the store and I could take the wagon and go up there tomorrow and surprise her. Is that not a romantic idea? I mean this might be my best and only chance to actually talk to her. What do you think?"

"I think you're crazy. But you already know that. What if you get caught. Then what?"

"What are they going to do to me? Put me in jail?"

"Well, they might--for trespassing or something. I don't know, but it seems risky any way you look at it. On the other hand, I personally have got nothing to lose, and it might be fun to see if you could actually pull it off. But if they do catch you, you know for sure you'll not be going up there again--not even for the Sunday services. So, you should think about that before you do anything you might regret later."

"No, I've got to see her. All this letter-writing is fine, but we can't keep doing this forever--just being pen-partners or something. No, I've got to talk to her, and this is my chance. Will you help me put together some sort of outfit from the clothes here in the store?"

"Now, this is where I could get in trouble. If this whole plan backfires, my dad's gonna blame me for givin' you the clothes."

"Well, what's he gonna do? Put you in jail alongside of me?" Asher says, laughing.

"Ok, I guess. Lucky for us my dad's not here. We've just got some new Shaker-style hats in the other day, so that's a good start. As your Dresser, I think I can make you look the part. The rest, of course, will be up to you--to play your part in this risky production of yours. We'll pick out your clothes today and you can take them home with you tonight and wear them tomorrow. But you gotta promise to bring them back tomorrow afternoon when you get back from Shakertown. That is, IF you get back from Shakertown!"

Wednesday was a sunny spring day. Asher got up and went to the church and to his regular janitor's job, taking a brown paper sack filled with the "Shaker" items he and Caden had put together the previous day. During his lunch time, instead of just eating a bag lunch there in the church, he changed into his Shaker outfit and climbed into the wagon he had brought from home that morning and headed off down the road and the seven miles to Shakertown.

Rather than driving his horse and wagon into the Pleasant Grove village through the main entrance, Asher decided to drive around to the back entrance along the river road. As he rode along the Kentucky River and approached the landing docks, he saw people loading onto the ferry that crossed the river. From the ferry dock, Asher turned his horse up the hill and towards the village's back entrance.

On Tuesday night, Asher had found a small Shaker book in his father's study that had come from Shakertown. In the little chapbook, there was a hand-drawn map of the village that showed the locations of all the buildings as of 1839. The little Shaker book lay beside Asher on the wagon's driver's seat as he entered the Shakertown property. He had studied it over and over that night, until he had it memorized, so that he would know exactly where the Dry House was located. He had brought his father's book with him, as a kind of security, so he would not get disoriented and be forced to drive around unnecessarily, or even worse, have to ask for directions and hence risk someone recognizing him as not being "one of their own."

Once up on the plateau and onto the property, he quickly got his bearings, having been there many times before, and was able to identify the Dry House, which was located approximately mid-village between the village farm and the orchard. To get there he had to pass the barns and gardens on the main road and then turn on a side road that went past the post office and continued on toward the orchard. Passing the post office was the most dangerous part of the route, as he might encounter people coming and going, or worse yet, milling around the post office in conversation. Luckily, his timing was perfect on this day. As he turned off the main road onto the smaller dirt road going south, passing the post office, there was no one in sight. He whipped the reins and added an almost inaudible "giiuup" to his pair of Morgan horses as he passed the post office and made his way toward the orchard and the little building that was already in view sitting just up ahead on a rise in the road.

It was the very moment when the Dry House first came into view that Asher felt a little knot starting to bind up in his stomach. He even felt a little light-headed coming around the curve and up the slight incline toward the small building that got a little larger with each clop of the horses' hooves. There was a brief moment when the idea of turning the wagon around and heading back crossed his mind. But his sense of determination was stronger than his feelings of fear he had of the unknown, and he continued on.

As the Dry House neared, he spotted a small turn-out area in the road about a hundred yards or so from the small wooden building. He steered the horses to the right and into the turn-out, pulling them up to a stop. For a moment, Asher just sat in the wagon-seat and stared at the Dry House across the road and at the road that made its way to the top of the rise. Beyond and all the way to the horizon, as far as he could see, were the tops of apple, peach and pear trees in full leaf--in a scene as idyllic as anything he'd ever read in books. In that moment, a kind of magic seemed to pervade the air, and he imagined that he, the orchards and the Dry House were part of some fantasy, some creation of his own making. And in that moment, he and the object of his quest, Kitt Leigh, were the sole inhabitants of that magic realm.

Asher climbed down from the wagon and tied the horses to a nearby apple tree. He checked his clothes for dishevelment and dust and his pockets for a special something he'd brought with him and took the first step toward the little building at the top of the hill....

There was no real latch or lock on the Dry House door, just a slat of wood on a nail to keep the door from swinging open in the wind. Asher noticed that the piece of wood was positioned straight up, indicating that it had been unlatched and that someone was probably inside. He drew a deep breath, pushed the smooth chestnut door open, and entered the building.

Kitt was opening the window in the back of the building and had heard the wagon coming up the road, but had paid it no mind. Busy with her refurbishing of the drying racks and the general cleaning necessary to get the drying room up and running for another year, she stayed with her work, that is, until the creaking sound of the old chestnut door announced the presence of someone entering the room.

"Sister Mary, is that you?"

When there was no answer, she straightened up and turned, facing the door.

"I'm sorry sir, I thought you were Sister Mary coming to see about my progress today. I heard your wagon as it came up the road, but I was too busy, I'm afraid, to look-see who it was that.... Oh, my goodness, is that you, Asher? What are you doing here!"

Asher stood there in the doorway for a few seconds admiring the view of her and the sunlight shining on her face from the nearby window before he became conscious enough to realize the situation he was in. As his face turned red, he took off his wide-brimmed hat revealing his blonde identity and somehow conjured up enough nerve to speak.

"Yes, it's me."

"What are you doing here? How did you get here?"

"I am here to see you. Only you. With my disguise and my wagon, and a little sleuthing, I have made it here."

"Did anyone see you?"

"No, I don't think so. I came in from the back entrance and everyone over at the farm was too busy to even take notice as I drove past."

"How did you find me, and how did you know I was here?"

"Love has shown me the way. In truth, your letter has brought me here. I come by invitation, in your own hand. I have committed it to memory. 'If you wanted to find me on a Wednesday, the Dry House is where I'll be.'"

"Did I use the word 'you'? It seems to my memory that you have changed my words to suit your fancies."

"This is how I took your meaning, even if a few words be changed. And I found the Dry House on a map in a little book that was made here by your society, which I found in my father's study. Once I found the orchard, it was easy from there. And once I saw the little house on the hill, no orchard's walls would have been high enough to keep me out. I flew past the stone wall at the bottom of the hill as if I had wings."

"Do you know what they will do to you, to us, if they find us, here, like this?"

"They will not find us. I am not afraid, for I am veiled in love's cloak. And it covers us both."

"I knew I had made a mistake when I wrote those words. I should have been more gamely and have put thee off. It is my fault then, that you have come. But I must confess, that even if my words were not intentional, there was probably a part of me that was wanting to see you. And now, look what we've done."

"Is this not right--that we are here together? Is this not some manifestation of all our written words?"

"It is too rash. Too sudden. Too risky. It seems more like a dream than something real."

"Don't you think that dreams, too, are real?"

"Asher, this is not the right time for philosophy or metaphysics. We live in two different worlds and ne'er the two do meet. This plan of yours is folly, though I admit that it is nice to finally hear your voice and to look upon your face without having to pretend I do not."

"You see, I was right in how I translated the words in your last letter. You said 'I am always thinking about the next time I will see you.' And 'I wish they would change the rules so we could talk.' You see, I have committed your exact words to memory. And I have changed none of these words this time. But, I have changed the rules, and have made rules meant only for the two of us. And our rules are 'No rules!' This is our rule, and ours alone. The others be damned. And now, here I am. You can see me, and I you. You can hear me and I can hear the wonderful music in your voice. And you can run your fingers in my hair."

As Asher moved closer, Kitt reached out spontaneously without thinking and ran her hand through Asher's curly, blonde forelocks.

"If you can touch my hair, I can touch your cheek. Fair's fair," Asher says as he reaches out and touches, gently, Kitt's cheek--now red with blush.

"Are we dreaming, Asher? Can this be real? Are we mad? Wait,

I hear something. What is that noise? Thank the Lord, it's only Brother Schricker in his wagon coming up the road. But I worry he has seen your wagon," Kitt says as she moves over to the window and peers out.

"Surely he will not know my wagon from any other in the village."

"We can't take the risk. As soon as he's passed by, you must go to your wagon and return to Herodsville."

"And leave you, so quickly? I have waited weeks. Months. And I have only just arrived. Let me touch your cheeks again--that my fingers commit you to memory, so that I might remember you when we are apart."

"Should I say yes, you would not think me a loose woman?"

"No, indeed. I would only worship you all the more."

"How do I know this for sure?"

"Because I have said so, and wouldn't lie to you for all the world. This day has been too long in the making and I would not be so foolish as to murder this moment with a lie."

"Let us save something to look forward to when we next meet. For now, this brave rendez-vous is sweet."

"You turn a seamless rhyme. Do you sew as well?" Asher says in jest. "And you do this just for me, as you know how I am in love with poems. I imagine we could write poems together some day."

"Brother Schricker has gone on down the hill into the orchard. Now is your chance to leave--before you are seen. The men will be coming from the orchard soon and will pass by this way. You must go before they come--or before someone else comes to fetch me. Two surprises in one day would be more than I could take."

"You say 'when we next meet.' So you swear there will be another time? Will you promise?"

"If it will help you to move from that spot, I will say it. And, thus, I will promise you that we will meet again. Although I know not when. You've got me speaking in rhymes, again. Now, get thee home before we are found out and all our promises disappear like the moon in morning light."

"Not before you have baptized me in our new love with a kiss."

"Get out of here, before I change my mind and take back everything that I have said."

"I'm gone, Kitt. How I love the way that word feels falling off my tongue. How my ears burn when you call my name."

"Go poet, and save all your verses to put onto paper tonight. And then send them with Sister Wicks to me next week."

"It will seem centuries 'til then. By then I will have written reams. Sister Mary will be delivering you a tome!"

"Go now, and take with you the memory of how I have loved your company today. As our favorite bard is fond of saying: 'go now, depart, away.'"

As Asher walked from the Dry House to where he had parked his wagon, Kitt watched him from the north window of the building. Watched as he unhitched the reins from the old apple tree, climbed aboard the wagon, turned it and the two horses around in the road and drove back the way he came toward the Kentucky River, a little dust rising into Wednesday's evening air from the wagon wheels as they turned.

A couple of beautiful spring days had come and gone following Kitt and Asher's meeting in the Dry House. Kitt and Eden were down in the basement kitchen of the Centre Family Dwelling washing dishes after the evening meal, talking quietly, so as not to be overheard.

"I have something to tell you, Eden. That is, if you promise not to tell a soul."

"Yes, of course. My lips are sealed. What is it that you wish to say?"

"You remember our earlier conversations about a certain blonde-haired boy?"

"Of course. The boy named Asher from Herodsville."

"Well, I talked with him yesterday."

"You talked with him? What do you mean you talked with him? Did he come to you in one of your visions? Tell me more."

"Well, actually, yes...he did come to me. But it wasn't in a vision."

"What, then?"

"He came to me while I was working in the Dry House the other day. I mean he walked in through the door--nearly scared me to death. I didn't recognize him, at first. He was dressed in Shaker clothes and wearing one of those wide-brimmed straw hats. When he took off his hat and it became clear to me who he was, I nearly fainted. But of course I kept cool and didn't let on."

"How did he get into the village? And how did he know where to find you?"

"Getting into the village was something he arranged according to his own devices. Something concocted between him and the friend of his who comes with him, sometimes, to Sunday meeting. I believe he said his name was Caleb, or Cane….no Caden. That was it. Caden. Sounds like Eden, and this is how I remembered it. Caden and Eden. That has a nice ring to it, don't you think?"

"Stop. And don't change the subject. How did he know where to find you?"

"I must have mentioned in one of my letters--you do remember that I have been writing him letters--that I worked on Wednesdays in the Dry House. I don't know what came over me to have written to him in such detail. But I did, and so he cleverly found the *Pleasant Grove Reader* that Brother Brent printed and published a couple years ago and found his way to the Dry House from looking at the map in that book. I have to say that the whole charade was wonderfully thought out. And as I said, I couldn't have been more surprised. If pleasantly. But I didn't let on that I was pleased. At least, not at first."

"Yes, of course I remember that Sister Mary has been delivering letters for you on her visits to town. Remember, it was I who was the messenger who put you on the trail of his name and who suggested Sister Mary in the first place. This story is all very romantic but aren't you worried that he was seen by someone and that there is someone amongst us who knows he was there with you in the Dry House?"

"Asher told me that he was quite sure that no one had noticed him drive his wagon into the village or had seen him pull up and park the wagon near the Dry House. And while he was there with me, only one wagon passed, and we watched it pass by and there was no suspicion that we could detect from the driver. Asher was not there in the Dry House for very long. I made him leave soon after he arrived, as I was getting nervous that someone would come and that we would be found out. And no one, not even anyone from the Ministry has approached me on this subject since."

"If this masquerade and secret meeting has gone unseen, then you have been lucky. Either that, or this Asher of yours is more clever than we think. I hope you were firm in telling him not to try this sort of thing again."

"At first, I was. It's true. But as he spoke and as I was there in his presence for a while, my resolve began to soften. And, in the end, I'm afraid that I may have left him with the impression that we would meet again. I can't explain to you, exactly, why I would say such a thing or why I would want to take such a risk. But it feels right. Not unlike being in the presence of Mother Ann feels right to me, so does my connection with our friend Asher feel much the same."

"Not OUR friend! YOUR friend! Remember, I warned you against this attraction of yours, right from the start. And I knew it would come to no good. And look what's happened. Already, he is sneaking in to the village to see you. Who knows where or when he will show up next? Perhaps he is skulking about, outside, as we speak."

"Don't be silly, Eden. I have made it plain to him that this sort of thing must never happen again--at least without my foreknowledge--as it is too dangerous. For both of us."

"Then, you have told him that you will meet him again and with your consent?"

"Not in so many words, dear friend. But neither have I told him I would not be willing to meet again sometime."

"I fear that there is no sanctuary safe enough for this clandestine behavior. And I fear for you both. But since it has happened and is now done, tell me, friend, what did you talk about?"

"Not much, my friend, as there was but little time. And in much of that time we did not talk. Just stared and touched."

"Touched!?"

"Nothing forbidden or improper, Eden. I once reached for his hair. To get a feel of his golden locks."

"And did he return your gesture? Or had he made one first?"

"We were standing close to one another, after being drawn to the window to watch the passing wagon go by. So when I reached for his hair, he reached for my cheek, in exchange."

"He touched your cheek? You let him touch your cheek? Did you not slap him, then?"

"No, Eden, it was innocent enough. An equal exchange. Finger-talk, is all. And, in parting, when he asked for a kiss, I denied him and sent him on his way."

"He tried to kiss you?!"

"No, but he asked. And, as I say, I sent him, unrequited, on his way."

"Oh, my. This liaison has already gone too far. I fear that this week's innocent intercourse is but a kind of aphrodisiac for further dalliance. Be careful, Kitt. Lest you find yourself in a God's plenty of trouble."

"Don't worry. I will be careful. And I will tell thee no more, in future, if you don't want to know or be involved."

"Am I not thy friend, Kitt? I will be thy confidante if you will also take my advice to heart."

"So much 'heart' in your speech, dear friend. And I will listen, I promise."

"I have to admit, that I rather enjoy being recipient of these tales, since I have no input in their actions."

"Oh, but we can add remedy to this distance, my good friend. As I said before, Caden and Eden has such a nice ring!"

Scene VII

On the banks of the Kentucky River, life in Shakertown went on, but not as usual. A wave of individuality had swept through the Shakertown society challenging the authority of the Elders, with spirit instruments giving fresh voice to the claims of the charismatic tradition. Out of concern for these alarming new developments, the Shakertown Ministry had written to the Elders at New Lebanon asking for guidance. New Lebanon had responded saying, "The true watchmen of Zion's walls must look out for the enemy. Mother has given to the Ministry and Elders there, spiritual spectacles that they may see clearly and not be deceived by false spirits."

While the central ministry in Shaker headquarters in New Lebanon acknowledged the positive aspects of the Era of Manifestation, they also sent warning, saying, "Those who can see into the spiritual world may be lost after all their great gifts if they do not attend to the orders and instructions given for the protection of the Believers. Beware that the want of true wisdom in the instruments lead the Believers astray." In a more poetic phrasing, Brother Seth Wells, one of the elders at the Shaker village of Canterbury, wrote to the Shakertown Ministry saying, "A ship or even a little boat, with a sufficient weight of ballast, will go safely through the water with spreading sail; while another without ballast is in great danger whenever her sails are spread; because she is greatly exposed to be upset with the first blast of wind that blows."

In his poetic interpretation of the general climate in which spirit instruments were active, Brother Wells was essentially saying that there needed to be balance between individual spiritual gifts and humility. "Beware pride lurking nearby, tempting the instruments and threatening to destroy union and order," he finished his letter to the Shakertown Elders.

Despite Brother Wells' warnings and the proclamations from New Lebanon, confusion in the Shaker settlements grew as religious excitement rose to a fever pitch. Shakerism, with its open canon, was ripe for continual expressions of the extraordinary. Once the spirit visitations caught the collective imagination of the Believers, the gifts could not be stopped. It seemed, to some at least, that there was nothing to be done but to let this phase of "spiritual revival" run its course. In some of the more extreme instances, even children could be heard addressing their elders in reversed roles. In his journal during these days, Brother Wilford Ranks wrote:

"Unusual spirit visitors fill the meetinghouse week after week-- angels with strange names, natives speaking foreign tongues, biblical figures from ancient times, political figures from the past. New songs have to be learned, new dances practiced, and preparations made for spiritual feasts and celebrations. Trances repeatedly interrupt the flow of daily activities. Sometimes meetings last into the early morning hours, with some special rituals lasting into the middle of the night. Our regular routines have, it seems, become victim to the manifestations."

With all this going on, tensions grew between those who supported Society members with charismatic gifts and the supporters of the status quo with their preference for a more structured order. It was almost inevitable, then, when conflict arose between the instruments and the ministry and a power struggle ensued, with each side claiming to be speaking for the will of God. A struggle of gift vs. order. At stake in this conflict was the very balance and future of The United Shaker Society.

Meanwhile, at the First Baptist Church of Herodsville, Rev. Matthew Pope was delivering another of his assailing sermons drawing swords against Shakertown and the Believers. In his lambasting sermon he addressed the younger members of his congregation, saying "Be ye sober in these times of travail. Be resolved not to give way to any wayward deeds or false prophets. Look to the cross, young people. Hold tight to the cross. Guard against your evil nature. The sooner you embrace the Son of God and his teachings, the sooner you will gain victory in this world. Take hold of your faith, young people. Embrace it, gladly. Beware the voices of Satan. Beware the false messages coming from Shakertown. Beware the antics and the enticements of the Devil. But be strong in your faith in Christ our Lord and in your resentment of the temptations of Satan.

"Go not today to 'the city which is built upon a hill'--to Shakertown--but rather go ye to the shores of Galilee and become one of His followers. Become, as Christ did, 'fishers of men.' Become fishermen, not fish--to be caught in the nets of those who cast them about because of their own spiritual hunger and in the name of spiritual starvation. Instead, mend your own nets and cast them in the seas of transgression and repentance.

"For those of you here today among us who go up to Shakertown to witness and participate in their Satanic rituals, if you must go, go in the spirit as did Christ into the heathen temples--to cast out the snakes and demons, there. Go to Shakertown and cast out the demons, there. Go, there, and cast out demons, young people. In the name of the Lord. In the name of Jesus Christ-ah. In the name of the one true God-ah. Stand up on their Meeting House floor and sing Halleluja--aahh. Halleluja-aahh. In his name-aah. Sing the sacred hymn, there, in the midst of their presence-aahh. Sing the words--aahh. " 'Mine eyes have seen the glory of the coming of the Lord....'."

After he had left the Dry House on that day of their memorable first meeting and was in the wagon driving out the dirt road away from the orchard, Asher realized that he still had his gift for Kitt in his back pocket. A poem--which he had written for her that expressed his true feelings and that he hoped would endear him to her, unquestionably, thereafter.

Now, he was back in Herodsville and into his normal routine of sweeping the sanctuary floor of the Baptist Church. His sweeping was like a meditation. The precise rhythm of the straw bristles of the broom counted cadence and created a kind of mathematics in his mind that, somehow, put his mind's monologue to sleep. In place of inner banter there was only silence, with an occasional image or idea that slipped in as if to test the water before committing to a swim.

In this particular moment of rhythmic contemplation and repose, Asher put down his broom and stopped his sweeping. He reached into his pocket and pulled out the folded, but now-rumpled, piece of paper upon which he had written his poem to Kitt in his best calligraphy. As he stood there in the front of the sanctuary propped up by his broom, he unfolded the sheet of light-brown paper and began to read the poem, aloud. Immediately the large room was filled with his voice echoing off the windows and walls.

Living on Mail
   for Kitt
It's not only hope,
It's the letters have kept me alive
All these months.
My mailbox

Like a big brown belly,
Always hungry,
Always dying of thirst.
Rumbling and grumbling for
Only the best of food.

Sometimes, during periods of drought,
There is not enough ink or love in the world
To go around.
My mailbox shrinks.
My body weakens.
And a time of darkness comes.

But bad times,
Like my old friend says,
Are the same as good times.
Neither lasts.

So I pick up thick books.
Take long walks.
And think of you all day—
Until the groans from my middle
And my mailbox cease.
And Sister Mary arrives
And there is mail.
And a child's unchained laugh
Echoing wildly through the woods!

  With his words still resounding in the hall, Asher folded the paper with the poem on it and slid it back into his hip pocket. He liked the poem, as it said what he wanted to say and what he was feeling. He was angry with himself that he had not remembered to give the poem to Kitt that day in the Dry House. And, now, it will be several days before she may even see the poem. Patience was not one of Asher's virtues. He anguished over the time and distance between the two of them. And he worried that the sentiments she had expressed to him would change during the days when they couldn't communicate with one another. He knew the poem would remedy this, but it was still there in his pocket. Distant from her eyes.

Still standing mid-church and leaning on his broom, he suddenly had an idea. He would see Kitt on Sunday if he were to go to the Sunday service in Shakertown. He will give it to her, there. Knowing the delicacy and the risk of that situation, he sat down in one of the pews there in the church and began brewing up another scheme that would result with the poem soon being in her hands.

Dear Asher,

I barely know where to start. But after wandering around at the farm yesterday here at Pleasant Grove, I became very wistful about what might have been for me had I chosen a different path for my life. I certainly thought a lot about you, too. The farm, with draft horses in the pasture taking a day off from late spring plowing, was very soothing to my somewhat restless soul. It took me back to my childhood growing up in Virginia and to my family's farm, where we had horses and from which my parents made their living--harvesting timber, growing grain crops, making sorghum molasses and, of course, growing a kitchen garden full of all kinds of vegetables. I also saw, today, my first mimosa blossoms of the year.

I came home from my walk over on the farm and re-read some of your letters and poems. I became more wistful for what might have been for us--had our destinies been different and had we been born into different lives. I, too, really don't know how we didn't connect earlier, but I feel that "our time" wasn't meant to be until now for some reason. Although I did feel very connected to you when we first discovered each other on the dance floor at the Shaker services, the timing was not right to get to know you. Maybe I was reluctant to do anything to encourage you or the feelings I was having each Sunday as we passed each other on the dance floor, because I was afraid if I did I would somehow alienate you and I didn't want to destroy something between us before it even had a chance to grow. Before that day in the Dry House, I was wondering why we feel so connected. As we've gotten to know each other these past weeks and months--mainly through our letters--this has become clearer to me.

I've found myself wondering, too, why it is that you are attracted to me, as there are many other young women in Herodsville and other places that would be more suited to you and the kind of life you dream of. I don't feel special in that regard. But there are other things. We both seem to love the simple life that comes from living in harmony with nature, the old ways, and growing things. We both have had experiences with Native peoples. We both have a deep curiosity about God and the Universe. We both have links to Scotland.

In one of your letters you mentioned that you felt that we were connecting in a timely fashion at this time rather than in the past. Given the quality of my good health, I may live for many more decades. So there may still be lots of time for us to be together if that is what is meant to be. Anyway, for now I'm very happy to experience the feelings we do have for each other, and I'll wait to see what the future may bring for us, if anything more. Now, it is our destiny, I believe, to be just close friends, given that you live in Herodsville and I live in Pleasant Grove--although we both now know that there is a possibility, at least, for us to see one another from time to time. But, I am not going to force anything and am not waiting for anything to come from you. What's meant to be will be and I will live with that.

Your description of your time spent over near Lexington with the family on the herb and wild plants farm sounds very interesting to me. This is something I would like to do, too. Harvesting and working with medicinal plants. But who knows. I may yet get to do this as a granny woman in my old age.

This is about all I have time to write today. I hope you are well and happy in what you do. I think of you.

your fallen friend,

Kitt

PS It is possible that my friend Sister Eden will be coming to town, sometimes, to do the errands either with or for Sister Mary. At least I have heard this, but not from Eden herself. If so, you will get to meet her on Tuesdays, as will your friend Caden. "Caden and Eden." Has a nice ring to it, don't you think?

Scene VIII.

Another Sunday had come and Brother Wilford, as The Watcher, found himself again in his familiar spot mid-staircase facing the small window that looked out over the Meeting Hall floor. As had been the case for almost every Sunday for the past year, the Hall was packed with Believers, but more so with visitors from the nearby Herodsville community--with their wagons lined up, as usual, along the highway from the front gate all the way to the rear entrance and on down the road leading to the Ferry Boat dock on the Kentucky River. Per usual, the service began with a period of silence, which was then broken by an a cappella singing of hymns, followed by a short "sermon" by one of the elder members of the Society before the beginning of the line dancing.

As was sometimes his habit, Ranks sat on the stair step during the formal beginning of the service and didn't show his face at the window until the dancing began. But once the dancing begins he got into his uncomfortable crouch and moved up to the window to begin his work of active watching. When Ranks appeared at the window, things picked up down on the floor. It was almost as if when the Ministry appeared at the windows, it was a signal for the festivities to begin. During this approved-of Era of Manifestation, the members of the Society became energized with the Elders' presence, wanting to give the dances, in all their escalating theatrics, their best efforts.

On this particular Sunday, the spectacle down on the floor was a bit calmer than usual. Word of the meetings between the Pleasant Grove Ministry and members of the Ministry at New Lebanon had filtered down into the Pleasant Grove community in general. There had been much talk amongst the villagers during the previous week, especially, and this was reflected in the gentler nature of the Meeting Hall service. But as the dances began, it wasn't long before an occasional Believer fell into fits on the floor, or went off whirling--out of control. But the difference, today, was that these theatrical events did not occur in such great numbers. Even the visitors were not as active on the floor as participants in the dances. Most watched from the fasteners or from outside through the large windows.

At one point, as Ranks was paying special attention to one of the Sisters reeling about the floor--out of line and out of control and speaking in tongues--out of the corner of his eye, he thought he saw something happen in the middle of the floor. Something going on between the two gender-segregated lines. A momentary flash of something white moving from one line to the other. Like a white dove scared frightfully into flight, or a burst of light reflecting from a small piece of mirror glass.

Ranks' eyes quickly moved to the middle of the Meeting Hall floor where the women's and men's dance lines were passing one another, moving in opposite directions. For some reason his eyes caught a glimpse of Kitt Leigh in the women's line as she was about to turn the corner when the line was bending and moving away from the north-facing front doors of the building. An instant later, his eyes caught Asher Pope disappearing from view as part of the men's line that had just passed along that same imaginary horizontal that differentiated the women's and the men's half of the room. Immediately upon catching sight of Asher Pope, The Watcher found himself recalling the incident of some months before, when there had been a somewhat harmless incident on the dance floor involving these same two young people. Although harmless enough, at the time Ranks had sensed something disturbing. Something other. It was only a feeling. But he had felt it. And now, he was feeling it again.

What had he seen? Ranks asked himself as he searched the Meeting Hall floor to find Kitt Leigh. But she had disappeared into the melee of the over-crowded dance lines and the town's people standing against the walls two and three deep and straining to take in everything that was going on. He was sure he had seen something. In that instant, with the blurred flash of white, he intuited trouble. Even with the source of the white flash unknown, his instincts told him whatever it was he had seen was not only unusual, but unblessed.

Wilford Ranks, while not being a particularly sociable man and not what most members in Shakertown society would call brilliant in that regard, was, according to his own opinion of himself, gifted in other ways. As a younger man, he had been an avid reader and student of philosophy. More recently, one of his few talents was manifest in his keen sense of intuition and natural instinct. About certain things he seemed to have an inborn proclivity, a native or natural clairvoyance. "That which is imprinted upon the spirit of man by an inward instinct," described by Francis Bacon. A second sight. Some members of the Shakertown society thought of Wilford Ranks' abilities as being nothing more than "knee-jerk" in nature. Others thought him a little scary and "not we" in his intimations and premonitions. All The Watcher knew was that he was rarely wrong in these forefeelings which he sensed in his bones. His was not a true *clairsentience*, but more in the manner of a hunch. *L'esprit de tact*. Knowledge without reason.

That night while lighting the kerosene lamps in the Ministry apartments above the Meeting Hall, Ranks kept playing the scene on the dance floor earlier that day over and over again in his mind. Each time he revisited the scene during the dances, the flicker of "white light" began to take on form. Until he was certain he had seen something tangible. And that there had been some kind of exchange.

A couple days had gone by since "the incident" in the Meeting Hall the previous Sunday afternoon. Wilford Ranks had become obsessed with the idea of something being exchanged between the men's and women's lines during the dances. He didn't think of it as an obsession, although he, at one point, began questioning himself and even his own sanity in the matter. While not being a man who exudes confidence in his god-given social graces, such as they were, he was, on the other hand, certain in his gift of insight and *apercu*. In this case he had become fixated on "the art of making truth prevail," as La Bruyere had put it so perfectly in one of his discourses on logic and morality almost two centuries before.

At that moment on this particular day, he was seated on one of the long benches that was still under construction in the Ministry Workshop, facing Sister Daniella, who was sitting more comfortably in a small Shaker chair opposite him and only a few feet away.

Wilford Ranks: Sister Daniella, I would much rather we were working here in the Workshop on our usual tasks as members of the community than being here about the work which has befallen us. But I feel strongly, bound by duty, discipline and decree to pursue this matter and the suspicions that have haunted my sleep these past two days. My instincts tell me that what I saw on Sunday somehow involved Sister Leigh. While I don't want to believe any of this, I can't seem to let it go. It seems a cursed situation we find ourselves in. If Sister Leigh was involved in something forbidden, we all lose. We lose her, and we lose her station in the community. And she loses her credibility and her dignity. If we don't investigate the matter, then we also lose. We lose in the sense that if anything did happen and is going on, then it could get worse and become a real incident. And part of our responsibility as members of The Ministry is to try and keep things in the community in a state of stasis. Am I not right about this, Sister Daniella?

Daniella Darrow: While I agree that we can't in good conscience turn a blind eye to things that might affect the community as a whole, I'm not really sure that in this particular case we should be holding an inquisition with Sister Kitt. Especially with such intangible and marginal evidence. I'm not at all convinced that what we are about today is a wise thing. What if you are wrong about what you think you saw--your "intuitions" as you call them? Think of the harm this could bring to the girl.

Wilford Ranks: I understand your concern, Sister. And I don't want to believe it either. While almost universally, everyone holds Sister Kitt in the highest of esteem, I also believe it is true that the exact opposite of what is generally believed can often be the truth. If this axiom has any validity, what are the implications if we don't do anything? If we don't ask any questions.

Daniella Darrow: Whatever it was that you think you saw the other afternoon, Brother Wilford, may have been nothing at all. By your own admission, you say that this may be the truth. And even if something did occur, what could it have been? How harmful could it have been given the circumstances? Sister Leigh is still just a young woman with little worldly experience. Women of her age are bound to commit small indiscretions from time to time that are of little or no consequence. You must remember, Brother Wilford, that children have neither a past nor a future. They are merely enjoying the present. A present that rarely, at our age, ever happens to us.

[*As Sister Darrow finishes this last sentence, the door to the Ministry Workshop*

opens and Kitt Leigh enters the room.]

Wilford Ranks: Sister Kitt, please come in. Won't you have a seat? [*He motions to an empty Shaker rocker near where Sister Darrow sits.*] Thank you for coming, today, Sister Kitt. Sister Daniella and I have been talking and we have some puzzling questions we are hoping, with your expertise, you can help us to resolve.

[*Kitt Leigh walks slowly over to the rocker and sits down, acknowledging Sister*

Daniella with a bowed head and a noticeable pursing of the lips.]

Kitt Leigh: Of course, Brother Wilford, how can I help you?

Wilford Ranks: Sister Daniella and I are in somewhat of a quandry concerning a recent occurrence and are not exactly in agreement as to how it should be resolved. We were hoping maybe you could help us.

Kitt Leigh: How can I be of help to you in such a matter? I am not a member of the Ministry.

Daniella Darrow: Sister Kitt, Brother Wilford thinks he saw something that may be dangerous for those involved. He is hoping that you might shed some light on this situation, as he says he has been losing sleep at night over this issue.

Kitt Leigh: I am sorry to hear that you are not sleeping well, Brother Wilford. I hope it is nothing serious.

Wilford Ranks: You needn't worry about my 'white nights,' Sister Kitt. But I am concerned about something I'm sure I saw last Sunday during Meeting. It occurred near to where you were at the time, and I thought that maybe you might have seen it too.

Kitt Leigh: Seen what, sir?

Wilford Ranks: I'm sure I saw some kind of exchange between two people in the men's and women's lines during the dancing part of the service last Sunday. I was hoping that you might know something about this.

Kitt Leigh: What was it that you saw being exchanged, Brother Wilford?

Wilford Ranks: I'm not really sure what "it" was, Sister Kitt. But I'm sure I saw something white being passed across the dance lines-- which, if true, would be unusual enough to get my attention, which it did, and improper enough to cause me concern, which it has. I know you were in the women's line at the time near to where this would-be exchange occurred and I just thought you may have seen something, yourself.

[*Kitt doesn't respond right away to The Watcher's story or suggestions, but sits in the rocking chair pondering what she has just heard. While a sinking feeling has suddenly appeared in her stomach, her mind has just as suddenly awoken to the situation and become very active. Many thoughts and many responses go through her mind in a matter of seconds, as she processes what she has just heard, including possible verbal avenues of escape. She is aided in her act of diversionary silence by Sister Daniella's intercession.*]

Daniella Darrow: Sister Kitt, this is not an accusation. Brother Wilford is not accusing you of anything. He just wants to know if you saw anything or have any information about any of this.

Kitt Leigh: [*Defensively addressing Sister Daniella*]
Sister Daniella, I don't think I saw anything resembling what Brother Wilford has described and haven't heard of anything unusual or out of the ordinary--which is a funny way of putting it, in light of what actually goes on at Shaker meetings. Most of the time, I'm not aware of what is going on around me, anyway, as I'm usually too involved with the songs, the spirits, you know....

Wilford Ranks: So, you saw nothing last Sunday afternoon that seemed different or strange to you in any way? You saw no one passing notes or objects to anyone during the dances?

Kitt Leigh: No, sir. I didn't see anything of this sort.

Kitt had never lied to anyone before. Not since she had been old enough to remember such things, at least. She didn't like how she was feeling as she sat there in the moments after her transgression, her "deed without a name." It felt beneath her dignity. It made her feel ugly. It made her thirsty. A flood of unrelated thoughts ran through her mind. Why had she lied? Who was she trying to protect? Did Sister Daniella and Brother Wilford know more than they were saying? Would she be trapped in her lie? Would God forgive her? Would Mother Ann forgive her? What would happen to Asher?

She realized in that moment that she was thinking of Asher. Was concerned for him. Was concerned for him and her, together. This thought shocked her. The weight of this thought alone frightened her. The implications of this thought frightened her even more. Her being frightened frightened her. Could Brother Wilford and Sister Daniella see that she was frightened and have deduced that she was lying?

That night as she lay in her bed on the second floor of the Centre Family Dwelling, Kitt wondered where Asher was. She wanted to see him. But she also wondered what Sister Daniella and Brother Wilford were thinking. Had they believed her? Or had they seen through her cover-up and her deceit? Suddenly, her safe and secure Shaker life had been disturbed. Had taken a tumble. Had fallen out of plumb. And she had, to the best of her knowledge, committed her first sin.

At the same moment as Kitt lay in bed with thoughts that kept her from sleep, Wilford Ranks was in deep meditation about the same subject matter in his little room in the Meeting Hall Ministry apartments. He had come away from the meeting in the Workshop feeling unsatisfied. Not that he wanted a confession from the young Sister or that he needed to be right in his assumptions about her in order to substantiate his faith in his intuitive abilities, but that he still had a nagging feeling that something was amiss. Something was not quite right in Sister Leigh's story. There was something unsettling in her denial of any knowledge pertaining to the events in question. Part of him was relieved that Kitt had said that she had taken no part in the event on the Meeting House floor that Sunday, as such behavior might have caused an unfortunate domino effect unhinging the whole of the

Society's upward momentum. A momentum that he and others in the greater Shaker Society felt to be timely and necessary in order to keep the Society growing and sustainable. Even as he felt some relief in Kitt's declaration of innocence, deep down he knew that in her denial were seeds of a greater lie.

Sister Daniella twisted and turned in her bed in the East Family Dwelling, almost as if the thoughts of Sister Kitt and Brother Wilford were concurrently invading her mind. In her small room there didn't seem to be enough air, and she struggled to get her breath and to relax. Her thoughts were mainly on Sister Kitt and this whole business of her would-be indiscretions. Kitt's welfare was her foremost concern, and she feared Brother Wilford's seeming obsession with the now notorious "event in the Meeting Hall." She hoped that Brother Wilford had been satisfied with Kitt's answers to his questions. She hoped that Brother Wilford would let this go. She hoped their life would go on as normal and that nothing more would be said or done concerning this issue, ever again. She tried to imagine Kitt involved in something the least bit dishonest, but she could not. In her mind Kitt was beyond reproach, guided and protected by the spirit of Mother Ann.

After opening a window and letting some of the dew-filled air into the room, Sister Darrow was able to catch her breath. She was convinced of Kitt's innocence and the misguided nature of Brother Wilford's concerns. And with these thoughts she was finally able to put her worries to rest, climb back into bed and fall asleep.

More manifestations. More tensions. More conflict. More dissension. More meetings. More division. More spirits.... Shakertown was, now, truly at a crossroads. Things were, in the eyes of some, nearing a state of anarchy in the settlement. This, coupled with the displeasure being vocalized by many of the local townsfolk had created a problem for The Ministry unlike anything they had ever faced. The meeting suggested by Wilford Ranks in his recent conversation with Sister Daniella had been called and had been an all-night affair with the four members of the Ministry going over and over all the issues and possible remedies. Following a riveting transmission from Mother Ann via Sister Kitt that same day--where the spirit of Mother Ann spoke out condemning certain practices and called for discipline and control--The Ministry was inspired by that afternoon's message: "Give up un-neccesary freedoms. Give up reading unprofitable books. Give up your keeping of journals. The young people should refrain from the use of rocking chairs. Sisters should no longer wear green veils. Purge all idols from Zion! Institute rules with great solemnity and the fear of God!" Kitt had pronounced during that afternoon session, and The Ministry, all of whom had been in attendance, had taken her words to heart--injected them into the spirit of their own private meeting that went on into the night.

What came out of the "Midnight Meeting" as it was to be referred to ever-after by members of The Ministry, were new communal regulations that were written up and then circulated throughout the community in manuscript form--to be accepted as formal doctrine that would be read aloud each year on the birth date of Mother Ann. In the new "Birthday Regulations," as they would be known to the Believers, instruments were required to share their visions with members of The Ministry, separately. This measure was instituted as a kind of check-and-balance regarding extremism, as well as integrity. The Ministry also authorized scribes to write down the communications. Under the guise of "preservation of sacred texts," this was really a measure instituted to control spirit texts that circulated throughout the community and the bishopric. The control of all meetings by the Elders was also a prominent feature of the new regulations. This regulation went so far as to encourage older and more experienced instruments in an effort to neutralize the more youthful inclinations and transmissions of many visionists. The Ministry was even granted powers to involve themselves in the selection of new visionists.

Right from the offset, these new "Birthday Regulations" created controversy. In trying to maintain the reins of control, The Ministry had, in essence, unleashed something of a monster into the community. Almost immediately, the already growing chasm between the older and younger generations was widened as the more youthful instruments felt the pinch of the regulations. Their power and position in the community had been ever-increasingly elevated during the past several years and this sudden "reining in" by The Ministry didn't sit well with many of the instruments and their devoted followers. The perception that many instruments were simply "playing to the visitors" during the Shaker Meeting and the dances, was addressed in the new regulations with a statement limiting the amount of uncontrolled behavior in the presence of "the World's people."

In his somewhat awkward public address to the Shakertown society--in order to give literal voice and justification to the new regulations—Wilford Ranks spoke sermonistically, if not naively, about the documents circulating within the community. "I felt a need to urge the necessity of keeping every order and counsel which has been given for our protection and increase in numbers. In all the ages of the world, God always noticed and protected his people when they obeyed the laws and statutes which were given them." In the end, what Ranks was ironically saying to his Society brethren and sisters was that the Shakertown Ministry was now in a position of defending the letter of the law against the spirits. While nothing could have been more controversial at this time in the history of the community, it was deemed as a necessary act in order to keep the workings of the community from falling into a state of chaos and disrepair.

The Shakertown Ministry had now set themselves up as a kind of benevolent police force. Unprecedented in Shaker history to this point, the almost inevitable "we and they" split this was bound to create actually began its own brand of manifesting. With relations strained and good will on the wane, Brother Wilford Ranks wrote to the New Lebanon Ministry asking for advice. In reply came a letter from Brother Isaac Newton Youngs saying "It is now the fight for us to come more into order and be more together, and not divide in the rooms, but for all that live in two rooms to come into one--and to have a Godly union, in order, nothing private. Take heart. All join hands to keep every order and to be united in every gift. Be sober in your decisions and resolve not to give way to any hard feelings, but be cheerful." In this upbeat, if arcane message from Brother Youngs, Ranks took heart, just as Youngs had suggested, taking the words from New Lebanon as an approval of the "Birthday" acts that they had initiated there in Shakertown. And with new resolve, Wilford Ranks and the members of his Ministry forged ahead.

On the Tuesday following the "flash of light" incident on the Meeting House floor at Sunday Service, no one from Pleasant Grove had appeared at the Herodsville General Store, and so there was no letter from Kitt. No word in response to Asher's latest poem. In a state of blighted hope and disappointment and with his "mailbox moaning and groaning from a lack of food," Asher had spent almost two weeks awaiting the mail that in recent weeks had become his life-blood.

As he cleaned the windows of Caden's father's General Store that Tuesday, he saw the Shaker wagon pull up to the corner of the store and the Sister climb down from the driver's seat gathering her shopping gear. A lightness immediately entered Asher's body as he anticipated the long-awaited response and an answer to his poem.

As the Sister entered the front door to the store, she didn't see Asher standing beside the front wall window, and so made her way into the large room with shelves to the ceiling, smelling of fresh meat, and with sawdust thinly covering the entire floor. Asher watched her, undetected, as she passed by. Asher thought he saw something different in the way the Sister carried herself. He watched her as she made her way across the room to the back counter where Caden was cutting some fresh beef that had just come in that afternoon from the Shelton farm outside of town.

As Caden sensed the Sister's presence, he looked up from his cutting board. With a quick double-take he noticed that he was looking at the face of a much younger woman than the one he had been used to waiting on on the odd Tuesdays when she appeared in the store. This younger woman was much fairer of skin, with large round blue eyes, and there was a hint of red hair peeking out from under her bonnet. Caden was somewhat startled and surprised at the beautiful young girl in Shaker dress standing on the other side of the counter, and he almost stumbled as he straightened up from his crouch over the cutting table and moved awkwardly up to the counter where she was standing.

"Hello, I am Sister Eden from Pleasant Grove and I have come to town today to do the shopping for Sister Mary. Sister Mary usually does the shopping for the community, but is busy with other duties today so couldn't come. I was wondering if you could help me in finding the things, here, on my list."

"Um, yes ma'am, I mean Miss Eden. I'd be happy to. What is it you are looking for today?"

"You must be Caden. I've heard about you from Sister Wicks, who speaks highly of you. She says that you are very helpful and can be trusted."

"Well, umm, yes, I mean I hope so ma'am, I mean Sister Eden. We try and do right by our customers. And that, of course, includes yourself and Sister Wicks."

All the while this exchange was going on between Eden and Caden, Asher was watching and listening from his vantage point over near the large window at the front of the store. He heard the soft lilt in her voice and saw the dance-like gestures of her arms as she spoke. He wanted to say something--to announce his presence. But he did not. Instead he stood stationary on the other side of the room, window rag in hand.

"Here is my list, then, if you would be so kind as to find these things for me. If you can't read Sister Wick's handwriting, let me know and I'll help you with that."

"Oh, I know Sister Mary's handwriting and can read it quite clearly. In fact I've often remarked to the Sister what good handwriting she has."

"As well as the shopping list, I also have this letter that I'm supposed to deliver to Mr. Asher Pope. I believe you know him? Sister Mary has told me that I can trust you with this letter and with the knowledge of the correspondence between Mr. Pope and Sister Kitt. If so, I would like to give you this letter from Sister Kitt--for you to give, in the strictest of confidence, to him."

"Yes, I will be happy to do as you say. But, if you would rather give the letter to Asher yourself, he is standing right behind you over by the far window."

Being taken by complete surprise at Caden's announcement of Asher's presence in the room, Eden whirled around, slipping a little on the sawdust on the floor and scanned the room with her eyes, as if looking for a ghost. Regaining her balance and her focus, she saw Asher standing across the room by the large front window of the store. As they stood staring at one another from long distance, Asher raised his arm and waved to her with the hand that was holding the window rag. The gesture was comically awkward and from across the room looked somewhat feminine--like a socialite waving her handkerchief, as if to say goodbye to a loved one leaving on a long trip. Eden smiled and a slight giggle came from her mouth, as she politely waved back to Asher from across the room.

"I'm Asher," Asher finally announced in full voice as he began walking toward her. "I've been listening to your conversation with Caden, and recognize your name from letters I have received from a mutual friend of ours, I believe. Kitt told me that you might be coming into town to run errands someday soon, and I see that you have made it. I'm pleased to meet you and am hoping that you might have brought something with you today that may be addressed to me."

"Oh, yes I have. And, oh, I'm pleased to meet you. I'm Eden and I do have a letter for you from Sister Kitt."

She reached for the letter she had just given to Caden, who placed the letter and the shopping list back into Eden's outstretched hand. Eden laughed at receiving the shopping list along with the letter and politely returned the list to Caden, who had already turned a little red with awkward embarrassment. Meanwhile, Asher had made his way across the room from the window to the large counter in the back of the store where Caden and Eden were still standing in a state of awkward engagement.

"It's been so long since I've heard from your friend Kitt that I was beginning to worry. That letter in your hand has relieved my mind, I can tell you. It's been one of the longest weeks I can remember. I thank you for bringing this to me."

"Since you brought it up, the word "worry" is appropriate and timely, as much has gone on these past weeks. I am a little reluctant, I must say in all honesty, to give you this letter I hold in my hand. I have my own personal reasons for saying this, but there have also been suspicions aroused by your little sleight-of-hand trick at Sunday services Sunday before last. Fact is, that Sister Kitt was called in to talk to The Ministry about this, as one of the members of The Ministry apparently saw you slip the piece of paper to Kitt during the dances when you passed her in line that afternoon. They asked her all kinds of questions about "the exchange" and she was forced to lie to the Ministry to protect herself and to protect you."

"Oh my God! I didn't know, of course. But 'protect me?' How and why would she protect me?"

"I'm not sure, exactly, as I've only just been able to talk with her once, and very quickly this past week while we were hanging out laundry at the East Family Wash House. You know they keep us busy up at Pleasant Grove and rarely do we get a chance to talk alone. All I know is that she said the whole time The Ministry was questioning her, all she could think about was you. Even so, I'm reluctant to give you her letter, as I've always been worried that someone would find out about the two of you and your letters--not to mention your showing up that day at the Dry House!"

"You know about that? I thought that I was able to get in and out of the village without being detected. Did someone see me? Do they know that we were together in the shed?"

"I'm Kitt's best friend, so she tells me a lot. She doesn't tell me everything, but I know pretty much about the two of you. So, of course I heard all about that meeting of yours in the Dry House. We don't think anyone noticed you coming or going that day, or that you were with Kitt in the Dry House, but it is indeed a miracle that no one saw you or got wind of what you were up to. However, apparently you weren't as lucky with your contact at the Sunday service!"

"I'm sorry about the Sunday service. I really didn't think anyone could possibly see me slip the piece of folded paper into her hand as we passed in line--the room was so crowded and with all that was going on...."

"Well, it's happened, and you should know that the Elders are suspicious. So, you best keep quiet and careful and not let your emotions get the better of your good sense. I'm hoping that you do have some sense about you. Kitt seems to think so, but I wonder, as she seems to be much too enamored of you and the thrill of this letter-writing."

"Enamored? Did she actually use the word enamored?"

"No, that is my word. But I can see it in her eyes when she talks about you and about your letters and your surprise visit. You've turned her head, Brother Asher, and I worry about her judgment and what could happen if anyone should find out about you two."

"I will promise to be more careful in the future. I don't want to get her into any kind of trouble. You must believe me when I say this. On the other hand, it's very hard--all this waiting--between letters. Between seeing her on Sundays at the Meeting Hall. And not being able to talk to her face-to-face. Do you understand?"

"No, I can't say that I do, never having been in this kind of situation, myself. But I'll have to take your word, I guess, about being careful and having Kitt's best interests at heart. And if I didn't give you the letter, as I promised her I would do, she would be very disappointed, even angry at me. So, since I promised I would, here is her letter."

Eden places the letter from Kitt into Asher's outstretched hand.

"Thank you for understanding and for being her messenger. You are indeed a friend."

"If a friend, then a reluctant one. While I love Kitt like a sister and want to help her in any way I can, I only want what's best for her, and I'm not so sure that you are what's best for her. I hope that you will prove me wrong in my suspicions and my doubts."

"I will try hard to win your confidence, Sister Eden. But I must get back to work before Caden's dad comes back. It was a pleasure to have met you and I can see why Kitt speaks so well of you."

Asher turned and walked back in the direction of the front of the store and the large window where he had left his bucket of soapy water and rags.

Eden blushed at Asher's parting line and looked embarrassed at Caden, who was also looking a little nervous and uncomfortable.

"Forgive him," Caden apologized, "he hasn't been himself lately. All these letters and everything have gone to his head. There's a bit of devilment in him these days that I've never seen before, and I've known him since we started school together, a long time ago. He's a good person and he means well, but your friend Kitt has gotten his total attention and it's practically all he talks about these days. Maybe between the two of us we can keep these two from making a mess. So feel free to talk to me anytime, as I'm probably sitting more on your side of the fence than Asher's concerning this unlikely liaison."

"Indeed I will, Brother Caden. I thank thee for thy confidence. It was a pleasure to meet you. And now, if we can find those items on my list, I'll leave both of you to get on with your day."

Caden gathered up various provisions around the store and

checked them off Eden's list as he went. He packed everything in the cloth bags Eden had brought in the store with her, took her cash, gave her change and a two-handed handshake in parting.

Asher waited until he got home after work to finally read Kitt's letter--an act which had taken all the discipline and strength-of-character he could muster. All the way home that evening he had thought about what Eden had said to him in the store-- about Kitt's ordeal with The Ministry and her having to lie. He was feeling guilty as he finally sat down in his upstairs attic room in the parsonage to read Kitt's letter.

Once into the words of the letter, Asher was swept back again into his preferred romantic state of mind and soon forgot about the bad news he had heard that day. He loved how she talked about growing up on a farm. About all the things she had said they shared in common. How she used words like "destiny" and phrases like "feelings we have for one another." But maybe even more so, he loved how she LOVED his poetry. He read the letter once. Then read it again. Read it a third time. The third time through, he could actually imagine he heard her voice. He was back in the Dry House and she was there with him. She was running her hand through his hair. He was gently touching her cheek. She was alive and present for him there in the attic. In this moment he was already plotting what he must do to see her again--so strong was the pull from the power of her words there in the leaden lines of pencil on the light brown pages.

Amidst the revelations and regulations in recent days and following her inquisition with the members of The Ministry, Kitt has found her new status in the community compromised. While all this was unsettling, her thoughts were on Asher. It had been days since Eden's trip to Herodsville. Kitt stood pensively alone in the Dry House with her thoughts, struggling with her work, awaiting word from Eden.

How long has it been? I have made many marks on my calendar. And have lost count. Where is Eden? The sun has gone up and down, up and down, again and again since last we talked. Even Cupid would not tease, this much, my sense of longing. Maybe she has been found out and at this very moment sits in similar council with Brother

Ranks and Sister Darrow that I, too, have lately been accustomed to. She knows of my interest, yet she has not come. Would I make her suffer so? Wait, what's that? Sounds like feet coming up to the door.

The door to the Dry House opens and Eden enters the room.

"Thank goodness, you have come! I was beginning to fear you had met a fate similar to mine and had been retained by our elders, who know nothing of our youthful anxieties. So, tell me Sister Eden, what news? And tell me no bad news, as I have had enough of this kind of gift in recent days. And if the news is bad, tell it to me with a smile."

"I can stay but for a minute, as I have been sent on an errand for Sister Mary--who sends her good wishes, by the way--and I am out of breath having run all the way from the East Family Wash House where I've been in a state of slavery to water and warm weather all afternoon. So, let me sit, first, and catch my breath so I can tell thee what I know you long to hear."

"But don't take too many breaths. Save some for your story and all the news. Meanwhile, I'll fill the time by asking questions. I know you went to town. Sister Wicks has told me this much. But how much more can you add? We have enough time, today, for at least a scene from that play. Tell me, how did the conversation go?"

"Well, I've got to say, that your Asher is quite the romantic. A strong presence, he has. But while his presence is great, he is no match, in looks, for his friend Caden. Now there is a true flower in the Herodsville garden!"

"Yes, yes, I know all this, as surprised as I am to hear such speech from your own lips. But what word do you have from Asher? How is he? Much has gone on, here, as you no doubt know, since last I saw him. I have been through such agonies and heard great insinuations since we last talked."

"Mercy, my heart is still beating like it would jump from my body. Give me a minute more and I will tell thee all."

"We haven't much time, as there is only room for four sonnets in a single Scene, and we have already spent time enough for one. You are the sonneteer. Don't keep me in suspense any longer; can't you see I'm dying to hear your tale?"

"I think next time you should go to Herodsville yourself. This would save us both a lot of strain and, in my case, a lot of breath. And you would have the satisfaction of getting words from his lips, first hand. And I think that it's the lips you really want. The words are but secondary. But I can only give you words, today, as he has not sent me with a package of his lips to share with thee. So, words will have to do."

"Eden, you have now spent the second sonnet's time in this sonnet sequence, and all my patience. Tell me what it is you have to say."

"I will sonnetize, lest your sororal feelings for me turn sorrel. Where was I?"

"At the beginning, if indeed you even got that far, fair sister."

"I went to Herod's store and, at first, saw only the handsome Caden there. But after we talked about our business and I told him of the letter I had brought for his friend Asher, he pointed to the window across the room where Asher had been standing in mode of eavesdropping all along. He quickly joined us and we were a threesome in our conversation, but then, I must say, he does not talk much, your boy."

"Even if only a few words, dear Eden, what did he say?"

"He was all hands. He couldn't snatch the letter fast enough from my fingers. He was like a man starved for food and the letter in my grasp a hunk of cattle beef. But he was polite and did not read it in my presence. How do you like my sonnet so far?"

"It has a sweet cadence, but only a little substance. Do you have another? For we have room for one more to make our four. Did he ask about me?"

"Indeed, he did. On and on, now as I recall. But in the end, the most news I got came from his friend Caden, who, after Asher had departed, told me that he had been pining for you for days and rarely would speak of anything else. While a good sign in other circumstances, perhaps, I was a little alarmed at this sort of news, and I told Brother Caden of my concern, the same as I had done to your Asher."

"Did you speak harshly to Asher? I hope you were not too motherly with him, as I know how you can be."

"I was only forthright in saying that if he, indeed, cared for you, he should be more careful in future about his comings and goings and what he does at Meeting, and that he should think of your well-being and not only his own selfish desires."

"You didn't use the words 'selfish desires!' I hope you didn't leave him feeling chastised. You really are the mother, Eden."

"No, not these words, but words to this effect. In the end we left each other on friendly terms. He listened well to what I said and was even apologetic for the trouble he had caused you, and was concerned. I think his concern was genuine, as he went on to promise me that he would be more careful in his actions from this point on. And this is the end of my sonnet, sister. I hope it has satisfied thee."

"It has, indeed. In as much as poetry can replace the sound of his voice."

"Good, now tell me some important news and about this

business with The Ministry, as there are only rumors circulating among the Sisters in Centre House. It is your turn to talk. Send me some prose."

"While I was treated with respect, the content of Brother Wilford's questions was not at all pleasant to the ear. He said he had seen 'something unusual' Sunday before last during the Shaker dances and wondered if I knew anything about it. He also asked about certain stories he had heard about letters being passed between young people in the Society and certain young people in Herodsville. Although he didn't come right out and say it, I felt that in a deceptive sort of way he was insinuating that maybe all this had something to do with me."

"Well, what did you tell him? Surely there are more chapters in this book?"

"Against my principles, and probably against God, I lied. I could not bring it upon myself to tell Brother Wilford the truth. Those beady eyes of his did not invite a truthful answer from my lips. Even Sister Daniella's compassionate words in my behalf couldn't wedge the words Brother Wilford was looking for from my mouth."

"Do you think they believed you, Sister Kitt?"

"I'm not sure of that, Eden, although I think that Sister Daniella was uncomfortable about the whole situation and very much wanted to believe in my response."

"How did Brother Wilford know of the letters? How did these rumors start?"

"Like all tales begin, I suppose. Two and two are put together and it makes five. For everyone's talk and intention of 'taking the higher ground,' humans love gossip-mongering more than almost anything else. It's a small world when it comes to the talk of the town."

"What busybody would have leaked your secret, do you think? Who could it have been? Surely Sister Mary would not have whispered such confidential information to anyone else. And even if such tabby is being whispered about in the streets of Herodsville, what other way would it have gotten back to the settlement other than through Sister Mary?"

"It's hard to know, Sister, since there is a good bit of commerce that goes on between the two camps. And who knows what is exchanged other than money during these meetings? While we will probably never know how all this got started, we do know that the bird is out of the cage and while Brother Wilford and Sister Daniella have no concrete proof, they seem to have plenty of suspicion fueling their fire. From now on, we must be more careful. And maybe even devise a different plan for getting the letters back and forth, and certainly be more cautious regarding any future physical meetings."

"Maybe the safest thing would be to stop the exchange of letters altogether, Kitt, before this goes any further. The atmosphere at Pleasant Grove is not all that 'pleasant' these days. Maybe you should just take the letters and be satisfied with what you have and put all this backdoor behavior behind you, while it's still not too late."

"I hear what you are saying, Eden, I know you are concerned. And I do not like the fact that I have lied to the Ministry. This is the worst part of the story, thus far. I've had more trouble wrestling with the idea that I lied to Brother Wilford and Sister Daniella than anything else. I am not ashamed that I have written clandestine letters and sent backstairs messages to Herodsville and to Asher. This was all honest and innocent enough. But I don't feel the same way about the conversation I had with the members of The Ministry and that I felt I had to lie. And did lie. This has become a great weight on my soul. While my heart is alive, excited, healthy, my soul is in grieving as if over someone's death. While my physical virginity is intact, I will never be spiritually innocent again."

"Don't be too hard on yourself, Sister Kitt, all this tattle being bandied about, all this talk over the back fence, will, I hope, pass, and the Believers will turn their focus to other, more important things. Besides, who is going to stand up in service and chide you for your deeds? Who is going to stand up as your accuser? The Ministry is not going to let this happen. Your visions of and messages from Mother Ann are too important to the Society as a whole to let such an unproved lie destroy you."

"This is water deeper than I dare to wade into, dear Eden. And this is where our 'reading' ends, for today. No more prose or fiction shall pass from my lips, nor more poetry from yours. The sun goes down in the sky as we speak and on our speaking, too. So, get thee back to thy washing and to Sister Mary. This colloquy is done 'tween me and you."

ACT II

Scene I.

Since his face-to-face conversation with Kitt and Sister Daniella, Wilford Ranks had become obsessed with the idea of possible improprieties going on between the youth in the Shaker community and certain young people in the town of Herodsville. Based on what he thought he had witnessed from his Meeting Hall window, coupled with the unsettling internal events of recent weeks, he was not only losing sleep at night worrying about the possible ramifications, but had come to some modicum of resolve that steps needed to be taken to gain greater clarity regarding these suspicions of his, and to take measures to protect the integrity of the people of Shakertown. With these thoughts giving him no rest, he arose one morning in the summer of 1842, put on his best clothes, hitched up a team and wagon in the stables, and set out for, what was for him, a rare trip to Herodsville.

Ranks had arranged and timed his trip to Herodsville so that he would be going on what would be the usual "town day" and could therefore conduct his covert business under the guise of running errands for the community. His wagon passed the Old Mud Meeting House on Dry Branch Road--a building that he had always admired, built of oak timbers, its walls filled with straw and sticks by a band of Huguenots who had settled there in 1800, coming from Pennsylvania. As he made his way along the seven miles of dirt road toward town, Ranks planned his strategy for what he would do once he arrived in this haven of "The World's People." It had been a long time since he had, himself, set foot in Herodsville. He drew a mental map of the town and traced his route in order to avoid getting lost or making any wrong turns that would result in his having to ask for directions or draw any unwanted suspicion to himself. In his mind, he also rehearsed what he might say to anyone he should casually meet or who might unexpectedly cross his path. He visualized and rehearsed, too, his movements and conversation with those to whom he had come, specifically, to speak: the employees of the Herodsville General Store.

The two Belgian horses pulled Rankss' wagon around the last corner before entering onto the main street of Herodsville. For a fleeting moment, he felt, for the first time, some trepidation creep into his consciousness, and for a split second he considered turning his horses about and heading home. But this thought passed, as there was no will in the hands that held the reins to his team, and so his two big Belgians took the corner and headed down Main Street to the large wood-framed store at the other end of what seemed to Ranks like a gauntlet of commerce and humanity.

As Ranks made his way as quietly as possible down Main Street, inside the Herodsville General Store Caden and Asher were going about their usual Tuesday duties unawares. Fresh produce was coming in from the local farms and Asher was busy unloading wagons onto the loading dock at the back of the store and putting some fresh vegetables in the cool storage room, while Caden put out a variety of select vegetables into baskets and wooden boxes in the produce section of the store. In the mid-morning hours of this Tuesday, for Asher and Caden, all was right with the world and life was going on, predictably. The two young men had just, only minutes before, been joking about and teasing each other over the previous Sunday's Meeting in Shakertown and Eden's last visit to the store in Herodsville. Asher had, since that day, been ceaselessly teasing Caden about the"Eden" ploy that both he and Kitt had hatched and kept taunting him with inuendoes that brought blushes to Caden's face and unconvincing denials from his lips.

The Shaker elder's wagon made its way down Main Street, as the buildings and names became familiar to him. It had been almost a year since his last trip to the town of Herodsville. Once a frontier town, Herodsville had been founded in 1774 as the first permanent English settlement west of the Allegheny Mountains. Quickly gaining the reputation as "the Williamsburg of the West" with its colonial architecture and its booming farmbelt population punctuated by its large Mercer County Courthouse constructed in 1785, the town had kept its fashionably rural appearances and charm over the years and feels unexpectedly appealing to Ranks. He drove slowly past the old courthouse, past the Boice family blacksmith shop and stables, and, finally, up in front of his destination.

There was quite a bit of commotion in and around the store on produce day, so Ranks was slow to climb down from the wagon, taking his time with the horses, all in an effort to try and calibrate his timing to synchronize with his intentions. After several minutes of fiddling with horses and wagon, and not wanting to draw undue attention to himself by his actions of avoidance, he noticed a momentary lull in the activity of shoppers coming and going from the front and back of the store and set his gaze on the store's double doors which were positioned directly under a large sign painted in bold red letters.

He pushed open the right-hand door and set his right foot onto the oak floorboards of the General Store as the doorbell rang, giving him a start that nearly caused him to trip over the doorsill with his next step. In the back of the store, Caden heard the bell ring, so knew a customer had just entered the store. Busy putting more fresh produce in the grocery section, both Caden and Asher were stocking the boxes and bins for the usual anticipated rush of Tuesday customers.

"Be right with you," Caden announced, responding to the bell but not bothering to look around to notice or acknowledge who this particular customer was. "Asher, can you bring me some more of the beets and turnips that Mr. Davis brought in this morning? I need some more to fill these bins we use for root crops."

"Sure thing. There's more in the cold room out back. How many you need?"

"Maybe a half bushel of each. That ought to be enough for today."

"Anything else while I'm out there?"

"No, I think we're set for everything else. So, just the beets and turnips."

"Back in a flash. Who knows, your friend Eden might just have woken up this morning with a hankerin' for beets and turnips today and be on her way from Shakerland to get a load as we speak. We don't want her to come all the way to town only to find half a bin of beets, now do we? Just think of her disappointment," Asher said, teasingly, as he turns toward the back door of the store that opens out onto the loading dock.

As the words fell from his smiling lips and he turned to leave the room, his eyes caught the sight of a large male figure standing stationary in the middle of the store facing the two young men. Asher's smile quickly turned downward as his face took on the expression of sudden shock, almost resembling terror. Caden, who was sorting new potatoes and bending over the open bins with his back to the room, felt Asher's astonishment; he empathically straightened up from his arched posture and turned toward Asher thinking to retaliate to his sarcastic comments about Eden with a measured volley of his own. Instead of the expected teasing smile, Caden saw the unnatural look of horror on Asher's face. Following the invisible beam of Asher's glance to the dark figure standing several paces away, he recognized the face immediately. As if framed and hung on a wall, it was a face he'd seen before. A ghostly visage. The large man's presence sent chills down Caden's spine. It was The Watcher!

The room got terribly quiet as Caden and Asher looked into each other's eyes with eerie disbelief and discomfort. "Wondrous strange" crossed Asher's poetic mind, as he stood there, dumbstruck, facing the man who watched from the window in the Meeting House wall. Caden saw an "unearthly" figure from a bad dream. Long seconds ticked by, the silence only grew heavier with both young men standing at attention, blushing with embarrassment as much as fear, facing their mysterious visitor. Both were certain they had been overheard. As if to break the silence with an axe, the eerie, ghost-like presence standing mid-room spoke, his voice sounding to Caden and Asher like the crashing sound of breaking glass.

" 'Morning boys. Didn't mean to interrupt you, as I can see that you're busy. But I came all the way to town today just to see you two. I'm glad that I found you, for I've got some very important questions I need to ask."

Caden looked at Asher and Asher at Caden with The Watcher's pronouncement, as if he was Sheriff Ashe and had come with a warrant for their arrest.

"Yes, sir," Caden finally was able to respond, after waiting, to no avail, for Asher to be the first to speak. "Sorry sir. We were just joking around. Tuesday is our busy day for putting out fresh produce and so we weren't paying much attention when you came in. We thought we were alone for the moment here in the store and were just jokin' around. Hope we didn't say anything to offend you."

"Actually, I did hear you say something about Sister Eden, which, as you might imagine, got my attention. In fact it was just this subject that I came here to talk to you both about today."

With Rank's statement Caden cringed and Asher's skin pigmentation suddenly turned ashen. Both young men looked at each other, as if they were about to run. But neither moved, glued as they were to the oak floor and heavy with the lead in their legs.

Ranks continued. "I could tell by your expressions that you both recognized me right away. That being the case, there need be no introductions, as I know who you both are, too. Am I not right in my assumption that I've seen you both at Shaker Meeting during the past year? In fact, I think I have seen you many times over the course of the last year or so. Am I correct in saying this?"

"Yes sir," both boys responded in embarrassed unison like choirboys singing off key.

"So, can I assume that you are benefiting from your visits to Shakertown on Sundays, then?"

"Yes sir," they both responded again, together, in one voice, this time in key.

"We in the Pleasant Grove community have been happy to have you, your kinfolk and friends, join us for Sunday services these past months. We open our doors trustingly with hopes that what we share will be of some spiritual benefit to you and yours. We enjoy the interaction with members of the Herodsville community in the spirit of a sense of shared learning, so we can all learn from one another. Don't you agree?

" Yes, sir," Caden responded, Asher remaining silent this time, tired of playing the fool and sensing that The Watcher was just toying with them and that he had something more specific on his mind, as he surely hadn't come all this way into town to chat or out of some sense of missionary zeal.

"Good. I'm glad we are in agreement--about this much, at least. But it's the word *trust* in my last remark that I want to emphasize, now. And to the word *trust* I'd like to add the word *respect*. By opening our doors to the people of Herodsville we have trusted that you would come to our community and to our services with a sense of reverence and respect. That you would understand that while there is much we share in common, there is also much that is different in our two communities. We would hope that you would respect those differences and would act respectfully when you are on Pleasant Grove property as well as when you are not. Do you understand what I am saying, here, boys?"

"Yes, sir." This time it was Asher who answers. "Certainly we didn't mean any disrespect by what we were talking about when you came in, sir. I'm sure that folks in Shakertown talk this way about us folks in Herodsville, too. Is that not so?"

"Let me get to the point, boys," Ranks responded, ignoring Asher's last remark and its accompanying question. "I know you are busy and I want to take advantage of this time that we have been given— to be alone and without interruption. I heard you mention Sister Eden's name as I walked into the store. I detected affectionate innuendoes in your remarks. What, may I ask, were your referring to? Is there anything between you two and Sister Eden that I should know about?"

"No sir," Asher spokeup quickly, not trusting Caden to give the right response. "We both work together on Tuesdays here in the store and we know Sister Eden as a regular Tuesday customer who buys for the whole Shakertown community when she comes to town. I was just teasing Caden, here, that we needed to have plenty of beets and turnips in the bins or Sister Eden would be disappointed that we didn't have enough of those for the community meals. I understand that you all eat together, and so whoever is doing the cooking will need a lot of any one thing to feed everyone at the same time. I know that you grow most of what you eat there in Shakertown, but that sometimes you need additional food and things from town to meet your needs," Asher rambled on, uncomfortably.

"You seem to know quite a lot about what goes on amongst us Believers. May I ask what is the source of your information and knowledge of our practices and beliefs?"

Asher became uncharacteristically nervous with this last question by the older Shaker man, and the suddenly tense language of his body gave him away as he attempted a thought-out response that he hoped would put an end to the older man's inquisition.

"Yes, sir, I am very interested in the Shaker literature and Shaker customs and practice. This is why I, we, Caden and I, come to the Meetings on Sundays. But to answer your question, I have learned most of what I know about what goes on in Shakertown from my father, who is the preacher at the Baptist Church here in town. You may know him."

"Indeed I do--or at least I can say that I know of him, never having met him face-to-face. What I have heard of and from your father leads me to believe he doesn't know everything about our life over in Pleasant Grove. I've also heard that he does not approve of everything we believe or practice. Be that as it may, I didn't come here, today, to talk about your father or his thoughts on Shakerism. I came, today, to talk to you both, and especially to you, Mr. Pope, about your visits to Shaker Meeting, your interests in Shaker faith, and your intentions and interest, specifically, in a particular young member of our community, Sister Kitt Leigh. Do you know of whom I speak, Mr. Pope?"

"I believe I know this Sister Leigh you speak of, sir. She is well-known and respected in your community, I believe--or so I have heard. She has been pointed out to me at the Shaker Dances. Since she looks to be about my age, I have often thought that it would be interesting to talk to her and to get her perspective on Shaker beliefs, since she is apparently so highly thought of. I'm assuming, of course, that she would know a great deal about all this--from both study and experience. Like I said, I am interested in Shakerism. I guess I'm just a curious person and am always looking to learn more--about everything."

"Boys, let me just put it to you as I see it. There have been what I hope are only rumors floating around our community in Pleasant Grove that there has been some rather covert communication, even interaction, going on between the young people in your community and ours. This has been a worry to us, especially the elder members of the community, since we are responsible for the welfare of all our members, especially the young. Unsupervised intercourse, of any kind, between the sexes is against our beliefs and customs. Even amongst our young Believers it is a deep concern. Having said that, you can imagine our reaction to stories of unsupervised intercourse among young members of the opposite sex between our two different communities. And it is this urgent concern that has brought me to town, today. Having watched the two of you from my vantage point of the window in the Meeting House wall all these months, I have intuited, although perhaps wrongly, that the two of you might know something of what I speak and would be willing to share with me any knowledge that you have on the matter."

Both Asher and Caden were somewhat stunned by the use of the word *intercourse* in The Watcher's proclamation, as both of them had only heard this word used in a sexual context. That said, both boys were surprised by the elder man's candor, and quite frankly his nerve--to be so openly and descriptively conversant with people he had not previously known. But as Ranks' monologue progressed, it was Asher who was first to figure out that the word *intercourse* must have more than one meaning and that it must have to do with some kind of non-sexual communication between two or more people. So, after a rather uncomfortable moment following Ranks' confession, the two boys struggled to recover from their momentary shock. They tried to formulate some sort of coherent, if not evasive, response. It was rather surprising to both boys that Caden was the first to speak, hoping that his act of intercession would spare Asher any embarrassment if not also self-incrimination.

"I can tell you, sir, that I'm quite certain that there are no sexual relationships going on between any young people in Herodsville and any young people in Shakertown. This is a small town and this store is something of a hub for gossip. If anything like this were going on, I'm pretty sure I would know about it. And I've not heard of anything like this. Believe me, it would be big news if anything like this was actually going on.

"Asher and I don't go to the Shaker Meeting every Sunday. We go when we can. Asher's probably more interested in your Shaker beliefs and practices than I am, but he has wanted me to come with him, sometimes, so that I could learn all about this, too. I have to say that life in Shakertown is quite interesting. But it's not for me. I'm just a homebody and this is my home and I can't ever imagine living anywhere or any way else. Of course I can't speak for Asher, but we're close friends and if he had heard anything regarding your questions, I'm sure he would have told me."

"I thank you for your ardent answer, Caden, but I would, in fact, like to hear what Mr. Pope has to say--to let him speak for himself. And forgive me if I gave you both the wrong impression. What I meant, of course, was simply verbal and written communication between our two communities. Mr. Pope?"

Asher winced slightly at The Watcher's paternalistic tone as well as at the thought of how he would answer his courtroom questions. Ranks noticed Asher's discomfort, but didn't interrupt the ambiance of the moment and let him speak.

"Yes, sir, I agree with everything Caden has said," Asher started off with diplomacy and caution. "I've not heard of any improprieties. Nothing between the young people in our respective communities anyway. And if Caden had heard anything I'm sure he would have told me about it. And as for the sex, I'm almost certain that there is none of that going on. I mean, how would that even be possible? Our worlds are so separate from one another and it is rare, if ever, that our young people interact face-to-face in any way. Don't you agree?" Asher interjected the question to keep from having to explicate, further, anything that might incriminate himself.

"Well said, Mr. Pope. But aside from the sexual question, would you know of any non-sexual relationships between any of our respective young people? It has been brought to my attention that you, yourself, might be involved in some secret communications with one or more of our young people. And I'm specifically referring to our own Sister Kitt Leigh, here."

Asher had been asked the question he had hoped to avoid. With Ranks' question he would either have to admit to the liaisons between himself and Kitt, or he would have to lie. To avoid further inquisition and to protect Kitt, he decided to lie. But first, he would try one further ploy to try and throw The Watcher off track.

"I'm not sure, sir, that this is the sort of conversation you should be having with the likes of us. Your concerns are grave and I can tell upsetting to you. Shouldn't you be taking up this matter with the elders in our community with similar social positions to those of your own? This sort of thing is beyond our ken and is really a more appropriate subject for you to discuss with your own peers."

Detecting Asher's efforts of avoidance, Ranks came right back at him with a savvy diplomatic response to the younger man's deviousness.

"Well said, again, Mr. Pope. You speak very well. Eloquently even. I am duly impressed. However, since I am here and we are talking to one another, and I can't imagine when such an opportunity might arise, again, I would still like to hear your side of the story, since you obviously have your hand on the pulse of the population of the younger generation in your community. Can I not convince you, as your good friend has done, to also speak to the matter of my concern?"

Asher thought long and hard before he spoke again.

"Very well, Mr. Ranks, I will answer your question."

"How is it that you know my name, boy?" Ranks snapped back at him like the cracking of a whip.

Caught in his own mistake, with this thoughtless slip of the tongue, Asher retreated into what he sometimes referred to as his "dumb mode." It was something of a time-honored tradition of self-deprecation and a kind of "playing possum game" in the Southern Allegheny mountains amongst certain members of the region whom Asher had had the opportunity to get to know while growing up, and in particular on trips he had taken with his father into very rugged and rural areas to spread the word of God. Since his "smart as a whip mode" (as Kitt had called it once in one of her letters) had not dissuaded Ranks from his tenacious obsession or his voracious hunger in getting at the truth, Asher was being forced to play his last card in this game of verbal poker with the man in the window in the Meeting Hall wall.

"Well, sir, I ain't really the right person, or even the brightest or knowing person to talk to about such things as this, but since you want to know what my answer is, I'll tell you. I go to the Sunday Meetings because I love to watch them whirling dances. And I love to listen to all the people talking in tongues. I like studyin' language and so I like to try and figure out if there are any words I know, and what languages people are talking in. I can't really tell, much, what languages they're speaking or what they're sayin', but it's fun to try. And I have to admit that I like watchin' the women doing them whirling dances, especially. And how their dresses spread out when they spin, well hit reminds me of those little wooden tops that spin and spin so fast. Why those women look as though they might just lift up off the floor and go right on up to the ceiling, sometimes. I'd never seen that before I went to one of your Shaker seances. Well, it seems like there's something new at these services every time! You can't get anything like that in Herodsville. I can tell you that. No sir, to answer your question, I don't know nothin' about any goin's-on between anyone in Herodsville and Shakertown, as I keep pretty much to myself and don't get around much."

Asher's self-deprecating response didn't impress the older man. By now, much time had gone by and the store was beginning to get busy with customers--which was Wilford Ranks' cue to leave.

"Well, thank you boys for your time and your willingness to talk," he said somewhat sarcastically. "I hope that you're right about this business of intercourse, I mean interaction, between the young people. I wouldn't want anything to jeopordize the good relations that Herodsville has had with Pleasant Grove over the years. It would be a shame if all of that came to an inglorious end just because of one man's lust or one person's self-centered short-sightedness. I hope that I won't have to talk to either of you, or your parents, about this again. Let's just hope these are unfounded rumors and that we all can get on with our respective lives in honor of the grace of God and all he has given us. I thank you, boys, and wish you a pleasant day."

With that benediction, The Watcher turned his back on the two young men and walked from the section of the store where the produce was sold, out the right side of the double doors ringing the door bell in reverse, setting foot on the wooden sidewalk that was a first step towards Shakertown and home.

In the summer of 1842, the Ministry at Shakertown declared an end to all public attendance of non-Believers at Shaker meetings and dances. The week before, on a weekday and around midnight, six highwaymen had broken into the Shakertown Post Office and robbed it--of a grand total of twelve dollars and change. They were discovered and the town bell was rung and settlement members gathered. Shots were fired from the ranks of the Believers--to scare off the bandits, who were on horseback. However, the robbers fired back--with the intent to kill. There was much gunplay, and as they retreated, they fired shots into the West Family Dwelling. The shots went through the front door and broke two of the banisters at the head of the stairs. The banister splinters from those shots hit Sister Paquette. One rifle-ball passed through the Water House and another was fired into the Yellow Shop. The next morning a meeting was called, from which the "Declaration of 1842" was drawn up that closed Shaker Meeting to the public.

While the Post Office robbery had certainly galvanized the populace of Shakertown against outsiders, it also gave The Watcher and his Ministry members an added excuse to tighten the reins on the extremes that had been occurring within the Society and the Pleasant Grove property boundaries. And so, from that day hence, the relationship between the Believers of Shakertown and the non-believers of Herodsville was forever altered. Dealings between the two camps would be limited to matters of business--of buying, selling, trading and tasks of manual labor beneficial to both, and occasional pleasantries shared around such interaction. No longer would there be any interplay between the two communities concerning spiritual matters. No longer would Shaker Sunday Service be used as a form of entertainment for the locals, nor would it be a stage for the acting out of supernatural utterings by the members of the Society. Rather, subtlety and spiritual sobriety would be the rule. This would have widespread ramifications amongst Shakertown Believers as well as upon neighboring Shaker villages right on up the line--all the way from South Union, Kentucky to Sabbath Lake, Maine. With this action, and with a few of the more ardent spiritualists immediately leaving Shakertown, either for other Shaker settlements or to return to the World, the Elders of Shakertown had set into motion what would, very soon, become the denouement and the eventual end of the Era of Manifestation.

Meanwhile, the Ministry at Shakertown went about the business of instilling the new regulations amongst its constituency. Fearing a whiplash effect and possible reprisals, especially from the young and a growing cohesive group of instruments and their avid followers, announcements and signs were posted at the borders and within the village. These signs, saying "Closed to all but the chosen people of Zion. Any persons coming with unclean hands and defiled hearts to make sport of the work of God will meet with sore affliction and distress," acted as spiritual roadsigns for one and all. In addition, a large, more formal sign was placed at the roadway entrance to the village which read "Enter not within these gates, for this is my Holy Sanctuary saith the Lord. But pass ye by, and disturb not the quiet, upon my Holy Sabbath." Hence in a single stroke in writing and in full public view, the residents of Herodsville were banned from Sunday Service. With this proclamation, Sunday afternoon outings to Shakertown by local townsfolk became a thing of the past.

While the Ministry felt its decision to close the meetings to the public was a prudent one, it did conflict with the idea that meetings open to the public were an important way of attracting new members. In light of the uncompromising statutes pertaining to celibacy and in order not to destroy the community with this new regulation, the Ministry created a proviso: "those who genuinely seek information about the religious faith and principles of the Believers will be welcomed at the village and will be duly attended."

Even with the institution of the "Birthday Regulations" at Shakertown, the existence and practice of spiritism continued, if in new and somewhat altered forms. Perhaps the most striking example of this was when Ranks began to receive spirit communications. No one was more surprised at this twist of fate than Ranks, himself, who was still in a state of self-doubt concerning his role as an Elder. For him to be "entertaining" a heretofore unknown spirit with the name of Tarjumanu-l-Asrar Khwaja, was perplexing to say the least. These messages from beyond were coming to him in the form of couplets. In his first visitation experience, Ranks had received the seemingly personal message that instructed him to:

Drink wine of the love for God. For neither by acquisition nor by choice is this being a lover of God;
This gift of his is given from the heritage of creation.

With this and subsequent visitations, Brother Wilford, The Watcher, became one with the ranks of those he was watching. Became one of the instruments whose actions he had voted to curtail. He had quite literally leapt into the fire.

As Wilford Ranks was having spirit visitations and indecipherable dreams in his room upstairs in the Meetinghouse, in the parsonage attic in Herodsville, Asher was having dramatic dreams of his own. With his dreams crowding his mind and as he tried to make sense of it in the days that followed, in nearby Shakertown, Asher's worst nightmares were coming to pass. His trip to the Shaker Services at the Meeting Hall that Sunday was shortened by his encounter with the new signs along the village road, and, then, with an elder stationed outside the hall waving all non-Society members away. The long, slow ride home gave Asher plenty of time to reflect upon the gravity of this new situation and its implications. With the wave of a Shakerman's hand, he had been cut off from his easy access to Kitt. His latest ploy to get to her at that week's Sunday Meeting derailed by subtle sabotage.

Now put in an adversarial position as an "unbeliever," Asher found his thoughts on the way home that afternoon drifted from one extreme to another. From horizon to horizon. From depression to depravity. He had been in the habit, now, for months, of at least getting a look at Kitt during the service and dances of the Sunday meetings. The gratification he had gotten from this, over time, had become habitual. Almost a craving. His week had been spent in anticipation, waiting for those brief moments on Sunday when she would pass him in the line of the dance. In recent weeks, those looks from her had come complete with smiles or with a certain coy message in her eyes. Now, being deprived of a glimpse of her face and form had split something inside him. His naturally poetic and romantic way of seeing the world had been altered, and all his poetry turned into politics. Sitting there on the buckboard bench behind the two large Morgan horses and with reins in hand, Asher felt an end to something. A dying. And it stayed with him all the way home.

Days went by and Sister Mary had come, again, to the General Store in Herodsville to discuss with Asher and Caden the visit by Brother Wilford. She told the two boys of the general situation in the Shaker settlement so they would have a proper picture of what was going on, and why. Finally, Sister Mary revealed to Asher that she had brought word from Kitt in the form of a simple message and a written letter. She handed Asher the folded letter which he took eagerly from her hands and wandered over to his favorite spot near the large windows in the front of the store where there was more light. He read the letter while Caden and Sister Mary talked and did their usual business of buying and selling.

Dearest Asher,

I write this to you with heavy heart. Here in Shakertown much has gone on since last we spoke to one another or have looked into each other's eyes. In some ways things have gone upside down in the past few weeks. There has been a major incident, here, of which I'm sure you've heard. A robbery of our Post Office in which there was shooting from both sides-- the robbers and two of our brethren. Almost immediately after that the Ministry handed down a resolution to all the members of the village--to end all visitation from people from town at Sunday Meeting. I know you know of this, too, as I caught sight of you driving up to the Meeting Hall last Sunday with your horses and wagon. (What lovely horses you have!) And I saw Brother Spires speak with you, telling you to move on. I could tell that's what he was saying to you, because of his hand gestures. He always says more with his hands than he ever does with his mouth. He really should have been a dancer, he is so expressive with his body.

What I am wanting to write to you about today is to share with you my sorrow over the present conditions here in the village that will only make our continued communication all the more difficult, if not impossible. It is because of this and because of my lack of clarity as to what to do about it, that I am writing to you to suggest that we meet face-to-face, if only for the last time, to try and come to some kind of mutual resolve or, in the worst case scenario, an amicable farewell.

I have arranged it with Sister Mary and Sister Eden to cover for me in such a way that I will be free during the services at the Meeting Hall on Sunday, and after--when the Society will be going to our annual end-of-summer picnic over at the river. We can meet in the graveyard on the west side of the village, a quarter of a mile from the nearest building and easy access for you coming from town so that you won't have to drive through or sneak into the village, itself. I will be there at 2:00, waiting.

I know that plans like these are not foolproof and anything can happen. But I feel I owe you this time together after all we have been through these past months. And, besides, in all honesty, I want to see you again, even if it is for the last time.

I will send this letter with Sister Mary, who will be going into town tomorrow to do the shopping. Please tell her if

you can meet me this Sunday, or if you cannot--so I will know. If you don't want to come, I will understand, although I will be disappointed. Please believe me when I say that I am sorry for all that is happening and the effect that it is having on our friendship. I look forward to seeing you and talking about all this with you in a few days. Until then, consider deeply what is in your heart and bring your resolve and your consolations with you, as we will need them to decide what it is we are going to do.
Til then,   with affection,

Kitt

Scene II.

That Sunday, from his window in the wall, Wilford Ranks scanned the floor of the Meeting Hall during the speaking part of the service. The services had been called for an earlier time on this day, as this was the date when the annual Summer Picnic was held over in the far fields along the Kentucky River. As he scanned the floor below, Ranks noticed that Kitt was not in her usual place on the women's benches. He thought it odd, as Sister Daniella had not mentioned to him that Kitt was ill, or had other commitments. He scanned the women's side of the room again--which was much easier, now, since the several hundred visitors from town were not there and filling up the fasteners and standing around the walls. Still he didn't see Kitt amongst the women. Looking directly across to the other side of the room and the women's ministry window, he could see Sister Daniella's finely-chiseled face, as she diligently did her duty of watching the men's side of the room, which was more visible from the westerly window's perspective.

The Shaker dances had ended early inside the Meeting Hall and Believers had gathered in the wagons and on foot moving east in unison down the road toward the banks of the Kentucky River. In the graveyard just outside the west end of Pleasant Grove proper, Kitt watched as Asher's horses and wagon moved at a fast trot up the dirt road in her direction, leaving a heavy trail of dust in their wake. As Asher and the wagon approached the graveyard, Kitt felt an excitement well up inside her, and at the same time: trepidation. In her mind she tried to weigh one feeling against the other--to determine which feeling was the stronger of the two. In the end, she couldn't choose the better emotion. Her body was conflicted. But she knew this already, which is why she had written her last letter to Asher and conceived of the "graveyard plan." As her heart beat almost out of her chest and her stomach sank, she watched Asher drive his wagon to the far end of the graveyard behind a small grove of trees, climb down from the rig, tie off the reins to a low tree branch, turn and enter the graveyard through the small west gate.

What Asher was feeling as he entered into the cemetery, was raw nerves. He was a bundle of them. All the rehearsing of the speech he had prepared for Kitt was leaking out of his boots like a small hole in an earthen dam. All his confidence, manliness and mettle had left him the moment he walked through the graveyard gate and had seen Kitt standing in the shade of some large boxwood bushes and a weeping willow tree along the north edge of palings that make up the picket fence.

Standing there in the sun's shadow at a distance and in amongst the rough stone markers that passed for gravestones, she looked like a vision from another world, another time. Asher was taken aback, as Kitt's picturesque presence drew a perfect picture in his mind. Asher filed away this image somewhere in the unused recesses of his brain, like a keepsake one would never want to part with, but would want to keep for viewing on another day. As he approached the cluster of gravestones that surrounded Kitt, he could see her face--spotlighted and framed by a beam of sunlight shining through the willow tree. And somewhere, far in the distance, he could hear the faint ringing of bells. In that moment it was as if he was seeing her for the first time--with the sun accentuating the beauty of her natural features. And under the cloth Shaker cap, he noticed that she has let fall her hair.

"Asher, you've come. Just as you said you would. It's so good to see you again. You look good. But, then, you always do. It's just that it's been a while and we forget when separation plays its pawky games with our minds. Do you recognize me?"

"I admit," Asher stumbled, "that these past weeks your image has taken on the heavenly nature of a goddess or even a nymph-of-the-woods in my mind's eye. But, as I look at you standing there, your person has exceeded even my most generous memories. You look as though you are of the same family as the willow tree that shades you, like it, too, was part of your summer wardrobe. You belong here, and in this moment it does my heart good to see you. I have long waited for this day."

"I think we are safe here--for a time. The Sunday services have ended. They have been shortened today, with little dancing, I am told, in order that the Society can make their way in ample time across the river and to the Family Fields, where our seasonal picnic is being held. All traffic will be headed east and away from our hiding place here in this far western part of the property. Everyone will be at the picnic, so we will have a place in time to talk. I pray that this is how our grave drama will play out."

"'Grave'? Why grave? While we do stand on them, they do not have to affect our mood. These dead pilgrims have nothing, now, to say. So, let's not let them ruin our play."

"Well put, my happy bard. We will put all our *grave* thoughts away. For this time and place is ours and above ground we can do anything we please. So let it be a pleasant visit and one that we won't remember poorly. So, tell me, Asher Pope, how have you been?"

"To be honest, I have missed seeing you. My moods, I must admit, have been heavy. When it's hot and humid, I'm jealous of the sun. If it hails or rains, I'm jealous of the lakes and rivers. Or the oceans from where rain came. Like a star, my heart wants to implode. I just want to see you. And I think of you with others and in other places--other than where I am--and I am jealous of all and everyone that is near you."

"Asher, you with your eloquent speech. How can I reply to such a soliloquy? But let me try and explain myself. Although my ramble won't be as poetic as yours, I hope that I can explain things to you in such a way that you will understand.

"In our Shaker society, we are as a whole. As a single unit. In that sense we are all parts of each other. As one functions, so does all of the society go. If one inspires, all are inspired. If one falls, all are fallen. This idea goes back to the beginning of our 'creation story' and the teachings of Mother Ann and the early Believers. There is an old Shaker psalm that says, 'Tis not one without the other,/That will keep the union strong;/O, do learn to go together!/Then you will be join'd in one.' And along with this sense of union, there is the doctrine of celibacy, as you know. Mother Ann was very emphatic about this practice. Only the other night when she visited me in a Quick Service in the East Family House, one of our new scribes wrote down her words on this subject. She said, 'God will bring down the haughtiness of man, and stain the pride of all flesh. Brother, if you have a sweetheart, let that woman alone. God will break into pieces the man and the maid. The marriage of the flesh is a covenant with death, and an agreement with hell. If you want to marry, you may marry the Lord Jesus Christ. He is my husband, and in him I trust.'

"So, you see, Asher, there is no simple solution to our situation. We live in different worlds."

"I understand what you say, but hear me out, so you can see the world--which your people seem to think is such a horror--through my eyes. I am not blind. And Jesus is not the only one with eyes. I can see for myself. It is because of everyone else's blindness that you and I can't see. What I have come to know is that desire is the purest form of prayer. And my prayers are always full of torrents and tears. In this 'heaven' of sadness, God doesn't care if I cry. All he wants is union with you and me. This is not heresy. This is only the voice of the wind wanting an audience for what it has to say.

"Even though there are NO TRESPASSING signs everywhere to keep me away from you, happiness never tasted this good. I have been trying to mend our problems in my sleep. And nothing that my father or your Mother Ann can say will disengage my love for you. Everyone knows, deep down, that nothing is really far from flesh. The Earth is a sacred garden covered in holy vines. So let's make great wines!"

"Oh, Asher, you are such a romantic. And in many ways I share your passions. Yet I am bound to this family at Pleasant Grove, as you are to your kin in Herodsville. My own parents are no longer living in this world and the Shaker Family has taken me in, given me shelter, food, and love. I can't just turn my back on them, ungratefully, and run out into the world with you. If I were to do such a thing, just think how it would likely end. I am thinking as I speak--of the words to one of the songs we sing at meeting. It goes:

> *Dost ever thou think O Darling*
> *Fair loved one of first we*
> *Stood linked in each other's*
> *Embrace.*
> *Dost think as thou goest on the*
> *Way of that time when my heart*
> *Was so full of love over-flowing*
> *That I spoke not but kissed thee*
> *And sent thee away*

This idea of my living in your world would inspire too much guilt. I would be torn and in that sense would never be yours. Can you not see this? In the end I would have to send you away, or you, me."

"We can't live our lives to please others. And who cares what is right or wrong? We can't change their minds. Tomorrow may greet us with ill health and a farewell to beautiful bodies and my terrible verse! And we'll be out of time, out of luck. If I die, the roses you put on my grave will only blow away. No memorial service will bring me back. Nor will pretty pictures painted by the blind. So let's grab this birdsong's hour of bliss, and be free. Let's celebrate this end to innocence. Soon I will be an old man. An old man, like my father, alone out on the water fishing for the moon. Kitt, this is our moment to rise. It is not a fall from grace. And this really isn't about sex, but the whirling of suns that have been locked up in a closet of empty dreams. I'm bored to death with the idea of 'doing good.' You and I are a fire in a cold universe."

"Asher, I can see you are resolved to make me over to a woman of the World. I fear I am too long gone from there to make that remedy work. It would be easier for you to become Shaker than for me to live with thee. Think on it. Let me make a list. Do you not also believe in the lean use of words? Do you not also believe in the heavenly nature of good work and praising thyself by good work done? Do you not believe in sincerity of the soul? Do you not relish contentment? Do you not abhor pride? Do you not love meekness? Do you not honor simplicity and education? Do you not enjoy the bounty of fresh good foods? Do you not enjoy the gracious company of others?"

"And what of love? Where does love fit into this perfect picture of us you have painted? When, again, will I ever see your hair? Your hair! I will never forget. That day. The accidental gesture. Something that simple has defined for me, forever, what love is. And what it wasn't before that moment. Something simple, like the way you talk about your Shaker beliefs. Yet, something as complex as the absence of wind in the trees. You are the girl who shakes her hair in my dreams. I think of this, now, as I stand here looking at you. I see the girl in my dreams. It is you. A girl with long brown hair. And she shakes it from side to side...."

"Oh, Asher, so lovely. How could a woman ever say 'no' to you? You could have any woman you wanted. Why me? Why impossible me?"

So, here they were, Kitt and Asher standing amidst headstones in a graveyard speaking from the heart. Each, holding their own brand of dialectic communion, conversing on everything from celibacy to the sublime. Kitt addressing Asher in Shakerese, Asher, her, in high-strung verse. This little eternity, this time-bent hour, had become the time and place for Kitt to convey to Asher the benefits of Shaker life and for Asher to try to convince Kitt--this cloistered "bride of God"--to fall in love with a mortal man. As Kitt scrutinized Asher's poetic paganism, he questioned her Shaker resolve. And so the conversation went. Back and forth. She trying to make a Shaker out of him, he trying to make an apostate out of her. She from a position of exegesis, he from eros.

Although Asher, in that moment, could see her hair, there was something about the fact that everything but her hands and eyes were hidden that made the mystery of her concealed body all that much more alluring, seductive. From those beautifully blinding eyes surrounded by flawless facial skin and a pair of snow-white dancing hands across from him came an apparition of a body no man alive could resist. It was as if her Shaker dress were skin-tight and every perfect eighteen-year-old curve and line were etched in a sensuous, expanding light only the eyes of second-sight could see. And Asher's penetrating eyes saw them like poetry pacing desert dunes looking for that one-and-only perfect rhyme. Yes, there was something in his heart that wanted to devour her. Sexually and spiritually possess her as part of himself. Looking into Kitt's eyes was, for Asher, like drinking good wine. Everything changed. Everything became intoxicating. Fragrant. Enticingly forbidding. Everything moved. Became exquisite. Became intimate.

"Where does the heart of a captivatingly beautiful young Shaker girl go when it wants to go out and play--to hide and seek, to gather stones, to break the habit of sex as *le petit mort* of prayer?" Asher asked himself as he stood there facing her in the cemetery, surrounded by tablets like the one brought down from a mountain on the other side of the world thousands of years ago with a list of rules that men and women ever since had been trying to live their lives by, never quite measuring up. Everything about Kitt that was being kept from him, including that which he couldn't see, lit up in his mind's eye in a kind of waking dream. She was everywhere. In him. Around and under him. And even though he could not penetrate the cloth-contoured outline of her body or die in her lap, it was all there in her eyes that filled, with welcome taboo, his hopeful heart.

While Asher and Kitt engaged in their graveyard encounter and their see-saw battle of the souls, Sunday Meeting had long since ended and the Pleasant Grove Family had, en masse, made its way down into the pasturelands on the eastern end of the village boundaries for the Summer Picnic. Like Kitt, but for his own reasons, Brother Wilford Ranks had decided not to join the other members of the settlement for this annual outing that included good food and some fun and games. Rather, he was holed up in his Ministry apartment above the Meeting Hall. Following the service, he had felt the pangs of a vision coming on, so he had begged off from attending the Summer Picnic and had retreated quickly to the solitude and quiet of the Middle Room upstairs, which had a desk and writing instruments for the use of both the women and the men.

Ranks didn't have to wait long before he was being "visited" by the spirit of Khwaja. And it wasn't long after that that he was taking dictation as it flowed through him like fresh water from a mountain spring.

Do you know what fame and fortune is? It's looking into the Beloved's eyes.

It's preferring a beggar's life to that of being king.

Anyone can kill himself and be lost from this life,
But try giving up friendships or life with one you love!

With my heart closed like a bud, I'll go into the rose garden that is

Full of thorns--to be stripped of my conceit and cocky ways.

O breeze, tell all your secrets to the rose.
Nightingale, sing again the melody of love's sweet song.

Go ahead and kiss the Beloved on the lips.
To pass up this chance is like putting a lock on an open door.

This house has two doors and a dozen windows;
You may never have this chance again.

O Beloved, don't forget to remember the dervish Khwaja;
And send me a message if You are ever coming by this way.

As Brother Wilford finished his transmission, he put the pencil aside and took a deep breath. This short exchange between himself and the spirit had uplifted him but at the same time he felt almost exhausted. Even so, he still had enough stamina and curiosity to go back and read what he had just written. Certain lines jumped out at him. He found that he identified with the image of the rose garden and one's heart being closed like a bud. *Go ahead and kiss the Beloved on the lips./To pass up this chance is like putting a lock on an open door,* Khwaja said. This couplet shocked him. Did he, or He, write this? "Heretically sensual," he thought to himself. *This house has two doors* reminded him of the very building in which he sat--an eastern door for the women to enter and a western door for the men to enter into the Meeting House or the Ministry apartments. And then, the last line: *And send me a message if You are ever coming by this way.* He thought, immediately of his recent visit to Herodsville and the whole business of these supposed letters flowing freely between the Settlement and the World. The voice in the message seemed to be saying that it was alright to express your love in a physical way and not to squander your chances at such an experience. *You may never have this chance again,* the message said. *To pass up this chance is like putting a lock on an open door.* In Shakertown, there were no locks. Not one lock on any door. But Khwaja was not talking here about physical locks, he was talking about psychological locks, spiritual locks, even sexual locks.

As Brother Wilford sat over his written transcription trying to decipher its meaning, he wondered to himself, *How much of this am I supposed to believe? We are taught to trust the spirits and their messages. Some of this message is disturbing. So, what if Khwaja visits me, again, and tells me that sex is ok, and that to avoid sex is 'like putting a lock on an open door?' Do I dare to share this sort of thing with anyone? Or am I duty-bound to share it with the whole community? Under the new regulations, any transmission by an instrument is supposed to be recorded by a scribe. Should I give this message to the scribe? Reading this message, there are those who might read this as a kind of Shaker heresy. It's certainly out of the ordinary, to say the least.*

With these thoughts, the Shaker Elder picked up the sheet of paper upon which he had written the message dictated by the Sufi spirit and took it into the reclining room which he shared with his male counterpart in the Ministry and placed it into a small paper file that he kept between the mattress straps underneath his bed. *For now,* he thought to himself, *I'll set these writings aside until I have enough to get some perspective on the transmissions and the transmitter. I don't want to be about the business of disseminating the words of an evil spirit. And evil spirits, like evil people, can be very tricky with their words and their ways. For now, all this will remain private.*

But Ranks couldn't get the image of "the message" in the transmission out of his mind. *And send me a message if you are ever coming by this way,* it had said. His mind immediately went back to the subject of Kitt, Asher, Caden and the Herodsville General Store and the rumors of "messages" (letters) coming from and going into town. In that moment, he knew what he had seen that Sunday on the Meeting Hall floor. That "flash of light" being passed from the men's line to the women's side of the floor. He had seen "a message" being passed from one of the men to one of the women. From Asher Pope to Sister Kitt? *Yes, I think that must have been it,"* he thinks to himself. *"I'm sure of it. What else could it have been?*

But with this new certainty about the incident on the Meeting Hall floor, came, just as quickly, the doubt created by that afternoon's transmission from Khwaja--predicated by the lines *Anyone can kill himself and be lost from this life/By giving up friendships and the one you love./Nightingale, sing again the melody of love's sweet song.* Wilford Ranks had lived his life for almost forty years by denying himself any kind of physical love. How many "open doors" had he put a lock on? Had he effectively "killed himself" by denying himself the experience of love? *Nightingale, sing again the melody of love's sweet song.* The line kept echoing in his head as he made his way down the western stairway of the Meeting Hall on his way to the Centre Family Dwelling—where he would greet the society members as they returned from the picnic and where he hoped to glean a little nourishment left over from the feast.

With the summer moving quickly into the fall harvest season in the hills of central Kentucky, and with the *denouement* of the Era of Manifestation taking its toll on the state's two major Shaker communities at Pleasant Grove and South Union, conflicts and uncertainties combined to create new regimens coming from both the leading instruments of the spirit manifesters and, on the other side, The Ministry, who had now found themselves in the business of resurrecting the status quo from earlier times. Regulations concerning diet, dress and daily routines poured forth from the instruments, making greater demands on the Believers. In some cases, these new regulations were ignored, and in some cases adopted by various enclaves within the Pleasant Grove community causing splinters within the society. As The Ministry attempted to crack down on the indulgences of the instruments and their ardent followers, a growing resentment from the youth against their elder authority figures had been unleashed. Their major complaint being the many orders coming down from The Ministry restricting their freedom. Some of the orders recorded at that time included: cologne water, or any kind of perfumery was to be avoided before attending meetings; the seats of the brothers and sisters in the Meeting House were to be no closer than five feet; all whispering or winking was prohibited; Sisters must not mend, nor set buttons on brethren's clothes while they have them on; restrictions on relationships with pets, including superfluously trimmed or ornamented animals.

This was during a time when the stereotyped image of the non-worldly people held in the minds of a predominance of The World's People would have been shattered had they known that Shaker life was not always as strict and austere as its principals suggested. Believers, in their efforts to eradicate natural affections in children, put on candy-making parties. Culinary favors were granted by kitchen sisters. Tolerance was practiced in the face of bad behavior. Elders took favorites and awarded them favors over other children. All this, in the name of the subjugation of carnal desire. In truth, the social order and much of the actual day-to-day practices of the members of the Shakertown community looked very much like that of the children of farmers in the rural countryside and in the nearby town of Herodsville. These special treatments combined with harsher regulations and restrictions that included the prohibition of secular reading, denying the right of private judgment and upholding the virtues of passive obedience, became exaggerated when children left their own order--the girls at age fourteen and the boys at sixteen--to take their places as responsible members of the Society. It was at this stage that resentment for authority was rising to the surface in Shakertown and becoming tactile. It was at this untimely and inconvenient moment that a controversy broke out amongst the youth over the banning of coffee, tea and pork--three staples of the Shaker diet and three food items dear to the heart of the Shaker youth--only adding fuel to the already burning political fire.

"Confusion of infidels," "fraud and chicanery," "mediums from the world visiting the villages," were all entries recorded in the Ministry journals during the summer and following fall of this most confused and controversial year. With all the "Rules and Orders" handed down in that season from the mother communities "up North," in a not so subtle way the insurgent instruments of spiritual manifestation, with their "holy laws" and "divine revelations," were claiming for themselves a spiritual superiority over earlier generations and guidelines with their rebellions. The "rappings" and "knockings" coming from the spirit world were a deafening roar in the ears of the Ministries in many of the Shaker villages, and Pleasant Grove was no exception.

Word had come from New Lebanon, from Brother Issac Youngs that summer, that the enclosure there had been vandalized: stone altars had been desecrated and broken down. At the same time the highly popular mountain feasts were discontinued, along with other social gatherings and entertainments, with the feast-grounds being returned to its natural wild state--all without much explanation from the offices of the Ministry. Ironically, it was at this exact time that one of

Shakertown's most earth-shattering events occurred. Quite literally, the Pleasant Grove property was shaken by a force even greater than its members' abilities to "shake and quake" in their services and rituals: an earthquake.

Even with all this turmoil and the rumblings in the earth, the seasons and the daily routines of work in Shakertown went on, if sometimes altered, in an attempt to harvest crops, to properly tend livestock and to manage the various cottage crafts industries. Flax was carded, soap was made, sheep were sheared, wool was spun, corn was picked, pickles were made, apples were crushed and cider was boiled, and hogs were butchered.

During these tempestuous times, one of the few aspects of Shaker society that truly flourished was the seed industry. As the first major Shaker industry, the raising and selling of garden seeds had begun in one of the northern communities in 1794 and by 1822 had taken root in Shakertown, where the business flourished, giving Shaker gardens the reputation of being "the most skillfully cultivated in the country." The famed naturalist Raffinesque was even known to have said that "The gardens of the modern Essenes, the Shakers, have the best medical gardens in the United States." While other American seed companies were selling and distributing vegetable and flower seeds in bulk--in cloth sacks--the Shakers were the first to come up with the idea of selling seeds in small, usable and affordable quantities in paper envelopes. This invention made the distribution and transportation of seeds easier and more widespread and serviced a whole population of non-farmers growing household gardens.

With such a large and lucrative industry being carried out in Shakertown, the East Family Brethren's Shop became "Operation Central" for the seed business, with the Brethren of the East Family effectively running the business. The Dry House was also used extensively in the drying and preparation of seeds, as was a section of the Scale House. In the late summer of 1842, as luck would have it, Kitt had worked long hours in the Dry House, often with the assistance of Eden and Sister Mary. A compatible, if not complicit trio. Many long afternoons were spent in the Dry House with the three women chatting, laughing and teasing, and plotting their imagined outings into the nearby town. In fact, the sorting of seeds and the rhythms of this often monotonous labor was the background music, the accompaniment, for their best-laid plans. Plans that had been thwarted, in recent days, by the Ministry's new regulations and by the resulting decrease in interaction with The World's People. But even with the new regulations and the new obstacles to "the adventures of Kitt and Asher," the late-day banter and high-pitched laughter flowed from the windows of the Dry House out into the fields and orchards, beyond.

While the production and packaging of seeds was certainly one of the most consistent sources of income for Shakertown, it wasn't the only enterprise that brought in an annual revenue. The unlikely brewing and marketing of "Shakers' Aromatic Elixir of Malt" was also a popular product marketed to the World's People. In fact about $2,500 a year was made on the sales of Shakertown malt elixirs where on the bottle labels one could read: "This elegant elixir may be used in all cases where the Extract is indicated and it will prove far superior for it is Carminative Nutrient and tonic. It may be administered in Consumption, Debility, the Loss of Flesh and Strength, Variable Appetite, Dispepsia, Headache, Flatulence, Diarrhea & etc. This preparation of malt is grateful to the most delicate stomach, and can be prescribed in many cases where the common extract of malt cannot be taken. It is also a good vehicle for the administration of Genuine Iron, Cod Liver Oil & etc. Manufactured exclusively by the Shakers at Pleasant Grove, Mercer Co. Ky. Under the supervision of R. B. Rupe, M.D. Pharmacist Rx. Aromatic Elixir seven parts; Pure Extract of Malt (our own make) eight parts. Dose for adults one tablespoonful three times a day after meals." Sold at six bottles for five dollars, Shaker Malt was a central Kentucky favorite, if not because of its price, then for its "punch." Even Believers were known to "nip" from the bottles of malt upon occasion, taking advantage of the old adage that "an ounce of prevention is worth a pound of cure."

While the Believers in Shakertown were sipping their "ounce of prevention" behind closed doors, Asher and Caleb were sampling a few drams of their own on the back porch of Caleb's family farmhouse just outside of town. It had been a tough day in the fields cutting and gathering hay that would eventually make its way into the haymows of the family barn. They had both soaked their "outsides" with water from the hand pump in the yard and were in the process of "wetting down" their insides as they sat on the back steps under the porch roof and out of the late afternoon sun.

"Damn, glad to be finished with that," Caden sighed loudly as he drew another sip from the bottle of Shakers' Aromatic Elixir of Malt. "You know, this stuff isn't half bad. A guy could get used to it. Guess it will do in a pinch. We've about emptied what was left in this bottle. So, if anyone asks, I'll just say that you got an upset stomach from eating green apples over in the orchard and needed a tonic."

"What we really need is some of that good homebrew that my dad secretly makes," Asher replied. "Chilled down, that would really hit the spot. This stuff is ok as a relaxing tonic and in small doses, but it's not meant to quench a man's thirst."

"You've drunk some of your old man's beer? I thought that was the best-kept secret in Mercer County and that he even kept that stuff hidden from the family."

"It may be a well-kept secret, but I know where he hides it, and I was bad to sneak down in the root cellar when I was in school and "test" the stuff. Can't say that I ever got hooked on it, but once in a while it was good when I had the blues over some girlfriend or for poetic inspiration, if you know what I mean."

"About the strongest drink around this house is this bottle of Shaker Malt and it's not exactly what you'd call "a good drink." You never told me about your dad's secret stash when we were back in school. Those evenings when our parents were all at Wednesday night church service and we'd go over to take the Parker girls for a ride in our wagon--now, that would have been the perfect time to have had some of your dad's hootch!"

The two boys both smiled at each other and laughed.

"Yeah, I thought of that, once or twice, but couldn't do it on account of if the word had gotten out that my dad was brewing beer in the basement of the manse, it would have cost him his reputation, if not his job. So, I just kept it to myself and took a nip ever now and again. But, I agree, it might have made a difference as to how our relationships with those Parker girls ended up. And, if so, it would have saved me all those nights with the bad blues. You know those Parker girls were two good-lookin' girls. Whatever happened to them, anyway? I haven't heard hide nor hair of them in over a year."

"Last I heard they were living over in Tennessee. Near Knoxville, I think. Had something to do with the logging business over in eastern Tennessee near the North Carolina line, and their daddy moving down there to make more money. That's the story I heard, anyway. But you know, there were also rumors going around that Cindy had gotten herself in the family way and that that was the reason they decided to move--since she wasn't married or anything."

"Preggers? I never heard that story. Who was she supposed to have gotten pregnant by? It wasn't me, I can tell you that. And it wasn't for any lack of trying on my part."

"Rumor was that it was Charlie Freed or Donnie Meyers. You know how tight those guys were and they were going out with both the

Parker girls right before they left for Tennessee."

Caden took another large drink from the Malt bottle and handed it to Asher who did the same.

"That makes sense, then. Ol' Freed was a mean som'bitch. I'll never forget when he cold-cocked Johnny Luxton. Knocked him plum out--just for going out with one of his old girlfriends. They had to take him to ole doc MacIlwaine to check for a concussion. You remember that? Ole Johnny was trying to put the make on Debbie Humphries, Charlie's long-time flame, and ol' Charlie drove in his old man's wagon all the way out the main road to the Ferry Landing out near Shakertown, where he waited for Johnny and Debbie to come back across the river from some place they'd gone over near High Bridge. When the ferry came back across from the other side of the river, on the last trip, ole Freed jumped right onto the ferry platform before Luxton's wagon even came off, and jumped ole Johnny right there on the ferry before he ever got a chance to climb back in the wagon, and cold-cocked him upside the head--right there in front of Debbie Humphries, the ferryman, God and the Holy Ghost. They say that ole Johnny never came to til he was half-way home. They say that it was the Shaker ferryman had to drive Debbie and Johnny home."

"Well, now that you've brought up Kitt and the Shakers... There was something else that I wanted to talk to you about. I'd almost forgot. This Shaker Malt must be getting to me. Must be better than I thought."

Both Caden and Asher laughed at Asher's last statement about the malt drink, and they both took another swig from the oddly-shaped bottle with raised writing on one side.

As Caden took a long draw from the bottle, he noticed the writing on the side and started to read the raised print. "Says here on this bottle that you should drink this stuff three times a day. Maybe we should get some more of this stuff, since it's so good for you. I bet we could even get it for cheap from Kitt or Eden. Eden could bring it from Shakertown on Tuesdays when she comes to the store. It says, too, that this stuff is good for Loss of Flesh. Guess ol' Luxton could have used a little of this malt elixir after ol' Freed took some skin out the side of his head."

"'Nough of all this strolling down memory lane. I need to talk to you about Kitt. Some serious talk, if you think you can handle it."

"Sure. I can handle it. But I'm almost afraid to ask. What is it you got on your mind?"

Asher almost looked surprised with Caden's easy acquiescence, and, in fact, choked on the dram of malt drink he was in the process of downing. Now, he was on the spot. A part of him wished he had never mentioned the business of Kitt and Shakertown, as it would have been much easier for him to have avoided the subject altogether. He wiped his mouth with the back of his sleeve to soak up the malt that was leaking from his lips and began to speak.

"I don't have to tell you that things are not looking good for yours truly concerning all-things-Shaker and our friend Sister Kitt. With the Sunday Meetings closed off to outsiders, not to mention the unexpected visit The Watcher made to the store to drum the fear of God into us, I've been thinking long and hard about what I'm going to do. The way I see it, I've got two choices: to give up the idea of ever seeing Kitt again, or to do something radical to be able to see her, be with her. Somehow, I just can't seem to accept the idea of not seeing her again. We were just starting to get close and to open up to each other. So, it doesn't seem right to have all that momentum that we've gained just go to waste. Besides, she's the finest girl I've ever met, and girls like her don't come a dime a dozen here in Herodsville, if you know what I mean. I mean, what are my options if I give up on Kitt? To settle for some "Cindy Parker" here in Mercer County and make babies? I don't think so.

"So, I've been thinking, and here's what I've come up with," Asher proclaimed as he took the bottle of malt elixir out of Caden's hands and took a stout swig before handing it back to him and continued with his oration. "Since Kitt has told me in no uncertain terms that she won't leave Shakertown and her life there to come and be with me here in Herodsville or anywhere else, for that matter, I figure it's up to me to make some kind of move. I've thought long and hard at what kind of "move" that just might be. Kidnapping is out of the question, as romantic and as appealing as that may be as a simple solution. Winning her over with some sort of Shakespearian sonnet of my own making is definitely a long-shot, even if I could pull it off, which I can't. Trying to make her jealous by creating some *faux ruse* of my being in love with another girl isn't going to work, either. So, the way I see it, if you can't beat 'em, you gotta join 'em."

"What do you mean: 'join 'em?'" Caden replied, almost inaudibly with the Shaker Malt bottle pressed up against his lips.

"I mean just what I said. I mean 'join 'em', man. Join up with the Shakers. Become a Shaker. Move to Shakertown."

"You gotta be joking. That's the bottle speaking. Not you. You don't mean it. I mean, you wouldn't do something like that. Would you?" Caden responded in inebriated amazement.

"I'm serious. What choice do I have? I came to this realization way before we started nipping on this bottle of Shaker Malt, here, today. I've been studying this whole thing night and day since ol' Watcherman paid us a visit."

"You're starting to sound just like those folks that live up in the hollers of the mountains around here. 'Studying'--what kind of word is that? I don't think you know what you're saying right now. This elixir is going to your brain," Caden summarized as he held up the bottle as if it were Exhibit A in a federal case down at the Courthouse.

"No, I'm serious. I've thought it over... About this time of year, Kitt says, there are people from Mercer County, and some from farther away, who come to the Shakertown Meetings and join the community. Become Believers. She says that they only stay through the winter, since there's no farm work anywhere at that time of year and nowhere else for them to go—'less they were going to live out in the woods with the animals. So, I figure that I could join the Shaker community as one of those 'winter Shakers'--I think that's what Kitt called them. The Watcher and all his ministers who run the place have seen me at all the Sunday services and dances, and I think I could convince them that I am a good worker and am interested in their beliefs and am willing to live according to their regulations and practices. I've already said as much to The Watcher the other day when he was in the store. Right?"

"Wrong... This whole idea is crazy. What you gonna do up there in Shakertown when you get tired of pretending to be a Shaker? And how do you think you're going to get to play kissy-face with Kitt. You know what they think about sex and how the men and women are always separated from each other all the time. Have you thought about that?"

"Yes, I've thought about that. I don't know. I'll figure something out--find ways to see Kitt alone. It can't be that hard, and I'll be right there on the property, close by, all the time. And I know that if I were willing to 'become a Shaker' just for her, that she'd think a lot more of me for doing so. That would only put me in her good graces, right?"

"Whatever you say, Asher. I can see that you've made up your mind. I only hope that you'll wake up tomorrow morning, after this malt has worn off, and have forgotten about this whole scheme. I mean, this is the craziest thing I've ever heard. With the Sunday meetings closed to folks in town, and with all their new policies, when will I ever see you? Hell, we've known each other our whole lives," Caden sighed, sounding a little sad.

"I know. It's been a hard decision to make--leaving all my friends and family behind. But I'll just be right down the road, and I'm sure things will ease up in Shakertown with all the new rules and stuff, and I'll be able to see you from time to time. It won't be like the old days, but nothing ever is."

"Damn, now you're beginning to sound like one of them philosophers you used to always read. What was that one? Saint August, or Saint September…"

"Saint Augustine," Asher answers laughing.

"Yeah, that old Christian who your father doesn't care for much, as I remember. Said he was too controversial in his day, just as he is today. Maybe you got all these wild ideas about joining the Shakers from reading all those philosophers like St. August."

"Saint Augustine, Caden."

"Whatever you say. You know I was never good with details in school. Could barely memorize my own name. My dad still won't even let me go near the financial books or the credit log at the store. He's afraid I'll mess everything up and he'll end up in poverty or something. Anyway, this whole conversation is givin' me a headache. You got anything to cure a hangover? If you do, I could shore use it about now."

"Yeah, I need to be getting on home. I've still got some figuring to do about how I'm gonna pull this whole thing off."

"You mean 'studying' don't you," Caden interrupted, making fun of Asher's choice of words.

"Yeah, right. Guess that's one for you, my friend. Thanks, I think, for the malt drink. Hope your dad doesn't miss it down at the store when he's 'studying' the inventory. I think that stuff is way over-rated. I'm probably gonna need a hangover pill myself tonight. But it was worth the inconvenience just being able to talk to you about this. I needed to talk to someone, and there really isn't anyone else I could talk to that would understand this or would be willing to keep it secret. You can keep a secret, can't you? If word of this gets out to anyone, especially my old man, I'll be sunk."

"Maybe what you need is a good ass-whupping'. Maybe that would clear your head. I have half a mind to run right to your father and spill the whole thing to him--if that would keep you from carrying out this crazy plot. But I know you'd just find another way to get what you want. I've known you for a long time and know how you are. Once you get your mind set on something, there's no changin' it. So, yes, your secret is safe with me. So, now, get off my porch and get on outta here. I've heard about enough of your insanity for one day."

"I can take a hint. We'll talk more about this soon, as it's not like I'm gonna rush right up to Shakertown and sign my soul away on the dotted line tomorrow or anything."

"I've heard enough. Now get your ass outta here before I change my mind about being a friend of yours, and start blabbing this story all over town."

Asher got up a little too quickly from where he and Caden had been sitting for a good long time, and was a little light-headed as he descended the porch steps and walked out across the dusty yard toward the barn where his Morgan horses and wagon were waiting for him. Caden just sat there on the porch, shaking his head as he watched Asher zig-zag his way on malt-liquored legs to the barn.

Kitt sits on her bed in her room looking out the large window at the night sky. She is thinking about Asher. She is thinking about herself. She is thinking of her and Asher together. She unbuttons the top button on her over-dress, and the question returns: "What am I going to do about Asher?" In something of a state of growing panic, and not thinking clearly and certainly not thinking confidently as she had been only minutes before, she begins creating a long list of excuses--of all the reasons why they could not be together.
He's not a Shaker.
He's not a Believer.
He's not really even a Christian.
He is too independent.
He doesn't like rules.
He likes the girls.
He's a poet.
He's the son of a Baptist preacher.

The list goes on until it becomes almost silly and is little more than word-chatter filling up her brain. The only real solution to their dilemma is if she were to leave Shakertown and move to Herodsville to be near or with him. The idea of her inexperience in interacting with the World's People all these years fills her with fear. Her mental reaction to that imagined scenario is "I wouldn't fit in. I wouldn't be accepted. This would be too hard on Asher, or on us as a young couple. And our children, would they grow up to be Shakers or Baptists?"

Her head is now filled with too many questions and not enough real answers. Irrationally wanting to come to some kind of resolve in that moment of impatience, Kitt becomes desperate. Without thinking, and acting totally on impulse, she makes her way back over to her bed, pushes the bed aside a foot or two and bends down, lifting up a loose board on the floor beneath the bed. From the empty space under the floorboard, she pulls out a pack of letters tied together with some baling string. As if she has suddenly metamorphosed from Kitt into Shakespeare's mad Ophelia, she crosses the large, high-ceilinged room to the far corner where a small Shaker stove sits waiting for winter in a state of dormancy. Quickly, she opens the hinged door of the small little three-legged cast-iron stove and throws the packet of letters into the black metal box. Not bothering to close the door to the stove, she rises up and goes directly over to the large piece of furniture against a nearby wall that doubles as a bookcase and a writing desk. She opens the desktop drawer and reaches in, pulling out a small tin box. She opens the lid of the little tin box and reaches in, taking out a red-tipped match. She puts the lid back on the tin box, puts it back in the desk drawer, pushes the drawer closed and makes her way back over to the stove--which sits there on its three legs looking almost alive, the open door like the mouth of a hungry animal waiting to be fed. Reaching the door of the stove, she strikes the match against the catch-plate and tosses the wooden fuse into the dark inner sanctum of the stove atop the bundle of letters. Immediately, there is a flash of firelight as the letters burst into flame-- the initial burst of flame being so loud it is almost a scream. The scream, it seemed to Kitt's ears is Asher's voice--coming from Herodsville--as if he has, too, been a synchronistic victim of the flames. As Kitt stands in front of the open door of the little stove watching the letters burn, she feels a burning in her heart. A pain, like nothing she has ever felt. A killing pain. Something that could stop the heart. She imagines, in that moment, that her heart has, in fact, stopped beating. That her life has ended. And that she will disappear--to wherever the girl in the mirror has gone. To that "other world" Mother Ann has spoken about so often and with so much reverence and longing.

As the paper from the pages of Asher's letters slowly burns, turning to but wisps of black ash, Kitt fixates on the irony of Asher's name. The word "ash." And now, all that is left of his proclamations of love for her is nothing but ash, lying at the bottom of the funny little Shaker stove. She worries, now, that her rash action might have more profound consequences. Might be harmful in some way to Asher. She tries to dismiss these thoughts as nothing more than superstitions, as the "rappings" of a misguided mind. But the thought remains with her. She now, on top of all else, feels guilty for what she may have done to Asher in her thoughtless haste.

She feels a pining for their love, symbolized by the smoke circulating in the stove and rising in the long thin stovepipe that disappears into the walls of the East Family Dwelling, that makes its way eventually into a brick chimney on a steeply-slanted roof of a brightly-painted building— rising, rising up and away into the wind of the early September air.

Scene III.

News of the outside world has come to Shakertown from as far away as Watervliet, New York, in the person of Brother Seth Y. Wells, an elder of the South Family there. Watervliet had been founded twenty years before the beginnings of Pleasant Grove. Brother Wells has arrived in Shakertown prior to the fall equinox as part of a trip to the "southern" communities on behalf of the Ministries from the north in an attempt to achieve some kind of universal cohesion between all Shaker communities in the system. He has also come as the result of a personal invitation from Wilford Ranks, who has been in communication with him earlier regarding the alarming developments among the younger instruments in the Shakertown community. At that time Brother Wells had responded to Ranks' long written discourse and listing of recent events at Pleasant Grove with a list of his own-- enumerating for the members of the Pleasant Grove Ministry a variety of gifts he had personally witnessed, including visits from an "antediluvian of a very tall stature" and "from the native American princess Pocahontas."

On this trip Brother Wells has been put up in the Farm Deacon's Shop. Built in 1809 as the first permanent structure in the village, it has in recent years come to be used as a sometime tavern for wayfarers, as well as the residence for the Pleasant Grove farm deacon. In addition, it has accommodations on the second floor for overnight lodging for village guests and visiting Shakers. The informal yet comfortable surroundings of the Farm Deacon's Shop served as a perfect environment for gatherings of small groups interested in hearing the "news of the world" from their occasional guests. During Brother Wells' visit to Shakertown he has already met frequently with members of The Ministry. On this occasion his business is of a lighter fare, as Brother Wells is there to hold forth as the bringer of more informal news from the northeastern Shaker communities as well as locations along the route of his recent travels.

A group of about a dozen Pleasant Grove Believers have all gathered in the tavern on the first floor of the Farm Deacon's Shop to listen to Brother Wells' tales of rumors and experiences amongst The World's People. On this particular occasion, the conversation has taken a philosophical and literary turn and Brother Wells is in an animated mood, having found renewed energy from a mug or two of the Farm Deacon's highly-prized homebrew. Before Brother Wells had left Watervliet on his "southern journey," he had had the opportunity to travel north to the Canterbury Shaker Village in New Hampshire and had stopped in the town of Concord, Massachussetts, along the way to visit a certain Ralph Waldo Emerson--a Unitarian minister turned Transcendentalist and a world-renowned lecturer who had become something of a legendary figure in the Northeast and had written several books on spirituality and nature. Brother Wells had heard him speak in the town's First Parish Church and then had had the opportunity to meet with him privately at his home in Concord.

"Mr. Emerson was in a state of grieving over the sudden death of his young son at the time of my visit to Concord, but he remained active in his speaking engagements and spoke with passion and a positive message that left the parishoners of the First Parish Church practically spellbound," Brother Wells begins. "And then in greeting me after his sermon, which was really more of a theological discourse than a sermon, he invited me to his home for supper that very evening. Upon arriving, I was greeted at his front door by a young man probably in his late twenties or early thirties who introduced himself as David Thoreau. I was to learn later that he was a boarder at the Emerson's home and had been living there for almost two years. I noticed after I'd been there a while, that he and Mr. Emerson were quite cozy--meaning that they were very friendly toward one another and with a great deal of respect.

"After a lovely dinner prepared largely by Mr. Thoreau and Mr. Emerson's wife, we sat in the parlor and began our after-dinner discussion, which I learned was something of an institution there in the Concord community. Mr. Emerson had only recently published a book of his essays that looked very promising to me at first glance. I have since had a chance to read his book, as he was kind enough to give me a copy before I left for Boston and the Hancock Village just outside of Pittsfield. I can tell you, for what it's worth, that Mr. Emerson is quite a wonderful writer, whose ideas on the world, God, and all of creation, left me in a state of wonderment and deep inquisition. The same holds true of his oratory abilities. During my visit there, I witnessed large audiences who flocked to hear him and were left spellbound by his orations and his spiritual presence.

"There is one particular essay in this new book that I have found especially interesting and upon which I actually heard him speak. It is entitled 'Self Reliance.' I have taken a few notes from that lecture, which

I will share with you, for I think you will find them of interest, too. Mr. Emerson begins his essay in the book by saying that 'to believe our own thought, to believe that what is true for you in your private heart is true for all men,--that is genius.' And he goes on to say that 'Nothing is at last sacred but the integrity of your own mind.' Then later that night, at the dinner table, when I asked him to elucidate on the subject of self-reliance, he said, 'What I must do is all that concerns me, not what people think. It is easy in the world to live after the world's opinion; it is easy in solitude to live after our own; but the great man is he who, in the midst of the crowd, keeps with perfect sweetness the independence of solitude.' I was taken with this statement and offered my opinion that this idea was in line with our own Shaker beliefs concerning the world and The World's People. He seemed very interested in my admission and questioned me extensively on our Shaker doctrines. Following my attempts at explanations of our beliefs, Mr. Emerson responded by saying, 'If we cannot at once rise to the sanctities of obedience and faith, let us at least resist our temptations. This is to be done in these harsh times by speaking the truth. So, live no longer to the expectation of deceived and deceiving people with whom you may converse. And see prayer in all action. The prayer of the farmer kneeling in his field to weed it, the prayer of the rower kneeling with the stroke of his oar, are true prayers heard throughout nature. What I see, today, is--that all men plume themselves on the improvement of society, and no man improves. And because no man improves, society never advances.'

"These words from Mr. Emerson about society and isolation could have been taken right out of our own texts. I think we were both struck by these similarities and he seemed truly interested in learning more about our Societies and practices. But we agreed to postpone that conversation until another time. Meanwhile, Mr. Thoreau, who was also there with us at the table during all this talk on self-reliance was quick to join in on the conversation and speak up. He was most loquacious about this subject. One might even say, obsessed in his enthusiasm. It turns out that he has just published, this year, in his own right, a much bally-hooed treatise on "The Natural History of Massachusetts," and with help from Mr. Emerson, is entertaining the idea of a project in which he plans to move out onto a piece of property outside of town and essentially live alone, there, as a solitary and in a state of self-sufficiency. In his own words, 'to be completely self-reliant.' He had read Mr. Emerson's ideas on self-reliance and had taken them to heart and had decided that, in his own words, which I have written down, 'it is not enough to merely think high-minded thoughts, but to put such thoughts into fruitful action.' He then went on to say that 'in society you will not find health, but in nature. Unless our feet at least stood in the midst of nature, all our faces would be pale and livid. Society is always diseased. To him who contemplates a trait of natural beauty no harm nor disappointment can come. The doctrines of despair, of spiritual tyranny or servitude, were never taught by those that shared the serenity of nature.'

"Mr. Thoreau's passion took those seated at the dinner table that evening by surprise. But apparently his outrageous enthusiasm is well-known amongst the local town folks and they prize his keen insight and wit. So, we did not interject our own thoughts during Mr. Thoreau's diatribe, but let him proceed. Which he did, saying further that 'We fancy that this din of religion, literature, and philosophy, which is heard in pulpits, lyceums, and parlors, vibrates through the universe, and is as catholic a sound as the creaking of the earth's axle; but if a man sleeps soundly, he will forget it all between sunset and dawn. How silent and soothing is the beauty in the recesses of nature. As for me, I love to be alone. I never found a companion that was so companionable as solitude.' And then he went on to pontificate about how etiquette and politeness and all our rules were like 'musty cheese,' I believe were his words. Quite a character is this Henry David Thoreau. If a little overbearing, he was certainly entertaining, and I can see why Mr. Emerson would be so fond of him while mentoring him along."

At this point in his soliloquy, Brother Wells pauses to take a long, healthy drink from his beer mug before saying anything further. The twelve members of his audience sit transfixed for some seconds before they, too, raise their mugs to their lips and drink--following his lead like a young ewe might mimic its mother. When all thirst is satiated, Brother Wells continues.

"I don't know how we got onto it, but at some point Mr. Emerson began talking about Hinduism, Islam and the religions of the Middle East. Something that I had to admit that I knew very little about. Mr. Emerson began talking about his admiration for certain tenets of the Koran and other religious books, and began speaking about a Persian poet from the 14th century whom he much admired, and whom he said he had come across from his readings of Goethe and that he had since been translating. This figure had a very long name, which I could remember none of except the first word, which I believe was Khwaja. Mr. Emerson told us that this man, when he was young, had memorized the Koran in its entirety and had become legendary for this and had been given the spiritual name of Hafiz, which in the Persian language meant 'he who has memorized the whole of the Koran.' At this point he began to recite some verses by this Khwaja. In my efforts to record these lines later that evening, I could only recall certain lines, which I have been carrying with me on the road these last few weeks and which I would be happy to share with you if you think you are at all interested."

All twelve Pleasant Grove members shake their heads in unison and in agreement, yet without speaking a word, encouraging Brother Wells to continue, which he does, taking some crumpled papers from his large coat pockets, unraveling them, and commencing to read his random passages.

"O philosopher, be sensible and don't speak out against love,
Have you some sort of bone to pick with God?"

"Because of the birds of grief that had broken our hearts,
God sent us Christ to take up our travail."

"Don't worry about property and money in this life. Even if you have enough
Friends to sell a hundred houses or family to live a hundred lives, it would
Not pay for His advice.

But be careful, for Satan will tempt you at every turn:
He is everywhere, so be silent and listen for the advice of angels and your heart.

Because of all this talk of money, the world has been ruined and there is
Little joy. To remedy this, let's bring out the harp. Beat loudly on the drum!"

"O Teacher, share some of Your wine with Your disciples.
What harm is there in wasting wine this way?

Remember: wine charms reason's wits and takes its rust away.
This vineyard will be here from now to Judgment Day!

Khwaja, you chose the path to the Winehouse, happily,
So from this path of prayer and love, don't stray."

There is a long, pensive silence following Brother Wells' recitations, and then a sudden and unexpected explosion of applause, which frightens everyone including those who were clapping. Perhaps the most enthusiastic applauder of all is none other than Wilford Ranks, who is one of the attending twelve that evening and already into his third mug of the Deacon's lethal homebrew. Ranks has become almost spooked with Brother Wells' mention of the Persian poet Khwaja, aka Hafiz, as he has never heard or read any other references to this figure from the 14th century who has become like a living presence in his life of late. But the lines Brother Wells is reciting are so familiar that they might have very easily been taken right out of those he, himself, had written down only a few evenings prior in the solitude of his apartment above the Meeting Hall. When Brother Wells has ended his recitation of the two-line verses, Ranks has heard himself let out an uproarious cheer, as if he has just witnessed an exhibition or feat of supernatural strength or physical skill. For the first time in many years, Ranks has felt the adrenaline rush of true excitement. But catching himself in this moment of exuberant celebration and a bit embarrassed by his own outburst, he settles back onto his bench aside the long wooden tavern table, trying to disappear into the proper, if appreciative, applause of the group.

At this point in the evening, Brother Wells suggests that they take a short break to refill their beer mugs and to catch their breath and their wits before he ventures on in the continuing discourse of his travels and his exploits in that "other" and more foreign world of American society.

Some fifteen or twenty minutes later, the enthusiastic, if slightly inebriated, group reconvenes, returning to their benches and straight-back chairs. Brother Wells reclaims his former position at the head of the dimly lit room and resumes his storyline where he had left off before the break. "Now from Concord, I traveled southward to New Lebanon and my home community of Watervliet in New York state. I spent some memorable time in both of these communities of Believers before pushing on further to the south and Philadelphia, where I spent a few days and attended a Quaker Meeting with the David Scull family who are a Quaker family I had been introduced to on a previous trip. From Philadelphia, I traveled to Baltimore. Although there are no Shaker communities there, I was given the name of a Quaker family named Heap and carried with me a letter of introduction from the Scull family in Philadelphia I had just stayed with. Baltimore was right on my route, so I used the Quaker family's hospitality as a rest stop before pushing on to the west and toward Kentucky.

"Quite unexpectedly, while in Baltimore my host family took me around to see the sights and to instruct me in the history of the city. As an addendum to all the history and politics of the place, I was also instructed in some of the local color in this eclectic seaport town. Perhaps one of the most intriguing evenings I spent in Baltimore was at a lecture and reading that was held at the Quaker Meeting House in the downtown area of the city. The speaker that evening was one diminutive and curious-looking gentleman named Edgar Allan Poe. I was told that he was an up-and-coming writer and was the talk of the town. The moment Mr. Poe began to talk I knew I was in for an interesting evening. And interesting it was, for Mr. Poe was certainly not your usual author who writes in the vogue of the time--about Indians and pristine nature. In fact, quite the opposite, he was gaining some recognition as a writer of mystery and horror stories, and in that sense I would call him an original.

"He began the evening by reading from a recently published story called "The Pit and the Pendulum" and had the whole place transfixed from the first page. I don't ever remember being so mesmerized by a piece of fiction, or nonfiction for that matter. After concluding the segment from the ghoulish prose piece, he read us one of his poems--based on stories from the Koran. In many ways, the poem reminded me of the conversation I had had a couple of weeks before with Mr. Emerson in Concord. Mr. Poe's poem was nothing like those of Mr. Emerson's Persian poet, Khwaja, as Mr. Poe writes in an original and very modern style.

"From there, Mr. Poe talked about and read passages from a work only recently undertaken which he called "The Tell Tale Heart"-- about murder, a vulture's eye and a body cut up in pieces that has been hidden under the floorboards of the murderer's house. Very eerie and disturbing was the short segment that he read to us. He also talked at some length of a novel he had written which was on the subject of a shipwreck, mutiny, cannibalism and various misadventures on the high seas. All in all, it was a very entertaining evening. While Mr. Poe's stories and poems were not for the light-hearted, they were certainly engaging, as he, himself, was a very dynamic speaker.

"After the formal presentation at the Quaker Meeting Hall, a group of those in the audience, which included myself, traveled down the street with Mr. Poe to what he referred to as his "favorite pub," where we were told we could get quite good food and plenty of good beverage to wash it down. It soon became apparent to all of us in Mr. Poe's entourage that he quite liked his drink. He began with a dram or two of the local beer even before we ordered our food. And it wasn't long before the eccentric side of his personality emerged and he began to hold forth, extrapolating on his various beliefs, ideas and opinions about all manner of subjects.

"It was clear from the outset that Mr. Poe seems to enjoy his writing and that it is not a chore for him. As macabre as some of his tales may be, he seems to have a true interest and devotion to his stories and their characters. I was also touched by his sense of loyalty and love for his young wife Virginia, as he mentioned her often that evening. Again, and not unlike my habit of taking notes during the talks and conversation of Mr. Emerson I was privy to, I jotted down notes, there in the pub, of Mr. Poe's conversation, driven by an instinct that he, too, like Mr. Emerson, was a figure that would be remembered and celebrated long after he was gone. Both men had that kind of presence about them. While

Mr. Emerson is something of a metaphysician, Mr. Poe certainly is not of that camp. Yet, he is not merely a macabre genius lost in the world of the grotesque, but can talk elegantly of things of the mind and the intellect and has strong personal opinions on all matters. For instance, I have written here in my little notebook that I carry with me on all such occasions some of Mr. Poe's tavern oratory." He takes a small bound notebook from the side-pocket of his overcoat. "Either the New World must be mine as I will have it, or it is a worthless bog. There can be no concession. We have snapped asunder the leading-strings of our British Grandmama, and, better still, we have survived the first hours of our novel freedom--the first licentious hours of hobbledehoy, braggadocio and swagger. I'd rather *the ice* than their way.'

"Mr. Poe, unlike certain others who are writing among us, such as Lowell and Bryant, is concerned with the soul, and his use of language is modern, his words are as clear as the most transparent sand, his characters, to use his own words, 'are those who belong properly to books.' On the subject of characters and language, Mr. Poe was quick to say, 'a character should speak to the people in that people's ordinary tongue.'

"Poe, I found to be a lonely figure, despite his gift of gab. He seemed to exude, along with his vivaciousness, a kind of sorrow and weariness and even disgust with mankind. Despite his having inhabited various East Coast cities for most of his life, there seemed to be a longing for solitude. This apparent paradox seemed to be causing him consternation. Hence, perhaps, his penchant for drink. Whatever the case may be, Mr. Edgar Allan Poe was at all times a gentleman and a man of considerable intellect and talent. He left us that night in the pub with a thought that I find I am still pondering, even tonight as I talk with you, here, in Pleasant Grove. He said: 'The highest order of the imaginative intellect is always preeminently mathematical.' I apologize to all of you for leaving you with this quote out of context, but it struck me so strongly at the time that I was forced to write it down.

"Well, enough, my patient friends, of my long-winded tales of my travels. It's getting late and I'm sure you have better things to do with your time than to listen to my tedious yarns."

With this end-line, Brother Wells bows to enthusiastic applause from those in attendance in the Farm Deacon's tavern, and all rise for a time of mingling and animated conversation before all mugs are emptied of beer and all banter and bodies exhausted. Wilford Ranks walks, that evening, slowly back up the wide dirt road that bisects Pleasant Grove in the light of a full moon, pondering what he has just heard. He is struck with the unexpected reference to Khwaja, by the wisdom of Ralph Waldo Emerson and his protege Henry David Thoreau, and is somewhat spellbound by Brother Wells' tales of Edgar Allan Poe. As he climbs the stairs to the Ministry apartments in the Meeting Hall, he feels his legs bend with fatigue. His body is heavy. His mind is full. That night he dreams of sailing ships, cannibals and the sound of a beating heart coming from the floorboards underneath his Shaker bed.

While the men in Shakertown were pondering and replaying the mental images and pithy quotes they had experienced the evening of what had already begun to become known as the legendary "Farm Deacon's Shop Discourse," Brother Seth Y. Wells made his way down the river road to South Union, Kentucky, and Asher Pope moved about Herodsville in a stew. He had talked Caden's ear off, even gone to the hills to consult with the eighty-year-old mountain man William Rayfield to get his sage advice. In the end, Asher had gone against all the advice he had been given and had made his own decision. One that was not going to make him popular amongst his kith and kin in Herodsville, but a decision that had come from his cogent mind and his impassioned heart.

As the rain fell in a downpour on a late Kentucky night in September, Asher was up late in his attic room unable to sleep and sitting at his desk writing. Writing a letter to Kitt.

Dearest Kitt,

It has been so long since I have seen you. More than a lifetime, it seems. I have been unable to sleep tonight, thinking about our situation and a decision I have made that hopefully will put an end to our anxieties and fears and will, once and for all, resolve the matter of our being together.

In recent days and weeks, I have listened to my heart and consulted with some of the wise friends I have in this community about my plight. Everyone has advised me to give up my love for you and to get on with my life here in Herodsville. But life here in Herodsville without you has no meaning for me. I'm not really here in Herodsville at all, as in my mind I'm always and constantly there with you in Shakertown. So what's the point of "getting on with my life here in Herodsville" when

I'm never really here. And what's the point of my staying here in Herodsville if I'm always (in my heart and soul) there in Shakertown with you?

Based on this thinking I have come to my decision. It is really the only logical decision for me. And that decision is–for me to come and live there with you in Shakertown. To become a Shaker. I feel like I've practically become a Shaker over this past year–so often have I been to Shaker Meeting, taking part in the services and dances. And then, of course, there is you, who have instructed me in "all things Shaker" by example and through our letters and meetings. So, I have sent word to Mr. Ranks (since I have met him, we have spoken, and he knows who I am) as a member of The Ministry that I would like to have an audience with him on this Wednesday to speak with him about important matters concerning my person and my future life. Although I have not heard any response from him as to my request, I will ride up to Shakertown on Wednesday to hopefully meet with him and talk. It is my intention at that time to tell him that I wish to become a Shaker and that I wish to join the Pleasant Grove community. Since I have been approached during Shaker Meeting about converting to the United Society of Believers, I'm hoping that my induction into the Shaker ranks will be little more than a formality. Perhaps I am being naïve about all this, in which case I'm hoping that my hidden intentions (which I will, of course, not divulge to him) and my gift of gab will pull me through any inquisition or ordeal I might face with him and/or his brethren and sistren (is 'sistren' a real word that is used amongst the Believers?).

So, my princess, that is my decision. I hope that you will be pleased. When I finally made my decision, a great weight was lifted off of me and I was inspired to write. What I wrote was a love poem. A poem to you. A poem to us. I end this letter with that poem, and seal it with a kiss.

Always yours,

Asher

Wind In a Galleon's Sails

Let the words flow through me
Like wind in a galleon's sails
And I will reach
To the nearest star
Pluck a thousand smiles
You will receive as roses
In a bride's bouquet.

For us the sun is taboo
We carry our hearts in cloth totebags
Strapped to the beginning of our lives

The muse is singing!
I have captured Her songs in the ink of my pen.

On one Fall day,
I am going to step out of my body
Become breeze over water
Like wind in the sails of a galleon
You are the ship of my existence
The anchor in my joy

Asher had written his letter to Kitt on Monday. He took the letter to work with him at the General Store in town on Tuesday and gave it to Sister Eden who had come to town to do the usual Shakertown shopping. Tuesday seemed like the longest day in Asher's life. All his thoughts were focused on Wednesday, and his meeting with his old nemesis The Watcher: Brother Wilford Ranks.

Tuesday night, he lay in his bed for what seemed like hours unable to sleep. As usual when he couldn't sleep, he got up and went to his desk. From his small collection of books lined up between two bookends made of metal, he removed the thickest book and opened it, at random, to page 1085 and began to read:

> *O woeful sympathy! Piteous predicament! ...*
> *Oh Nurse, Spak'st thou of Juliet? How is it with her?*
> *Where is she? And how doth she? And what says my concealed*
> *Lady to our cancelled love?... But that a joy past joy calls out on me,*
> *It were a grief so brief to part with thee....*

With his spirit and insomnia calmed by the synchronicity of Shakespeare's words and his own predicament, he made his way back to the horsehair mattress on his bed, lay down, shut his eyes and didn't wake until Wednesday's sunshine was pouring in through his attic windows and the rooster in the barnyard had filled his ears with anticipation and with joy.

After a morning's worth of chores and garden work in the barn and around the house, Asher took a quick washbasin bath, put on appropriately clean clothes, found some cornbread and a bowl of canned applesauce in the kitchen and he was out the door and moving with purpose toward the small barn behind the manse. He made his way to the back of the barn, opened the stall where the two Morgan horses had stayed the night, fit them with halters and led them out of the barn to the side-shed where the wagon had been parked under cover and where Asher had left it after returning home from town. He hooked the team of two large horses up to the wagon, fed them a couple palm-fulls of oats and cracked corn, then climbed up into the seat in the front of the big-wheeled wain. With a single flap of the reins and an enthusiastic "giyup" he drove the tandem from its garage in the old barn, around the driveway that circled the west side of the house and headed out onto the dusty dirt road toward Shakertown.

Ministry Edler, Wilford Ranks, sat on one of the fastener benches in the Meeting House. Alone in the large empty room, he felt crowded by the spaciousness of the room and the silence. He had eaten an unusually large mid-day meal in the basement dining area of the Centre Family Dwelling--thinking too much of his appointment and how that might go, so he had taken a little extra nourishment to get him through his interview with the young Asher Pope. Now, as he sat on the fastener bench in the Meeting Hall, he was bloated and uncomfortable and with too much of his mental and physical energy going to digesting what had amounted to a mid-day feast.

Sister Eden had delivered Asher's letter to Brother Wilford the previous evening upon her return from Herodsville and the General Store. He had read it with great surprise, if not interest, and was immediately struck by the lines: "I think I am a good candidate for Pleasant Grove and that this should prove to be an answer and a solution to your suspicions and concerns about me as you expressed them to me personally only recently." On a second reading, he was even more struck with how similar these words were to what his own thoughts had been on the subject and the conversation he had recently had with Sister Daniella. The rest of Asher's letter, which wasn't overly long or wordy, merely expressed his interests in the various tenets of Shaker spiritual beliefs and Shaker life and work. Although still a bit suspicious of the young Asher Pope, Ranks found that the younger man's letter had a compelling ring to it and he found himself being drawn in to the alluring personality of Asher's writing style. All this was going through his mind as the men's entrance door to the Meeting Hall opened and the sound of the door closing followed by footsteps on the wooden floorboards caused him to cease his daydreaming, turn, and notice a thin young man with bright blonde hair moving elegantly across the room toward where he sat.

Although elegantly, since he had the gait of an athlete and dancer, Asher moved with some trepidation toward the lone figure who sat on the fastener bench where he himself had sat on many occasions observing the Sunday meetings and dances during the past year. Being back in the building that housed many of his best memories from the last twelve months created a sense of nostalgia in him. Although the emptiness and silence of the Meeting Hall at that moment seemed a little strange, he was able to put himself back in time as if the room were full of shaking, quaking bodies engaged, full voice, in song as he looked up toward the west wall and the small window where the visage of The Watcher had been a fixture like the wall or the window itself.

Asher's daydreaming was broken by the echo of a voice that sent a chill down his spine, as if The Watcher were speaking to him, god-like, from his watchtower in the wall. "Good afternoon, Mr. Pope. I see that you have found me and that we meet again."

Pulled quickly back into the reality of the moment, Asher turned his gaze away from the window on the wall and found himself standing before The Watcher who was rising from the fastener bench as he spoke. "I have received your letter and I understand that you have something that you'd like to speak to me about." Brother Wilford extended his hand in greeting, which Asher took and shook shyly. "Please, Mr. Pope, sit down here on this bench and let us talk. You should be comfortable here, as you have spent many a Sunday on this very spot, so this should be a familiar and congenial place for us to partake in conversation."

Barely able to utter a sound, Asher somehow managed to get out "Yes sir. Thank you sir. It's good to be back, here, again, sir."

"Let's forgo the formality Mr. Pope and just speak man to man. Equal to equal, as this is the Shaker way. You have something you want to speak to me about and I'm interested in what you have to say. In short, my young friend, I'm all ears."

Asher hardly knew where to begin. While he had been preparing his delivery to The Watcher during his wagon-ride all the way from Herodsville, in this uncomfortable moment all his loquacious, god-given gifts seem to have deserted him. But there he was--in the moment of reckoning, the moment of truth--and he had to begin somewhere. So he did. "Thank you for meeting me, sir, er, Watch...I mean Brother Ranks. I am glad that you have gotten my letter and that we have this opportunity to talk. I wish to speak with you about Pleasant Grove and about your Shaker faith. As you know, I have been here regularly on Sundays for the past year and have found a deep interest in what you believe and how you live."

"I have no doubt in your sincerity, my boy, but maybe you can be a little more specific about this and why it is you have come here today, as your letter implied some more pointed interests. And please, call me Brother Wilford."

"Uh, yes sir, I mean Brother Wilford. You are right. I do, in fact, have something more specific on my mind, and I'll just go ahead and say it. I have given this a lot of thought and have come to the decision that I would like to become a member of the Pleasant Grove Society of Believers. I feel that I am well-acquainted with the practices of the community, both spiritually and physically. I also feel that I am well-qualified, since I have been coming religiously to Shaker Meeting this past year. And I feel that I am of age and able to make up my mind for myself about such matters and which direction my life should go. That, sir, uh, Brother Wilford, is, in short, what I have come here to say."

"Yes, my boy, I knew this was your interest from reading your letter. Being as this is the case, I have given this idea much thought--even a bit of prayer. In the end, and even though I
have some misgivings about certain matters I have afore expressed to thee, I have been able to clear away those thoughts and come here today to talk to you with an open mind. I am very interested in what you have to say and what has led you to this decision. As you know, we encourage converts from the World's People to join us here at Pleasant Grove if they are spiritually called to do so. In that sense, I am interested in

talking to you about this would-be revelation of yours."

"Yes, I think I am ready, sir, to take this step. As you know, and speaking in my own defense, I have on more than one occasion been approached during the Shaker Dances by members of the community who thought I was ready to 'come into the fold'--I believe these were their words on both occasions. So, clearly, there are some people here at Pleasant Grove who must have thought I was ready to take this step."

"Yes, I remember those incidents, very well, Asher, as it was I who initiated them. As you no doubt know, I am present at almost all of the Shaker services that take place in this building. While I am not a participant, very often, on the floor of the hall, I am able to witness most everything that goes on from the vantage point of the little window on yonder wall." Ranks raises his arm to eye level and points out across the large room to the small window on the facing wall. "From there, I have watched you and your Herodsville friends with much interest, and have even witnessed things that I wish I had not seen. Be that as it may, I have been very impressed, if not concerned, by your faithful attendance and your interactions with us--on Sundays, as well as in our business at the General Store."

"Yes, sir, I have been very interested and very happy to have been a part of your community in these ways. I have enjoyed all my interactions with people from Pleasant Grove and feel I have learned much from the time I have spent here, as well as what I have learned on my own about Shaker life. And after this past year and all I have observed and experienced, I feel I am ready to join the other brothers and sisters here at Pleasant Grove and to partake in Shaker life and practice."

"I am impressed with your enthusiasm and your sense of commitment, but are you sure you are ready for this kind of change, especially at this stage in your life? And are you sure you understand what it would mean for you to convert to our way of living?"

"I think so, sir."

"You understand, for example, that we live by certain rules here in Pleasant Grove. By certain tenets, if you will. Life in Pleasant Grove, or "Shakertown" as I believe your friends and family from Herodsville call it, is very different from life as you know it and as life exists in the rest of the world. Are you aware of this, Asher? Surely you must be. But in case you are not, I will spell it out for you, now, lest you have been misled or are mistaken about the tenets and regimen by which we live. We often have people coming to us, here, with unreal fantasies and illusions about what the Shaker life is all about. Many come to us full of expectation only to leave a short time later disillusioned and full of disappointment.

"For instance, Asher, in our document which we refer to as *The*

Testimony and in our earlier documents of *The Candid Statement* and the even earlier *Concise Statement*, there are spiritual principles and certain life rules by which we all abide. In other words, what you are willing to live and die by. So, if you will be patient with me, I will spell them out for you in case you aren't familiar with the central tenets of Shaker life here at Pleasant Grove.

"First and possibly foremost, we believe in a conscious separation from the world. By living in our own communities and being as self-sufficient as possible, we are able to shield ourselves from some of the less than wholesome influences of mainstream society. Hence, you see us seldom walking amongst you in the streets of Herodsville.

"Secondly, and most obviously--at least to those who live in mainstream society--is the tenet of celibacy. While this is probably the hardest of our rules for humans to live by, it is one of the most important. This idea of ours that prevents cohabitation is a reminder to us that lust resulted in man's expulsion from the Garden of Eden. Hence, we have all taken vows of celibacy and have dedicated ourselves to living lives of purity, giving up exclusive relationships and instead living together in families as brothers and sisters.

"Thirdly, there is the principle of equality. We believe in equality for all people regardless of race or sex. Equality between males and females--for this was clearly God's will at the time of Creation. And this includes black peoples and native peoples, as well as us European white folks.

"The fourth precept concerns the sharing of goods. None of us owns anything individually. When we become Believers, we turn over any and all property and personal belongings to the community, to the Society. We believe in the maxim of share and share alike.

"The fifth guiding principle is that of pacifism. Like our cousins the Quakers, we don't believe in war. We are, in fact, conscientious objectors to war and refuse to serve in wars of any kind, which has included the Revolutionary War.

"Finally, we have the standard procedure of the confession of sins. Each new convert must confess his or her sins to a member of the Ministry and at specified times thereafter. Now, Mr. Asher Pope, do you think that you could abide by all of these imperatives? And are they all clear as I have described them to you?"

"Yes, sir, I am familiar with your basic rules and laws. I have studied them deeply before writing my letter to you and asking for this audience. So, I guess you could say that I know what I'm getting into."

"And the dictates of celibacy and separation from the world. Have you thought hard about these two directives, in particular? As these are the two that young people of your age have the most problems with.

And it is these two tenets that I am most concerned about in your case, Mr. Pope. You are a very handsome young man and very agile and healthy. I can hardly imagine, at your age, that you wouldn't be attracted to girls and they to you. And what of all your friends and family in Herodsville? Won't it be hard for you to just pick up and leave them-- you may rarely see them, as you'll be living here in Pleasant Grove, even though it is only a few miles away. Have you thought hard and prayed about these two instructions?"

There was an uncomfortable silence after Brother Wilford's long soliloquy on the tenets of Shaker ground rules while Asher contemplated what he had just heard and how he was going to respond to The Watcher's charge. In a sense the whole past year had come down to this moment. This moment of truth. This moment when he would have to fabricate some kind of untruth, some lie that was convincing enough to persuade The Watcher to not only believe in his faux sincerity, but to accept him into the Pleasant Grove community. This moment, which would be a leap of faith for them both. For The Watcher in terms of blind faith acceptance. For Asher in terms of his determination and will to achieve his desired goal: to be nearer to Kitt Leigh.

In that moment of hesitation and uncertainty, Asher heard himself utter the words "Yes sir, I have, sir." And having uttered these unfamiliar if awkward sounds, he found himself entrenched in a deep grave of his own digging. In a single breath, Asher had made a commitment from which he could not retreat, yet to which he could not fully travel. He struggled to come up with words that were an adequate answer to The Watcher's loaded question.

" Yes, sir, I have," Asher embarrassingly heard himself say again. "I have thought long and hard about what it is that I must give up in order to become part of this community. I have weighed one thing against another. And I have realized that carnal divisions prevail among the denominations that belong to the Antichrist, which cling to legal ordinances and live after the flesh," he mimicks--from words he had heard coming from his father's mouth in a sermon given to his Baptist congregation only just that Sunday. And in having uttered these words he knew he was lying. Knew he was perpetrating a ruse that may one day come back to haunt him. But so strong was his intent and his determination to pull the wool over The Watcher's eyes, that this concocted utterance from some blasphemy taken in vain from biblical scripture had served its purpose and was therefore, at least for the moment, secure in Asher's mind as acceptable truth.

"Well, Mr. Pope, that was quite a statement. Quite frankly, I'm surprised by this declaration coming from someone as of-the-world as yourself. Is there any reason that I should be doubtful of your word and your seeming convictions?"

Asher, again, paused before he spoke. But thoughts and words were coming to him more easily now, as he found himself "living his words," as he referred to the process when taken over by the muse while writing a poem.

"No sir, Mr. Ranks, sir," Asher said, lying. And he continued along the lines of how he had begun in response to The Watcher's first question, taking liberties with some of his father's sermons and at the same time inventing scripture as he went. "I see Pleasant Grove as a safe refuge of souls. I have come to understand and to despise cities and the works of Babylon. I understand the Shaker tenets as the true nature of the work of Christ. And it is by this path that I wish to travel for the remainder of my life--by a strategy of withdrawal from the world. I am different from other young men in Herodsville who chase after the girls and lay up drunk on the weekends. People that know me will tell you that I am sort of a solitary and that I spend a lot of time alone--with my writing and my thoughts. I think I can live up to your dictums and your rules."

"Again, you surprise me. But I know that your father is, in fact, a Baptist minister. So, I can only assume that you will have known all this from years of growing up in his house. Nevertheless, I cannot fault you for paraphrasing the scripture or question your integrity, as I know you not and in that sense I must believe that what you tell me is true. Can I believe what you say, here, today, as gospel truth, young Asher Pope?"

"Yes, sir," Asher lied, again.

"Then let me put it to you formally, Mr. Pope, and in this context: We have a practice here at Pleasant Grove of accepting people into the community based on need and extraneous circumstances. Many of these people join us during or after the harvest season because they are out of work and are destitute in one way or another. And, of course, there are those who come to us with the best of intentions, as converts, to the Shaker faith. The seasonal laborers and those who are desperately in need of sustenance of one sort or another usually stay over the winter months and then leave us in spring when the weather is warmer and there is more need for laborers for farming and things. If I were to accept you into the community of Believers at Pleasant Grove, into our Shaker Society, would you come in as one of our "winter Shakers," as we call them? Would you come in on a trial basis--to see if you found it was a good fit for you and, reciprocally, if we thought you were a good fit for us?"

Without as much as a second thought, Asher responded immediately to The Brother's proposition. "Yes, sir, Mr. Ranks, sir. This would be ok with me."

"Well, then, if you're certain that this is what you really want to do, we'll have our informal preliminary instatement now, where we make things official--on a temporary basis, remember--and then in six months or so, after your trial period, you will meet with the Ministry and will go through a very informal confession of sins and a signing of a covenant, in which you will sign away your earthly possessions, properties and wealth. Upon signing of the covenant, you will officially be a member of the family of the Society. There will be no public welcoming ceremony or celebration, no formal indoctrination or public ceremony upon joining the community. Do you understand and will that work for you, Mr. Pope?"

"Yes, sir. That works just fine."

"Well, then, let's get on with our little ritual. Do you, Asher Pope, accept the gospel, the role of Christ as an example for Believers, and the function of obedience in the process of justification, and the goal of a sinless life? And do you understand the Shaker practices of confession, celibacy, joint interest, and withdrawal from the world, designating these as marks of the true church of Christ? And do you accept and agree to separate your body and your beliefs from your natural family and integrate your body and beliefs into a Shaker family? Will you cross that threshold into a new life as a Shaker and leave your old way of life behind?"

Asher paused a second or two after Ranks had finished with his ritual questions, then gathered himself, took a deep breath and uttered, "I do."

"Asher Pope, you have answered to me this day that you will live by and uphold the tenets of The United Society of Believers in Christ's Second Appearing. Because of your affirmation I am vested with the privilege of saying to you that....God has created man an active, intelligent being, possessing important powers and faculties, capable of serving himself according to his needs and circumstances; and he is required to devote these powers and faculties to the service of God. To devote only a part...is to render an imperfect service.

"God has created nothing in vain. The faculty of dancing, as well as that of singing, was undoubtedly created for the honor and glory of the Creator. God has created the tongue of man. He has also created the hands and the feet, and enabled them to perform their functions. And shall these important faculties be active in the service of sin, and yet be idle in the service of God?

"As union is the distinguishing characteristic of the true followers of Christ, so it is an essential part of the worship of God. To render this unity of spirit the more perfect, a uniformity of exercise is necessary. All are invited to share the feast of the Lamb, to strip off our garments of sin and worship God in the dance.

"With this invocation I invite you, Asher Pope to join in the circle of our Shaker family. Let us consecrate this gesture with the singing of a verse of one of our sacred hymns."
The Watcher reached over to a nearby walnut hymnal stand at the end of the fastener bench where he was seated and handed Asher a hymnal. He turned to the appropriate page, pointed to the verse in question, and encouraging Asher to do the same, started to sing:

'Tis not one without the other,
That will keep the union strong;
O, do learn to go together!
Then you will be join'd in one.
Be not anxious to go forward,
And to leave your brother dear;
You may happen to fall backward,
And your brother forward steer....

After the exultation and the singing of the song, Brother Wilford drew silent, looking deep into Asher's eyes--looking for some sign of his commitment or possible unease. When he found neither sign in the young man's face, he raised his arm and placed his hand on Asher's shoulder, as would a king place the blade of a broadsword on the shoulder of a newly invested knight, and nodded with a positive sign of his acceptance as a virtual embrace that brought Asher formally into the Pleasant Grove family of Believers. Finally, he spoke: "Remember, you are part of one body, Brother Asher—if I may now call you that. You may return home now to make your peace with your family and friends. When you return, you should seek me out and I will take you around the village and introduce you to the children of Zion--the Brethren and Sisters of Pleasant Grove. And we will fit you in the proper clothes and with proper lodging among other Brethren who, like you, are new to Shaker life."

With this, Asher nodded in approval, turned and walked the long walk across the large room toward the men's entrance, noticing, again, The Watcher's window on the far wall as he went. His heart sank as it leapt in paradoxical elation with the realization of his new status and his soon-to-be new life. Asher's first thought as he exited the Meeting Hall door and made his way out into the September afternoon and down the stone steps, was of Kitt. He wondered where she was at that moment. He imagined her coming up the wide, dirt road to meet him. Embracing him and welcoming him into the community--the extended family of the Brothers and Sisters of Zion. He looked for her--first to his right, then to his left--as the stone walkway ended and he reached the wide dirt road.

She was nowhere in sight. But although she was not there to greet him, Asher knew that he would see her soon.

As Asher made his way in his wagon back down the wide dirt road to Herodsville to collect his belongings and confront his family with the news of his imminent move to Shakertown, Kitt sat on the edge of her bed in the room that she shared in the large Family House. Having just read the letter that Asher had sent her by way of Sister Eden, she held the letter in her lap with both hands, gazed down at it in a state of muted shock and disbelief. Many minutes went by before she rose from the side of the bed and made her way over to the small table that served sometimes as a desk, sat down, took a sheet of brown paper out of the thin table drawer, picked up a pencil that had been left there by someone else, and on a light-colored pine writing box began to write.

Dear Asher,

Your latest poem is lovely, and I am indeed flattered that you would write something of such significance to me. The lines lift me out of my present misery and my sweet dilemma, which is your letter. O, what deadly news should be sent in so sweet a package! The news of your intention of joining The Society and coming here to live amongst us has come to me as if from a deceiver's tongue. And, now, I am at a loss to know with what tongue I should use to call your name.

I know I had mentioned this possibility to you when last we talked on that sweet afternoon there amongst the dead, but I thought we had decided that this was not the best solution to our problem and that I had convinced you of the folly of this path. Now, it is apparent that you were not convinced. Or maybe I misunderstood, being as I was so taken by the moment and our time together. This is all my fault. Have I mis-led you to this reckless act, this dubious end? Whichever the case, your news comes as a shock, as I realize that while I am reading your letter, you are most likely somewhere here in Pleasant Grove meeting with Brother Wilford and possibly making an informal commitment. How helpless I feel, knowing all this and not being able to intervene or to talk to you before you take such hasty action.

    O, what will we do, now, my impulsive poet? What rash result will your quick move bring? While your words of longing and love touch me deeply, at the same time the thought of you as a Believer rubs at me the wrong way. You are too much the poet, a free man, a free-thinker who loves to be alone with himself, with his thoughts and his words. How can such a renegade as yourself be at home inside his own frame and at the same time within the confines of the rock walls of Pleasant Grove?

    Think you, now, that the two of us will live in a mortal paradise of sweet flesh? A pair of saints or would-be angels dove-feathered in nature's bower? Such fantasy, my precious rogue! This plan, these wrongly-written words make me feel old. If thou hast taken the Shaker vows then I am too late to blister thy tongue and to keep it from giving voice to such a wish. The thought of you amongst us, here, is no better than if you had been banished. I fear your romantic mind has painted a false picture into which you have leaped.

And what, dear Asher, will your family say? I know you are old enough to make your own way in the world. But my instincts tell me that this will not go down well with them, nor with your good friend Caden. The two of you have been like brothers since you were mere boys.

O, Asher, your sweet words have left me in exile of thy love. What cruel irony is this that leaves my heart in such shambles. When I see you next, you will be dressed in the shackles of Shaker dress. How will I recognize you in such strange clothes? Will your voice even sound the same? And your name-- It will be Brother Asher and not just Asher any more. What was once an open field is now the Dry House door. What was rich between us is now poor. O Asher, are you sure....this is what you want to do?

I write these words to you. They are the tears which I cannot shed. I wish that they were tears of joy. You deserve joy. It is your rightful compliment. And if I cannot in this fateful moment exude for you this joy, then what does that say about how good I am for thee? Maybe I am not your "Juliet". But more like Romeo in skirts and you be Tybalt slain. Your poetry but a corpse in Shaker's shroud. O, Asher, I fear for you and what this Shaker life will do to your verse. You are more akin to falcons and feathered friends than to those of us who have severed themselves from the world, who wait for an end-time and the promise of the return of Christ which will *likely never come. O, what have I done?*

Exhausted from what to her seemed like a pointless exercise occurring outside of time, Kitt put the pencil down, and on the wooden tabletop buried her head in her arms in despair.

Scene IV.

Asher arrived home as his mother and oldest sister were preparing dinner in the kitchen. His father helped the two women by peeling onions over on a cutting board near the sink. There had already been much discussion there in the kitchen during the previous hour or so concerning the mysterious absence of the horses and wagon, and of Asher's secretive behavior of late. As Asher entered the back of the house by the kitchen door, all heads turned towards him in tell-tale silence.

He had been dreading this scene, this altercation. As much as he had tried to skate his way around it with various deceptions, part of him knew what was coming. And, now, there they all were --looking at each other with expectant stares and with no one wanting to strike the match that would ignite the inevitable. Asher nodded in silence to his family members as he stepped from the doorway into the kitchen and then took a first step toward the hallway that led into the rest of the house. Seeing where Asher was going with that one evasive step, the Rev. Jacob Pope was having no part of it and broke the silence with a single word that, to Asher, sounded like a billion cracked church bells.

"Asher!?"

Asher stopped where he stood, barely closer to the hallway, and turned his head a little sideways to acknowledge his father.

"Asher. We'd like to have a word with you. There are a few things you need to explain."

Asher's father had never been known to mince his words or to be anything other than direct.

"Yes, sir," Asher replied almost timidly, as he turned his full body around toward his family and walked to a point in the center of the room.

That evening in Herodsville, Rev. Pope and his flock of Baptist "faithful" gathered at the Baptist church for Wednesday evening service. Rev. Pope is anxious to get into the pulpit and so the usual opening songs and announcements have been postponed as he is hell-bent to address his crowd.

"Please, everyone take your seats, for I want to speak to you tonight. My heart is heavy tonight. I can't bear to wait even for the songs. For my heart is heavy tonight. God has come to me and has said to me, 'Preacher Matthew, I want you to talk to your people tonight. I want you to speak your heart. For there is much to be said.' So, I want to speak tonight to all of you who work, eat and sleep here in Herodsville about what lies so heavy on my heart and mind. Let us begin with prayer.

"Oh Lord, we come here tonight as sinners. But because of your mercy and your gracious gifts we can be saved. We know that we backslide, Lord, but you have given us prayer and your mercy has pulled us through even the toughest of times--Amen. Oh Lord, I come here tonight in one of those times. In one of those moments of backsliding. My heart is heavy tonight, Oh Lord, as one of this congregation has fallen. Has lost his way. Has fallen in the gaze of thy grace. Oh Lord, please give me the strength and the clarity to speak thy will and thy words tonight to these good people of Herodsville. That together we may know and be recipient of thy ultimate counsel--Amen. And Lord, we ask that you be in the hearts and souls of those whom we pray for here tonight. That they may also know thy will. And that thy will be done. On earth as it is in heaven--Amen.

"Good people of Herodsville, I come before you tonight with a heavy heart. One of our flock has fallen. One of our young ones has strayed and has been taken by wolves. I come before you tonight to ask for your prayers. For your help. And for your forgiveness. For, as the father of this young lamb, I, too, have failed. Have fallen in my duties to lead the young lamb down the straight and narrow spiritual road to safety and a life in the Lord Jesus Christ. Friends and neighbors, I ask for your forgiveness. I ask for your help in finding one of our young lambs who has strayed, and leading him home--Amen.

"Good people of Herodsville, I have learned only a few hours ago that my eldest son, Asher, has taken vows to become a Shaker and to join the Christian cult in Shakertown. As we speak, and at this very moment, he is packing his things at our home in preparation to leave. We have had no warning of this decision and so we were unprepared to take any spiritual actions to help young Asher along the way. Now, at this late hour, we, you and I, must come together in Christ's love and find a way-- to bring back our young lamb who has strayed--ah. Who has become lost and has taken up the company of heathens--ah. But the great spiritual song says: "I was lost, but now, I'm found," and we, friends and neighbors, must find it in our hearts to forgive young Asher--ah. To find the lost member of our flock--ah. And to bring him home--Amen.

"I am reminded, tonight, neighbors, of the words from the book of Deuteronomy that say: 'Their foot shall slide.' And just as he that walks in slippery places is every moment liable to fall, he falls without warning. And I am, too, reminded of the words from the book of Psalms--that say, 'Surely thou didn't set them in slippery places; thou cast them down into destruction.' O Lord, our young Asher has slipped--ah. His foot has slid--ah. And he is falling, tonight, toward destruction--ah. We ask for thy help--ah. We ask that you catch him as he falls from Your grace and into destruction at the hands of the infidels at yon protestant monastery who are among the enemies of Heaven and Earth, who turn the water at the marriage feasts of this poor world, not into wine but gall. For we know that to fall out of thy hands is a horror beyond our expression, beyond our imagination--ah. And we know, Lord, that when men talk of a little hell, it is because they think they have only a little sin, and they believe in a little Saviour. We know, Lord, that there are those that believe that if Christ is not for you, Buddha will do, or for that matter anyone or anything else you choose--ah. But we know better than this--ah. We know, Lord, that when you get a great sense of sin, you want a great Saviour, and feel that if you do not have him, you will fall into a great destruction and suffer a great punishment at the hands of the great God--ah. For we know, Lord, as you have told us--that Hell is the turning point between Christianity and other false religions. It IS the critical doctrine--ah. You can't get rid of it--ah. We must therefore look matters in the face--ah. For God has told us--in the book of Deuteronomy, chapter 29, verses 23-25--that 'your children will follow foreigners who come from distant lands. And calamities will come to them and to the land. And everyone will ask: Why has the Lord done this to our young people and to the land? And the answer will be: It is because they have abandoned the covenant of the Lord, the God of their fathers, and have gone off and worshiped with other people and other gods.'

"O Lord, our young Asher has gone off to follow foreigners who have come here amongst us from distant lands. To worship with them, with their pride and vanity and their Shaker gods. We ask for your compassion, here, tonight, O Lord, and your forgiveness for our young Asher and ask that you may find him and spare him the calamities of which you have warned us. He is among dangerous people, Lord, and we know, as you have told us, that there is nothing that keeps wicked men at any one moment out of hell, but the mere pleasure of God. So, we pray for the people of Shakertown, who think that happiness lies in bread and butter, that they may come to see the light and the error of their ways--Amen.

"We know, too, Lord, that the foolish children of men miserably delude themselves in their own schemes, and in confidence in their own strength and wisdom, and that they trust to nothing but a shadow. They say to themselves: 'I think I should contrive well for myself. I think my schemes are good.' But we know, Lord, that they are only flattering themselves, and pleasing themselves with vain dreams of what they would do--ah. For God is under no manner of obligation to keep them for even a moment from eternal destruction--ah. Without His blessing and His embrace the devil is waiting for them--ah. Hell is opening its doors for them--ah. The flames gather and burn about them, and the firey rain comes down to swallow them up--ah.

"These Shaker neighbors of ours, who are known to take in persons so young that they cannot know their own minds, like wiley wolves, have lured one of our young lambs into their den. He is in peril, and he knows it not. He is deluded by his own willfulness and determination. As he packs his bags to join these spiritual despots, these mysterious worshipers in Shakertown--with their mirth and revelry--he cannot see or feel the heat from the flames of hell that wait for him, there. We must help our young Asher, neighbors, and enlist God's help--Amen--for there is nothing that keeps those who have strayed at any one moment out of hell, but the mere pleasure of God--Amen. Young Asher's feet are sliding. Let us join together, in prayer, and catch him before he falls--into the clutches of these shaking Quakers, and therefore into the fiery flames of hell--Amen.

"Let me end, tonight, with the words of Hosea, chapter 6, verses 1-3, where he says: 'Come, let us return to the Lord. For He has torn us, but He will heal us, He has wounded us, but He will bandage us. So, let us press on to know the Lord. And He will come to us like the rain. Like the spring rain watering the earth'--Amen. Please, people of Herodsville, pray tonight and in the days to come that the Lord's rain will fall upon the mind and spirit of our young Asher and that he will, once again, know the Lord, who will heal and bandage his wounds--Amen. That when we come together next time we will have reason to rejoice, and to sing again--in His name. Amen and Amen."

Wilford Ranks was not only having trouble sleeping at night, he was also having disturbing dreams. One wouldn't call them nightmares, but then again, and from his perspective, these were little earthquakes that shook him awake at night—large tremors in his sleep. He had woken before daylight on this particular night from a dream with a young woman sitting by his side and a young man pushing on his chest as if to break it. In the dream, the pain became excruciating and when he awoke he thought that he was having a heart-attack and that the young man in the dream was somehow symbolic of this physical occurrence that seemed to be actually taking place. It was true that his heart was beating quicker and louder than it should, but soon the ticking inside his chest slowed, the pain subsided, and he began, again, to feel almost normal. Normal, that is, except for the anxiety caused from the memory of the dream that came flashing back before his eyes and that seemed more real than the waking moment in which he was remembering it.

In the waking dream, now he saw the young woman more clearly. She was beautiful. She had long flowing auburn hair. She sat beside him on a kind of day bed. He reclining, she sitting on the side of the bed and looking away from him toward the center of an empty room. After imbibing the vision of himself lying there beside the girl, suddenly he realized that the girl in his dream was someone he knew. Someone from Shakertown. The young woman was Kitt Leigh.

Shocked from this realization, yet at the same time a bit tantalized, his inner vision now focused on the memory of the young man as he approached him in the dream. The young man was upset. He clearly intended to harm him as he began pressing on his chest as if to break the bones that surrounded his heart. As the boy got closer and Ranks began to feel, again, the artificial pain from the pressure of the boy's hands on his ribcage, he realized that it was Asher Pope who was trying to do him harm. In the dream Asher seemed to be acting out of jealousy. In a kind of rage. A rage directed at Ranks and the fact that he had caught him in a somewhat suspicious and compromising position with Kitt. Clearly in Asher's mind there was something going on between the two--between the older man and the girl. As Ranks revisited his dream again in his mind's eye, he saw that there was, indeed, a kind of intimacy in the connection between himself and the girl in his dream. He realized that Kitt was innocently and quietly responding to his silent advances in the dream by her mere presence there on the edge of the daybed--looking sexy but sisterly. This thought troubled Wilford Ranks as much as it excited him lying there in the dark room contemplating the meaning and the implications of his dream. Not only did the situation of the dream trouble him but the fact that the two others in the dream were Kitt and Asher made the whole thing seem all too real.

As he lay there, he admitted to himself that the dream was representative of feelings and emotions he had experienced of late. The feelings of attraction for Sister Daniella. Yes, he had to admit, those feelings were real enough. And, yes, he had perhaps even had similar thoughts about Kitt Leigh. This realization bothered him the most. He found this realization and these thoughts somewhat despicable and unworthy of his position in the community. Was he having some sort of spiritual crisis, he wondered to himself there in the mid-morning dark? Was this curiosity of his about Kitt and Asher Pope based on some sort of jealousy? Was he being warned in the dream that he should desist? Or was this more than a warning and in fact a threat to his very life? Questions, outrageous questions, and such emotions! All these were engulfing him as his heart was beginning to beat loudly and more quickly again. Now, he was beginning to feel disoriented. He felt as if he was beginning to go a little insane. As his heart beat louder and faster, his mind began whirling and he felt a wave of panic flush through his body. He had never experienced such a thing before. It frightened him. He sat up in the bed and moved to the bed's edge and sat listening to the sound of his heart beating strongly inside his head. As the heartbeat grew stronger, the sensation of panic grew in intensity. Surely he was going mad.

    Ranks was up off the bed and onto his feet. Groping in the dark he felt around atop the bedside table for the little grease lamp. After clumsily knocking over a glass of water and listening to the water fall from the table--the sound being magnified in the dark like a waterfall onto the wooden floor--he finally managed to find the lamp. Having found the lamp, he felt around the top of the table for the rectangular tin box of matches that would allow him to light the lamp and shed some light upon his inner darkness as well as that which enveloped the room, hoping that the light would also serve as an antidote to the escalating panic that was not only threatening his mental stability but seemed to have a wild grip, now, on his soul. Perhaps he was having some sort of heart attack, he thought to himself, again, as he struggled to strike a match against the tin matchbox. After more than a few tries, he was able to light the match, and with unsteady hands, he worked awkwardly to ignite the wick. Suddenly, the room was filled with light and the Shaker elder could, as if for the first time, see the space surrounding him and the objects that defined that space. Recognizing the space as his bedroom, he felt a slight tinge of relief in knowing that he was, in fact, in his bedroom in the second floor of the Meeting House and not in the room he had experienced in his dream. But the moment of relief was short-lived as the panic, the fear and the pounding heartbeat again claimed the space where relief had fleetingly resided. Feeling as if he were truly going to lose his mind, and with his heart near to bursting right out of his chest, he impulsively made an instinctive move for the door.

    Before he knew it, and with only a candle in hand and the faint lamplight leaking from the bedroom, he was out in the hallway and moving toward the Center Room of the Ministry apartments. Able to negotiate his way through the Center Room with its scanty shelves of books, the large pine secretary with desk lid, and the perfectly positioned large cane-bottomed rocking chairs, Ranks soon found himself at the end of the hallway of the upstairs Meeting Hall apartments occupied by the two women members of the Ministry. His flight-from-fear had been abruptly brought to a halt by a large wall and window. To his right there was a door. Thinking only of escape--escape from the fearful thoughts roiling around in his head; escape from the confinement of the building he felt had entrapped him; escape from the vision of his dream that kept playing out like a kineograph before his mind's eye-- he reached for the knob on the door. The next thing he knew he was standing in the middle of an unfamiliar place, with only the dim light from the just-rising sun outlining a few of the larger objects in the room. Where was he? What was he doing in this room, he wondered. Then, suddenly, he knew. He had come here seeking help. Assistance. Guidance. Something or someone sane.

"Sister Daniella!!" the desperate dreamer called out in the semi-dark. "Sister Daniella, I need your help!"

There was a garbled scream that came from the far corner where Ranks could barely make out a bed. A noise made in the spirit of combat that was created from instinct, from fear. Nothing quite of this world, yet very much a part of it.

"Who's there?!" the voice managed to articulate, more as a means of self-preservation than curious response to that which had woken the room's occupant from deep sleep.

"Sister Daniella, it's me--Wilford Ranks, I need your help."

"Brother Wilford? What on God's earth are you doing here in the middle of my room in the middle of the night?" Sister Daniella managed to say in a state of semi-consciousness.

"I need your help, Sister. I am troubled and need help. Forgive me, Sister, but I am desperate and need a calming presence."

There was a fumbling sound coming from the corner of the room where the Sister's voice came. And suddenly there was a burst of light that illuminated the room and Ranks could see the corner bed and bedstand and a body clothed in a long white gown rising up from the bed like a specter, like a ghost.

"Sister Daniella, is that you?" Ranks asked in an almost frightened tone. Daniella Darrow standing by the side of her bed gazed in curious disbelief at the figure of Wilford Ranks who still stood, helplessly, in the sparsely-furnished, high-ceilinged room. After identifying her intruder as being the person he claimed to be, she spoke: "Mr. Ranks, what in the devil ails you? Why have you come into my room in such a state? Have you been over-indulging in the Farm Deacon's home brew?"

"No, no Sister, I assure you, it is not that. I have woken up in the middle of the night with a racing heartbeat and a mind that is leaking its sanity like water from The Water House main. I fear I am going insane, Sister, and that my heart is about to burst from anxiety. Do you have something in your medicine box that might help? Or a word or two of wisdom to calm my nerves? Even a soothing smile would be welcome for this state I'm in."

"Mr. Ranks, have you come in here in the middle of the night to chase my affections? If you have, you had better get your sixty-year-old body out of here before I take a switch to it."

"No, no, Sister, I am indeed in trouble and in need of help. Please believe me, Sister, I have not come to you like this for any other reason than out of sheer desperation."

Daniella Darrow could now see the panic in Wilford Rank's eyes and hear the desperation in his voice. She moved away from the bed and walked towards him there in the middle of the big empty room.

Ranks began, now, to notice the details in the room in which he stood. Having never before set foot in a room on this side of the building, he noticed the wooden straight-backed caned chairs hanging on wooden pegs on a wall where a bonnet and hand-made day dress hung on hangers between two windows. On the facing wall was a solitary Shaker high-press of pine and stained red. At the foot of the press-of-drawers there was a ladder-like footstool for climbing in order to reach up and into the highest drawers. In the near corner to the door there was a small black Shaker woodstove with a narrow stovepipe coming from the top of the stove and extending up high to a right angle turn where the pipe disappeared into the whitewashed wall. On the floor at the foot of the single cherry bedstead were elaborately woven floor rugs. Everything was clean, spotless, and in its proper place--which was the Shaker custom, and in fact the Shaker purpose.

"Sister Daniella, you have quite a nicely-kept room, here. I've never looked in here before. But I can see that you are living comfortably and in appropriate style," the disoriented man mused.

"Brother Wilford," Daniella Darrow addressed the lost man standing in the middle of her boudoir, "as you have pointed out, this is not a social call. If you have come for medical assistance then let us keep our focus there. I would hate to think that you have come under false pretenses simply to gain entrance to my room in the middle of the night."

"Oh, no, no, Sister, I assure you, I have need of your help. Have you nothing to calm a man's fears or to soothe my brow?"

"I might be able to find a calmative for you, Wilford, but as to soothing your brow, I think we'll have to find an appropriate alternative to that request," Daniella answered rather sternly. "Sit yourself down in that rocker over by the window and let me look into my medicine-box and see what I might have that will help you. I'm pretty sure that I still have some of that 'nerve tea' concoction I made a few months ago--with chamomile, lemon balm and hibiscus." She stirred around in a small chest that sat at the end of her bedstead before exclaiming, "Yes, right here it is," holding up a canister as if for the whole world to see. "Here's a potion that's also got some pink rose petals, spearmint and sarsaparilla in it, too. If this won't help you to wind down then I don't know what will, she said in a physician-like tone and hoping to put a positive perspective on an otherwise very awkward, if not unprecedented, situation.

"Wellness comes when one combines amazingly flavorful teas with a fertile imagination and some other good things from nature," Daniella discoursed as she worked at spooning some of the tea from the canister into a wood-handled tin teapot that was sitting on the floor beside the cold cast-iron little woodstove. "I'll have to heat up this stove so I can boil this tea for you. This might take a few minutes. Will you be alright while we wait?"

"I think so, but I feel like my mind's about ready to explode, Sister. I've got such hateful thoughts running around in there that I hesitate to even give voice to them lest they turn into curses that might come true. I've never had such a set of nerves that I can remember. I don't know what brought this on, 'cept for maybe a dream I was having right before I woke."

"Would you like to share your dream with me, Brother Wilford? There might be some hint, there, as to why you're feeling like you do."

"No, no Sister, I don't think I want to do that, right now, thank you. I don't really want to get into it again, as I'd be embarrassed to tell you, as some of it is rather scandalous."

"Oh, I see, Brother Wilford," Daniella replied, in a rather sarcastic tone of voice. "So you've been out galavanting again at night in your dreams, have you?" she continues, with a smile coming to her face.

"No, no, nothing like that, Sister. It's just something that I'd rather not talk about--at least until another day when I'm in a better frame of mind and a little more relaxed."

"Well, as soon as this fire gets going and I can boil this pot of tea for you, we'll see if we can't get you at least on your way down the road to feeling better. Meanwhile, why don't you give me a few more details about your symptoms and the short history of how all this came about. That might help my diagnosis and I might be able to better assist you. But just you remember--keep your hands to yourself." Sister Daniella laughed as she placed the perfect old teapot on the stove.

Asher stood looking out the large window in a second floor room of the two-story white weatherboard building that had been rebuilt from its brick and stone noggin-frame original incarnation in 1817. What he saw were hills upon hills of cleared fields and pastures rolling away almost as far as the eye could see. His new home in the North Lodge with several other male converts and new inductees seemed strange in that he wasn't used to living dormitory style with a group of men. Yet in its strangeness there was a kind of calming nature about the place. Its sparseness and orderliness in terms of décor, its lack of distractions, its focus on detail rather than decoration. It was a peaceful place. Maybe too peaceful, he thought as he viewed the Shakertown landscape and beyond. Wistfully, Asher turned and faced the retiring room that would be his sleeping quarters for the next several months...white plaster walls lined with dark-colored pegboards from which four long maple wall sconces hung; three small bedsteads in a row on the south wall with black and white striped quilted blankets folded neatly near the footboard; a painted pine step stool; large rag rugs covering the floor upon which the three beds, from where he stood on the other side of the room, seemed to float; a nook that served as open closet, dressing room and tripled as a washroom--with washstand, large pitcher and bowl, a towel rack and a 12" x 18" mirror; a single cane-bottomed rocking chair; a tall cupboard and case of drawers made of light poplar wood with an orange-brown wash in the west corner; a small work table and a cherry and maple rocking chair against the east wall; a yellow wash ash and pine handling carrier next to the ever-present Shaker-design black woodstove with matching flu pipe rising and bending high up into the middle of the southern wall. Home. Such as it was. His new life. Sparse and spartan. Clean and without clutter.

Luckily Asher was a bit monkish by nature, so the minimalist surroundings didn't bother him. In fact, he quite liked the look and feeling of the simplicity of it all. Less clutter meant less distraction and, hence, hopefully more focus on what mattered. "A poet's place," he mused to himself. Yet, how would it be sharing this space with the two other men, both much older and from places unknown to him and very far away. One of the men was a man named Enoch Jacobs who had, upon his arrival at the North Lodge, referred to himself as a Millerite, from Cincinnati. The Millerites, Jacobs had proclaimed, were a spiritual sect founded in 1822 by a Baptist layman and farmer named William Miller who heralded from the "Burned over district" of New York state. Having a fixation for Bible prophecy, he had very publicly predicted the second coming of Christ on or before the year 1843. The actual "Millerite" movement had begun sometime around 1830 and had quickly become a national movement that was spread mainly through various Millerite publications, such as small newspapers and pamphlets. The other occupant of Asher's retiring room was a man named Anders Bloomberg, who was originally from Sweden but had migrated to Shakertown from a place called Bishop Hill in Illinois that consisted of a community of followers of the Swedish missionary Erik Jansson. The Bishop Hill "Janssonists," as they were called, were a utopian community who were dissidents from the Church of Sweden who believed in the perfectibility of nature and the possibility of living without sin. Both of these men had come to Shakertown and the Pleasant Grove community because they recognized a measure of common cause with the Shakers.

While Brother Jacobs had brought several other converts with him to Shakertown from the Cincinnati Millerites, he was the only one remaining of those who had found the Shakertown society attractive because the Believers took the Second Coming seriously. The others had found the principle of celibacy too difficult and had left, with one man, so Brother Jacobs recounted, stating that he "would rather go to hell with his wife than live among the Shakers without her." As for Brother Bloomberg, he, too, had brought with him and been visited by fellow Janssonists during the short time he had been there--many of them coming to Shakertown directly from Sweden--with almost all of them leaving soon after arrival. In Shakertown the colloquial term for the migrating Janssonists was the "Swede Stampede" and their coming and going was sarcastically referred to by the Pleasant Grove mainstays as "Swede trotting."

So, there Asher was in the North Lodge as part of the "Gathering Order." As he contemplated his fate he wandered over to the open closet area at the dark end of the room to the washstand with the basin and the pitcher of water. He took up the pitcher and poured an inch of some of the clear well water that came from the holding tank inside the Water House nearby into the large white porcelain bowl. He bent over the bowl, and with both hands cupped, scooped up as much water as his hands could hold and splashed it on his face, letting the water run off his forehead, eyelids and chin and back into the bowl. He did this two or three times and then reached for a cotton cloth hanging on the wooden rack to his left with which he hoped to dry his face and hands. As he soaked up the wet beads of water from his face with the fresh towel, he rose up to a normal standing posture and when he did he noticed that he was looking into the simple wood-framed mirror that hung from a peg in the pegboard that ran along the wall at a height of about six feet. In the mirror was his own face. A face, now, that he barely recognized with hair all trimmed in a Shaker bowl-cut and body adorned with simple, yet stylish Shaker peasant garb. As he stood there looking into the mirror-image of his own blue eyes, his visage began to change into something else. Change into someone else. Standing there looking into the 12" x 18" mirror he was looking at Kitt. As if Kitt were perusing her own perfection. Her own beauty. That angelic face. That mane of hair.

Asher imagined her hair, as he stood there in front of the mirror, being a chain of flowers. Wild and natural. Pleasurable poppies and clinging vines of wisteria. The beautiful eyes of tulips and the lasting beauty of stock. The comforting cones of petunia and the loyalty of pansies. The purity of lilies and the innocence of lilac. The bounty of hellebore and the warmth and virtue of garden mint. The wisdom of columbine and the grace of calendula. All these in braided chains framing her face and shoulders. Instead of the Medusa of Snakes, Asher's vision of Kitt was that of the Venus of Flowers. Something splendid. Someone who had emerged from a heartland of ferns, cyclamen and English ivy as opposed to the purlieus of stinging nettle and poison oak.

For days, now, Asher had gone without seeing her. Had, in fact, not even heard from her by story or by mail. Gradually, and in this moment before the mirror, he had become possessed by his image of her. An image that had come to him like Rapunzel in her tower. Hidden. High. Out of reach. Rather than something that was real, with white skin, dark pink lips, and magnets for eyes, she had turned into someone in one of his mother's tattered books that had sat untouched for years on a shelf in the livingroom. Lotte from Goethe's *Young Werther* perhaps. And like Werther's letters of love to Lotte, Asher had courted the young beauty Kitt. Both couples remained unrequited in their love. Asher ached as the realization passed through him, and he remembered Goethe's ending to his romantic coming-of-age saga. While Asher was not contemplating taking his own life as did young Werther, he did feel that part of his life had been taken away from him. Taken away and hidden somewhere in the world of silence. Somewhere in a world absent of form.

Asher looked into the mirror and again he saw himself. Again she had left him. Again she had disappeared. It was as if her presence, the fact of her, was something he imagined, and that the work of his imagination had created her from the very beginning. In this moment, he worked his imagination trying to bring her back. Bring her back into the mirror. Back, into this room. Into a body. A body he had felt with his hands. A body whose perfumes he had taken in with his nose. Whose music he had taken in with his ears. Whose brilliance he had taken in with his eyes. Where was she? When would he see her again? How would he see her again? Where would he see her again? The Dry House? The cemetery? The fields…in fresh-mown hay?

Asher believed in destiny. He believed in the power of love. The power of beauty over hatred and fear. But maybe even more than all of these, he believed in himself. He believed that he was born for a reason. That his life had a purpose. And that he was meant to fulfill that purpose, that "destiny." Why else, against all odds and breeding, would he have become a poet? Why else would his mother have read him books full of children's verse as a boy before bedtime, over and over, even after he could read on his own? Why else would he be standing in this barrenly beautiful room as a Shaker? Why else would he have found Kitt in the dance line and fallen in love? These questions ran through his mind like a stampede of wild horses. They ran around and around his face in the mirror. Her face. Her face that was also now his face. There was something inextricable in this thought. He was entangled in her. Just as the flowers had been entangled in her hair. Now, he was a part of her hair. That part of her that had become him. That was him being her. Being her body. Her otherness and how she was different from everyone else. Everything else. This moment of his aching to touch her. To hear the song of her voice. That self-made song that was him, in her.

"Is this too much to ask?" Asher spoke softly to himself, careful not to elevate his voice that others lurking but unseen might hear him talking to himself and think him queer. "Is this too much for a poet to ask?" He continued this train of thought in his mind, not allowing his thoughts to escape through the imperfect lock on his lips. "I want it all. And she is everything. She is It. The map of love. A map I have memorized. Each contour of hills. Each road. Each trail of blue water that weaves its way through pages of her skin. Over flesh mountains. Through laurel hells and bush. Down rock face and slippery slopes. Fields of grass…. The length of distance. The miles. The time. Since I have seen her. Until I will see her again."

Late afternoon; upstairs in the East Family Sister's Shop-- location for Shakertown silk worm and silk weaving and production enterprise. Kitt is working at what is her regular job of the moment as Eden enters the room.

Kitt: Oh, Eden, there you are. I was beginning to worry, wondering if you would come.

Eden: Sorry I'm late Sister Kitt, but I was detained. I hope that you've not had to do too much of the work because of my tardiness.

Kitt: No, it's ok. You're only a little late for your work duties, and I've covered for you. It's been a pretty slow day here at the silk farm today, so no damage done. But I've been anxious to talk to you, to get caught up, as we've not had a chance to have a real heart-to-heart conversation in some time. This time of year is always so busy with harvest and there are a few things on my mind that I'd like to share with you.

Eden: Sure. Let me take off my cloak and we can talk while we're working.

Eden goes to the pegboard on the wall behind the door she entered from and hangs her coat on one of the pegs. She comes back to the loom bench sitting up upon a wooden throne near a south-facing window that faces the spooling area where Kitt is working with what look like small spinning wheels.

Now, where were we? Show me what I need to do to help, as I've not worked much with the silk, and we can talk as we work.

Kitt: Here, let me show you about the silk and what we're doing. Over in the corner of the room you can see those large flat racks covered in netting. Those are where in the spring we put the worms when they are in the pupa stage. We feed them lots of mulberry leaves that we get when the leaves are tender and green. The silk worms gorge themselves on the mulberry leaves and soon they grow larger and begin making cocoons that are made of spun silk thread. Then, over there in that vat and fireplace, near the racks, is a big pot that is filled with hot water. The cocoons are placed in the pot of water to dissolve the cocoons. When the cocoons are dissolved, they are taken out of the water and the tiny threads of the cocoon are unraveled and rolled onto reels. Finally, this thin fiber is spun with other silk strands of thread to make an even stronger thread.

What we will be doing, because it is already fall and there are no cocoons to feed or put in the water-bath, is working with the reels and combining the strands to make a larger, stronger thread. These spinning wheels have been invented to do this work. As you can see, they work together--with three spools at the back of the machine that feed the separate threads through the eyes in the center and then twist them together and come out at the front, where we're sitting, and roll onto this single spool. It's our job to make sure the strands are feeding onto the single spool properly and to watch to make sure the threads coming off the three smaller spools at the back are not breaking as they come together in the center. If the threads should break, then you'll need to stop the wheel and re-connect the smaller, single threads to the centerpiece. You got all that?

Eden: Sure, I think so. This is all new to me, but it's very interesting. I know that the Society has been doing this ever since I came here, but I really don't know much about the history or the process. You'd think that I'd have done more with this as long as I've been here.

Kitt: Because it's so labor-intensive, it's done by the adults. That's why those of us who are younger don't know much about the silk production in the community. Sister Mary told me that we've been making silk and weaving silk since about 1820. It's not like the Seed business where most of it is sent out in the world and brings in a good income. Most of the silk products that are produced here in Pleasant Grove stay in the community or are sent up to some of the New England communities. All the bonnets, scarves, clothes linings and things that you have that are made of silk come from right here. I think that they have a silk production process down at the South Union community, too. Sister Mary says that the reason there are silk worm 'factories' here in Kentucky and not up in Virginia and in the north is that the geography is better here. Meaning it's better for silk worm raising and for growing mulberry trees.

So, there, that's a short lesson about the silk-making. You have any questions?

Eden: No, I don't think so. Just start up your wheel, there, and let me watch you while we talk. I'll get the hang of it pretty quick, I think.

Kitt: Good idea. Here, I'll start my wheel and you can watch. Meanwhile, I want to talk to you about a few things. I am in the throes of a grave dilemma and have no one to share it with, but thee. You know, of course, that our Asher has joined The Society and is somewhere, here, on the Pleasant Grove grounds as we speak.

Eden: Yes, I do know of this. And how I have come to know and all that goes with it, I will share with thee, later. But do go on....

Kitt: I got a letter from Asher a couple weeks ago, delivered by Sister Mary, telling me that he was going to join The Society. By the time I got it, it was too late for me to reply or to arrange a meeting and try and stop him from this folly. Now, I hear, he is already living in the North Lodge with the other new converts and inductees. Oddly, I've not seen him since he arrived, as I've been so busy with my work here at the silk farm and with the increase in the evening gatherings at the East Family Dwelling, that I've not been eating my meals at the Centre House. But sooner or later Asher and I are bound to run into each other, and I'm very troubled about that inevitability and how I will react and what I will say.

Eden: I'm surprised that he has not already sought you out. You know how he is when it comes to finding a way to get to you. He's very inventive and takes a kind of delight, I think, in his covert acts in the interest of love.

Kitt: Yes, you are right. I, too, have expected to see him appear at any moment and at any place--even here, today, for instance--which is why I am all ashambles with this whole situation. I never know what he will do next, or how I am going to respond.

Eden: What will you say to him when you do see him?

Kitt: I don't know. At first I was very upset and even angry with him for what he has done. Since getting his letter, however, some time has gone by and I find that I'm softening on that position. I have even, in fact, caught myself having feelings of tenderness and heightened anticipation of that first meeting. There's no doubt that I have deep feelings for Asher, and were this a different world or a different lifetime I have no doubt that we would be together. But our situation, as it is, is impossible. I tried to convince him of this at our last meeting and in my last letter to him. But you know how he is--when he gets an idea in his head, especially a romantic idea, he becomes blind to the realities around him and becomes single-minded in finding ways to manifest his idea. And that is just what has happened and I fear for him, as he really doesn't belong here amongst those of us who are trying to live separately from the rest of the world. He is a man of the world and belongs to it. He is the world's voice. He is a poet.

Eden: I hate to say it, but, if you'll remember I warned you early on about how all this could turn out. And, now, it turns out that my words have been somewhat prophetic. I'm not trying to gloat, here, in the face of your problems, but, I did, I told you that you were pursuing a dangerous, dead-end path by writing those letters and encouraging Asher. But, I'm not in a position to judge your situation or to even give advice, as there is something you don't know. I alluded to this when I arrived, as my excuse for being late. And now it is my turn to share a few intimate secrets.

Kitt: What do you mean?

Eden: Well....all these weeks since last spring when I have been carrying your letters and your messages to Asher at the General Store in Herodsville, you have been joking with me and teasing me about Asher's friend Caden. "Caden and Eden" you say, playing off the similarity in our names. Well, I think between your letters and your entanglement with Asher and the part I have played in all that, what you were experiencing became enticing for me, and so a similar sort of relationship began to develop between myself and Caden. We, too, began writing letters to one another. And since I was the one making trips into town for The Society, I could deliver my own letters, or, even better, respond to Caden's letters in person when we would talk at the store. So, all this time Caden and I have been doing our own version of "Kitt and Asher" on the sly.

Kitt: Why didn't you say something? Why didn't you tell me?

Eden: I was tempted to, of course, but with your work and your position in the Society, and the trying times you were going through with Asher, I just didn't want to burden you with my exploits. Besides, I knew you wouldn't approve and so I didn't want that rift to come between us. And....I have to admit, it's been fun sneaking around and getting to know Caden. You know, he's a very nice person, and smart, and not too hard on the eyes.

Kitt: "Sneaking around?" What exactly are you referring to when you say "sneaking around?"

Eden: That's the part that I was getting to and is the reason I was late to work, today. Caden knows about this place just south of here that's in a remote part of the woods along the river. It's a cave, in fact. An old "Indian Cave" Caden calls it. He's never really explained the

Indian part to me, but he says it's a place that very few people know about, and those that do use it as a secret and illicit meeting place. You know, a "rendez-vous." At least that's what Caden says. So, this is where I was this afternoon and why I was late. The ferryman who runs the ferry line across the river got busy on the other side of the river when we were ready to come back across, and we had to wait for about thirty minutes or so for him to come back and get us.

Kitt: So you and Caden were meeting in that cave today? How long have you been meeting him there? Does anyone know that you are doing this besides me?

Eden: You're the first person I've told. I tell you, now, as I know you will understand, since you have been doing similar things with Asher. I guess Caden and I have been going to the cave for the last month or so. Maybe a little longer than that. As you know, it's hard to find times and situations that allow us, here in Pleasant Grove, to get away. Especially without anyone knowing about it.

Kitt: Well, that ferryman knows about you and Caden. Don't you think he'll tell people and the word will get back to certain Believers and even to Caden's family?

Eden: I thought of that, too. But Caden knows the ferryman, as he does his business there at the store in Herodsville. Caden's worked out some sort of trade where he gives the ferryman credit for goods bought in the store, and for that service the ferryman has promised not to tell anyone of our little secret.

Kitt: I just hope you're right. While I think you're taking a big chance, here, I'm in no position to judge you, either. It's interesting to me, though, that you, of all people, would be behaving this way, as it was you who was so vehement in telling me not to do, essentially, the same thing by getting involved with Asher....

Well, aren't we a pair--with our illicit meetings with men in graveyards and old caves.

Well, now that I've been enlightened, let me just ask you what you think I should do about Asher, now that he's joined us and is living in Pleasant Grove. I'm sure you, yourself, have had to ponder such questions, since what you are doing has similar implications. So, now I'm coming to you as "the expert" for a change and asking for your wise counsel. Do you think I should write Asher a letter? I could send it by way of Sister Mary. It's important that we talk. But we can't be too obvious, as the Ministry is already suspicious of us and we certainly don't want to fuel Brother Wilford's fire.

Eden: Yes, isn't this a reversal of roles! Well, the way I see it is--we are both kinda in the same boat, and since this boat is headed upstream, we need to help each other row. That is, if we're going to get safely and in good time to where we're headed. While I don't have any real answers to your questions, I will say that I've come to believe that you have to follow your heart. We're taught to follow our Shaker doctrine and the social rules that have been set up for us, and for the most part I agree with them, but I'm beginning to think that there's a whole other part of life that we're maybe missing. And, like you, I've decided to explore that a little bit to see what it's all about. What do you think?

Kitt: I'm not the right person to ask, given my own behavior these last several months, but I guess I kinda agree with you--that there's more to life than only a lot of rules. And, who knows, maybe Mother Ann didn't have all the answers, after all. We're all only human, and so was she. So we're all fallible. And I've been thinking, lately, more about her early life and the fact that she lost at least one child, a daughter named Elizabeth, when she was young. And then there were her troubles and eventual divorce from her husband Abraham Standerin. And, then, all the violence that was perpetrated upon her during her time in jail and afterwards because of her unorthodox spiritual beliefs in England. I'm beginning to wonder if Mother Ann's attitudes about sex may have been a result of her own negative experiences regarding sex and its outcome. I've been re-reading what little historical record that we have on Mother Ann, and these questions have come about because of my recent reading. So, I guess you can say that I'm not real sure about all of this, right now. I'm as confused as anyone. And just because I get transmissions from Mother Ann doesn't make me any the wiser about these central questions surrounding our beliefs. Maybe Mother Ann will come to me one day in her usual way and set the record straight. That would be nice. But I don't really expect that will happen. Meanwhile, women like you and me stumble on about our lives and just hope for the best.

Eden: I hope you're right. I guess we're just doing the best we can. What else can we do?

Kitt: Well, good luck, Eden. I'm glad we've had this little chance to chat and get caught up with one another. Just you take care, and be careful. Now maybe you can help me untangle all the silk from this spool. I've really made a mess of things not paying enough attention to what I was doing and too much attention to what I shouldn't be doing.

Scene V.

The "Indian Cave," as it was known to the locals around Herodsville, or "The Devil's Lair" as it was known to the more pious Baptists in the county, was an old cave on the far side of the river from Shakertown which was so-named due to the many petroglyphs and symbols carved into the cave's limestone walls. These pictographic images of bears, deer and birds along with other symbols and "strange markings" had been there for a "long time." A long time according to Caden's parents, who had told him that they had first heard about the cave from their parents, or Caden's grandparents, which would mean that the markings had been there at least since around the turn of the century. The "devil" connotation was largely a myopic reaction from the local Christians who considered any kind of animistic, pantheistic or mythical worship to be nothing less than "the devil's work." On the other hand, there were a few people of a more historical and scholarly persuasion in the community who believed that the glyphs, symbols, and especially what looked to be a sort of strange lettering, were somehow associated with the famous Cherokee chief Red Bird-- who had been buried for a time in the cave. These more open-minded folks, including some of Red Bird's own kinfolks still living in the area, were very vocal about the fact that Red Bird, himself, had created some of the petroglyphs while he was still alive and before he was tomahawked to death in 1796 by two white men in a fur trading dispute. These relatives and local historians believed that the pictographic images of the bears, deer, birds and bats were definitely the handiwork of Red Bird.

Then, there was the question of the strange symbols and the lettering. Caden's father had told him that a Cherokee man named Sequoyah had relatives who lived near the cave and that they had told him that Sequoyah had invented an alphabet and a system of writing that he later taught to others and that became the first written language for any tribal peoples living on the upper part of the North American continent. Caden's father had told him, for instance, that Sequoyah had taught his syllabary to Cherokee boys who were studying at a local school called the Choctaw Academy. Since it was known that Sequoyah visited the cave to pay his respects to Red Bird and for inspiration while he was working on his Cherokee alphabet, it seemed reasonable enough to Caden that Sequoyah, or one of his students, could have carved these letters, which seemed to be based somewhat on rock-art motifs, into the cave's limestone walls. Near the strange alphabet-like letters there was, also, a date: 1808.

On one of Caden's early visits to the cave, he had taken Asher, and the two of them had spent all afternoon one Sunday after church studying the glyphs, making up their own interpretations of possible meanings, as well as imaginatively extrapolating upon their origin. It was right about this time that Asher had shown a real interest in poetry, and his perceptive sensitivity had picked up on the fact that there were certain rock-art motifs in some of the individual symbols engraved into the walls of the cave and in the fifteen or so Cherokee letters from Sequoyah's alphabet.

"You see, Caden, how these stylized images over here on the wall are similar to these three alphabet-letters over here?" Asher had recently pointed out to Caden, while trying to break the code and interpret the images on the limestone walls of the cave. "If the picture symbols were made first, then these three letters in Sequoyah's alphabet were probably taken, or at least influenced by the old rock art images--which were, in their own way, a kind of picture-language. You see what I'm getting at here? If I'm right, then what we're seeing on the walls of this cave is of great importance. In essence, it's where prehistory meets history. Where the old meets the new."

Asher had visited the cave many times in the early days trying to make a poetic translation of the letters and symbols, thinking they must all be linked together to form some sort of "ancient poem"--as he would refer to his imagined unified theory--that combined all the disparate elements his creative mind could conjure. While this was way beyond Caden's abilities of perception, he went along with Asher's theories and fantasies to humor him, while at the same time poking fun at many of his translations and ideas. One of Asher's story lines for the Indian Cave glyphs told the tale of Little People living in caves and a magician who gave the animals voices and a language. In this story the bears and deer had wings and could fly in the sky with the buzzards and the bats. All this was told by a wise rabbit to his friend, the snake. In the story the buzzard had been sent out of the cave, where all the animals had resided for all time, to find water for them to drink. The buzzard came back with stories of a beautiful land with waterfalls and rivers and oceans. Excited by the buzzard's stories, the other animals begged the magician for wings of their own, so they could also fly out from the cave and see this beautiful world for themselves. And so the magician granted their wishes and one by one each of the animals took their turn flying out of the cave and coming back with their own tales of the places they had visited.

Asher had a way of telling this tale as he pointed to each of the pictographs, symbols and alphabet characters as he went along. Caden enjoyed these storytelling sessions, as each time Asher told the mythic tale, it would be a little different from the time before. And, so, over the years, the two boys had visited the Indian Cave and the tale of the mythic animals and the Little People had evolved.

Asher, too, was fascinated by Caden's telling of his father's knowledge of Sequoyah and the story of how Sequoyah had watched white settlers make marks on paper--what he had referred to as "talking leaves." Sequoyah believed, local lore had it, that these talking leaves were the source of the white man's power and success. This observation and belief, according to Caden's father, is what inspired Sequoyah to make the creation of a Cherokee alphabet the main mission of his life. Asher instinctively understood the intricacies of Sequoyah's passion about language. He, too, as a boy, had played around with inventing his own languages, each with its own set of characters. So, Sequoyah's story was an inspiration to Asher and fueled his escalating interest in language, literature, and poetry in particular--which to him was a symbolic language, unique from other forms of writing. He saw poetry as a kind of magic script born of magicians and scribes from other times and other worlds. For these reasons and others appropriate to the natural inclinations of boys and young men, Asher, and sometimes Caden, made the cave a primary destination in their excursions away from the confines of Herodsville, and visited there often.

Asher and Caden sat at the back of the old Indian Cave watching the rain pounding down on the red clay earth outside along the banks of the river. It was the first time that Caden and Asher had seen one another since Asher's move to Shakertown. Asher was there at Caden's invitation as Caden had been missing his old friend and was anxious to know how he was doing, as well as to hear the stories about Shaker life. Wednesday was Caden's day off from his duties at the General Store, the same as it was Asher's designated day to work on the farm. But the rains that week had saturated the fields and had prevented Asher's being able to work at harvesting the fall field-corn, so an impromptu meeting had been set up between the two. As they sat in the back of the cave and out of the rain, they found themselves discussing the rock carvings and the graffiti just above their heads that had appeared there in the cave in more recent years.

"You know, it's been a long time since you and I have been here in this cave together, my friend," Asher reminisced. "I remember you telling me about it for the first time when we were back in school. Your dad knew about it and had mentioned it in passing to one of his customers in the store and you had overheard their conversation. The next day, you and I were out tramping along the river looking for the cave. I remember it took us damn near all day to finally find it. But we did, and were immediately drawn to the rock carvings and the lettering and all."

"Yep, I remember. Then you went on about what the writing probably meant and kept coming up with all kinds of crazy translations every time we'd come out here. Finally, my dad told me about the connection to the Cherokee Sequoyah and the Indian alphabet. Oh, and don't forget the time that we brought Debbie Humphries and Wanda Ferrier out here, thinking we were gonna get lucky. I'll never forget that fiasco. Debbie got drunk and got spooked by your made-up Indian ghost stories and went running out of the cave and fell into the river. I remember we had a helluva time getting her out of the water and then back home without her parents finding out--which of course they eventually did and she was grounded and you were banned from the Humphries' house for ever thereafter. Yep, those were the days."

"I'd forgotten about that. Yeah, that was a disaster. One of many, I might add. Boy, if she wasn't a piece of work, that Debbie Humphries. It's probably a good thing that she got drunk that day and was forbidden to see me again. It wasn't long after that, I remember, that she mysteriously disappeared from school. Story was that she had been sent up to Frankfort to live with her aunt. I always thought that was a little odd--that she would suddenly up and move to Frankfort. Then, just as mysteriously as she disappeared, she came back--about a year later--and finished up with school in Herodsville."

"I agree. And you know, since then this cave has become pretty popular, as I guess about everyone knows about it, now. You see up there on the wall near all those Cherokee letters you used to try and translate? There are all kinds of new carvings on the wall. People's names and dates. Some with hearts around them--like that one, there, that says 'CF loves DH'. Looks like ole Debbie brought Charlie Freed back here and showed it to him. Maybe this is where they 'did it,' you know? And why she had to leave and go up to Frankfort to live with her aunt. And over there's another one. 'TD + KD'. Don't know who that could be, but I bet people come here from far and wide to meet in secret. Maybe some of them come to see the cave drawings and all, but this place has a reputation for being a place for couples to meet and make out. Me and Eden have been coming here recently. I've been meaning to tell you about that, but you're so hard to hook up with these days."

"You've been seeing Eden? Here at this cave?!"

"Yeah, ever since she started comin' to the store and bringing those letters between you and Kitt, I've had my eye on her. Then after you left to move up to Shakertown, we started getting pretty close. Then before we knew it we were coming up here to the cave and sparking."

"Sparking?!" You and Eden have been comin' up here to the Indian cave and sparkin'?!"

"Well, yeah. After all, it was you and Kitt that kept teasing us and trying to put us together."

"We were only teasing you. But, now that I think of it, both Kitt and I probably wished that the two of you would get together--so we'd have some companions in crime. But I had no idea you were actually seeing her. And sparking!"

"How could you have? You've been hid out up in Shakertown doing whatever you do up there--which I imagine is mostly chasing Kitt around like she was a bitch in heat. Us folks who still live in Herodsville, we have lives, too. You should be happy for us. After all it was you and Kitt that lit the spark that started the whole thing."

"Ok, I'll take the blame, but ain't you takin' a big risk meeting that girl here to have sex?"

"You should talk! I bet you've been into Kitt pretty good by now, seeing that you're livin' within a few feet of each other up there in Shakertown."

"No, as a matter of fact, I haven't. In fact, I've not even had a chance to talk to her in person since I moved in up there. She's been busy over at the East Family House with her visions and manifestations and as an 'instrument' of all that at night, or over at the East Family Shop working with the silk worms during the day. Either way, I don't ever even get to see her. But, I wanted to show you... I got this letter from her just yesterday."

Asher pulled a rumpled-up letter from his back pocket and handed Caden the piece of paper that he began to read..
"In here, she writes that she wants to see me. Here, you can read it for yourself."

Dear Asher,

It has been such a long time since I have seen you. I know you are here, now. But where are you? Eden says that she has seen you once or twice from a distance and that you are staying in the North Lodge with The Gathering Order. I hope that you like it there and are making friends with the other men who are coming into the Society. But I am not writing this letter to you to chit-chat. I know why you are here, and I feel responsible for that--even though your becoming a Shaker was not my idea. I really think that we should meet. There is so much, now, to talk about, and I worry about you and about your choice to live here amongst us. I don't think this segregated life we live, here, is a good fit for you. And I worry about your expectations about us--and our ever being able to be together. Yet, at the same time, I like knowing that you are near. I can't explain it. It's almost as if we were together, but aren't. I can feel you just a couple buildings away at night, and that gives me an odd kind of comfort. Oh, I can't go on, here, about my feelings for you. It isn't fair to either of us. We need to talk. Can you meet me somewhere sometime this week? Since I have been staying at the East Family House lately, I have been given my own room since a few of the newer women have left us and there is temporily some extra space. This not only gives me some privacy, but allows me a certain amount of freedom of movement--especially at night. I will wait to hear from you about where and when......

Caden looked up from the paper and gazed at Asher, who had been running his fingers over the old Cherokee script tracing the lines and forms on the cave wall.

"Sounds to me like she's wantin' to spark. Am I wrong?"

"Yes, you are wrong. That's not the way Kitt is. She's not one of those floozies, like those Parker girls. She just wants to see me. I knew that once I was actually living in Shakertown she'd warm up to the idea of my being there and my being close by. It's probably been a good thing that we haven't run into each other as yet. I think that this has given her some time to think, and to miss me. You know what they say--absence makes the heart grow fonder."

"So, what you gonna do?"

"Write her back, I guess. Set up a meeting. Now that it's getting colder at night, we'll probably have to meet inside somewhere. So, I'll have to think of a place that is cozy but not where we are likely to be seen together. That'll take some thought, as it's like a spider's web livin' in Shakertown. Not much chance for alone time or opportunities for secret liaisons."

"Lee-ay-zons? What kind of word is that? There you go, using those fancy words, again. I can see nothin's changed. You're the same old Asher. Shaker or no Shaker."

"Yeah, ok. But what I want to know is: what are YOU gonna do?"

"What do you mean?"

"I mean, what are you gonna do about Eden? With you two sparkin' and all. What if she gets pregnant? You thought of that?"

"Eden says that since she was a virgin our first time, that we're safe until she gets her next period. That's coming up pretty soon, so then we'll have to think of something else. Don't worry, I ain't takin' any chances."

"Alright, my friend, just don't do anything stupid. I worry about you, you know. You being such a knuckle-head," Asher said, laughing.

"Look who's calling the kettle black. If your joining the Shakers isn't the most knuckle-headed thing I've ever seen, I don't know what is."

"Ok, Caden, I've got to get back to Shakertown for dinnertime, or else I'll be missed. Let's stay in touch. You can send letters, or we can plan to meet pretty much as often as we like. The Ministry doesn't mind, I don't think, that I see my old friends and family once in a while as long as it doesn't interfere with any work. Working is what these folks are all about. So, take care my friend, and I'll send you my new theory about the translations of these Cherokee letters and symbols when I get it all written down. I'll give you a hint--I think it's a story about the bear and the deer falling in love, and the bird is carrying messages between the two of them."

"Just what I would have expected you'd say. You know, you'll never change."

Kitt waited impatiently underneath the large wooden tank in the Water House for Asher to arrive. She held his letter in her hand. The one he had written in response to her own, which included a plea for reason, yet was filled with hidden passion and evocative enthusiasm. At least this is what Asher had read into her words. On the other hand, Asher's letter, while exhibiting some discipline and restraint, had been filled with poetry. His poetry, as it always did, had overwhelmed Kitt, and had led to her agreeing to meet him in such an unromantic place for their first tryst.

The Water House was located a hundred yards behind the Centre Family Dwelling on an almost imperceptible rise in the landscape. A small inconspicuous two-story wooden structure, it was built to hide from sight and from vandals the ungainly structure of the large wooden water tank and to keep the water cool in the summer and from freezing in the winter. The water storage tank at Pleasant Grove was concealed in a building that blended in with the other buildings around it that were constructed as residences for members of the Society. Fed from a nearby underground spring or and powered by a horse or mule-powered pump system, the large eleven-foot-in-diameter wooden tank was girded by iron bands and sat on three large piers built of chiseled stone. The tank was elevated enough for water to flow freely to cook-stove boilers and other apparatuses in the Centre Family Dwelling, the East Family Dwelling, as well as the Wash Houses and several other community buildings. A perfect and unlikely place for a covert meeting between two young lovers.

As Kitt waited for Asher's arrival, she untied the string that wound around the folded paper that was the letter, and by the light of a full moon coming in through the small, solitary window on the front wall of the Water House, began to read.

I am disappearing
Into the side of your body.
Your body, which when it lifts
And turns, also moves the Earth.
I have given up the toys of my childhood
And my ambitions for old age.
And have moved deep within
The walls of your silver skin.

> I am through with my love of suffering.
> And the words that describe that love.
> I am going to carry on a magnificent
> Affair with the wind
> From the inside of your body
> Where we both sleep.
>
> Friend, I am going deeper, even
> Deeper inside than the animal
> Or a blade of grass-
> I am looking for the stones.
> The stones that lie to the side
> And in the bed of the Great River.
> Among those stones,
> There is only one rock with my name.
> I will pick it up
> And hold it high above my head
> In the inner light.
>
> I will know many things.
>
> Outside, with your body, you
> are teaching the world to dance!

As she read the words of Asher's poem written in his usual fluid and artistic handwriting, she felt tears coming to her eyes. With the soft cotton sleeves of her overcoat, she brushed away the water that was flowing freely with gravity, as if it were coming from a reservoir of the heart. She felt so very close to Asher in this moment. The poem had had its effect. But she didn't want him to see her crying, even though she was crying with love.

Sitting near the front window, yet at an angle where from outside she cannot be seen, she could hear the cast-iron latch upon the door to the Water House move. She watched as it began to open and the form of a man in Shaker clothing, limb by torso by limb, stepped through the threshold. It took her a moment to see the full figure and to recognize it as Asher. Once inside, Asher gently shut the door behind him. At first, he didn't see Kitt sitting over to his right against the wall and by the window, her brown frock and bonnet serving as a kind of camouflage blending in with the aging wallboards. As Asher took a few steps into the building and moved past the first wall of stone piers holding up the 10,000 gallon wooden tank, the sound of her voice calling out his name startled him. From where she sat, Kitt watched Asher's form disappear behind the stone pillars, then stared in surprise as his face appeared from around the corner and behind the stones like something she had seen in a puppet theatre performance as a child.

"Hey there!" Asher proclaimed, smiling and with a bit of an impish grin. "So that's where you've been hiding from me all this time! How are you, my love?

" Would that I knew I were."

"What's that. I didn't understand. Can you say it again?"

"How much you look like a Shaker. As if you were born to be one. Let me look at you--to make sure you are really the same Asher I used to know," she comes back, avoiding his question and her previous comment.

"Shaker. It's only a name. I am still the same Asher who met you in the Meeting Hall one afternoon and who loves to send you poems from my own pen."

Kitt took the letter from her lap and held it up so Asher could see it. "Then, I'm so glad it is you. For I have been reading this poem and it has moved me much. I had come here, a lioness, with the intention of beating thy brow for the acts you have taken of late. Instead, you send me a poem that has made a lamb of me. How is it that you can have such influence over my soul?"

"I don't know, angel. All I do is write and things appear on my paper that I cannot, in all my humility, claim to be author of."

"Oh, Asher, so little time has passed since we last met, and yet so much has changed. What will we ever do?"

Asher took a few steps away from the stone wall and moved closer to where Kitt was seated. "We are doing it, now, my sweet light. Even in this dreary place, the moonlight shines on thy face and makes planets of your eyes. Even in this damp house of water, when you speak my name the place does fill with light."

"Now I remember, again, how I do love your company. Say something more. Tell me a story, and if not a story, convince me of your love."

"I have come but a short distance to be near you. From Herodsville to Shakertown, only. Yet, I would have crossed oceans with the same ease of resolve to find myself again at your side. You must believe me."

"You're making me blush, Asher. Your words, your poems, your voice. I have no resistance, no defense, no resolve. Would you take advantage of me? Surely you have known all along what effect your words have on me. I feel like a ripe raspberry, red and ready to be plucked."

"Would that it were so. I would savor the taste of you as much as I do the sight. Surely you would be pleasant to the lips as much as you are to the eyes. Perhaps we should have a taste and see." As Asher moves closer to Kitt, he reaches for her hand. She lets go of the letter in her lap and freely gives it. Asher takes her hand and formally raises it to his lips and kisses her on the palm.

"How do you find it--the taste of my palm?"

"Just as I imagined--like sweet raspberries, and with a touch of sage."

"Does it make you want more. Is my taste that good?"

"Oh, yes. Not only would I love more raspberries, but I would love to have some of those peaches, too! And do I not also see some luscious plums? Ah, and there an apricot! All this fruit has made me hungry, my love."

"You have used that word, again. It comes so easily from your lips. Do you mean it, or is it just a favorite phrase?"

"What word is that?"

"The short little word that starts with L."

"Luscious? Lips? Like? Light? I have used all of these. Which one is the one you mean?"

"Oh, Asher, stop playing with my emotions. You know very well that the word I mean is the word 'love.'"

" Oh, that one. I apologize, but my memory is like that of my grandfather, it loses track of things and cannot find them. I will say it again if you will show me your mane of hair.

Kitt paused at Asher's request, but moved, almost unconsciously, to obey--untying the strings of the bonnet beneath her chin and removing the cotton cap from her head. When she did this, her long, heavy auburn hair fell to her chest almost audibly as Asher continued his soliloquy. "Oh yes, how I have been longing to look again upon that mane. It is your best part."

"My best part?"

"The best part of all the parts I have seen--which are few--since most of you is covered up with your clothes."

"What are you saying, Asher?"

"I'm saying that if it were not for your clothes, there may be other parts of you that I could see that I would like--dare I say "Love" again--more than your hair."

"Would you ask me to take off my clothes?"

"Those are your words. But these are my eyes," Asher says pointing with his index finger on his right hand to his eyes. "And these eyes would love--sorry, I've said it again--to see more of you, especially since I've seen very little of you, of late."

"Since you are wont to use the word so freely, do you love me? Do you mean it when you use that word? And what does that word mean to you, oh poet, for I know you love to play with words. Would you play like this, too, with my heart?"

"Which question do you want me to answer first? You have asked me four and within but one breath."

"Choose any one you like, but in answering answer them all. If I am to disrobe before thee, your true answer depends upon it."

"You do put me to the test. Having never been in this position before, I don't know what I will say."

"Well, you better say something soon, as this night is not getting any younger, and neither are we. I need to hear what you have to say lest we have little to say to one another but of the weather or of our pet peeves."

"I won't mince words, then, Kitt. I love you. I have since the day I saw you--there in the dance-line on the Meeting House floor. I think you know that. I could see it in your eyes. And I felt the same love coming from you. I love you, maybe even more when we are apart. No matter where I have been, whether in Herodsville or in the Dry House here in Shakertown, I have loved you."

"You swear?"

"Yes, I swear. I swear by the moon outside that window. I swear by the water in that tank," Asher utters as he motions to the water tank looming large above them. "I'll swear by anything you like."

"Simply swear by your own self. And make me believe thee. Then I might show you more than my hair."

Asher took Kitt by the hand and raised her up from her seat on the plank by the window. He drew her to him, looking her in the eyes, and kissed her gently on her lips. "This is my pledge, my troth. Now do you believe me?"

"Will you leave me so unsatisfied? You think that from one little kiss I should give so much of myself. You think my worth so small?"

"Here, let me try again. I didn't want to be so bold and run the risk of scaring you away. Let me give you a second and then a third, or as many kisses as you like. For you are worth every one and all the rest that may be left undone."

"Oh you are forever reaching for a rhyme, aren't you my poetry-man? But trade your rhymes, now, for kisses and give me my due." As Kitt speaks these words, Asher pulls her to his breast and kisses her--a long, sensuous kiss that takes Kitt's breath away. "That's more like it. My self-respect is coming back. But I may need yet another to set the scales back into a balanced place. Have you something more to place upon the scales?"

"Indeed I do, my red raspberry," Asher says as he kisses her again. "Now, where do we stand with regard to your pride and fair market value?"

"I am convinced, and I have been paid in full. It has been a pleasure doing business with you, sir. But if this business deal of ours is to be consummated, I have one more question to ask of thee."

"Ask away. For you, I am an open book."

"If your sworn testimony of love is honorable as you say it is, and if you would have me give my honor and all my love to you in return, then what are you willing to pay?"

"What is the price you would ask, my princess? Everything I have is yours. I would give you everything. Even that which I don't possess."

"And does marriage come as part of this package deal?"

"If marriage is your asking price, then I will pay it. And as for your scales, my lovely friend, you are worth your weight in gold."

This time it was Kitt who took Asher by the arms and pulled him to her. She embraced him and kissed him fully on the mouth before speaking. "Then let this kiss consummate the sale. Sworn testimony of love in exchange for a glance at my body, naked, and without clothes," she promised as she kissed him again.

Following the last kiss, Kitt began to disrobe. Slowly and even shyly she took off one element of clothing after another as Asher watched with increased longing. When Kitt had taken all the clothing from her body, she stood tall facing Asher, her long auburn hair covering her shoulders and breasts and part of her belly. For a time the two of them stood in an aura of disbelief and just looked at one another in admiration and awkward surrender. Then, just as awkwardly, Asher took off his coat. He followed this by taking off his vest and shirt before undoing the suspenders to his trousers and letting them fall past his knees to his feet, covering his shoes. Kitt let out an almost inaudible giggle as Asher's pants hit the floor with a thud and as he bent down to untangle his legs from his pants and remove his shoes. Soon the two of them were standing face to face and totally disrobed. They looked for what seemed like a long time at each other's body, much as an explorer might gaze for the first time upon a map of a newly-discovered land. Finally, the silence was broken and Kitt spoke.

"I'm cold, Asher. We need to do something to get warm."

"Sure. Yes. Let's make a little pallet back here between the stone pillars and underneath the water tank, where it's a little warmer and there's no cool breeze blowing in from around the window and underneath the door. I'll make a pallet and my body will keep yours warm. Promise."

Asher picked up his and Kitt's clothes that lay in two separate heaps on the hardwood floor, gathered them all to his chest and turned and moved toward the middle of the Water House and between the second and third row of stone piers, where he spread his long greatcoat down on the floor and then placed the rest of his clothes, and then Kitt's, ritualistically on top of the coat, giving the make-shift pallet as large and as soft a texture as possible. When he had finished with his mattress-making, he lowered himself onto the paillasse of clothes and once seated motioned for Kitt to join him at his side.

The two embraced, and as Asher felt the silk-like warmth of Kitt's skin, and as second by second the time that they shared went by, he experienced, for the first time, himself becoming complete, becoming whole. He stroked her mane of hair and she kissed his neck. As they knelt there on the Water House floor, Asher had an epiphany. He was experiencing Beauty. Beauty in its complete sense. Male and the female. Wholeness and emptiness. In this moment, he leaned slightly away from Kitt so that he could just look at her, wanting to revel in the beauty that was her face. That was her body. That was her supple spirit. If the "chase" had been as exhilarating as it was exhausting, "the capture" or the union of their two bodies was, for Asher, approaching ecstasy. Kneeling there on the bolster of clothes facing Kitt, Asher felt himself being overwhelmed, almost to the point of tears, by the beauty of her body. For a long time, it seemed, he just knelt there admiring her body as one might admire a work of art. And her body was, if anything, a gloriously organic piece of God's best work. The contours and ridges of her kneeling figure were like a mirrored replication of the Pleasant Grove farmland itself. And Asher, there in the midst of the harvest about to pick the fruit.

The next thing Asher knew he and Kitt were rolling around on their make-shift bed. What was happening wasn't sex, it was poetry. This was "Lass With the Bright Brown Hair" entwined with him there. Running his "yearning fingers through her silk brown hair." His fingers running through her hair "like rivers from his soul." Her lips, "like tidal pools, those little bowls" beneath him. From Kitt's perspective, she may as well have been the maid in Burns' "The Lass That Made the Bed To Me"--as she had invited Asher into her "chamber fair" and there, with her "cheeks like lilies dipped in wine," she had "wrapped her arms about his neck" on "a bed both large and wide"--as there on their bed of Shaker rags this old Scottish verse had come to life.

After the flames that had been ignited by their body friction finally died down, Asher lay there next to Kitt in a physical state of stunned reverie. There were no words that came to his mind. "No words for a poet?" the fleeting question crossed his almost empty mind. Yet, then, one word appeared and remained. The word was "love." Kitt's word: love. Earlier he had not really known from where she had been coming with their games of word-play and probing for depth of honesty and commitment when she had referred to love. It was just another word that he was parrying as if the two of them had been in a fencing match where there were no winners or losers, and where only pride and cleverness were at stake. But now, in this moment, Asher was realizing what Kitt meant by love, what that word meant to him. Asher also knew in this moment that although he was in "heaven," that there would be hell to pay. But that thought quickly vanished from his mind, as the overwhelming love that he was feeling for this woman, for this woman's body, for the incredible spirit that this body encased was all that mattered. Was his whole world.

"My wild pup, are you ok?" Asher asked, breaking the silence like the sound of a large rock entering a small body of water in the woods.

"Yes, and you my blonde-haired Shakespeare, are you ok?" Kitt replied.

"There's an owl outside that is hooting. It seems to be talking to us. Maybe it is warning us that someone is coming, or that we ought to leave."

"Or maybe it is just singing to the music that we have been making together. The sounds of our bodies moving together like a violin. Our groans and moans like all of the Believers in Shakertown at Sunday Service singing Shaker hymns. But you're right, soon it will be daylight and we need to be back in our respective rooms where we are expected to be. Although I don't want to move from this place, I know we must. So let's get up, pick up our pallet, put our clothes back on, and say our farewells."

They both rose from their bed-of-clothes and began sorting out one piece of clothing after another and putting them back on their bodies. Soon they were fully dressed and standing in the same facing position where they had begun the evening, gazing at one another with a kind of innocent knowing. This time it was Asher who broke the silence.

"Just give me one last kiss and I'll go."

"This is so hard. This is even harder than it was at the beginning. I don't want to leave you. Ever. Promise me that I'll hear from you every day. And if I don't hear your voice or see your face, I will receive your words on paper. The next week will seem like years."

"I will make every effort to see you every day and to hold you when I can, and to tell you how much I love you. Do you believe me now, when I use this word?"

"I do."

"Then with those two words, as if a marriage vow, we are betrothed--in spirit, since no Shaker service or body will acknowledge our pledge--in this holy place where we are surrounded womb-like by water."

"In God's eyes I believe we are as one. I only hope that each time we meet it will be to exchange sweet words to one another and not a list of woes. While I feel almost nothing but joy when I look at you in this moment after our first time making love, there is also a hint of sorrow in my soul that makes me want to weep."

"Tears of joy, is all they are, Kitt. Tears of joy. All will be well."

"I hope so, Asher, but if I know anything I know that God is fickle and that what sometimes comes as brightness is not always light. I feel shadows in my joy, Asher."

"It's only fear, love. A fear of firsts. A fear of the unknown. Everything will be fine."

"Spoken like a true poet. I love you, Asher. Go now. And go in peace. And take my love. Carry it with you always, near your heart. Although, physically, my body may be elsewhere, from now on, within your chest is where I live."

"Farewell, and feel no sorrow. For I will see thee 'gain tomorrow."

"Oh, you and your Shakespeare. Go on before your words turn, again, to nothing but wit."

Asher turned and headed toward the Water House door, but turned back as he crossed the threshold and with a sweeping gesture of his arm and in a grande Shakespearean salutation, uttered: "Sweet dreams, princess."

Scene VI.

Fall was casting its last shadows on Shakertown. As the leaves fell and the chill of the coming winter made its presence known, so, too, would life amongst the Society experience its fall from grace. In one of his poems written that autumn from the confines of his residence in the old North Lodge, Asher's words seemed prophetic in his references to love and its similarities to the seasonal changes he had noticed in his natural surroundings.

> *Fall is the season of the poem!*
> *The cold breeze of the mind*
> *As it talks to the earth*
> *In the language of fallen leaves --*
>
> *When I say to the woman I love, "I love you,"*
> *All she hears is the voice of my pain.*
> *It is when I reach for her hand that my heart speaks!*
>
> *What is winter saying to this fall?*
> *Is it some sweet goodbye?*
> *Or the lullaby of an ancient kiss?*
>
> *It is this:*
> *From the seed that once gave birth to the tree,*
> *To the tree we will return and embrace.*
> *Each year. As fallen leaves.*
> *From grace.*

As the leaves left the deciduous trees in Shakertown and fell molted into winter and the Millerite predictions of the end-of-the-world that would occur with the turn of the new year, all of these things, as well as Asher's poem, seemed to be stark indicators, if not signposts of what would come.

As the weeks and months passed, and the recently-adopted Millennial Laws were brought into full enforcement to try and negate the excesses in the practices of spiritism that had swept through the Shakertown colony during the past few years. These new regulations--which focused to a large extent upon laws dealing with intercourse between the sexes and all the regulation's "forbidden practices," coupled with a goodly number of new as well as old Believers leaving the community due to the severity of the regulations banning communication and relations between the sexes--had an overall calming, if detrimental, effect upon the Shakertown Society. These so-called "holy laws" that served to more clearly define the boundaries between the Society and the world, had raised the so-called "standards of purity" among the Believers, and had given the Ministry more power by enlarging their areas of supervision. Aside from these provisions in the Millennial Laws, there were rules focusing on appropriate behavior in the Meeting Hall and during worship services. One of the orders actually read: "All should go into the meeting in the fear of God walking on their toes." The impact of the enforcement of the regulations of the Millennial Laws was considerable. Traditional patterns of communal living were emphasized and obligation to maintain neatness, cleanliness, quiet and civil conversation were also given heightened priority. In short, Shakertown had become "a much more safe and civil place," to quote one of the members of the Ministry. A place where there was a lot less tolerance for innovation and excess.

Despite the progress toward the status quo in Shakertown, in Herodsville Reverend Pope continued his crusade against the Pleasant Grove Believers.

"The facts are clear. All their miserable pretence of cleanliness and neatness is the thinnest superficiality. These neighbors of ours, these Shakers, are a filthy bunch. Their utter and systematic lack of privacy, the close function of man with man, and supervision of one man over another--it is disgusting to think of. The sooner the sect is extinct the better. From what I have heard and the way things are going up there in Shakertown, it looks as if their end could be drawing near, I am happy to say," Reverend Pope railed from his pulpit. "The tales coming out of Shakertown these days are shadowy omens of disappointed hope and unavailing toil. Indeed, their wished-for apocrophal end-times could very well be coming sooner than they think."

In this changed environment, Kitt and Asher continued to carry out their various modes of communicating, as well as their occasional rendezvous, as their relationship grew and one could even say blossomed, given all the restrictions and hardships imposed upon them by the very nature of Shaker life. They found ways to overcome the obstacles imposed by social limitations by becoming somewhat creative in their means of communicating as well as in their place of assignation. While the Water House was and would always be a favorite love nest, other places on, and off, the Shakertown premises also served as pallets for their well-thought-out trysts. The East Family Wash House was, they found, a safe place to meet anytime after a certain hour at night. The same was true of the Cooper's Shop, as no one worked there after meal time in the evenings. The farm and all its various barns and outbuildings, in the company of the livestock, became a popular place for the two. Even the Indian Cave across the river was used as a trysting spot on rare occasions--in keeping with the long-standing rendezvous tradition of the community of Herodsville and surrounds. On one occasion, they ventured into town--to the home of Asher's parents and his former residence--when he knew that his whole family would be away on one of his father's preaching tours to other churches in the southernmost counties of the state. While Asher's relationship with his father had never been what one could call close, due largely to the differences in their personalities and in their spiritual paths, he had tried to maintain some kind of communication with his family and, in fact, saw them on a fairly regular basis despite his father's attempt at disowning him after his move to Shakertown. His mother, on the other hand, maintained her support for Asher's spiritual and literary endeavors and continued to be a pillar of uncritical love.

While that winter had been something of a blessing for Kitt and for Asher, it had not been so generous to others. Along with the first snowfall in late December, tragedy struck Shakertown sending a shock wave through the community. On the morning of December 23rd, only two days before the Christmas holy days, as a light snow descended upon the Shaker enclave, a loud cry was heard throughout the village. This foreboding scream came from none other than Sister Mary Wicks, who in coming from her breakfast duties in the Centre Family Dwelling along the main road that bisected the village, passed the Old Stone Shop on her way to her residence in the West Family Dwelling. She happened to look over toward the Old Stone Shop to admire the snow that covered one of the larger mulberry trees in a small grove beside the building. As she passed the building and looked back over her shoulder to get one last glance at the snow-painted mulberry trees, something caught her eye. Something odd about the appearance of the west side of the building. Something that looked from a distance like a large sack of field corn or potatoes that was tied to a long length of rope that came from a third-floor window. Upon closer scrutiny it became clear to Sister Mary that what hung from the long lead of hemp rope on the third floor was not a large burlap sack full of field corn, but a body. And upon even closer examination the elder sister could see that it was the body of a young woman. The body of Eden McNamara. Then came the painful scream.

The news of Eden's suicide hit the society hard. Especially Kitt. When they found the note she had left in the third floor room from whence she had tied the rope to the bedpost before she had tied the other looped end around her neck and jumped, the reason for this shocking act became clear. In her child-like script she had written, in apologetic tones, that the reason for her final act had been because of her sense of guilt and her sins against God and her Family of Believers. The fact of her pregnancy and her inability to confide in anyone due to the overwhelming shame she felt, and her lack of being able to come to any resolution as to what to do about her condition had led to her fateful decision. In her letter she had asked for the forgiveness of her brothers and sisters in the Society. In a postscript, she addressed Kitt by name, asking her to not blame herself for the act she was about to commit. She also asked Kitt if she would be the one to deliver the news of her death to Caden and to comfort him and to assure him that he, as well, was in no way responsible and should not harbor any guilt. Her last words to Kitt, with which she ironically ended the note were: "You have been a great friend to me. We have had many wonderful times together. All that is about to end. But we will see each other, I know, in the hereafter, where we will walk with Mother Ann and the prophets in a state of grace. Take care of yourself, my sister, and god-speed in ALL that you do. Your faithful messenger, Eden."

It took Kitt many weeks to come to terms with Eden's last syllable of recorded time and her leap into the abyss of death. The finality of it. The unnecessariness of it. The paradox. This all weighed heavily on Kitt as the days passed and successive snows piled upon the ground, rooftops and trees, as one year turned across its upward axis and began its downward descent into another. A new year that had begun bitterly for Kitt as she felt sorely the sting of loneliness and loss. This turning, this turn of events caused her to think deeply and to turn more inward than she had ever done before. The quiet isolation of winter became a kind of meditation for her as she contemplated her future and her life. In some ways Eden's suicide seemed to Kitt to carry with it a kind of foreboding. While she hoped that there was no basis for this thought and that it was not rational, she could not seem to shake it from her consciousness. But mostly she simply missed her best friend, who had been more of a true sister to her than she had ever had. And Kitt wished that she had been more of a friend, more of a true sister, to her and had been more supportive in her deepest hours of need. In this sense, she felt that she had failed Eden as a close friend and confidant. Except for Asher, now, Kitt felt very much alone.

1843 had arrived and Christ had not appeared. As weeks and months ticked off, more of the Millerites had left for greener pastures or more likely places where Jesus might show up. Ranks, The Watcher, during these days, was, as usual, watching. But much of the watching he was doing in earnest was of a limited scope.

Yes, there was the Meeting Hall with all of its obligatory observations, but more to the point his mirror had become the main object of his aging gaze. The mirror, Sister Daniella, and Kitt Leigh. These had become his obsessions. His focus. His belated mid-life trial.

After the shock of Eden's suicide and the coming to light of her relationship with the Herodsville boy, it had become clear to him that Kitt and young Brother Pope had also been seeing one another on the sly during the preceding months. In fact, he had seen them more than once in transit to one of their trysting venues. He hadn't had the nerve to actually follow them to their final destination, and so hadn't learned of their whereabouts. But it was obvious to him, now, that all his earlier suspicions had been borne out to be true: Kitt and Asher were breaking the most stringent social rule in the Shaker statutes.

As weeks passed, following his sighting of the couple making off together in the direction of the river road, and then the word that had come from one of the members of the society that Kitt and Asher had been spotted on the outskirts of Herodsville and headed toward town, he had, in essence, become an accomplice to their spiritual crimes. He wrestled with the fact that he was not giving due diligence to his duties as a member of the Ministry, but was, rather, fulfilling another role. The role of their protector. In this guise, he had, perhaps, been fooling himself as well as the other members of the Shakertown community. But the mirror on his reclining room wall saw all. It could not be fooled.

It was probably his lack of awareness of the Caden and Eden affair and the guilt he felt following her death, coupled with his co-conspiracy with Kitt and Asher and his inability to resolve within himself that hypocrisy that led to his decision late that winter to resign from his position on the board of The Ministry of Pleasant Grove. The fact that he knew in his heart-of-hearts that he was not going to expose Kitt Leigh and her accessory in crime, Asher Pope, to the rest of the Society was probably the issue that broke the back of his former resolve. He could no longer, in good faith, keep up the charade of being both a member of the Ministry and Kitt's protector. For, in the end, it was The Watcher's concern for Kitt that was driving him to do what he was, or in this case, wasn't, doing. So, on an overcast day in early March and after, yet another, winter snow, Brother Wilford Ranks called a meeting in the Center Room of the Ministry apartments with the three other Elders in the community and spoke his resignation--citing unspecified conflicts of interest and a crisis of faith as the reasons for his decision. In fact, after his resignation and as an unusually harsh winter began to melt into spring, Wilford Ranks, now no longer The Watcher, and having handed over his Meeting Room window duty to his roomate, Brother Joseph, was feeling a huge weight lifted from his shoulders. The sense of freedom his resignation had afforded him was as if someone had opened the door of the cage that had been his life and released him into a world of nature and pure inner flight that he had only known, briefly, as a child. Ranks reveled in his new-found freedom, as now he was simply another member of the Shakertown family where the only high standards he was being held to were his own. Now, on Sundays during Service and Shaker Dance, he was no longer the one watching from the small window on the wall, but one of the many being watched. This felt right to him. In fact, this felt good.

        Things were changing for Wilford Ranks and his relationship with Kitt Leigh. For one thing, since his resignation from the Ministry, the relationship between the two had changed from Ranks being Kitt's nemesis to becoming, gradually, a kind of confidante and father-figure. They found, over time, that they shared not only the act of being instruments for the voices of spirits living on 'the other side,' but other things, as well. The love of music, for instance. The love of poetry--which in Kitt's case was primarily the love of Asher's poems, while in Ranks' case it was the verse of the Transcendentalists and the English Romantics, especially Wordsworth and Keats, all of which was superceded, of course, by the verse that came through him from Khwaja. All this and the love of Celtic history and lore. Especially the histories of the Knights Templar and the biblical bloodline connections to the Scottish clans. All these topics and more filled the conversations that occurred between Kitt and Brother Ranks during the spring of that year--which was predestined to be forever, if erroneously out of season, known as "The Fall From Grace."

    While Kitt and Brother Wilford were falling into friendship, and as Kitt's love for Asher grew with each meeting, she found herself, one afternoon, sitting at the little desk in her reclining room in the East Family Dwelling with pen in hand, writing. She was not trying her hand at writing verse today, or trying to respond to one of Asher's brilliant poems, in kind, but was writing him a letter, as she had done many times before. If one were to have been able to witness the expression on her face and the language of her body as she paradoxically forced her words onto the page, one would have remarked at the somberness of mood in which she now wrote.

Dear Asher,

While we have known each other and have been together only a short time, I feel that we have known each other over lifetimes, over eternities. I feel a sense of agelessness when I am in your presence. I also feel a sense of calm. The kind of calm one feels when one is completely understood, accepted, loved unconditionally. This is the kind of love I feel from you, my prince. It made me so very happy that night in the Water House when you were leaving and called me "princess." Since then, that has become your pseudonym and nickname for me. I have enjoyed this affectionate name, this sobriquet coming from your lips. We have had such fun these past few months and my respect and love for you has only grown with each sighting of you in the distance, with each kiss from close quarters. How will I write you, here, what I have to say?

Since you came to Pleasant Grove to live amongst us, things have gone smoothly and evenly between us. There have been no ups and downs. We never argue. We always treat each other with courtesy and respect. We have always seemed interested in the same things. Reading the same books. Singing the same songs. When I would imagine us living together as a couple, it would be in a place and in a relationship where balance reigned and love led the way. But since Eden's death, something other has taken hold of me. Her intimate friendship with your friend Caden began to intersect with what you and I share. They became us, and we them. Sometimes I have not been able, in more recent weeks, to distinguish which is which. Who is who. What is what. Even where is where--so disoriented at times I have become. For the first time in my life, fear has become a companion. I think of Eden, I think of Caden's pain when he thinks of her untimely death, and I think of you and me, and I fear for us--that something similar could happen to either of us, or to us together. I don't know why this is happening, my sweet prince, but it is. At night, when we are not together, I worry for you. I fear for us. Sad thoughts surround my sleep--if I am able to sleep at all. Oh, I ramble on, here, and am saying nothing....

  O, Asher, it is so hard for me to get to the point of this letter. To tell you what is really on my mind. I don't want to read what I will pen, now, any more than you will when you receive this in a couple of days. I want to put this off, to procrastinate, til the last possible second, so that up until that moment I can continue to swim with you in that sea of love where we have spent, lo, these past months. In fact, I am pausing between every word, reflecting on specific memories I have of us, as I write--to prolong our wonderful run of good luck.. But I must get it out, as it is not fair to lead you on this way.

  Asher, when you get this letter, I will already be on my way to somewhere that is far away from the place we have known and what you call "Shakertown" and what I have known for most of my life as Pleasant Grove. And a "pleasant grove" protected and away from the world it has been for me. But, now, all that is about to change, for I have decided to leave the Pleasant Grove Society and all my Believer friends and to start my life anew elsewhere. I am not doing this for selfish reasons, but for reasons that I feel are best for everyone--mostly for you and for the Society. Since Eden's death I have not been the same person you knew me as when we began writing secret letters to one another, which Eden would deliver to you at Caden's father's store in Herodsville. Over these past months since she died at her own hands I have continued to worry about what might happen to us. The worry has turned to fear, dear Asher, and it is the fear that is driving this pen across the page.

In order to spare you and the good people of Pleasant Grove a similar kind of trauma as a result of our indulgent, yet beautiful, relationship, should we be found out, or worse, I want to take the opportunity to act, now, before it is too late--to spare our love and the faith that the Believers have put in me, and take my leave so that all of you may live out your days in peace and without the unhappiness which is bound to follow in our hallowed wake. O, Asher, this is so hard for me! My hand can barely steady itself enough to write these words. I can already hear what you are thinking. Your thoughts speak to me even as I write and before you even read these words. I know you will not approve of what I am saying, here. But I cannot, in good faith, put my Shaker family (which now includes yourself) through another casualty such as what Eden has put us through, bless her soul. Nor do I intend to embarrass or in any way compromise the reputation or the good name of the people of Pleasant Grove by my presence here, should our intimate relationship come to light. Do you see what I am saying, Asher? Can you understand? While we are not hurting anyone else by our being together, if we were to be discovered and others were to find out, then it would give the whole community a bad name and cast shame on all of us Believers in the eyes of not only the World's People, but also, here, especially with my high profile in Pleasant Grove as well as in the more Southern Shaker communities. You see the position I'm in, dear Asher? There is too much pressure on me and the odds are not in our favor--at least in terms of no one ever finding out about us--in which case both of us would have to leave your "Shakertown" and find a new place to live. So, I'm only anticipating the inevitable and moving away before some dark cloud covers Pleasant Grove and all our lives, blotting out the sun.

  I know that you are probably feeling hurt and abandoned as you are reading this, but I am thinking of you, most of all. By my leaving, your reputation won't be tarnished and you will be free to either stay in Pleasant Grove with your new life there, or you could reasonably return home, to Herodsville. I hope you will see the positive side in my reasoning, here, and not only the negative.

  You should know, and I am telling you, now, in the strictest of confidence, that there is one person who knows of my decision and who, in fact, knows about us. This will come as something of a shock to you, as it did to me when I first learned about it, but please accept what I am about to say, now, with an open mind. In the past few months, Brother Wilford, whom you used to refer to as "the Watcher," has discovered the true nature of our relationship. He came to me with this information and this time I didn't lie to him or pretend ignorance. Since my admission, he has been very supportive of me and my situation and has kept our secret to himself. This was a heavy burden upon him, given his position as a member of the Ministry in the community. He, like me, struggled with the moral and spiritual implications of his silence and his deceitfulness prior to his resignation from the Ministry. We have been strange friends and confidantes in all of this, but it has served both of us well in allowing us to get through these difficult times and for me to finally come to the resolve that I have and about which you now know.

    O Asher, I know this will be hard for you and I know you well enough to know that you won't take this sitting down and will probably comb the countryside looking for me. But, I beg you, don't try to find me. Don't come looking for me. That would only make things harder for both of us. Maybe later, after I've found a new home and things have settled down for me, then we can communicate again and see how things look-- that is, if you still want me after what I have put you through. But, for now, please try and accept the fact that I am gone and what has occurred is for the best, at least for now.

The other day, after I had told Brother Wilford that I had decided to leave Pleasant Grove, he responded, as he often does, with some philosophical line or two from one of his favorite philosophers. On this occasion he quoted Jean de LaBruyere, whom I believe you are familiar with. In an attempt to console me and support my decision to leave, he quoted LaBruyere saying: "At the beginning and at the end of love, the two lovers are embarrassed to find themselves alone." Then he went on to give me another quote and to explain what LaBruyere was saying and what he meant by that. The second quote was: "All of men's misfortunes and all of their unhappiness spring from their hatred of being alone." The best that I could understand from these two quotes and from his explanation is--that the fact of our aloneness will be the hardest part of this forced separation. But while it's true that most people are uncomfortable even with the idea of being alone, much less the fact of it, I know you, Asher, and of your ability and love of solitude. I think, too, of my previous life and that I had never been in love or had taken a lover. Knowing this gives me comfort and the certainty that we will both have had much previous experience of aloneness and can draw from this during the days ahead. I am counting on this to help us through the difficult times that are coming.

Please, Asher, forgive me for not having the courage to tell you this to your face. But face-to-face, from lip to lip, I couldn't have explained myself to you in this way. And, in the end, you would have only tried to talk me out of it and I wouldn't have been able to resist your charms, the way I haven't been able to resist them up until now. To do what I felt I had to do, I had to do it this way. So, please my dear prince, let your princess go. Let our love be a pleasant memory and know that I will come to you in your dreams. And there we can romp and play as we please and as we have these past months--where it is safe and we can enjoy each other's company without fear and without deceit.

Go in peace and with my love wherever this life takes you, and if we should meet again, may it be as if it were merely the extension of the last time we spoke--with love on our lips and fire in our hearts. God-speed, my prince, I will be thinking of you, as I hope you will remember me in your glorious poems, which I hope you will, forever, continue to write--for all to enjoy as I have. You have a rare gift, Asher, and I hope you will use it. Your wonderful words make this world a better place.

As once you recited to me, as if a kiss I return these words of your beloved Shakespeare to your lips....

"Our separation so abides and flies
That thou, residing here, goes yet with me,
And I, hence fleeting, here remain with thee."

        Kisses, from your

Princess

Kitt

Asher walked frantically down the wide dirt road from the post office toward the Centre Family Dwelling where he knew he could find Sister Mary Wicks working at her time-honored job of preparing the Monday mid-day meal. So quickly had he bolted from the small post office building after reading Kitt's letter that as he approached the large Centre Dwelling he still held the letter unsheathed and crumpled in his hand.

Asher found Sister Mary in her usual spot in the downstairs kitchen area at the large painted pine bake table which was positioned in front of the brick wood-fired ovens. She was busy pounding dough that would eventually become loaves of wheat bread for the day's main meal. As she took a long-handled paddle from the wall and placed three perfectly-shaped loaves of dough onto the flat metal surface at the end of the baking tool and as she slid the loaves through the open oven doors, Asher came bolting into the room in full voice.

"Sister Mary, Sister Mary, can I have a minute with you, please!" Seeing that Sister Mary is in the middle of an important and somewhat delicate act, there in front of the stove, he stops mid-room and waits until she can finish setting the loaves inside the oven, withdraw the long-handled spatula and hang it back up on its hook on the wall beside the brick structure. As she puts the spatula back in its place, she turns and looks over her shoulder for the first time to identify the source of the loud voice that has come bursting into the room.

"Well, Brother Asher, aren't we in a mood this morning. I think Brother Pious could hear you down at the barn. What is it that's got you in such good voice today?"

"Sister Mary, I've got to talk to you." Asher holds up his right fist, which is still wrapped around the crumpled letter, and announces "I've just gotten this letter at the post office and I need to find Kitt. I've not looked, but could you tell me if she is working today in the silk shop? Or if she is not there, where she might be? I don't know why I didn't go looking for her there, myself. I guess I thought I could save some time and a few steps by talking to you, first, since you and she are usually so inseparable. Anyway, I'm here and I'm desperate to find her."

"Slow down, slow down, lad. I can see that this letter has put you in a tizzy, but sit yourself down there in that chair at the end of the bake table and we can talk while I finish kneading these last loaves of wheat bread. I can't just stop and chat with you, as the Believers have to eat and we can't have them waiting up there in the dining room for the bread to bake with their stomachs growling, now can we?"

"No ma'am, I guess not. I'll sit down here, then, and we'll begin again." Asher walks over to a small straight-back chair positioned at the far end of the long work table and sits down. "Sister Mary, Kitt has written me this letter." And again he holds up the crumpled letter still tangled in his fist. "In the letter she says that she is leaving Pleasant Grove for some very obscure reasons and doesn't even say where it is she will go. I've got to find her and talk to her before she does something foolish. Can you tell me where I can find her? I'm hoping that she only left this letter at the post office this morning and that I still might have time to find her before she carries out this plan of hers. Do you know where she is today?"

"Brother Asher, I wish I could tell you where you could find her, but I'm afraid that I cannot. The last time I talked with Sister Kitt was on Friday evening at her usual Friday evening transmission sessions over in the East Family House. I haven't seen or talked to her since."

"But what did she say to you, then? Did she say anything about leaving Pleasant Grove or where she was going?"

"We did have a little time to talk after her session with Mother Ann, and she did tell me of her plan to leave. In fact, we said our farewells at that meeting. She wasn't all that specific as to her reasons for leaving, except to say that it was the best for everyone that she do so. She also mentioned that she thought she needed to share her transmissions from Mother Ann with members of some of the other communities and that she felt it was her duty to do so. I, too, was shocked at her sudden decision, but I respect and trust Sister Kitt's sense of dedication and responsibility. She didn't offer to tell me where it was she was going, and I didn't ask. But she did say that she was writing some letters to a few select members of the Pleasant Grove Family and that she wanted to get them to the post office by the next morning at the latest, since the post office would be closed by noon on Saturday and not open again until Monday morning."

"So, she mailed the letters on Saturday? If that's true, then she could be god-only-knows-where by now!"

"When we talked on Friday evening, she said that she was planning to leave right away. She wasn't specific, but I can tell you that I haven't seen her since our talk on Friday evening at the East Family House and rarely a day goes by when we don't see one another. I've just assumed that she must have left over the weekend--to wherever it was she was going."

"She didn't say anything to you about where she was going? Not even in what direction she was headed?"

"No, she really didn't, which I thought a little strange. But I've come to trust Kitt's judgment in such matters and so I figured that if she wanted me to know where she was headed, then she would have told me. She did say that when she got settled she would contact me and let me know where she was. So, hopefully, if she has already left, which I'm sure she has, then I'll be in touch with her sooner or later. I'd hate to lose touch with her as she and I have been so very close for a very long time."

"Is there anyone else, here, who might know where she is or where she has gone? I feel as if there's not a minute to lose and I don't want to waste my time running around the village looking for her when she might be stepping into a wagon as we speak and headed out the front gate."

"Well, she has been pretty friendly with Brother Wilford, of late. It could be that she has confided in him as to where she planned to go. Besides Brother Wilford, I can't think of anyone else who might have the kind of information you're looking for. Her closest friend and most likely confidante, Sister Eden, of course is no longer with us, so you'll not get any help from her, rest her soul."

Asher got up from his seat in the straight-back chair and took a few anxious steps in the direction of the stairway from which he had entered the kitchen. "Thank you, Sister Mary, you have been most kind in sharing with me what you know. It has been most helpful. And let me just say that since we are here alone and talking about Kitt, that I want to thank you for all that you've done for both of us, especially in those early days when you were our messenger and taking our letters back and forth from Herodsville to Pleasant Grove. I won't forget the risks you took doing that and putting yourself in what was a precarious position, to say the least. And I know that Kitt appreciated it, too. Now, let me go, as I know you have things to do and I need to find Brother Wilford before it's too late and Kitt gets too far away. Truly, thank you for your honesty and for your help."

"You're very welcome, Brother Asher. It was my pleasure to help you two young people all those months ago. And I have to admit, it was kind of a thrill being your Pony Express Rider and the messenger for your budding friendship. I know it must have been a hard decision for Kitt to have made--to leave what has been her home for most of her young life. But, as I said, I trust her judgment, as she must have had good reasons for doing what she has done. And it must have been hard for her to have left you, too. When she spoke of you, recently, she did so with tears in her eyes."

"Did she say anything about me that I should hear? Did she leave you any message for me?"

"No, I'm afraid that I have told you all I know. I wish I could massage your heart with some tender words or a roadmap that would lead you to her, my boy, but she left me not with such gifts."

"Thank you, again, Sister, but I must go. Time is not on my side. As we speak, she may be putting distance between us. Farewell."

"Good luck in trying to track her down and let me know what you find out."

"I will Sister Mary, and thank you again."

With that salutation, Asher bolted from the downstairs room and up the stairway. Once outside the Centre Family House, he headed for the road and turned right, heading to the Carpenter's Shop where he hoped to find the man he had formerly known as The Watcher.

As luck would have it, his timing was good and Asher caught Wilford Ranks just as he was coming out the door and leaving the old building that was once the blacksmith and wagon shop. Rather than descending the steps, Ranks stood on the stone and concrete landing just outside the door and watched Asher coming at him in full trot. From several yards away, Asher looked up from the ground and saw Ranks standing in front and above him. Even at such close distance, Asher called out to make sure that Ranks wouldn't get away.

"Brother Wilford, Brother Wilford....wait! Can I talk to you for a moment?"

Almost out of breath from his dash from the Centre Family Dwelling, Asher reached the bottom step of the stone stairway leading up to the small building. Ranks had not moved from the time he had seen Asher running down the walkway toward the building and just stood there and observed the young man who was now standing before him. He looked down from his parapet at Asher there below him and out of breath, and spoke.

"Well, my boy, where's the fire? What's got you in such a state? Let me guess...." Ranks noticed that Asher had some kind of document wrapped up in the fist of his right hand and quickly came to a conclusion.

"You must have gotten a letter from our Sister Kitt and you've been dashing around Pleasant Grove all morning trying to find her and someone told you to come and ask me if I knew where it is she's gone?

Is this it?"

Somewhat stunned by Brother Wilford's abilities of perception and clairvoyance, for a few seconds Asher found himself tongue-tied. Finally, he was able to blurt out the words "Yes. Yes sir. How did you know about the letter, sir?"

"Because you've got it right there balled up in your hand. Anyone could see that."

"But how did you know that I was coming to ask you about Kitt, er...Sister Kitt, sir?"

"Why don't you come on inside, Brother Asher, and let's have a little talk. It's cold out here this morning and you look as though you could use a rest," Ranks replied in an almost patronizing tone.

Asher replied to Rank's invitation with a "Yes, sir," upon which Ranks turned and opened the front door of the Carpenter's Shop and stepped through the threshold. Asher ran up the four steps to the entrance and, like Ranks, disappeared inside, closing the heavy wooden door behind him. Inside the building, they moved from the short hallway and turned right into the workroom where Ranks had just spent the better part of the morning sanding and finishing the legs and drawers for a small Shaker table. He sat down on the shop workbench and motioned to Asher to take a seat in the one cane-bottomed chair in the room that was designed for more comfortable sitting.

"I can see that you have come with a sense of urgency, Brother Asher. What is it that you wish to know?"

"Yes, sir, I mean, yes I have, sir--come here as a desperate last resort to hopefully find out where I might find Sister Kitt. I've just come from the Centre Family kitchen where I talked to Sister Mary, hoping that maybe she would know something. Turns out that she couldn't answer my question as to Sister Kitt's whereabouts and suggested that I come and talk to you."

"Why would she think that I would know anything about Sister Kitt, my boy?"

"She seemed to think that you and Sister Kitt have become friendly of late and that she might have confided her plans to you....as you said....to leave Pleasant Grove. Do you know where I might find her? Has she left? If she has when did she leave? Do you know where she has gone?"

"Slow down, there, my boy. One question at a time. I can see you're in a state, and are looking for some quick answers, but let me just say a couple things to you before I attempt to answer your deluge of questions.

"For some months, I have known about you and Kitt. As you know, I have suspected there was something going on between the two of you going as far back as the end of last year. But it has only been recently that my suspicions were confirmed and that I knew that there were certain improprieties, shall we say, going on between the two of you."

"You did?" Asher interrupted, feigning ignorance. "How did you know that?"

"Never mind how I found out. The fact is: I know, and have known for some time. Now, as I was saying....Upon having my suspicions confirmed, rather than going to the Ministry Board and revealing the facts of what I knew, I found myself in the unenviable position of, instead, keeping what I knew a secret--in order to protect the integrity and reputation of our Sister Kitt. From there, things just happened organically and before long Sister Kitt had confided in me and, I, in her. Consequently, I became something of a confidante for her and a kind of platonic father-daughter friendship ensued. And that friendship, that confidence has existed until this day.

"Now, as to what I know about her present whereabouts..... Yes, I knew that she was going to write you the letter that you clutch like a talisman in your hand."

In embarrassment Asher looked down at his right hand resting on the side of the Shaker chair and noticed that he was still carrying the piece of paper with Kitt's handwriting all over it in his hand. Blushing, he folded the letter and quickly stashed it in the pocket of his overcoat with a gesture that he hoped Ranks would not see.

"We talked about it when she came to see me early last week-- when she was making up her mind as to what she was going to do and how she was going to go about it. So, you see, I'm not a mind-reader after all, I'm sorry to say. But you showing up the way that you did, today, and with that wad of paper clenched in your fist, it didn't take much to put two and two together and come up with an appropriate welcoming response to your arrival at my doorstep. So, yes, I have known for some time about Sister Kitt's plans to leave."

"So, then she is already gone."

"Now I will answer your questions. To answer the question as to where you can find her, I can tell you unequivocally that you won't find her anywhere on the premises of Pleasant Grove. And, yes, she has already left, my young man. It is my understanding that she left on Saturday morning. She told me the last time we spoke before she left that she was going to mail the few letters that she had written and then depart directly after that. So, my man, I'm afraid that she left us on Saturday morning and is no longer here."

"Then, if she is not here, where has she gone? She does not tell me in her letter. How am I going to find her?"

"Slow down, slow down, I'm getting to that part of your inquisition, too. When we spoke just before she left and after we had settled on what the Society owed her—a horse and wagon and a small amount of cash—as we would any member in parting, she told me that she preferred not to tell anyone about her final destination. She wanted to make a clean break with her life and family here in Pleasant Grove and especially with yourself, as she knew that you would be upset and would try and follow her."

"She told no one?"

"As far as I know, that was her intention and her plan."

"Not even what direction, what state she was headed for?"

"Not even what country, for all I know. She was intent upon being totally secretive about this. And I can't say that I blame her, given her state of mind and the concerns she had, not only for herself, but for all of us here in the Society. So, given these facts, you might as well give up your search-and-find mission, as I'm afraid it will only help you in getting more riled up and out of sorts. You best resign yourself, as have those of us who know she has left us, to the fact that you will have to carry on with your life without her."

"I mean no disrespect, but that's easy for you to say! But consider my situation. This news is not easy for me to accept and I'm not sure that I can just 'carry on without her' as you so casually put it."

"Just let me say that it is not easy for me to say. In my own way I will miss Sister Kitt as much as anyone. Maybe not as much as you, young Asher, who has a more intimate connection with the girl. But those of us who knew her well, will certainly miss her. Yes, she will be sorely missed."

"I'm sorry, sir, I meant no disrespect. But since you know all about us, then you can appreciate how I must feel."

Asher patted his coat pocket where the letter was with his hand, and he continued:

"While she tried to explain to me in her letter why she was leaving, she really didn't give me any tangible reasons. So I'm still not clear on why she would do such a thing, and in such haste."

"All I know is that she was concerned about bringing shame to the community and the society and couldn't live with the knowledge that her actions might shed a derogatory light on Pleasant Grove. She is a very sensitive and responsible young woman, as you know, Brother Asher, and her sense of loyalty and duty must have been stronger than her own desires. This is all I can tell you, I'm afraid. So, this will have to suffice. She cared greatly for you, I can tell you that. But in the end, she couldn't sustain the level of affection she had for you, given the circumstances in which she was living. Those two polarities were warring with each other within her. Her sense of responsibility and duty won out, and she has left us. I'm sorry Brother Asher, but these are the facts and you'll just have to accept them and learn, as we all must, to live with them."

"Perhaps you are right, sir. But the pain of her leave-taking is still too fresh in my veins to take all that you are telling me at face value. And if there is no one else in Pleasant Grove who you can send me to who might know where she has gone, then I'll just have to find my own way of dealing with this. And, quite frankly, I don't know where that might lead. Right now, I'm only thinking about one thing, and that's finding Kitt. Until I do, or until I come to the kind of resolve that you and the other members of the Society have come to, I'll have to deal with this news on my own terms. So, thank you, sir, for sharing with me what you know. And thank you, too, for your willingness to keep our secret--Kitt's and mine--to yourself. I do appreciate that more than you'll ever know. I know that you didn't do it for my benefit, but no matter what your motives were, it gave Kitt and me some time together and that has been a true blessing and a gift to me. So, in a way, you have given me something, whether you meant to or not. And I thank you for that. Now, I must leave, as I've got many miles to go--whether only in my head or by foot--in trying to find Kitt's trail."

"Very well, son. And God go with thee."

With that, Asher rose from his seat and exited the Carpenter's Shop. At a fast clip, he made his way down the wide dirt road that was Pleasant Grove's link to the rest of the world, and toward the stables. Here he found a horse and wagon that would take him down the road, past Herodsville, and into the mountains where he knew of a person who could find any animal in any kind of weather. A tracker. A woodsman and hunter. Just the kind of person who might be able to lead him to Kitt.

Old mountain man William Rayfield's reputation as a tracker and a man-of-the-woods was unsurpassed in the environs of Herodsville. As Asher rode up the steep and narrow old dirt road on the south side of Scaly Mountain in the horse-and-wagon he had borrowed from the Shakertown stables, he was thinking to himself that if there was anybody that could find Kitt for him, it was old man Rayfield. The old man, now in his early seventies, didn't spend much time anymore out in the woods or on the trail of his favorite wild animal; his knowledge of the woods and the world was still intact, and his mind was as sharp, now, as it had been on the day he was born. Asher had known old man Rayfield since he was a young boy and had kept up their relationship all throughout the years, considering him a teacher and someone of like mind and spirit. Asher cherished his time with "Cuss" Rayfield, as he was known to his more intimate friends, due to his penchant for using certain four-letter words in private conversation. He thought of him as a kind of surrogate father. But now, he needed his old friend to be the legendary tracker and trapper that he had been in his prime, for what Asher was hunting was not some side of wild meat, but the love of his life. And as the minutes passed by that day, her trail was getting colder. As his horses pulled the wagon up the slope of the winding road on Scaly Mountain, Asher felt the urgency and he slapped the rear of the big Belgians with his reins.

Old man Rayfield must have known they were coming. When Asher drove the horse and wagon rig into the dirt yard of the old mountain house where four generations of Rayfields had raised their families, the old man was standing on the porch cloaked in a pair of blue overalls and looking like a bird of prey perched on a branch of a tall sourwood tree, inspecting his surrounds.

"Well, what brung you all the way up ole Scaly so early in the day? I hear'd you jinglin' afore ye got pert near within gunshot. And by the looks of you and that there hitch you're in, I don't expect that you're just cooterin' around or that you come all the way up here for some of my bumblins," Cuss Rayfield shouts with a smile on his sagging, unshaved face as Asher pulls up and parks the horses and wagon in the yard.

Asher jumped down from the wagon seat, kicking up a small cloud of dirt dust as he hit the ground, as old man Rayfield continued with his back-woods greeting. "You're a sight for sore eyes. I ain't seen you in a coon's age. Where you been keepin' yourself Mr. Pope? Or is that Brother Pope? Hell, I hear'd that you go by "Brother" now that you're shed of them Baptists and been hellin' around with them holy rollers up there in Shakertown. Turned heathen on us, have you? Well, heathen or no, come in out of the yard and set a spell up here on the porch with me. H'its been so long a time since I've seen you that I jist want to look on your face a while to memorize you again."

"Good to see you, too," Asher replied in kind as he tied the reins from the Belgians to the brake handle on the wooden wagon. "How you been? You're looking spritely enough. And I can see that you've already plowed a patch for your garden over there on the south side of the house."

"Come on up out of the yard, boy, and lets quit all this nonsense and blatherin' and get down to business. I know you ain't up here on no social call. What can I do fer ye?"

Asher climbed the wooden slats that were the ten steps that led up to the porch of Cuss Rayfield's mountain house and greeted his old friend with a warm handshake and a smile. The two men moved over and took their places in two old hand-built cane-bottomed rocking chairs that looked out over the valley beneath Scaly Mountain and in the direction of Herodsville that was one ridgeline over from where their eyes could see.

"Well, boy, lets get to it. I had it in my head to plow some more today, but since you showed up I don't reckon I'll have to now. I'm a little het up from all the plowing I done yesterday anyway. I ain't no spring chicken, you know."

"If there's anything I can do to give you a hand with any of that, just let me know, as I can still trail a team as good as anyone. Been doing a right smart of that sort of thing over in Shakertown lately, myself. But, you're right, I didn't come up here to gab, but to get some advice and maybe some help. I've kinda got myself in a fix and I figured that you were the only one who could help me with this particular problem."

"What ye gotten yourself into now? You always was bad to find yourself on the wrong end of a hick'ry stick--ever since you was a young'un. So, what kind of devilment you been up to?"

"Well, it's a long story, and I won't bore you with the whole thing. Besides, it sounds like you've already heard a good bit of it, from what you said as I rode up into the yard."

"Shore 'nough, young'un, word travels like wild fire up here in these hollers and I heard tell that you took up with them Shakers on account of you were courtin' one of their women. A right purty one, too, I've been told. At least you ain't lost your good taste, even if you have lost your good sense. So are you here on account of that girl?"

"Yes, sir, I'm afraid I am."

"Well, then, what kind of fix you gotten yourself into? I swear I don't understand what you'd want with one of them wimmin up there in that Shaker town, who I hear tell are all wropped up with lots of clothes and don't never take 'em off to spark, nohow."

"Like I said, it's a long story, and I won't bore you with the details of how this whole thing came about. Let's just say that I lost my head over one of the girls one afternoon when I was up there for their Sunday Meeting. But that's been a long time ago, now, and since then we got to know each other and that's what made me decide to move up there and become a Shaker--so I could be closer to her. Her name is Kitt, by the way."

"Kitt, like in a fox pup?"

"That's right. But I don't think she was named after the animal. I think Kitt is short for Katherine or something like that."

"Ok, so far all I've got of your yarn is a smidgin.' What else have you got to say fer yourself?"

"Well, Cuss, she's up and left. Over the weekend she packed up and just disappeared. And no one seems to know where she's gone. Didn't leave any notion or indication of where she was headed, or anything. All I got was this letter, which was in the mail today when I went down to the post office in Shakertown." Asher reached into his coat pocket and removed the crumpled up letter.

"Seems right quare and there must be more to it than you're lettin' on. You ain't scared her off due to your chasin' after it, have you, boy? Boys your age can get mighty hard up for a little sugar now and again. I know, I was a young buck like yourself once, too. Let me see that letter, boy. Maybe I can scare up some meaning out of this letter that you ain't seen. I reckon life's problems is a lot like trackin'. It's more about what you can't see than what's right under your nose. Let me see if she ain't left nary a trail in this here letter of yourn."

Asher handed Cuss the letter. Cuss unraveled it and read. For a few minutes there was silence there on the porch of the old house. Asher could hear the sound of a hoot-owl coming from the woods behind the house and the raps of a pileated woodpecker far off in the valley below. Finally, Cuss finished reading the letter and put it down in his lap, looking out over the valley and the ridgelines of the Kentucky hills before he finally spoke.

"Well, she really ain't said much in this here letter, I gotta say. At least not much 'cept for a lot of gushing and howdy do. And she's holdin' to her story--such as it is. She makes a big hellaballoo out of how she don't want to hurt nor hinder nobody. But the tracker in me says that story ain't worth a hill o' beans. While she may be one good woman, and I know you think the world of her, I've never heard tell of anyone who was sech a saint and would run off from home when they ain't done nothing, yet, to run off from. You see what I'm getting' at, here, boy? I think there's more to the story than what's she's said. She may be gwine and only dust on the road, but she's left a mighty big part of her behind. At least that's what I've culled from this here letter."

"So, can you help me find her? Did she leave any clues in that letter that I just couldn't see?"

"Not tracks, if that's what you mean. She's leavin' a heap o' heart-tracks and mind- tracks, to be certain. But she's been pretty clever in not leavin' no footprints that a man could foller. The whole thing puts me of a mind of the time my second cousin Eula disappeared all them years ago—headed her self over the mountain to see some granny doctor a'cause she wuz in the family way. She didn't tell no body where she was goin', neither, then came back about a week later as if nothin' had happened. You don't think maybe your gal has gone off to see some granny doctor or something do ye?"

"I don't know, Cuss. It sounded like she wasn't just going away for a short time. It sounded in her letter like she was going away for good. And she was clear about not wanting me to try and find her. She's always been honest with me, which is one of the reasons why I love her. I have to believe that what she's saying there in her letter is the truth."

"Maybe so, but wimmins is awful clever when it comes to hidin' somethin' they don't want no body to know. 'Specially when they get in a tizzy, or if they's avoiding a fray. Maybe your Kitt is like that fool's gold. Hit's yaller and shiny and mocks gold right smart, but you hit it a tap and 'stead o' flattening, it busts into pieces."

"I've got to find her, Cuss. My heart's a bustin'. And what am I gonna do stuck over there in Shakertown all alone?"

"Well, I'm afeared I can't help ye in terms of trackin' her down. Not unless she or the good Lord sends you some fraish signs--sich like in another letter or somethin'. I can see that you're a fool about this girl. I can see that much for damn sure. And you can take out in that wagon of yours and scour the land a-lookin' fer her, but it aint gonna do you no good more 'en likely. And it ain't gonna do you no good to sulk around or sull up like some ole stump-water while you a-waitin' for her to show up again. Hell, I ain't got no stummick for that sort of thing. They's too many trout in the river to be chewin' and swallerin' old bones. You catch my meanin', boy?"

"Yeah, Cuss, I know what you're saying, but that don't make this pain in my belly go away. How am I going to fix that?"

"Well, hell, maybe you're the one that needs you a granny doctor!" Cuss laughs as he says this and looks at Asher and winks. "You got a sour stomach, maybe it's you that's in the family way! Either that or you've been eatin' green warnuts." Cuss smiles again at Asher. "Time'll fix it, boy. Never you worry yourself about that. You best be gettin' on about your life and whur you're gonna live and what you're gonna do. Are you gonna just end up no count and worry yourself to death and end up like a tree that's been wind-thrown and busted to kindling' and just wigglin' and winglin' around for the rest of your life, or are you gonna go by what I'm tellin' you, here, and stay vig'rous and be the pop-cracker I've always known and get on about your life?"

" If you really don't think I can find her and shouldn't be wastin' my time trying to track her down, then maybe you're right. But it's not going to be easy for me just to do nothing to try and get her back."

"I understand, Asher. Hell fire, I've been in your shoes before, so I'm' not just speakin' out of the side of my mouth. When I was in such a fix as you, I'd go to them poke suppers and bid on one of them pokes of food that the wimmins had made, and I'd get to eat with the girl who fixed it and then carry her home. That way I got to sweet-heartin' again and plumb forgot that other'n who had cut out on me like I was pizen. So, I don't want to hear no tales of Brother Pope takin' no pizen on account of some play-pretty having left him for some polecat over in Tennessee. You hear? So, don't do like that boy in that book you was readin' a few years ago--that Romero, or whatever you called him--who pizened himself on account of his girlfriend who was only playing possum."

"Not to worry, Cuss, I guess I'll be ok. Eventually. I'm not going to poison myself or do something stupid. But how am I going to get her out of my mind?"

"Time, my boy. Time heals all. Speakin' of which, it's time to sing Old Hundred and for you to get back home--to Shakertown or wherever you're callin' home these days. And remember, you never know who you'll meet up with just around the next crook in the road. That next fox cub with blue eyes may be there waitin' on you just when you least expect it. So, stay in the saddle, boy, cause a man who's been horse-thrown and is afraid to ride ain't gonna get the chance to turn that curve and see what it is that's waiting there fer him. Now, git your hind end and god's biscuits outa that there chair and take that poke of creasy greens and miners lettuce that I picked today with you, and make a mess of them tonight for those friends of yours over in Nice Grove, as I bet they've never had anything like that. 'Sides it's good for the croup this time of year. You tell 'em that, too."

Asher thanked Cuss for his advice and for the go-away bag of greens and climbed back into his wagon, turned his big Belgians around and headed out of the front yard of the old mountain home-place and back down the narrow dirt road off Scaly Mountain in the direction of Herodsville and Shakertown beyond. Cuss Rayfield sat in his ancient rocking chair, rocking back and forth, with a smile on his face and chewing on a piece of ginseng root he had taken out of the chest pocket of his overalls as he followed the dust of Asher's descent down the mountain. There was a look of concerned knowing on the old man's face, and if you were to look closely, you could see a twinkle in his eye.

ACT III.

Scene I.

Asher struggled with his separation from Kitt in the days and weeks that followed his conversation with Cuss Rayfield up on Scaly Mountain. It seemed to Asher that as quickly as Kitt had come into his life, she had that quickly gone. He had found no trail of her departure from Shakertown or her whereabouts since she had taken leave and he had received her parting letter. As the weeks and then months passed, Asher made the decision to remain in Shakertown and to continue with his life as a member of the Gathering Order. His decision was partly due to a notion that Kitt might decide to return to Pleasant Grove and the place that had been her home for the majority of her life. But as the months passed and Kitt did not return, Asher resigned himself to the idea that she would probably not return and that he might never see her again. During this time, his trial period as a member of the Gathering Order had ended and he had gone through the formality of the signing of the Covenant, accompanied by a rather informal confession of sins, thus becoming an enrolled member of the Pleasant Grove United Society of Believers.

From that day forward, time passed very quickly for Asher and the residents of Shakertown as the winds of change blew through central Kentucky and beyond. By the mid to late 1840s Shaker worship and practices had normalized enough so that the public was again allowed to attend the Shaker services and dances on the sabbath. This meant that Asher was able to connect with friends and family from his old life in Herodsville on a more regular basis, including his friend Caden, who for a short time had considered becoming a member of the Gathering Order. In 1847 one visitor from Herodsville described the reformed Shaker services thusly: "First came a spiritual hymn or chant, sung standing, to a very homely, humdrum, secular sort of tune, with a brisk jog-like motion. It was sung in unison, all the voices on one part. There reigned the same neatness and correctness in this performance, as in their costume and their clean floor; no false notes or slips of time. The most singular thing about their singularities was the absence of all fanatical intoxication. In the songs and dances we saw nothing of that violence and frenzy which have been reported of them; all was moderate, deliberate and self-possessed; no distortions, whirlings round on tip-toe, groans or frantic shouts. The Spirit did not seem to wrestle with them, but to descend upon them soothingly."

By the 1850s all the extraordinary behavior such as the spinning and convulsive ecstasies had ceased. But while things were normalizing with regard to their spiritual services and practices, the Shakertown Believers were beginning to assimilate into the culture of the World's People and were increasingly conforming to the ways of the world. The fashions of the United States which surrounded them became more and more evident in Shakertown proper. Things that had been forbidden by the earlier Millennial Laws were now in evidence. Looking glasses, wigs for men, cologne and jewelry for the women became popular and in keeping with the society's growing interests in physical appearance. The men, in many cases, abandoned earlier standards and began sporting beards. Clothing styles changed, allowing for more individualism. Houses and other dwellings were painted in brighter colors and were furnished and decorated in a more elaborate and worldly way. Even the Shaker diet was transformed. Coffee and tea were available again and meat-eating, including pork, was permitted.

During these years, Asher found himself dividing his time between Shakertown and Herodsville and his family and old friends. Now secure in his decision to remain a Shaker and to remain a part of the community that Kitt had introduced him to, he went about his daily chores and activities with gratitude and grace.

By 1860, as the society was changing, Isaac Newton Youngs, who was still a highly-regarded member of the New Lebanon community in New York and a long-time friend of the Pleasant Grove Society, sent a letter to the Ministry at Shakertown airing his displeasure at all the changes that were taking place and of his concern for the implications of these changes on Shaker society in general. "Dear Friends," he wrote. "From a spiritual perspective, the United Society of Believers is wading through much tribulation and is greatly exposed to outside sources causing discouragement from various causes. The increasing use of hired help from the World's People is creating an undesirable situation which is, I believe, damaging to the Believers' spiritual travel. Likewise, members have become more and more experimental and daring, about clothing and articles of fancy, including the use of high colors, than is virtuous or proper. In this time of great improvements in the world in which there is much free thinking and freedom of investigation, and in a time when there is much interaction between Believers and the World's People, the world is insinuating itself powerfully among Believers, which is very injurious to their advancement in the gospel. In fact, during this time when temporal things are prospering, there now exists a disorderly union between Brethren and Sisters. Indeed, Zion is wading through deep waters of sufferings and tribulation that includes much apostasy, much weakness, darkness and loss. The same elements that are rending asunder the kingdoms of the world are also surging in the ranks of the Believers, especially a worldly carnal sense and feeling."

If worldly values and fashions were not enough in helping to compromise the status quo of the lives of the Believers in Shakertown, the war that was raging between the North and the South was the final nail in the coffin. The official position of the central Ministry for all Shaker Believers during the war years was, as stated: "Believers, who are obeyers, cannot, under any circumstances engage in military servitude of any name or nature." Despite this spiritual statute, Shaker societies, both East and West, were inevitably drawn into the conflict. Most of those who were members of the Shakertown Society who were enscripted into the draft refused service, but the draft still continued to cause problems. Added to this, wartime levies and taxation on Believers, which were considered "enormous," took their toll. Even as the Pleasant Grove Believers maintained their neutrality consistent with their pacifism, as early as 1862 they were experiencing profound hardships at the hands of the secessionists. In the diary he had been keeping since Kitt's disappearance many years earlier and en lieu of the letters he loved to write, Asher wrote in the fall of 1863:

"Our position on neutrality in this war is driving us into poverty. Our resources are being taxed to the limit by both the Confederate and Union armies that are passing through here. The demands for food and lodging are exceeding our capacity to meet them. Hay and fodder are being requisitioned by the soldiers. Horses and wagons owned by our Believers are being pressed into service by military officers or are being paid for with worthless script. Thievery by guerrilla bands is common. Fires, too, are destroying our property. Only recently, twenty thousand oak fence rails were burned in federal camp fires. I have to agree with the sentiments of Eldress Mary Wicks, who is now a member of the ministry and who

the other day called this war 'the most singular and sad spectacle that has ever been witnessed since the creation of the world.' Both sides taking part in this conflict seem to have ignored the unparalleled prosperity, peace and happiness that had existed in this country and go on fighting like dogs, butchering and murdering each other, and glorying in their deeds of blood like demons.

We, here in Pleasant Grove, are repeatedly forced to feed large companies of soldiers that are moving through our village or are encamped on our lands. This autumn, large crowds of barefoot, ragged, greasy and dirty troops marched into our yards and surrounded our wells like the locusts of Egypt, and struggled with each other for the water as if perishing with thirst; and they thronged to our kitchen doors and windows begging for bread like hungry wolves. We nearly emptied our kitchens of their contents, and they tore the loaves and pies into fragments, and devoured others if they did not divide with them. No matter the frequency or the numbers of the hungry-sometimes as many as 1,000 in a day--bedraggled soldiers coming to our village, we have never denied them food. The sisters sometimes get up in the middle of the night to cook for them.

During all this upheaval, and in order to protect ourselves, we have taken certain measures to try and keep from giving up our horses and protect our dwelling houses. We keep lookouts at night and sometimes hide our horses far from the village. John Morgan's guerilla band with Captain Breckinridge came through here recently and stole two horses from the West family. If we hadn't acted in a hurry and hidden the rest of our horses, the Rebels would have, no doubt, taken them, too. We are so inundated by this war that we can scarcely give any attention to our everyday affairs. In October, 10,000 Confederate troops passed through here after the Battle of Perryville. We set up tables along the road in front of the Trustees House. We were able to feed about 1,400 soldiers, which almost depleted our food cellars. Our stores of foodstuffs are all but exhausted, now, yet troops are coming through here daily by the hundreds.

We supply them with what we can afford. Meanwhile, we sit and wait for the next round of clumping feet, clatter of wagon, boom of cannon belching forth death and destruction and the war's impending menace that comes, continually, to threaten us. For us, there seems to be no sanctuary from the war."

The ravages of the Civil War took their toll on what, through the 1850s, had been a prosperous agricultural economy in Pleasant Grove. During these earlier years, Shakertown residents had built and purchased modern cultivation and reaping machines. Because of these purchases there was an abundance of corn and wheat that was ground at the Mill on the Kentucky River, much of which was traded at ports down river. The gardens at Pleasant Grove were equally as productive, where the women and girls grew, canned and preserved fruits and vegetables. Also during this period, the Shakertown Believers began growing a type of oriental sorghum that supplied them with sugars and syrups. There were plenty of garden seeds to sell through the booming seed business and plenty of cattle to sell to markets as far away as Illinois. But during the war years and all the skirmishes and guerrilla activity in central Kentucky that continued through 1864, Pleasant Grove took a beating from which they were never able to fully recover. They were unable to continue with their normal trade routes for their various small businesses during the war and as a result were never able to fully restore them. Even though, eventually, peace was restored to Shakertown, the dynamic and enterprising qualities that defined the Pleasant Grove community would never be regained.

In contrast to all those things lost to the Society at Pleasant Grove during and following the Civil War, there were a few things that one could view as possible improvements over what they had been in previous years. A good example of this was the attitude of Believers toward books and printed material. While, previously, Believers had feared the contaminating influences of books, by the mid to late 1860s, books written on arts and sciences were deemed to be useful and necessary in order that Believers should keep up with current trends in American society and industry. There grew a new openness even with books concerning religious themes. Believers no longer would fear the printed word, but rather would seek it out. This was, of course, good news to Asher, who seemed to thrive during these years, so much so that he began to achieve a kind of prominence and reputation as an accomplished writer amongst the Shaker colonies, and beyond. This shift to a more accepting attitude and practice of beliefs and lifestyle was emblematic of a greater change that spread through all the Shaker colonies. Yet, this did not alter the turbulence that they experienced during the war years which depleted their numbers.

By 1870, with the gospel and the religious element "running out," as some of the Believers were saying, Shakertown was only a shadow of its former self. In an almost desperate effort, a written message was sent out to all members of the community that began with the words "God forbid that his Zion should perish; for, She is His vicegerent on the earth." The circular went on to propose that all Believers in every family should unite each Sunday evening at half past seven in a "universal gift of prayer," beginning on August 7 and "continuing until God shall return unto Zion in mercy." On the designated date, the Believers at Pleasant Grove did exactly that. With this prayer service established, the Ministry appealed to everyone to "spread the Gospel Testimony among the world" in an effort to reverse its recent loss of members and to, again, bring stability to the community. And so, a missionary program was launched, in which members traveled alone, in pairs, or in large groups, and lectured about the Shaker gospel to anyone who would listen. This missionary program culminated in an article that appeared in the *Atlantic Monthly* titled "Autobiography of a Shaker," which presented Mother Ann Lee as a gifted visionary and seer of comparable importance to such "true scientists" as Confucius, Plato, Jesus, and Swedenborg. In this essay an interpretation of the Apocalypse was given that featured "the history of the seven churches, from the Pentecostal to the Shaker Church." Membership into this "new Shaker society" required a new requisite "belief based on rational inquiry and scientific investigation--that the same Christ Spirit that created the primitive Pentecostal church, composed of Jewish Israelites, has made its 'Second Advent' upon this earth, and has created Pentecostal Communities, composed of Gentile Israelites."

During these turbid times of change, having found his place amongst the Shakertown Believers and the ranks of the "shaking Quakers" at large, Asher remained steadfast and in many ways could be said to have flourished.

Scene II.

In only a matter of months after

Kitt had left Shakertown and after formally resigning his position as a member of the Pleasant Grove Ministry due to, in his own words, "a conflict of interest and a privation of faith," Wilford Ranks had taken his much-altered personal ministry to New York state, where he began a new and decidedly non-ecclesiastical and more secular life amongst the World's People. After lying to Asher about Kitt's whereabouts the day that Asher had received his dismissal letter from Kitt at the Pleasant Grove post-office, Ranks had decided to take his mazed mind and his temporal imagination far a-field from Shakertown and to settle in a community in upstate New York that was along the Hudson River, and only a stone's throw from where Kitt had gone and where she was, also, making a new life for herself.

No longer the official "Watcher" at Pleasant Grove, Ranks had spent the twilight years of his life watching out for Kitt's welfare from his nearby "watchtower." He had also joined the Abolitionist Movement that he had been introduced to by his new friend and acquaintance, a young man by the name of Walt Whitman. Through Whitman, who at the time of Ranks' move to upstate New York was staying with friends in a small borough along the Hudson River, he became a stalwart in the early organizational activities that launched the movement into prominence. Since then, and with Whitman having returned to the hamlet of Huntington on Long Island before moving in to New York City and eventually over to nearby New Jersey, Ranks had continued with his early activism in behalf of the Freedom From Slavery Act and all that this activism subsequently implied. He had also become interested in the study of nature from his friendship with a man named John Burroughs, whom Whitman had introduced him to some years after his move to upstate New York, and who had bought a farm on the outskirts of nearby West Park. Burroughs, a naturalist and writer, had come to Ranks' attention in 1860 from an article he had written and Ranks had seen and read in the *Atlantic Monthly*. While both Burroughs and Whitman were inspirational and enabling figures for Ranks, so too did Ranks serve as a kind of mentor and patriarch to the two soon-to-be-famous controversial writers.

By the 1850s, Ranks had long since put his vows of denial and celibacy behind him, due in large measure to certain circles he had been introduced into as a result of his association with his activist friends. During these early post-Shaker years, he had, on occasion made good on his earlier lustful visions of Sister Daniella Darrow and his sexually explicit transmissions of Khwaja. While he had spent the major portion of his life in the company of both men and women during his Shaker years, he had never allowed himself the freedom to explore the possibility of anything more than cerebral and surface associations regarding physical sex. So, he had become aware of what, to his surprise, was a natural, if late ascending sexual proclivity. He spent his remaining years in the pleasant company of certain like-minded females who were either widowed or divorced, while all the while watching over and caring for Kitt as her patron, and as if he were duty-bound and she were not only a surrogate daughter, but also, spiritually, a kind of saint.

Scene III.

In August of 1870, Asher celebrated his fiftieth birthday. By this time an established poet in the state of Kentucky, to celebrate and to mark this half-century event a book of his poems was published by a Kentucky publisher in Frankfort. The book, titled *Learning To Dance* was a controversial collection of love poems spanning the arc of some thirty years, focusing on poems written when the author was in his twenties and thirties. Praised by newspapers across the state of Kentucky and a few literary journals as far away as the east coast, copies of the book had found their way to a small general store in an Amish community just outside of the town of Middle Hope, New York, on the Hudson River in the foothills of the Catskill Mountains. It was here, in the little general store in Middle Hope that Kitt had been shopping and had seen the title of Asher's book from a distance on a display table and had serendipitously picked it up out of curiosity.

Meanwhile, and almost a thousand miles away in Shakertown, Asher was seated in the stairwell of the Meeting House Ministry apartments. Behind the small window pane of glass high on the wall he looked out over the Meeting Hall floor. Ironically, now, "The Watcher," Asher sat at his station watching the Sunday service and the Shaker dances in a nostalgic frame of mind… The line of men at one end of the hall, the women's line snaking around at the other end. Folks from Herodsville sitting in the fastener benches against the walls. The singing. The Shaker songs….

    'Tis not one without the other,
    That will keep the union strong;
    O, do learn to go together!
    Then you will be join'd in one.
    Be not anxious to go forward,

And to leave your brother dear;
You may happen to fall backward,
And your brother forward steer.

During the singing of the Shaker song, Asher reached for the latch on the small window and opened the pane and sash on its hinges out into the room so he could hear better the words of the song. As the words slipped into his ears, memories flooded his mind. Memories from an earlier time, when he was just a young lad sitting on the fastener benches crowded with townsfolk and the floor of the Meeting Hall full of moving Shaker bodies in all manner of order and disorder, in all manner of tranquility and trance. While the room on this Sunday was not nearly as full of either Believers or the World's People as it had been in those earlier years, the service, Asher's presence, and the Shaker hymn had made him mindful of those more halcyon days.

Looking down from his perch in the wall at the line of women dancing, he thought of Kitt. His memory of her was so vivid that, for a moment, he thought that he saw her in the line of women moving and bowing back and forth across the floor. This apparition startled him and he shook his head to clear his vision and his mind. But the thought of her remained, and he followed the thought forward and through its natural progression of that youthful year during the Era of Manifestation. The letters. The clandestine meetings. His conversion to a Shaker life. Their first meeting in the Water House and making love to her there on a pallet on the floor underneath the giant wooden water tower. Her letter. Her leaving. His anxiety and angst. And he remembered sitting in the fastener benches and watching the face of Brother Wilford Ranks up in the watcher's window and how the moniker of "The Watcher" had first slipped from his lips as he talked to his friend Caden. All these thoughts flooded his mind, all these images flashed before his eyes as he sat in the stairwell window seat.

Asher thought, too, of his meetings with Brother Ranks, and how he had, in earlier days, thought of him as a kind of nemesis. A foil for his burgeoning love for Kitt. And he thought, too, of the irony that it was now he himself who was sitting in the window seat. It was he who had become The Watcher. And he wondered how many young men there on the fastener benches had used that epithet to describe him. As he watched the younger men and women on the Meeting Hall floor partaking in the line-dancing, he wondered who among them were secretly meeting at odd hours in the Old Mill down by the river, in the old Indian cave, or in the Dry House. And how many letters had been carried by messengers from the society to the Herodsville General Store. He thought, now, of Caden, who after Eden's death had recovered from that shock and later married a girl from Lexington and taken over his father's store to support his young family. So many memories. So many changes. So little distance between the past and the present. It seemed to Asher as if it were all happening now and in the same moment. All of it: the images, the thoughts, the emotions. And Kitt... Where was she? What had she done with her life? Was she safe? Was she even alive? He wished he had answers to these questions. He wished he knew. She had been his one and only love. My "Juliet," he thought to himself, as tears began to well up in his eyes.

Meanwhile, down on the Meeting Hall floor the brethren and sisters had started up a new song. The lyrics drifted up into the rafters of the large room and through the open window where Asher had retreated from view and was sitting on the stairway steps wiping the tears from his eyes with the sleeves of his hand-woven cotton shirt.

I'll sense the awful situation
Of the souls that turn away;
They lose all hopes of their salvation,
For them Believers cannot pray.

Just as Asher had thought the flow of tears had stopped, with these lines from the Shaker hymn ringing in his ears, a new flood of water began raining from his eyes as he buried his head in his hands.

T he next day was a Monday and Asher's first stop each Monday morning was the post office. This had become a ritual for him ever since Kitt's leave-taking and his receipt of "the letter" that she had left for him on that symbolic Monday those many years ago. Since the regional mail rider would deliver a goodly amount of mail to the Shaker village over the weekend when the post office was closed on Sunday, there was usually more mail waiting for Believers on Monday morning than any other day of the week. And since Asher's Ministry duties included communication and correspondence with the other Shaker communities in Kentucky and beyond, Monday was usually a day when such important social and spiritual correspondence would arrive. Because of his proclivity for writing, he had become identified in Shakertown as not only "the author," but the mailman. A part of his routine, on Monday morning after breakfast at the Centre Family Dwelling and after his Ministry chores, he would pick up the mail at the post office and go about delivering it to people throughout the community. Of all his business and duties as a member of the Ministry, this was his favorite job. He often thought to himself during his

Monday mail rounds that he "had been born for this job." And so he approached his work as the Pleasant Grove mailman with a sense of destiny and with vigor and in good spirits. Everyone in the village was happy to see him coming along the roadway and paths on Mondays--with his leather satchel full of letters and small packages--like a kind of Santa Claus, sans beard, that would greet one and all with a smile and a gift.

On this particular Monday, Asher opened the door and entered the small post office edifice which had been moved from its original location behind the Ministry Workshop on the road to the orchard to a small but more substantial building along the main road next to the Trustee's Office. He sensed something different in the energy that enveloped the inside of the building. As he stepped across the threshold, he was greeted with unusual enthusiasm by the village postmaster Brother David Lee, who was no relation (or so he said) to Mother Ann Lee.

"Why, Brother Asher, there you are. Running a little late, are we? Was beginning to wonder if you would be making your usual Monday run around the village, today. Thought maybe you were busy working on another of those scathing books of poems of yours and had lost track of time. Anyway, glad to see you are here and in good health, as always."

Asher looked over at Brother Lee, who was standing behind a long counter that reached from one wall of the rather small room to the other. Behind the counter was a wall of cubby holes, all of which were numbered from 1 to 400 beginning at Asher's left. Asher could see something of an impish glint in Brother Lee's eyes as he stood there behind the counter waiting for Asher's reply to his greeting. Asher hesitated, not saying anything and waited to see if Brother Lee might speak again, revealing what lay behind that teasing glint that was, now, bleeding down his face and had caused an upwards crease in the left side of his lips that was trying very hard not to turn into a smile. "Yes, running a little late, this morning," Asher finally replied. "Not because of any writing or anything. Just had a couple things to take care of, first thing, over in the Ministry Shop. But I'm here now and rarin' to go about the business of delivering the Believers mail. You got anything for me today?"

"Yes, I've got a right smart of mail in general for the village," Brother Lee said, motioning over to his left and the large pile of letters and packages stacked on the far end of the counter. "But to be more precise in answer to your question--yes, I DO have something for you. A letter from New York. I don't think it's from New Lebanon, as the return address is from some place I've never heard of. 'Hope, New York,' I think it was--no, 'Middle Hope,' New York, that was it. And it's addressed to you in a mighty nice hand. And it smells real nice too," Brother Lee added along with the smile of a crafty old cat, as he reached out with the letter in his hand at full arm's length in Asher's direction.

"A letter for me? From New York? Don't know who that could be," Asher responded, lifting the letter from Brother David's grasp and looking at the handwriting on the face of the letter.

"Better smell it first before you open it," Brother David joked.

Asher looked at the postmaster suspiciously and shook his head with a sarcastic nod, in agreement. At first glance, his impression was that the handwriting looked familiar. Yet, he couldn't place it. The New York address was throwing him off track. It looked like a woman's script. But he knew no one of the female gender from the state of New York or even New York City. Just as he was about to give up with his private guessing game, he got a strange sensation in his stomach and an eerie feeling came over him. He could actually feel the hair standing up on the back of his neck. He was unexpectedly thinking of Kitt. It was as if Kitt was standing right there next to him in the room. Her presence was palpable. The queasy feeling in Asher's stomach had turned into a knot. "New York? Wonder who that could be?" Asher finally blurted out in a forced and awkward response and in an effort to break the silence that was almost tangible, now, in the small room.

"Don't know," Brother David Lee came right back with his response. "But I sure do like the smell of that perfume. That's gotta be that big city high-priced perfume. You don't get a whiff of anything like that from the sisters around here, I can tell you that. I know that's a fact, as the post office is the best place in Pleasant Grove for smellin' perfume. The sisters come in here looking for their mail, or to mail a letter, and I can smell the perfume all over them, here in this little place. 'Specially in the winter with the windows and doors shut and the woodstove goin'. Why this place is a regular perfumery. And I've never smelled that fragrance before. Smells like honeysuckle, don't you think?"

Asher blushed a little at Brother David's remarks and was reluctant to follow the postmaster's lead, but slowly relented and drew the letter up to his nose and took what he intended to be a token smell from the letter he now held in his right hand.

He liked the smell and Brother Lee had been right--it smelled like fresh June honeysuckle vine. That, too, now seemed familiar. Not the honeysuckle, but the perfume. Where had he smelled it before? Of course, he thought to himself, it was Kitt. Kitt had always, to him, smelled like honeysuckle. It was the natural fragrance of her skin. The thought of her skin sent shivers up Asher's spine, causing him to blush again, thinking Brother Lee could probably read his mind and that his emotions were certainly visible.

"Well, Brother David, I best be on my way with all the mail that's come in over the weekend. It'll take me at least until dinner time, or longer, to get these letters and packages to everyone. We can't stand around here sniffin' letters all morning."

Asher smiled as he delivered this last remark, as did Brother Lee in return, both parties now engaged in a kind of silent conversation being carried out by pantomime as well as by some extra-sensory method neither one of them was fully aware of. Asher walked over to the far end of the counter and started loading the pile of mail into his large leather bag, packages first and then the letters. When he had gotten all the mail tucked neatly and orderly in the pouch, he threw the long leather strap attached to the bag over his right shoulder and turned toward the door to exit.

"Be seein' ya Brother. Sorry to have to take the perfumed letter away from you, knowin' how much you like the smell," Asher quipped. As he opened the door and disappeared through the entrance, Brother Lee nodded, winked and gave him a salutary wave of the hand that carried with it the meaning of 'get on outa here' rather than the normal and more cordial Southern salutation of 'y'all come back.'

Some hours later and having finished his mail delivery rounds that day, Asher made his way down the little path towards the Ministry Workshop, his satchel still hanging from his shoulder with, now, only one letter left in the bag. He looked down into the brown leather pouch and the letter lying in the bottom of the sack. He could see the handwriting with his name in fluid, artistic letters: *Asher Pope*. It was all he could do not to stop there in the pathway and reach down into the bag for the letter, so loud was the sound of the voice from within calling out to him. Instead, and controlling his almost uncontrollable impulses, he made his way to the Ministry Shop door and was able to get inside the building and close the door behind him before tearing into the bag and ripping open the letter that had been there taunting him all day.

There, in dark blue ink on a sheet of light brown parchment paper, as if awoken from the spell of an apothecary's potion and staring at him, was Kitt's handwriting.

Dear Asher,

First, let me apologize to you for my bad behavior all those years ago when I left Pleasant Grove under a cloak of secrecy, leaving you with only a letter to explain my actions. I know this had to have been hard for you and I wouldn't blame you if you never forgave me for doing what I did and the way that I did it, but I thought it best at the time and it was the result of a desperate young girl's mind being jangled and out of sorts.

O, Asher, it has been so long! How are you? Are you still in "Shakertown"? If not, where are you and what are you doing with your life? Do you still see Caden? Do you go together to the old Indian cave like you used to? And how is Sister Mary? O, I have so many questions. But this is not fair to you, as I know you have questions, too. By telling you about my life over the past twenty-five years or more, maybe I can answer some of your questions. I owe you at least that much.

Yesterday, I was in the general store in the little town where I have been living since I left Pleasant Grove, and I saw your book of poems--Learning To Dance--on the book table there in the store. I bought the book and took it home with me and read the whole thing last night. I was, of course, overwhelmed when I recognized the poems you had written to me those many years ago, and then the newer ones which I had never seen. I took the whole thing--the fact of coming across your book in that way and the content and subject matter of the poems--as being serendipitous, if not some kind of strange omen. That being the case, I decided right then that I needed to write you a letter. In truth, I have been writing this letter to you in my head for years. But finding your book the way I did was a kind of sign, or signal, that I needed to, finally, write that letter. So, here it is.

When I left Pleasant Grove all those years ago, I traveled overland a long distance and settled in a small community here along the Hudson River near the small town of Middle Hope. Here I have been ever since. I was told about this place and this community by Brother Wilford Ranks, who had heard of it from members of the Ministry at New Lebanon, and who, it turns out, was looking for a place to move to, himself--which, of course, as you know, he did--not long after I had, myself, left. So, Brother Wilford, as I have referred to him for, lo, these many years, shepherded me to this place—this gentle community--where there were many Quakers who were people of like mind and spirit, even if not Shakers, who took me in and have treated me like family. I gave up being an "instrument" of Mother Ann upon arrival and have been happy here and have had a good life. Brother Wilford, as I say, moved shortly after I did--to a little town just down-river from Middle Hope, called West Point. There, he made many new friends and began a new life for himself that fit with the changes that he was going through during the years when we knew him in Pleasant Grove. He, for some reason, felt a need to be something of a guardian for me, and in this role he was most generous and gracious. At first, I was suspect of his intentions, but soon it became clear that he truly had my best interests at heart and so we became close in the way that a father and daughter would. I think this was good for both of us, with me never really having a father and he never having children of his own. Sadly, Brother Wilford died a few years ago, after living a long and productive life. Myself and a few of his closest friends--which included John Burroughs, the nature writer and Walt Whitman, the poet (maybe you know of them?) buried him in a little cemetery in West Point.

I have liked living with the Quaker people, here. They are, in many ways, like our Shaker brothers and sisters. The major differences being: that they don't practice celibacy, do have a biological family unit and do not hold property in common. Otherwise, there are an amazing number of similarities. They accepted me and my condition, right away, and didn't judge me in any way, but rather took me in and nursed and nurtured me during the days of my pregnancy and then the birth of my, our, son. Yes, you read this right, WE have a son! You are a father, Asher. And this is the real reason I am writing you this letter--to tell you about the existence of your son, whose name is Christian, named after our beloved Savior.

O, Asher, I know this will come as a shock to you. I know that you might be hurt, confused and even angry. But please try and understand and to see things from my perspective. I thought at the time that I was doing the right thing--in leaving Pleasant Grove and leaving you the way I did and sparing you and everyone the shame and embarrassment that the news of my pregnancy would have brought--both to the community and to yourself. I was young. Maybe now, faced with a similar situation, I would do things differently. But I was young and I was scared and I was also thinking of you, believe it or not. And I know it's not fair to tell you all this, now, after so much time has gone by. But, I felt, after finding your book yesterday in the general store, that both you and Christian deserved to know about one another. That it was the right thing to do--to tell you about each other now, even though it would be hard for you both. I hope that I have not made the wrong decision in telling you about this, now. If so, it's already too late and what is done is done.

   O, Asher, Christian is such a beautiful boy. But he's not really a "boy" anymore, but a young man. Only a little older, now, than you were when you and I last saw one another, he has grown into a wonderful person. He looks a lot like you and has many of your wonderful traits. That Scottish light in his eyes. Your athletic build. Your love of language and literature. All of these things. And, you should also know, and you might laugh, that he, too, has an eye for the girls. I haven't told him a lot about you, as he rarely asked when he was younger. But recently, he has wanted to know more details about you and your family, your writing, etc. and I have told him everything that I could remember--which wasn't much, since we were still both so young and only beginning our life's journey. But he does know about you and has, in his own way, expressed an interest in knowing who his father is.

I'm sorry that you have to digest this all at once and in such an impersonal way. Are you ok, dear Asher? Has this news been too overwhelming for you? If I were there, I'd take you in my arms, the way I did once upon a time, and hold you. I wish I could. I think about you often, and the way we were. You should also know that I have not been with anyone but you--even after all these years. You have been my one and only lover. For a long time, I felt that I needed to stay solitary for Christian's sake. But, then, after a while, I just got used to the idea of being alone--just the two of us, Christian and I-- and I never really met any men that I felt attracted to. In short, no one could ever measure up to you, Asher. At least not the 'you' in my memory.

I guess this brings us to the 'big question' then of what we are going to do. I have talked to Christian this morning about all this (we can talk to each other about anything) and he is alright with the idea of finally meeting you. That being the case, I'd like to make a suggestion. You can feel free to accept or reject this and I will understand, completely. What I would like to suggest is that we plan a 'family meeting.' That the three of us decide on a place and date to meet somewhere and to spend some time together--so that you can get to know your son, and he, you. My feeling is that it would be easier on all of us if you could come here. The families that I live with here know about my story and would have no problem with your spending some time with us, here, in our little farmhouse. I dare say that I don't think the environment would be as receptive there in 'Shakertown'. I don't think it would be a generous atmosphere for a first-time meeting between you and Christian, nor would it be an open-arms reception for me, given my early and then subsequent history. But I am open to your suggestions about this and will remain flexible, as I understand that at this point everything can't be on my terms, alone.

O, Asher, I'm so sorry. I hope you can forgive me. I don't know how I'll ever be able to make this up to you. I'm just counting on what I remember as your innate inner wisdom to get you and get us through this. I know that there is a possibility that you won't want to bring me, and now Christian, back into your life. Especially if you have given your life to the Society. Whatever you decide, I will accept. But please know that both Christian and I await you with open hearts and open minds, and I, especially, look forward to our reunion (dare I say 'rendezvous'?).

Yours even after all these
years,

Kitt

For the next few days, everyone in Shakertown noticed that Asher was "somewhere else." "Turned around." "In a daze." "Off the track." "At sixes and sevens." Even Asher would have admitted to himself that he was not fully present at Shaker Meeting or at meals or when delivering the mail. His mind and at least part of his ethereal body were somewhere up along the Hudson River in a small rural enclave near a place paradoxically called Middle Hope. He wandered around Shakertown in a trance, rereading, over and over again, Kitt's letter in his mind. After a few days, he had memorized it and could recite the letter in its entirety to himself. He kept searching in and between the lines of the letter for hidden messages--like an invisible secret code. In the end the whole message from Kitt was right out in the open, and soon he realized that he would have to accept this and just take the facts, as they were, at face value.

By this time, a whole week had gone by. Asher was no closer to making a decision or to responding to Kitt's letter than he had been after his first reading. He needed to talk to someone. But who could he talk to about this? Certainly no one in the Society. How could they be objective. How could they help him in any way? He couldn't jump in a wagon and ride up to Scaly Mountain and get old man Rayfield's wise counsel as he had twenty-five years before, as old Cuss had passed on to that great forest in the sky a long time ago. The only person who would understand his situation would be Caden. *Yes, Caden,* Asher thought to himself. *Hadn't he been through a different but similar crisis with his first love, Eden? He, too, had lost Eden, if more violently, as I later lost Kitt. Now he has his own family. Surely he would understand.*

Scene IV.

It was Sunday, after the Shaker services, and Asher and Caden were sitting together on the fastener benches in the old Meeting Hall as they had as boys in earlier days. Now, instead of watching the spectacle of the Shaker dances, they were discussing the spectacle that had become their lives.

"Well, we really made a mess out of things, didn't we?" Caden said after a long silence and after listening to Asher's long story about Kitt's recent letter and his subsequent lament. "We certainly took the back roads in this life to get to where we are today, didn't we? And all this time I thought it was I who got the rougher deal. Well, guess I was wrong about that. It was tough for a while after Eden died. But there was at least a kind of finality about everything in the end. In your case, you never really did get that kind of storybook ending, or, what do you call them, an 'epilogue' at the end of the book that is a resolution or at least ties up all the loose ends. So, now, twenty-five years later, she sends you the last chapter in the book. And what a zinger it is! She ought to get the 'book of the year' award for this story! So, what do you think? You gonna hitch up the wagon and head east?"

"Don't know, Caden. I've got mixed feelings about the whole thing. One minute I'm as good as gone, the next I'm damned if I'm going anywhere and set myself up for another fall like the first one I had. I say to myself, 'you got to be crazy, Pope, to go all that way only to be played for the fool again.' Besides, how do I know that she's being totally honest with me? Maybe she just needs money, or wants me to bring the boy back to Shakertown to live, so she can have some free time for herself. But then I remember her as she was way back--the beauty, that long auburn hair, the feel of her skin, that seductive smile….. If it is possible for a living man to feel the tortures of hell, I'm that man."

"I get it, friend. Our situations are not so very different. I, too, spent a long time in a deep black place. I thought I'd never find my way out from under that damn dark cloud. But I did, and I moved on, and I'm glad I did. Otherwise, I'd have never met Angela and never had our boys. All I know to tell you is what I know to be true for me, and that is: you gotta just put yourself back in control and get back out on the ole 'road of life.' And to do that you've got to take some chances. Take some risks. I mean, what have you got to lose? You've already been through the worst of it. It can't get no worse than what you've already been through. Right? If you agree with that, then, hell, you might even get lucky and the whole situation could turn out real positive. You'll never know unless you go and check it out for yourself. You still have a chance to be the one to write the ending to this book. If you stay here and don't go, the only ending to this story you'll ever know is the one she wrote. If you go on out to New York and check things out, you may be able to write your own ending. Now, since it's *your* life, you don't want someone *else* writing the ending for your story, do you?"

"I get your point, Caden. And I appreciate everything that you've said here. It makes a lot of sense."

"Well, that's a first," Caden laughs. "In the old days, it was always you who was considered the sage, and I was always coming to you for advice. Guess what they say about time being the great leveler may have some truth to it after all. Anyway, I'm happy if I've been of some help to you. You asked for my opinion and you got it."

Asher rose from the fastener bench there in the Meeting Hall. The creak of the old wood planks echoed around the room as he lifted his six-foot, one-hundred-and-eighty-pound frame up from his seat. "Really, thanks for listenin' to all this. I know you've got better things to do than to listen to all of my problems. But as old Cuss used to say, I'm gwan to git on outa here and go 'study' on what you've said for a while and try an' figger it out."

"You bet. It was good seein' you again. Just like old times. We ought to do this more often. Who knows what kind of devilish ideas we could come up with if we really tried. We sure were good at that sort of thing when we were younger. Hey, you ever hear what happened to those Parker girls? You reckon they ever came back to these parts? We ought to look into that."

"You're crazy. I'm gonna get out of here before things get more complicated than they already are, or before I get myself into more trouble than I'm already in. You take care. I'll let you know what I decide. You'll be the first one I send the last chapter in that imaginary book."

With that caveat, Asher took his leave and departed the Meeting Hall. But instead of turning to the right and following the stone path that led around the corner of the big white building and to the door that would take him up the stairs to the Ministry apartments on the second floor, he kept walking straight. Straight out to the dirt road that runs through the village of Shakertown. Straight out the dirt road for about a quarter of a mile past the community gardens to the stables and the barnyard. Straight through the large sliding doors of the big black barn. Straight back to where two of the Societies best Belgian horses were locked in their stalls. Straight out of the stalls to where the little blue buckboard was parked. Straight out of the barn with the team hitched to the wagon--to the dirt road again. Straight out on the dirt road for about two hundred yards to the main highway and then left. Straight north on the wide road, all the way to Lexington. Straight up the steps of the platform of the Central Pacific Railroad. Straight onto the train car waiting in the station. Straight down the tracks and straight on into morning and the sunrise that came up in the east. Straight on to New York City and the heart of the World's People. Straight north by boat up the Hudson. Straight past Manitou, West Point, Balmville and Orange Lake. Straight to hope. To the middle of hope. To the town of Middle Hope. To the sound of a voice like music. Like bells. To the absence of sweet bells jangled.

Credits and Acknowledgements
THANKS TO:
Charlie Hughes—who took me there
Nan Watkins—who shared the journey
Susan Hughes (Education Director/Pleasant Hill, KY) - for her quick answers to my tedious questions
Dixie Huffman (Archivist/Pleasant Hill, KY) - for allowing me to peruse the handwritten journals
Lawson Whitt - for his Shaker stories about Pleasant Hill and his offer of a place to write
Georgie Riddell - for showing me "the window in the wall"
Larrie Curry – for keeping it all together for posterity
Darryl Thompson (Canterbury Shaker Village, NH) - for his generosity and invaluable knowledge
Joe Parker Rhinehart – for the support, enthusiasm and the box of books
Karen Dill and Wayne Caldwell – linguistics teachers of Old (mountain) English
Diana Kirk—for taking the first look
Nancy Barton—for opening doors
Glenn Barefoot—for the polish

=========================

Books referenced:
The Shaker Experience in America/Stephen J. Stein/Yale Univ. Press/1992.
One Shaker Life/Glendyne R. Wergland/Univ. of Massachusetts Press, 2006.
The Simple Spirit/Samuel W. Thomas & James C. Thomas/Pleasant Hill Press, 1973.
Drunk on the Wine of the Beloved: 100 Poems of Hafiz/Shambhala, 2001.
The Shaker Communities of Kentucky: Pleasant Hill & South Union/James W. Hooper/Arcadia Publishing, 2006.
The People Called Shakers/Edward Deming Andrews/Dover Publications, 1953.
God Among the Shakers/ Suzanne Skees/Hyperion, 1998.
Gather Up the Fragments/Mario S. DePillis and Christian Goodville/
Yale Univ. Press, 2008.
"Romeo & Juliet"/William Shakespeare/*The Works of William Shakespeare*/Black Readers Service/1937.

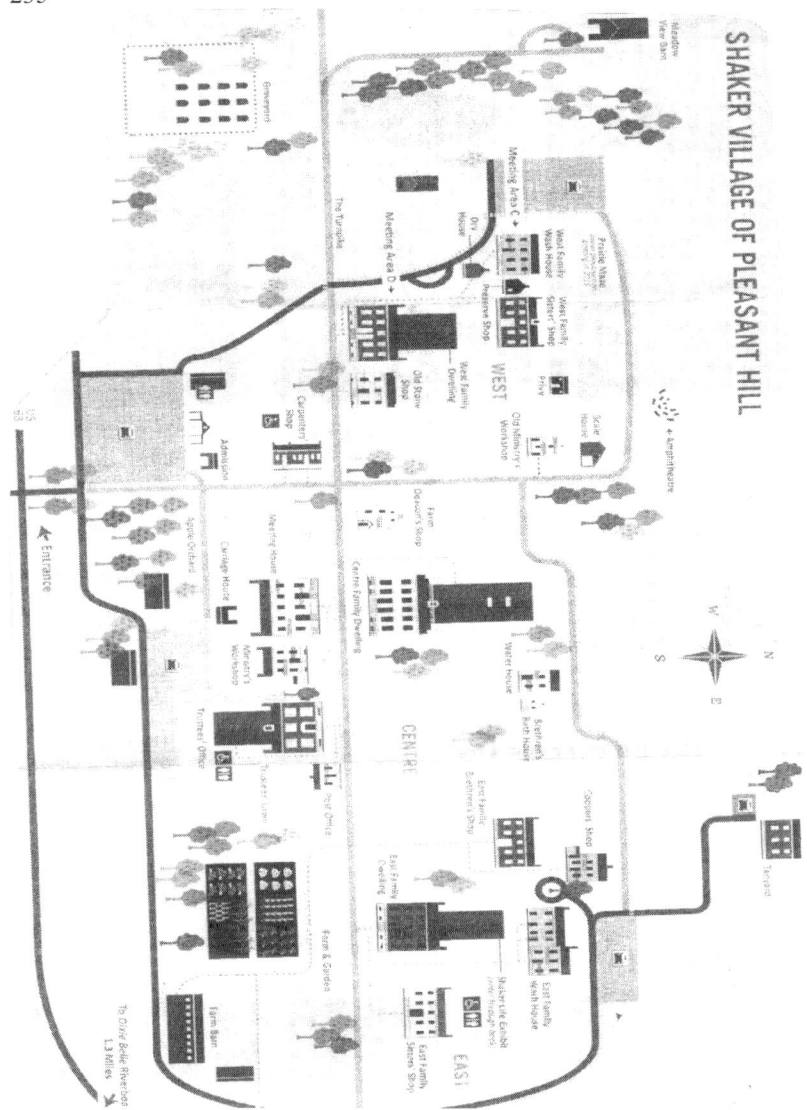

Author Thomas Rain Crowe in front of the Meeting Hall at Pleasant Hill, KY

Photo by Nan Watkins

AUTHOR BIOGRAPHY

Thomas Rain Crowe is an internationally-published author of thirty books, including the multi-award winning book of nonfiction *Zoro's Field: My Life in the Appalachian Woods*; *The End of Eden: Writings of an Environmental Activist (essays)*; *A House of Girls* (short stories); *The Laugharne Poems* written in Wales and published by Welsh publisher Carreg Gwalch in 1997; and edited the classic Celtic language anthology *Writing the Wind: A Celtic Resurgence.* As an editor, he has worked with *Beatitude magazine, Katuah Journal* and the *Asheville Poetry Review.* He is founder and publisher of New Native Press. His literary archives have been purchased by the Duke University Special Collections Library. He lives in the Tuckasegee community of rural western North Carolina.

Made in the USA
San Bernardino, CA
25 April 2015